KU-529-926

For Marcin Dymalski of the Wrocław Agglomeration, Robert Kuczera, the Director of the Wołów Criminal Department, and Iwona Bawolska. With gratitude for their invaluable assistance in making the Graham Masterton Written In Prison Award in Poland a reality.

When Beatrice carried the basket of wet laundry out to the yard to hang it up, she saw that Noah's hobby horse was lying on its side close to the pigpen, but there was no sign of Noah. She had seen him riding around not ten minutes earlier, waving his pudding cap and shouting to his imaginary militia to follow him into battle. Now he was gone.

She laid down her basket and went over to pick up his hobby horse. It had been made for him for his fifth birthday by William Tandridge the carpenter and painted shiny white, with huge staring eyes and its teeth bared as if it were snickering. William Tandridge had asked for no money for it, and Beatrice suspected that he had been trying to win her favour. She was a widow, after all, and he was a widower. His wife had died of typhoid fever three winters ago, along with three other wives in the village, and five children.

'Noah!' Beatrice called out. 'Noah, where are you? It will time for your supper soon!'

She lifted the hem of her dark brown dress a little so that she could walk out across the grassy slope that led down towards the river. The afternoon was bright and windy, with white clouds tumbling overhead. She called out Noah's name again, but all she could hear was the rustling of quaking aspen trees and the whistling and chipping of vireos.

'*Noah!*' she called again, and this time her voice was shrill with anxiety. How could he have disappeared completely in such a short time? Perhaps he was playing hide-and-seek to tease her, but she doubted it, because he had become very serious and protective since Francis had died, even though he had been so young. He teased his sister Florence, of course, but with Beatrice he behaved almost like a miniature husband.

She hurried further down the slope, stumbling two or three times. The river was narrow and weedy and shallow – so shallow that it barely reached up to Noah's knees when he paddled in it – but she had forbidden him to play in it unless she was there to watch him. She prayed that he hadn't disobeyed her, and been floating his toy boat or trying to catch pickerel.

Twenty yards from the river's edge she saw his horsehair-stuffed pudding cap lying on the ground, and her chest tightened in panic. He loved that hat, and would never go off anywhere without it. He had even wanted to wear it to bed. She went over and picked it up, looking around desperately to see if he was anywhere in sight.

'Noah, where are you? Noah! I hope you're not playing games with me, young man, because this is not at all amusing! *Noah!*'

There was still no answer. Beatrice went right down to the river's edge, and walked along its margent until she reached the grove of aspen trees, peering down into the rippling water to make sure that Noah wasn't lying underneath the surface, drowned. She saw a few silvery pickerel swimming between the weeds, but that was all.

Eventually she stopped, calling out his name again and again.

Please, dear Lord, don't let anything terrible have happened to him. I couldn't bear to lose Noah. He looks and speaks so much like his father, and he may be all I have left of my dearest Francis.

She climbed back up the slope towards the parsonage. Just to make doubly sure that Noah wasn't playing a game with her, she walked up and down all the long rows of beanpoles in the vegetable garden, and in between the apple and plum trees in the orchard at the side of the house. She opened up the green-painted shed where all of the gardening tools were kept, and she even let herself into the pigpen where her three Red Wattle pigs were snuffling around, bending down so that she could see if Noah were hiding inside their sty.

Of course the chance that he was hiding from her was remote, but then so was the chance that he would drop his beloved pudding cap and leave it lying in the grass.

As she walked back to the house, Beatrice could hear Florence crying. 'Coming, Florrie!' she called, and hurried inside, making her way through the kitchen and up the narrow stairs.

Florence was standing up in her wrought-iron crib, her cheeks red and her blonde curls damp from sleeping. Beatrice picked her up and hugged her, and brushed away her tears with her fingertips.

'There, there, Florrie, don't cry. You can have some milk now if you're thirsty. But then we'll have to get you dressed and go out to look for your big brother. I don't know where he's disappeared to. I just pray to God that he's safe, and hasn't been hurt.'

Florence frowned at her and said, 'Where's No-noh?'

'I don't know, my darling. But we'll have to find him before it gets dark.'

She unbuttoned Florence's white cotton nightgown and lifted it off, gently laying her down on a folded blanket on the table in the corner of the bedroom to change her soaking-wet diaper. Her mind was in turmoil with thoughts about what could have happened to Noah and she changed Florence so hurriedly that she pricked her finger with the long diaper pin, so that it bled and she had to suck it. She prayed that it wasn't an omen.

It was so difficult for her to decide what to do. The long-case clock in the hallway had only just chimed four, so there were still more than three hours of daylight left. Yet how far would she be able to search for Noah by herself, carrying an eighteen-month-old child with her?

Her cousin Jeremy had been living with her, but two weeks ago he had gone to Portsmouth to start work with a shipping company, and there was no way to send him a message in anything less than a day. To find anybody to help her to look for Noah she would have to harness her horse, Bramble, to her shay and drive into Sutton, or else walk there, which would take her at least twenty minutes. Whichever she chose to do, nearly an hour would be wasted, and supposing Noah came home while she was away, frightened or injured and in desperate need of attention?

She dressed Florence in her maroon cotton gown, and tied on her apron and her bonnet. She would try calling out for Noah one more time, but if she still heard no answer she knew that she would have to go down to the village and ask Major General Holyoke if he could raise a search party. It was easy for children to get lost in the woods around Sutton: little Tommy Greene had disappeared last autumn and it was only by luck that a cottontail trapper had come across him three days later, more than four miles away, starving and dehydrated and his curls thick with dried leaves and twigs.

She carried Florence down to the kitchen and sat her in her high chair. She filled her drinking cup with fresh milk and gave her a shortbread cookie, and then she went outside again to shout out for Noah.

The wind was beginning to rise, and the clouds were thickening, and there was a tang of rain in the air.

'*Noah!*' she screamed. '*Noah, where are you? Noah!*'

Eventually she went back into the kitchen. Florence looked at her worriedly and said, 'Where's No-noh?'

'I don't know, Florrie. I just want him to come home.'

She picked up Noah's pudding cap from the kitchen table. Maybe she should let her black Labrador, Seraph, out of his kennel so that he could sniff it and pick up Noah's scent. She was not sure how far this would lead her, though, or how long it would take, and she would still have to be carrying Florence.

She was still trying to make up her mind when she heard a knocking at her front door. A single, hesitant knock, followed almost immediately by another, a little louder.

'Mama, that's No-noh!' said Florence, with her mouth full of cookie.

'I don't think so, darling,' said Beatrice. 'But let me go and see.'

She opened the door and found Goody Harris standing outside in a long grey cloak with the hood raised, so that she looked like a visiting spectre. Goody Harris was the wife of William Harris, the horse-breeder, who owned the largest stud farm in Rockingham County.

'Goody Harris!' said Beatrice. 'I'm afraid you've come at a most desperate moment! My little son Noah is missing and I have to find a way to go looking for him!'

Goody Harris pushed back her hood. She was young, no more than twenty-three years old, and exceptionally pretty, with blonde ringlets tied up with a ribbon, cheeks red with rouge, and enormous blue eyes. Her husband was fifty-four – a big, grumpy, grey-haired man – and Goody Harris was frequently mistaken for his daughter.

'Oh,' she said. 'I came for your help, Widow Scarlet. But if you need mine, I will do whatever I can.'

'Is your need urgent?' asked Beatrice.

'In its way, yes, but not as pressing as yours.'

'It's not life-threatening is what I meant.'

'It could be, if William were to find out. But it can wait until you have found your son.'

Beatrice saw that Goody Harris had come in a calash, and that a young man was sitting in it waiting for her. As he turned around, she recognised him as John Meadows, the son of Sutton's gunsmith, Walter Meadows.

'Would you and John go back post-haste to the village and call on Major General Holyoke?' she asked. 'Explain to him please that Noah has disappeared and if he can raise a party to help me to find him, I would be grateful to him for all time.'

'Of course,' said Goody Harris. 'We'll go instanter.'

Beatrice watched her hurry over to the calash. She climbed back up to her seat and Beatrice saw her speaking to John Meadows. He nodded, and then he raised his whip to acknowledge to Beatrice that they would be going to get help.

As they rattled off along the oak-lined driveway, Beatrice pressed her hand to her mouth and her eyes filled with tears. The sky was even darker now, and the first drops of rain were beginning to fall. She felt that the end of the world was coming.

2

The men arrived within the hour, nearly a score of them altogether, some on horseback but most in their carriages. They had brought lanthorns, too, because the darkness was gathering fast.

Beatrice was waiting for them in her long black cloak. She had been outside several times to call for Noah, but it was drizzling persistently now, and because Florence had recovered only recently from a cold and she didn't want to risk her catching pneumonia, she had left her indoors.

Major General Holyoke climbed down from his carriage and came stamping across to the porch. He was a short, stout man with wiry grey whiskers and a black eyepatch over his left eye. He was wearing a tricorn hat and a brown oilskin watchcoat which made him look like a walking tent. He had been Sutton's magistrate for more than seven years now, and although he was known for the severity of the sentences he handed down for thieving and assault, he was also acknowledged for the kindness he showed to anyone in the village who needed assistance.

'Widow *Scarlet*!' he said, in his usual growly shout, as if he were addressing a jury. 'Goody Harris tells me that your *Noah* is missing!'

Beatrice nodded. 'He was playing outside not an hour ago. I went down as far as the river and I found his cap but other than that there is no trace of him.'

Major General Holyoke laid one hand on her shoulder and then he turned around to the men he had brought with him, and shouted, 'Spread out, fellows! Down to the river and into the woods! And keep on calling out the little man's name!'

He turned back to Beatrice and said, 'Let us go inside, ma'am. There is no reason for you to be standing out here in the wet. We don't want you ill as well as upset.'

Beatrice stayed in the porch for a moment as she watched the men making their way around the side of the parsonage. She knew all of them, of course, and one or two of them tipped their hats to her, although some seemed anxious not to intrude on her distress, and looked away.

She led Major General Holyoke into the kitchen where Florence was still sitting in her high chair pretending to feed her doll, Minnie, with a large wooden spoon.

'Say "how do you do" to Major General Holyoke,' Beatrice prompted her. Florence stared at the major general's black eyepatch but said nothing.

'*Florrie*,' Beatrice admonished her, but Major General Holyoke said, 'Not to worry, Widow Scarlet. I must present quite a fearsome image to her, poor child. Besides which, I have something of considerable importance to tell you.'

'Go on,' said Beatrice. Through the kitchen windows she could see several members of the search party making their way down towards the river and up towards the aspen grove.

'There is no point in my being anything but direct with you,' said Major General Holyoke. 'I was given news yesterday afternoon that a band of Ossipee Indians have been marauding in the area, and that they have burned down two farmhouses in Epsom and stolen horses and guns and other property.'

'What?' said Beatrice. 'I thought the Ossipee were long

gone!' She was dreading what Major General Holyoke was going to say next.

'The Ossipee are all resettled now in New France, and as far as I know, this was only a small band of them,' he told her. 'I don't know if they have been raiding us out of resentment for occupying what was once their territory, or if the French have sent them in order to cause us alarm and disruption. But apart from stealing and causing havoc, they have also kid-nabbed three women and several children.'

'Oh, dear God,' said Beatrice. Women and children from several families in the area had been taken away by Indians, but there had been no abductions for over three years now. Some had managed to escape and return to Sutton, and the stories they had told of being forced to walk nearly two hundred miles to Canada without food or drink had been horrifying. Most of them had been faced with no choice but to stay, and to be integrated into Indian tribal life.

'Of course your Noah may simply have wandered off,' said Major General Holyoke. 'Let us pray that we find him safe and well, and find him quickly. But I have to warn you that there is a likelihood that the Indians have borne him away.'

Tears were running down Beatrice's cheeks now, and she had to lift her apron to wipe them away. Florence looked bewildered, especially when Major General Holyoke embraced her, and held her close, and said, 'There my dear, there my dear,' gruffly in her ear. He smelled of tobacco and stale beer and oilskin, but Beatrice needed his comforting right then. She knew that he wouldn't have told her about the Indians unless there was a real possibility that they had taken Noah. He wasn't the kind to cause a mother anguish unless he knew he had to prepare her for the worst.

Florence obviously sensed that something was badly wrong, because she suddenly started to cry. Beatrice picked her out of her high chair and shushed her, rocking her from side to side.

Major General Holyoke said, 'It looks as if the rain has eased. I'll go out and see what progress has been made.'

The search for Noah continued long after twilight, when scores of brown bats flocked around the parsonage roof, as they did every night. Beatrice sat at the kitchen table, her hands clasped, and her pain was made worse because there was nothing else that she could do except comfort Florence and wait for news.

Soon after the clock chimed ten, she saw lanthorns swaying in the pitch-darkness outside, and heard men's voices. There was a knock at the kitchen door, and Major General Holyoke reappeared, along with David Purbright the grocer and Ebenezer Banks the carriage-maker. They all looked exhausted, and their knee boots were wet and muddy.

'I'm sorry, Widow Scarlet,' said Major General Holyoke. 'We have combed every inch from here to the mast road to the west, and as far as the Wilmot farm to the north, and the woods, too, and Abnaki Lake. There's not a sign of Noah.'

'There's no profit in searching for him any further, not tonight,' David Purbright put in. 'We'll return at first light, though, and we'll bring a few dogs with us. Nigel Porter has two fine bloodhounds and if they can't track your boy down...'

He was about to add '... he'll be lost and gone forever,' but he closed his mouth instead, and gave Beatrice a sympathetic shrug.

'Do you want to come into the village tonight and stay with us?' asked Major General Holyoke.

'Thank you for the offer, but no,' said Beatrice. 'What if Noah comes wandering back during the night and there's nobody here?'

'In that case, I recommend that you lock your doors and keep your windows closed tight. I would expect the Indians to have left the locality by now and taken their booty with them, but there is always a chance that some may still be lurking around. You have a musket? You have powder and shot?'

'Yes,' said Beatrice. When they had first arrived at the Sutton parsonage, Francis had bought a flintlock longrifle and taught Beatrice how to load and fire it. She had practised over and over again until she could tamp the gunpowder and ball into the muzzle and prime the pan within less than fifteen seconds. She could shoot accurately too. One October morning she had brought down a grouse from over thirty yards away, and they had eaten it for supper, with sweet potato soup.

All the men left, and after she had heard their carriages and horses clatter away down the drive, she went upstairs to make sure that Florence was fast asleep. Usually she went to bed herself soon after Florence, because there was very little mending for her to do now that she was alone, and very little preparation in the kitchen. It saved on candles, too. This evening, though, she knew that she wouldn't be able to sleep, and so she went back downstairs to the living room to write in her diary and to continue reading her novel, *Pamela: Or Virtue Rewarded*, which her friend, Sally Monckton, had brought her from England.

Alone in the parsonage, though, except for her sleeping Florence, all she could write by the flickering light of her candle was *I beg you, Lord, to shield Noah from any harm and to deliver him back to me unscathed*. She looked at her leather-bound novel, but she couldn't even begin to think of reading any more about the virginal Pamela and the way she conveniently swooned every time a lecherous man approached her, bent on seduction.

Her grief had been almost overwhelming when Francis had been murdered, but she found it even more agonising to think of losing Noah. Francis had at least lived out some of his life, and loved her, and married her, and come to New England with a vision of bringing his Christianity with him. Before he had been killed, Francis had at least been aware that he was facing a challenge from men who were determined to do him harm. Noah was only five, and his only experience of life so far had been play, and singing songs, and he knew nothing whatsoever about evil.

Beatrice sat there all through the night. She nodded off after two or three hours, but she jerked awake when the wind rose up again, and shook the kitchen door like some intruder trying to break in. She strained her ears and she could hear crying and whistling in the woods, but it was only the whippoorwills and the nighthawks. Just before dawn it started to thunder, and to rain again heavily, so that all she could hear was the water gushing out of the eavespouts.

She went to the kitchen window and looked out over the yard. Her basket of laundry was still there, becoming more and more sodden, and there was Noah's hobby horse lying on its side. Rain was drifting up from the river like a cortège of ghosts.

She closed her eyes and said another prayer for Noah, but even as she did so, she accepted that she might never see him again, or ever discover what had happened to him.

3

Later that morning, Major General Holyoke brought his search party back to the parsonage, and they came with Nigel Porter's bloodhounds, but even after they had sniffed Noah's pudding cap they could find no scent of him outside. They circled around and around and sniffed at his hobby horse but then they came back, panting, with their tongues hanging out.

'I regret that I am even more persuaded that he was kidnabbed, because of that,' said Major General Holyoke. 'If he had strayed away on foot, he would have left a trail that the dogs could follow, even after all this rain. But if he was picked up, and carried away in the arms of some abductor, then of course there would be no trace at all.'

'Is there not someone you know who has dealings with the Ossipee?' asked Beatrice. 'Some trapper or some trader? What about the militia? Do you not know any officer who could send out rangers? Perhaps they might be able to catch up with the Indians before they take Noah into Canada.'

'I know of no trappers or traders who might have contact with them, I'm afraid, and as you are aware, all of the Abnaki tribes are hostile to a high degree. I know a militia officer with the First Battalion, Colonel Andrew Petty, but he and his men have more than their hands full keeping those damned perfidious French at bay, and in any event I doubt if I could even manage to get in touch with him.'

There was a long silence between them. Then Major General Holyoke said, 'We will search further and wider, Widow Scarlet, but I am afraid that we must accept that the worst has probably happened, and your Noah has been taken from you. Let us pray that his captors treat him well.'

Florence appeared in the kitchen doorway, carrying her doll, Minnie. Beatrice had disliked Minnie from the moment that her former housemaid, Mary, had first given it to her, because of her madly staring eyes. She looked as if she had just escaped from a lunatic asylum.

'Where's No-noh?' she asked, frowning. 'I want to play.'

Three days went by. Several members of the search party rode further afield to see if they could find anybody who had witnessed a small white boy being taken away by Indians. Two farmers and a drover said that they had seen a small band of Ossipee Indians heading north up the Merrimack River valley, maybe fifteen or twenty of them, but they had been too distant for them to tell if they had Noah or any other white captives with them.

Beatrice wrote a message to Jeremy and gave it to the post rider to take to Portsmouth, informing him that Noah had gone missing. Meanwhile, Major General Holyoke sent word to Colonel Petty, asking if his militiamen could keep an eye open for any sign of white women and children being abducted by Indians. He was aware how unlikely this was: the Indians only travelled at night, and very quickly, and by the most devious routes.

At midday on the third day, Beatrice was sitting in the kitchen eating pease-and-ham soup with Florence when she heard a carriage outside, and then a knock at the door.

It was Goody Harris again. The day was windy but sunny and she was wearing a light-blue cape and a matching bonnet. As before, John Meadows was waiting in his calash on the opposite side of the driveway.

'I have heard that your little boy has still not been found,' said Goody Harris. 'I cannot imagine how concerned you must be.'

'Come inside,' said Beatrice. 'Does John not want to come inside, too? He is more than welcome.'

'He wants to let me speak to you in confidence, Widow Scarlet. He is feeling sufficiently guilty as it is.'

Beatrice led Goody Harris through to the kitchen. Florence had been trying to feed both herself and Minnie with the thick green soup, and both of them had it smeared all around their faces.

'Florrie, just look at you!' said Beatrice, wiping her face with a damp muslin cloth. Then, 'Sit down, Goody Harris, please. Can I offer you anything? Some tea, perhaps, or would you care for a bowl of soup? There's plenty, and, as you can imagine, I have very little appetite myself.'

'There's no word of your boy at all?'

Beatrice shook her head, and said, 'None.' She didn't like to think how frightened and hungry and exhausted Noah might be. 'But what help do you need?'

'I am mortally ashamed to tell you this,' said Goody Harris, lowering her eyes and twisting the ribbons of her embroidered purse around and around between her fingers. 'Since the first day of July, John Meadows and I – well, we have been lovers.'

'I see,' said Beatrice. 'I assume by "lovers" you mean that you have lain together.'

'Yes,' said Goody Harris, so quietly that Beatrice could hardly hear her, especially since Florence was rocking Minnie in her arms and singing to her at the top of her voice: *'Hush-a-bye, baby, in the treetops.'*

Beatrice said, 'Hush, Florrie, and please sing some other song.' 'Hush-A-Bye Baby' had been inspired by the Indian custom of suspending a baby's birch-bark cradle from the branch of a tree so that the wind would rock it to sleep. She couldn't bear to think of little Noah trying to fall asleep in the open, in the chilly wind, surrounded by hostile Indians. As it was, he had always been afraid of the dark.

'You're not with child?' she asked Goody Harris.

'No. But John went to Boston on business last month, and when he returned he had a soreness and a slight yellow weeping. We thought little of it, but soon afterwards I too began to feel sore.'

'Do you have other symptoms? I notice your eyes are quite red.'

Goody Harris said, 'Yes. I have a nagging pain in my stomach, which comes and goes. My privates are swollen, and I have a burning sensation whenever I relieve myself. I have sometimes left spots of blood on the sheets after we have lain together, and I have also been bleeding in between the usual time for my flowers.'

'Emma,' said Beatrice. Although she didn't know Goody Harris well, it seemed ridiculous to address her formally when they were discussing such an intimate problem. 'Do you have a discharge too?'

'Yes, and it is most unpleasant. Yellowish, like John's.'

'Did you consider going to Doctor Merrydew?'

'How can I? Doctor Merrydew would insist on knowing how I acquired my condition, and he is one of William's closest friends. They play quadrille together twice a week.'

'Have you been intimate with William since you began to feel sore? You realize that you could pass this on to him, and then he would be certain to find out about your relationship with John.'

'William lost interest in the intimate side of our marriage over two years ago. We sleep in separate rooms and he relies on me only for running the household and book-keeping. He wanted children – a son, especially – and when we discovered that I was unable to conceive, I think that took away his sole motivation for having physical contact with me. He doesn't even embrace me or kiss me these days. Can you blame me for seeking comfort with John?'

Beatrice said, 'I might be a pastor's widow, Emma, but I am not a judge of others' morality. However, I have to ask you if John has explained to you how he came by this disease.'

Emma's cheeks flushed, and she twiddled with her purse strings even more furiously, as if they were some kind of frustrating puzzle.

'He admitted that while he was in Boston he had missed me greatly, and that one evening he had been thinking about our lovemaking and that had aroused him beyond endurance. He had been directed by one of his colleagues to a house run by a woman called Hannah Dilley, where men could lie with whores.

'He said that immediately afterwards he had been filled with remorse, but his remorse had not been enough to cleanse him of the pox that the whore had infected him with.'

'Well, it is best that you came to me,' said Beatrice. 'I have no idea how much Doctor Merrydew knows of sexual diseases, but I do know that he is still prescribing lunar caustic for your condition, which can stain your skin irrevocably and cause even greater sickness or even death. My late father was an apothecary in the City of London, and taught me everything he knew about diseases and their treatments, and of course he frequently had to prescribe medicines for the same disease that you and John are both suffering from. I am reasonably certain that you have gonorrhoea, Emma – commonly known as the clap.'

'I suspected so,' said Emma, without raising her eyes. 'I prayed and prayed that it would cure itself but it has been growing progressively worse for both of us each day. Can you cure us?'

Beatrice stood up and went across to the cupboard on the other side of the kitchen. Inside the cupboard were all the powders and pills and medicines that she had prepared herself to treat those villagers who came to her instead of Doctor Merrydew – either because they were too embarrassed about their complaints, like Goody Harris, or because they knew that Beatrice had all the very latest and most effective treatments. She took out a large brown-glass bottle with a cork stopper and set it down on the kitchen table.

'Like Doctor Merrydew, most physicians will prescribe a metal for gonorrhoea – arsenic or antimony or bismuth. One physician we knew in London would suggest that a woman should sit on a commode and fumigate her private parts with cinnabar, mercury and sulphur, which would be placed on a hot iron plate underneath her.

'But *this* treatment I came across when I met a ship's doctor in Portsmouth. He had recently arrived from Brazil, and he had discovered it while he was treating some of the natives there. It's a balsam taken from a tree called the copaiba and the natives use it to calm sores and skin inflammation and as a cough medicine. They also use it to ward off hexes, although I don't think you will be requiring that particular attribute unless William finds out about your liaison with John.

'This ship's doctor tried applying the balsam to sailors who had contracted gonorrhoea after visiting whores in various ports, and he found it to be most efficacious, without the staining and other side effects of lunar caustic.'

'Widow Scarlet, I can't thank you enough,' said Emma, and she was in tears. 'What do I owe you?'

'I wish I could let you have it for no money,' Beatrice told her. 'Unfortunately the church pays me only a meagre widow's pension, which is why I have to supplement my income by preparing and selling my medicines. Two bits, though, will be more than enough.'

Emma took a quarter dollar out of her purse and set it down next to the bottle. Then she stood up and held Beatrice close and whispered, 'Thank you. God bless you,' in her ear.

Florence sang, '*Ring-a-ring of roses! Ashes! Ashes! All fall down!*'

4

Two days later, Jeremy arrived from Portsmouth. When he stepped down from the carriage, Beatrice could see at once that he had put on weight, and that his wavy brown hair was cut shorter. He looked pasty and tired and his long brown coat was covered in dust from the journey, but after he had taken off his cocked hat and brushed himself down, he held out his arms to her and gave her the saddest of smiles.

Beatrice hugged him and pressed her cheek against his chest. It gave her a huge sense of relief that he had come to console her, and that she now had someone with whom she could share her grief. Ever since Noah had disappeared, she had only been able to sleep when she was so exhausted that she was almost delirious, and she had eaten hardly anything except for corn chowder and pumpkin bread.

'How are you, Jeremy?' she asked him.

'Fair fagged out, to be truthful. The carriage lost a wheel at the nineteenth milestone and we had to wait for over three hours for it to be repaired. But I had to come, my dearest. It is just too terrible, what has happened to young Noah. You must be devastated.'

Jeremy took off his coat and hat and they went inside. Beatrice called out to Florence, who was playing with Seraph in the back yard, throwing a wooden spoon for him to fetch.

Florence came running in and Jeremy swept her up off her feet and kissed her.

'My lovely Florrie! I've only been away for a month and how much you've grown!'

'No-noh's gone,' said Florrie. 'Mommy's been crying and me too.'

'Yes, Florrie. I know that. But don't you worry. We'll find him and bring him back to you, I promise you that.'

When Florence had run back outside, Beatrice said, 'You shouldn't raise her hopes, Jeremy. Nor mine. Major General Holyoke sent men to search as far north as White Mountain, and he has advised an officer in the militia that Noah might have been taken by Indians, so that his men can watch out for him. But if the Lord has kept him safe, and he has survived, I doubt if I will ever hold him in my arms again.'

She started to cry, with deep painful sobs that made it hard for her to breathe. Jeremy held her close and kissed her forehead and said, 'Bea, Beatrice. If I believed that I could possibly find him, I would go looking for Noah myself.'

'I know you would, Jeremy. You have always taken such good care of us. But I really fear that it is hopeless. It would have almost been more bearable if he had fallen sick and died. Now I shall never know if he is alive or dead, or what kind of a man he has grown into, if he is still living.'

They spent the next few hours in the kitchen, while Beatrice mixed dough with wheat flour and corn mush and molasses to make two large loaves of bread, and then prepared a chicken pot pie with onions and carrots and celery. Jeremy sat at the table with a mug of hard cider and tried to keep her mind off Jonah by telling her all about the antics that he and his fellow clerks got up to after a day in the shipping office.

'You must miss Mary,' he said.

'She still comes in to help me sometimes,' said Beatrice. 'But of course I can't afford a maid these days. Still – we have only the two of us now, me and Florrie, so there is nothing like the washing and the cooking that there used to be. Francis was always so particular about having clean stockings every day, and he did love his chowder.'

Jeremy got up to stoke the cast-iron Franklin stove with more wood. When he sat down again, he said, 'I missed you a very great deal in Portsmouth, Bea. I am enjoying the work, without question, but I think of you constantly.'

'I miss you too, Jeremy. I have many good friends here in Sutton, but it can be lonely, especially at night. Florrie is adorable, but it would be enjoyable to spend an evening talking about something more grown-up than dollies and doggies and when are we going to bake some more snickerdoodles.'

Jeremy put down his mug and said, 'You nearly smiled then.'

'I will have to learn how to smile all over again, Jeremy. From the moment I realized that Noah was missing, I have been incapable of any other humour but dread.'

'You know why I followed you here from England, don't you?'

'Jeremy, we have spoken of this before. I am fully aware of your affection for me, and I am most warmly disposed to you, too. But there is a difference between affection and warmth and true love. Besides which, I have yet to recover from losing Francis, if I ever will. As I hope you never discover for yourself, you don't stop loving people just because they have died.'

'But it has been almost three years since, Bea. And isn't it possible that you could grow to love me at least half as strongly as you loved Francis?'

'Jeremy, you have been wonderful, and you saved my life, for which I will always be grateful. We are cousins, though, and I simply cannot think of you as a lover and a husband.'

'I have a handsomely paid job now, Bea, and even if it took you some time to see me as a husband, I could support you financially and comfort you emotionally in your time of grief.'

Jeremy paused, and took a deep breath, and then he said, 'I love you, Bea. I love you with every fibre of my being. If I have to wait longer, then it will hurt me, but I will endure it. So long as I know that one day you will be able to give me your hand.'

Beatrice stopped kneading her bread dough, and closed her eyes. She felt as if she were falling down a black and bottomless well, falling and falling with no end in sight. Jeremy had never tried to make a secret of his attraction to her, ever since her parents had died and she had been taken in by his mother, her Cousin Sarah in Birmingham.

He had been drunken and feckless when he was younger, but he had grown up to be hardworking and loyal and Noah and Florence adored him. He was handsome enough, although his eyes were small and Beatrice always thought he had looked a little sly. His lips, too, were full and red for a man, and she couldn't imagine kissing him in the way that she and Francis used to kiss.

She thought that it was deeply unfair of him to ask her to marry him when she was so distraught about Noah, but he probably knew it, and had seen it as his best chance. She did badly need somebody to take care of her, because she had almost no savings left, and she could see no future for herself if she stayed in Sutton. The money she made from selling salves and medicines to people in the village was barely enough to cover the cost of their ingredients, and how long would the church go on paying her a widow's pension?

She opened her eyes to see Jeremy looking at her with his eyebrows raised, as if he were expecting an answer. He was young, and he was far from ugly, and he loved her, and who else did she know who would make her a suitable husband? All of the men in the village were already married, with the exception of Henry Nobbs the bootmaker who was fifty-five years old and bald and almost always intoxicated.

Very few of the married couples she knew appeared to love each other as fiercely and as passionately as she and Francis had done, but they lived and worked cheerfully together, and they seemed to be content. Why could she not have a marriage like that with Jeremy?

At last she said, 'I appreciate your offer, Jeremy, but I cannot give you an answer, not today, and probably not for many weeks to come. I am far too distressed at losing Noah, and he is all that I can think of.'

Jeremy looked down into his cider mug with a frown, as if the mug had spoken to him, instead of Beatrice. Without raising his eyes, he said, 'I understand, Bea, and I am sorry if I have been too forward. I thought it might help you in your time of need to know that you are loved and valued, and that I would do anything to protect you.'

'Jeremy – there is no need for you to apologize. I would rather you expressed your feelings for me openly than keep them bottled up. And at any other time, I would have been flattered.'

'But what do you think you might have said, at any other time?'

Beatrice finished punching the big lump of dough into shape and lifted it into an earthenware basin to prove.

'I cannot tell you, Jeremy. If there is one thing I have learned about time, it is that it takes no notice of our dreams or our desires. It sweeps us along helpless as twigs in a flooded stream.'

She went in to see Florence before she went to bed that night. By the light of her candle she could see that Florence was deeply asleep, but all the same her lips were moving as if she were talking to somebody in a dream. Beatrice bent over her crib and kissed her.

She went to her own bedroom and undressed. She could hear Jeremy's bed creaking in the bedroom next to hers, and the sound of him closing the door of his wardrobe. Once she had put on her long white nightgown she blew out her candle, but before she went to bed, she looked out of the window. It was a clear, breezy night and the stars were out, millions of them. It brought tears to her eyes to think that Noah was somewhere out there, looking up at those same stars, but scores of miles away from her by now.

Eventually she climbed in between the sheets. She still slept on the left-hand side of the bed, as she had done when Francis was sleeping next to her. Somehow it seemed as if the right-hand side was still his – chilly and empty as a winter landscape, but still the side on which he had preferred to sleep.

It took her over an hour to get to sleep. She had several bottles of her own sleeping tincture in the cupboard in the kitchen – a mixture of opium, musk, nutmeg and brandy – but whenever she took it she still felt drowsy the following day, and she knew that if taken too frequently it could be addictive.

The gibbous moon came up, so bright that it was almost like daylight. She whispered a prayer for Noah, and then closed her eyes and sent him a mother's love, to be delivered by whatever spirit might be listening.

She turned over so that she was facing the window, but as she did so she heard the soft squeak of her bedroom door being opened. She lay still, listening, and after a few moments she could hear breathing. She turned around again and saw Jeremy standing in the doorway in his knee-length shirt.

'Jeremy!' she whispered. 'What is it?'

'I thought you might need comforting,' he said, hoarsely.

'I need to sleep, that's all,' she told him, but without saying anything else he came across the bedroom, lifted the blankets and slipped into the bed beside her.

'Jeremy! No! Get out, please!'

She tried to sit up but Jeremy put his arm around her shoulder and held her down. She could smell brandy on his breath.

'Bea, it's all right. I won't harm you or take advantage of you, I promise. All I want to do is hold you and reassure you that you're safe.'

Beatrice struggled and pushed him, but he was much stronger than she was, and he continued to hold her pressed down against the mattress. She tried to kick him but her legs became tangled in her nightgown.

'Jeremy, you cannot do this! If you don't leave go of me and get out of this bed at once I shall have to throw you out of the house for good!'

'Why would you do that? You know that you need me! You know how dearly I love you!'

With that, he took hold of her left hand by the wrist, and levered it downwards towards his crotch. Through his cotton shirt she could feel his penis, as hard as her bedside candle. He tried to make her take hold of it, but she managed to twist her hand away. He shifted himself nearer to her, trying to kiss her.

With her right hand, Beatrice reached under the pillows and found the butt of the loaded coat pistol that she kept there every night in case of intruders. She was still trying to push

Jeremy away with her left hand while she cocked back the pistol's hammer with her thumb.

'Jeremy, get *away*!' she panted, as if she were reprimanding a naughty dog, but he was growing more and more excited by the second.

'Bea! I've never touched another woman! I've always kept myself for you! Please, Bea! If you don't permit me to take you, I shall surely explode!'

Beatrice pulled the trigger, and the pistol went off with a deafening bang. The pillow burst open and the whole room was filled with a snowstorm of goose feathers, shining white in the moonlight. The pistol ball had hit the wall on the opposite side of the landing, and buried itself in the plaster.

Jeremy sprang up, clapping his hand to his left ear. He lost his balance and tumbled backwards off the bed and thumped onto the raggy rug, hitting his head hard on the bedside table. He lay there, stunned, staring up at the goose feathers as they softly see-sawed down on top of him.

Beatrice got out of bed on the opposite side and came around to stand over him, still holding the pistol.

'I thought you'd killed me,' Jeremy croaked up at her.

'It was lucky for you that I didn't. You swore to me that you would take care of me and that you wouldn't take advantage.'

'You'll have to speak louder. I've gone deaf.'

Beatrice knelt down beside him and shouted, 'You know how grief-stricken I am, at losing Noah! You swore that you would look after me!'

'I wanted nothing more, except to hold you in my arms. I swear it. I thought you would find it comforting.'

'I'm sorry, Jeremy. You gave me hard evidence that you wanted more than just an embrace. I have a good mind to reload this pistol and have done with you.'

Jeremy's lips puckered up and he started to make deep sobbing noises like a donkey. 'I beg your forgiveness, Bea! I have wanted you so much, for so long! I couldn't help myself!'

Beatrice stood up. 'Go back to your bed, Jeremy. In the morning I will feed you breakfast and then I want you to leave. Go back to Portsmouth and your office and I hope that you become prosperous and one day find yourself a wife. I shall never know, because after you have gone I have no wish to see you again.'

Jeremy reached up and held on to the side of the bed so that he could heave himself onto his feet. Brushing feathers from his sleeves, he looked down at Beatrice with a beaten expression on his face, but said nothing. He had known her long enough to appreciate that she meant what she said.

He shuffled out of her bedroom and returned to his own, closing the door behind him. Beatrice went in to see Florence and wasn't surprised to see that her eyes were open, although she wasn't crying.

'There was a *bang*!' she said.

'Yes, my darling, but it was only God moving his armchair. He wanted to sit where he could see you better, and make sure that you stay safe.'

'I heard you shouting. Are you cross with Uncle Jeremy?'

'No, I'm not. But sometimes people pretend they can't hear you, because they don't want to hear you, and then you have to shout to make sure that they have.'

'Is No-noh coming back in the morning?' asked Florence.

'I don't know, Florrie. We can only pray that he does.'

'Are you going to give me a kiss?'

Beatrice bent over her crib and said, 'Yes, my darling. Tonight, tomorrow, and always.'

She went back to her bedroom and locked the door. All the

feathers had settled now, but she would pick them up in the morning. She would have to change the sheet, too, because it had been peppered with black spots when the flintlock had discharged, and the pillowslip had been torn to rags.

She eased herself wearily into bed and closed her eyes. In spite of what had happened, or perhaps because of it, she fell asleep almost immediately, and didn't wake up until her bedroom was filled with six o'clock sunlight.

5

After she had washed and dressed and stepped out onto the landing, she saw that Jeremy's door was open. He hadn't bothered to tidy his bed, but he had probably guessed that she would strip it and launder his sheets, if only to rid them of the smell of him. His big leather travelling bag had gone, and he had left his wardrobe door open, and it was empty except for some crumpled brown paper and a long-handled shoehorn.

When she went downstairs, she realized that he had left without staying for breakfast or saying goodbye. She hadn't heard a carriage, so he must have walked into Sutton to find a driver to take him back to Portsmouth. He hadn't even left a note.

She stood in the porch, looking down the driveway with its line of oak trees rustling in the sunshine, and she felt immeasurably sad. The only family she had now was Florence, and she couldn't even be sure that Francis was Florence's father. Shortly after Francis had died, she had been attacked and brutally raped by an evil chancer called Jonathan Shooks, and if Jeremy hadn't intervened, Shooks might have killed her too. But now she had even lost Jeremy.

She looked up at the huge white cumulus clouds sailing across the sky and she couldn't help thinking, *God, are you really there, and if you are, why are you hiding behind those clouds?*

She went back inside to dress Florence and to give her a bowl of porridge for breakfast. She decided that she would harness the shay that morning and go down to the village to buy some more provisions. She had been keeping her diary so religiously that she had run out of ink, and she also needed more wool.

She was clearing the ashes from the stove when she heard a knock. Florence looked up at her expectantly, but she doubted that it was anybody bringing her news of Noah. She went to the front door and found that it was the Reverend Miles Bennett, from the neighbouring parish of Canterbury, who had been standing in for Francis since his death.

The Reverend Bennett was a tall, kindly man, skeletally thin, with a flapping wing of grey hair that looked as if an exhausted pigeon had settled on his head. He had near-together eyes and a large, complicated nose, but he always had a benevolent smile on his lips.

'A very good morning to you, Widow Scarlet,' he said. 'I had been hoping to pay a visit to you earlier, as soon as I received the intelligence about your son, Noah. Unfortunately, I was delayed by important church business and also by my poor wife's sickness.'

'How is your wife?' asked Beatrice.

'Not at all well, I regret to tell you. She has been suffering for some weeks now from chin cough, and no matter what treatments she has been given, they seem to afford her only temporary respite.'

'You should have come to me earlier,' Beatrice told him. 'I have a preparation which I have twice administered to children in the village for chin cough, and it gave both of them great relief. It's a mixture of spring water and a syrup of pale roses, with a grain of hemlock-mass.'

'Hemlock? Surely that is toxic.'

'Not if sufficiently diluted. And one must balance the risk of death from hemlock poisoning against the risk of death from chin cough.'

'Well, if you recommend it, Widow Scarlet, I will surely take some and see if it can relieve my wife's agony. With every spasm it feels as if she is coughing up her very soul.'

The Reverend Bennett followed Beatrice into the kitchen. Florence stood up to give him a curtsey, which made him smile even more. She had been kneeling in the corner, using one of Beatrice's bake-kettles as a pretend boat for Minnie. Beatrice no longer allowed her to play outside on her own. Even though she was reasonably sure that the Ossipee had long gone, she was still fearful that one or two of them might double back and snatch her, too.

She went to her cupboard and took out a small dark-green bottle. 'Here,' she said. 'One teaspoonful three times every day, and two before retiring. That will be half a dollar, I'm afraid.'

The Reverend Bennett took out his leather purse and paid her, but then he said, 'The purpose of my visit was not to tell you of my wife's sickness, Widow Scarlet, although I am heartily grateful that you have given me a cure.'

'Please, go on. Can I offer you some tea?'

'I am sufficiently refreshed, thank you. But I have to inform you that a new parson has been appointed to this parish, and he and his wife will be arriving next week. They came from Lincoln, in England, and at the moment they are in Boston, awaiting the remainder of their belongings.'

'So that means Florence and I will have to leave?'

'I regret that it does. The Reverend Mills and his wife have three children, and they will need all of the accommodation that this parsonage provides.'

'I see,' said Beatrice. 'So what is to become of us? Will the church continue to pay my widow's stipend?'

The Reverend Bennett reached into the pocket of his coat and produced a letter. He unfolded it and held it up. 'Reverend Mills brought with him this invitation from the Reverend Edward Parsons, the church's superintendent minister at Windmill Hill, in London. He asks if you would consider returning to England to assist at St Mary Magdalene's Refuge for Refractory Females. He is aware of your expertise as an apothecary, and believes that would be of great advantage.'

Beatrice said, 'My son Noah is here, Reverend Bennett. How can I possibly leave New Hampshire and return to England until he has been found? That would mean I had abandoned him.'

'I understand entirely, Widow Scarlet,' said the Reverend Bennett. 'But if he has indeed been abducted by Indians, as you suspect, then the chances of him ever being returned to you are so slim as to be negligible. And that is to assume that he has survived his ordeal, although we pray of course that he has come to no harm.'

'Do you know what you are asking of me?' said Beatrice. 'You might as well ask me to cut off my right hand and throw it in the fire. Noah is my flesh and blood and, more than that, he is the flesh and blood of my dearest Francis. He is all that I have left of him.'

The Reverend Bennett looked across the kitchen at Florence. She had overturned the bake-kettle so that Minnie had fallen out, and now she was calling out in a squeaky voice that she was drowning. Beatrice saw him looking, and although he said nothing, she could guess what he was thinking. *Is Florence not Francis's flesh and blood, too?* 'If I may, I shall leave you to think it over,' said the Reverend Bennett, folding the letter and placing it on the table. 'The cost of your passage to England will of course be met by the church, and you and your daughter will be accommodated free of charge at St Mary Magdalene's. On top of that, you will be paid nine guineas per annum for the help you give to their young girls.'

He hesitated when he saw that Beatrice had tears in her eyes, but then he said, 'Widow Scarlet, I assure you... the Reverend Mills will be instructed to look out for Noah, in the event that by some miracle he should return here to the parsonage. He will also encourage the residents of Sutton village to stay alert for any sign of him. Apart from that, there is little more that we can do.'

'I know,' said Beatrice, miserably. 'It is just that the pain of losing him is too much to bear. I can still hear him singing, inside my head. I can still feel him in my arms.'

'There is little more that you can do yourself, Widow Scarlet,' said the Reverend Bennett. 'If Noah were to be found, he should be sent to join you in England by the first available sailing. We are thinking only of your own welfare now, and the future that you and your daughter have to face.'

Beatrice picked up the letter and then put it down again. 'Thank you, Reverend Bennett, and God bless you.'

The Reverend Bennett laid his hand on top of hers and said, 'God bless you and protect you too, Widow Scarlet, and bring you comfort in your time of sorrow.'

After the Reverend Bennett had left, Beatrice opened the letter and read it. Had she not had Florence to take care of, she might have considered staying here in Sutton and finding herself some employment, even if it was only as a housemaid or working in John Levinson's bakery. But she would need a nursemaid for Florence, and she would simply not be able to afford to hire one, even if it was only one of the girls from the village.

Besides, she had been brought up in London, and she still had many friends there. Compared to New Hampshire, it was overcrowded and filthy, but it was familiar.

She went into the living room and looked at herself in the mirror over the fireplace. The glass was slightly distorted, so she always seemed to have a secretive smile on her face. But in her plain black dress she was surprised how young she still looked now that she was nearly thirty, with her wide blue eyes and her brunette ringlets and her perfect oval face, like a Madonna from a Renaissance painting.

I have a whole life behind me, she thought, *but then I have a whole life ahead of me, too*. And it was then that she decided that she would have to find a way to contain her pain about Noah, and go.

6

Shortly after noon, when she had bought all she needed in the village, she drove her shay to the north-east end of the triangular green and tethered her horse outside Widow Belknap's house.

This corner of Sutton was where the poorer residents lived, artisans and smallholders and odd-job men. Their homes were ramshackle and crowded together, and the grass outside was deeply rutted with cart tracks and reeked of horse manure. Clara Belknap's house, though, was set well back, and she had a triangular front yard that was overflowing with flowering weeds – yarrow and dame's rocket and fleabane.

It was an odd house – five-sided and strangely proportioned, like an optical illusion. It had a lean-to kitchen and a dairy at the back, which added to the oddity of its appearance. It used to be pale yellow but Clara had recently had it painted a shiny sea green.

Beatrice carried Florence up the path between the flowers, but before she had reached the porch the front door opened and Clara came out. She was a thin woman of about forty, and although her face was as pale as a midsummer moon, she was quite beautiful, in a very unusual way, with green, feline eyes and thin bow-shaped lips. As always, she was wearing a black bonnet and a black dress. Beatrice had arrived too late in Sutton to have known her late husband, but Clara continued to dress in mourning, year after year.

'Gerald is still inside me,' she had once told Beatrice. 'I shall only be able to cast off my widow's weeds and dress gaily once he has gone, and that day may never come. He clings on. He whispers in my ears. He is terrified to leave me, and to fly out into the spirit world by himself.'

Beatrice had hesitated to ask her if Gerald's spirit could be exorcised, although she knew an exorcist in Salem, the Reverend Sparks, who had been a friend of John Wesley.

'Beatrice!' said Clara. 'What brings you to my door? Not that you aren't welcome.'

'I was wondering if you could kindly tell my fortune for me,' said Beatrice.

'I have heard about Noah, of course, and my heart bleeds for you. Do you want to consult me about him?'

'Partly. But I would also like to find out what might become of us, Florence and me. I have been told that a new parson is coming to Sutton next week, and we will have to leave.'

'Come inside,' said Clara, and ushered Beatrice and Florence into her parlour. The room was so filled up with furniture that it was more like a shop than a parlour – five Windsor chairs and a brocade-covered ottoman, as well as side tables crowded with candlesticks and figurines and framed pictures of various relatives. Almost every inch of the walls was hung with dark oil paintings of angels and engravings of monks and ghosts and extraordinary animals. Florence had been in here before, but she still found some of the pictures frightening, because she clung close to Beatrice's skirt.

Apart from all the furniture and pictures, the room was also filled with a strong aroma of incense and cloves and stale tobacco smoke. Beatrice didn't find it unpleasant, but she always felt when she entered the Widow Belknap's parlour that she had entered into another world – a shadowy, claustrophobic world of mystery and magic. If she hadn't been able to see the sunlit green outside the window, she could have felt that she was being carried away in the captain's cabin of a supernatural ship.

'May I offer you tea?' asked Clara. 'Or I have some cider if you prefer, and apple juice for Florence.'

'Yes, a glass of cider would be welcome,' said Beatrice.

Clara went into the kitchen, but while she was there she called out, 'I didn't think you really believed in my fortune-telling, Beatrice. Doesn't the Lord light your path for you?'

'He lights it, yes, but he doesn't give me a map of where it will lead me tomorrow, and in the days after that.'

Clara came back with a jug of cider and two glasses, a mug of apple juice, and a plateful of thumbprint cookies filled with blueberry jelly. Florence immediately detached herself from Beatrice and sat up with a smile.

'Nothing like cookies to overcome your fear of the Devil,' said Clara. She poured out the cider, and then she said, 'You brought a luckybone, I trust?'

Beatrice reached into her pocket and took out the wishbone that she had saved from the last chicken that she had cooked. Clara held out her hand and they both hooked their little fingers around it.

'One, two, three – what will we see?' chanted Clara, and they snapped the bone apart. Beatrice had the larger piece, and she shook her head in amazement.

'Every time we do this, I win,' she said.

Clara tapped the side of her nose. 'We witches, they train us to do that from birth. It takes much more skill to lose than it does to succeed. Now, I used the crystal ball last time to look into your future, didn't I? But only last week my cousin sent me a pack of new fortune-telling cards from London. She claims they are wonderfully exact in predicting what will happen in the months ahead.'

She pulled out a drawer underneath the low table between them, and produced a cardboard box of cards. They looked like ordinary playing cards, with clubs and diamonds and hearts and spades, and royal cards, too, but each of them had a four-line rhyme printed at the bottom of them.

'They have been newly produced by John Lenthall of Fleet Street,' said Clara, as she shuffled them. 'He has produced many types of cards, but these are the first that can tell your fortune. There are only forty-eight of them, instead of fifty-two. As your conjuror I am commanded by the Oracle of Delphos to multiply the twelve signs of the zodiac by the four seasons of the year, and no more than that, which means that the four aces have had to be excluded.'

She laid all forty-eight cards face-down on the table in six rows of eight. Florence stopped pretending to feed Minnie with a thumbprint cookie and watched in fascination.

Clara said, 'Now, Beatrice, place your right hand on your left breast and say, "*Honi soit qui mal y pense.*" Then pick out a card. If you do not wish to reveal what it says, you can return it to the table and choose another, but whatever your lot, that second card must be abided by. You may pick four cards altogether, one for each coming season.'

'Will they say when No-noh is coming home?' asked Florence.

'They may,' said Clara, gently. 'Let us hope so. But most of all they will say what your mother can expect.'

Beatrice said, '*Honi soit qui mal y pense,*' and picked out a card. It was the seven of hearts, and the rhyme said, *Now the seven I'll maintain, Shews thou hast not lov'd in vain, Thou wilt have the golden prize; But with maids 'tis otherwise.*

She read the rhyme, hesitated, and then placed the card back on the table without telling Clara what it had said. She then picked up another card, and this was the three of clubs. The rhyme said, *You who now this three have drawn, Will on cursed Harlots fawn, Women who do get this trey, To their Acts do answer Nay.*

Beatrice passed the card to Clara and said, 'What does it mean? I'm confused.'

'It means that you will meet women of easy virtue, but you will stand up on their behalf and protect them from being exploited by men.'

'I have been invited to work for a society in London for refractory girls,' said Beatrice. 'How could the card have known that?'

Clara shrugged and smiled. 'I told you... they are very exact. I read my own fortune with them, and so far everything has come true. I drew the king of hearts, which foretells for women that they will soon be preferred by a very amenable man, and that is exactly what has happened. Two weeks ago I met the new master who will be coming here next month to teach at the school and we took an instant liking to each other.'

'You didn't tell me that? What about Gerald?'

'I believe that once Gerald realizes that I have found happiness, his spirit will leave me. He loved me passionately, after all. But I don't know how soon this will happen. I also drew that ten of diamonds, which says that I will be wed again, but "*none knows when*".'

Beatrice picked up her next card, the five of diamonds. *He who draws the no. five, Where he lives he will thrive, But if drawn by woman-kind, They better luck abroad will find.*

After that, she picked the queen of spades, and this card told her that *The Queen of Spades likewise, Shows thee will to riches rise, Women by the same will have, What they both desire and crave.*

'I have no wish for riches,' said Beatrice. 'I desire and crave only to have Noah back in my arms.'

'If that is what you want, then you shall,' Clara told her.

'But these are nothing more than cards. How can I believe them?'

'Because they are so much more than cards, Beatrice! They are like *signposts*, which show you which way you can go. And they are mirrors, too, which reveal to you those qualities that you sometimes fail to see in yourself – how strong you are, how attractive you are, and how you will get what you want only by taking risks and following those signposts wherever they point.'

Beatrice picked one last card, the two of diamonds. *Hast thou drawn the no. two, Thou'lt wed one that is true, But if Woman this shall have, Beware of a fly cunning knave.*

Clara looked at the card and said, 'Well... be warned by this. Remember Jonathan Shooks.'

Beatrice looked at Florence, who had stood up now and was wandering around the parlour, showing Minnie some of the strange creatures in Clara's engravings.

'How could I ever forget him?' she said.

After the card-reading, Beatrice and Clara went out into the back yard, and walked around in the sunshine while Florence jumped up and down and threw Minnie into the air, pretending that she was an angel.

Clara lit a small clay pipe and thoughtfully puffed it as they walked around the apple trees.

'I know you're frightened, Beatrice,' she said. 'And I also understand how much you're grieving, not only for Noah, but for Francis, too. Grief is a kind of illness from which we never completely recover. But the cards have told you that you have to venture abroad, and that you will one day find happiness. That is not to say that I shan't miss you. I shall miss you dearly.'

She wedged her pipe into the crook of the nearest tree, and then she put her arms around Beatrice and held her close, and kissed her on the lips. It was strange to be kissed by a woman whose breath smelled like that of a man, but she knew that she would miss Clara as much as Clara would miss her, and she touched her moon-pale cheek with her fingertips, and kissed her back, and for a long moment they stared into each other's eyes and shared the pain of understanding that they might never see each other again, except in heaven.

7

Beatrice had forgotten how foul the stench was in London's streets, and she was sure it had grown worse since she was last here. She was thankful when their carriage at last left the narrow cobbled lanes of the City with their kennels overflowing with sewage, and arrived at Windmill Hill, by Moorfields, one of the last grassy spaces left in Shoreditch.

It was a chilly, fresh morning, with a north-east breeze blowing. All the same, it had rained during the night and the muddy churned-up road outside the meeting house was shoe-deep in wet horse manure.

'It's so *funky*!' complained Florence, as the coachman swung her down from the hackney.

'Ah, you wait till the summer, young lady!' the coachman grinned, showing his gappy walnut-coloured teeth. 'You and your dolly will be having to hold your noses!'

Beatrice climbed down carefully, lifting up her skirts so that they wouldn't trail into the muck. She gave the coachman his fare of six shillings, and two pennies as a vail. Then she trod with hesitant steps over to the meeting house, as if she were playing hopscotch.

Francis had brought her here to the Foundery before they had set off to America, to meet some of the church's ministers. It was a collection of five large pink-brick buildings, just to the north of Bethlem Hospital for lunatics. Originally it had been built as a factory for the casting of brass cannon, but Francis had explained to her that forty years ago a shattering explosion of white-hot metal and steam had killed not only seventeen bystanders but the foundry's owner. For safety's sake all munitions-making had afterwards been removed to Woolwich, and eventually the damaged and derelict factory had been taken over by the Nonconformist church.

Beatrice could see that buildings had been extended since she was last here, and the rooftops had been repaired with new slates. As she approached the maroon-painted front door she could hear children singing from the courtyard at the side.

She knocked, and the door was opened almost immediately by a smiling young girl with a scrubbed-looking face and a long white apron.

'I am Beatrice Scarlet,' said Beatrice. 'The Reverend Parsons is expecting me, I believe.'

The Reverend Parsons must have heard her, because he appeared in the gloomy hallway behind the young girl, with a loud bray like a horse and a cry of 'Widow Scarlet! You have reached us safely from across the ocean, thank the Lord! Welcome to Windmill Hill! You are heartily welcome!'

'This is my daughter Florence,' said Beatrice, and laid her hand on Florence's shoulder to push her gently down into a curtsey.

The Reverend Parsons had short-cropped gingery hair and ginger eyebrows. He looked excited to see her, but Beatrice would soon learn that he always looked excited, from morning till night, as if the entire world and every minute he spent in it was a huge surprise. He was big-bellied, so that he had to leave five or six of his waistcoat buttons undone, and she doubted if he ever managed to button up his black tailcoat at all.

The smiling young girl stepped outside and directed the coachman to carry Beatrice's two trunks around to the side of the building. The Reverend Parsons meanwhile ushered Beatrice and Florence inside, and into a large mahogany-panelled drawing room.

The room was austere, with dark brown curtains and comb-back chairs, and the only picture hanging on the walls was a large oil painting of Jesus at the pool of Bethesda, healing the sick. But a bright log fire was crackling in the grate, and a tortoiseshell cat was sleeping close beside it, much to Florence's delight.

'Please, sit,' said the Reverend Parsons. 'I am sure you must be extremely weary after so long a voyage. How many days was it?'

'Twenty-seven, because we had some very stormy weather around the south coast of Ireland. One night I was even fearful that we might be run aground.'

'I am a very poor sailor myself,' smiled the Reverend Parsons. 'All I can say for my one and only visit to the colonies was that my seasickness helped me to lose a considerable amount of my girth! I am afraid that much of it has been returned to me, though, courtesy of too many Kit-Cats.' He was referring to the popular mutton pies that could be bought from Christopher Catt's pie shop in Shire Lane, and which had been a favourite of Beatrice's father, too.

It was probably the effect of exhaustion, but Beatrice suddenly had the feeling that she had never left London, and that her life in New Hampshire had been only a dream. If Florence hadn't been kneeling by the hearth, stroking the cat, and if she hadn't been carrying around her own neck a silver pendant with a miniature portrait of Noah inside it, which Francis had given her for her last birthday, she could almost have believed that the last three and a half years had never happened.

The Reverend Parsons lifted his pocket watch out of his waistcoat and sprang open the lid. 'Goodness, it is almost one o'clock! Mrs Smollett should be here at any moment. She has been running St Mary Magdalene's refuge for over eighteen months now, and since she has taken it over, it has proven to be a wonderful success. She has arranged gainful employment for many a penitent prostitute, and also for young women who are either abandoned or destitute or whose conduct has caused them to be expelled by their families.'

'I heard children singing when I arrived,' said Beatrice.

'Yes! We have expanded the meeting house so much in the past eighteen months... well, almost as much as *I* have expanded, myself. But now we have a school here for some sixty-odd ragged children, with two masters. We also have an apothecary for the distribution of medicines to the poor, *gratis*, as well as a surgeon who visits from St Bart's twice a week to conduct minor operations such as lancing boils or amputating gangrenous toes. We are thinking, too, of building and opening an almshouse.'

'You are doing excellent work, Reverend,' said Beatrice, tiredly. All she wanted now was to change her clothes and bathe and retire to bed for the rest of the day, although she knew that she would have to find somebody to take care of Florence while she slept. Florence didn't seem to be tired at all, but then she had slept until it had been time for a lighter to row them upstream from Deptford, and ashore.

A long-case clock in the hall chimed one, and almost as soon as it did so, the door opened and a woman bustled in like the female figure popping out of a weather house.

She had a dead-white face, except for two crimson spots on her cheeks, and she was wearing a curly reddish wig with two long ringlets, and a slate-grey bonnet which matched her slate-grey dress. Plain as it was, this dress, it was widened so much by the panniers on her hips underneath it that it brushed against the door frame on either side.

She was in her mid-thirties, Beatrice guessed, although it was difficult to judge her age exactly because of the masklike whiteness of her face. This had been achieved by the application of a thick lead-based paste, and the two rosy circles on her cheeks had been dabbed on with vermilion. Her lips were a little bee-stung pout, although she had painted them only the faintest pink with beeswax and carmine. She hadn't wanted to look like an actress, or a prostitute.

Beatrice was conscious that her own face was unfashionably suntanned from tending the vegetable garden at the parsonage, which made her look like a working woman. But she knew that when lead was absorbed through the skin over a period of time, it could be lethal, and that many fashionable young women had died from using it regularly to make up their faces. Vermilion was even more toxic: it was made from cinnabar, which was sulphide of quicksilver.

She would say nothing, though. It was so fashionable for women to make up their faces like this, and who was she to tell them that they shouldn't? Some women even spread white lead paste on their cleavage and painted blue veins on their breasts to make themselves appear to be even more anaemic than they actually were. And for all Beatrice knew, this woman had unsightly smallpox scars on her cheeks which she needed to cover up, and she didn't want to embarrass her.

As her father had always said as he mixed up his medicines in the outbuilding at the back of his shop, 'The most virulent poison of all, Beatrice, is vanity. Most of us would sooner be dead than ugly.'

The Reverend Parsons stood up and held out his hand to the woman in greeting. 'Ida! You are looking a picture as always! Let me introduce you to Beatrice Scarlet, who will be assisting you at St Mary Magdalene's. And of course to young Miss Scarlet here.

'Beatrice, this is Ida Smollett, who has transformed our home for refractory young women beyond all of our expectations. I trust the two of you will be the very best of friends and companions.'

Ida nodded her bonnet and puckered her lips into a smile. In spite of her appearance, she spoke with considerable fluency and warmth, as if she were used to addressing an audience.

'It is such a pleasure, Beatrice, if I may be so familiar. Our work at the home has become almost overwhelming, and with winter approaching I will be sorely in need of assistance.'

'Let me arrange for us to take some tea,' said the Reverend Parsons, and left the drawing room while Beatrice and Ida sat side by side in the upright wooden chairs.

'How many young women do you currently care for?' asked Beatrice. Sitting so close to Ida, she could smell her perfume, a musky amber toilet water, but she could also smell cinnamon, which was commonly used to sweeten bad breath. Among other side effects, such as blackening the skin, white lead rotted the gums and attacked the enamel of the teeth.

'Presently we have thirty-six,' said Ida. 'They are mostly girls who have become estranged from their families, for one reason or another. Either their parents were so destitute that they couldn't afford to feed them or clothe them, or else they were too sick to care for anybody except themselves, or they were drunk – or in many cases, deceased. I don't know if any intelligence of it reached you in the colonies, but there was a mortally bad plague of consumption here in London last winter, and hundreds died. So many bodies were stacked up in coffins in the Quaker cemetery that they toppled over into the next-door brickyard.

'Some of our girls managed to survive by thieving, or by begging, but the majority kept themselves alive by prostitution. I expect you have seen them yourself, some of them as young as twelve or thirteen, loitering around outside the theatres after the end of each evening's performance, trying to catch the eye of some dissolute fellow with five shillings in his pocket.'

'So how do you lift them out of that life?' Beatrice asked her.

'We shelter them, we feed them, we teach them simple arithmetic and to read and write. We give them moral education, too, and catechism classes. After that, with the generous help of several benevolent businessmen and factory owners who are members of our church, we find them gainful employ.'

'It all sounds most gratifying,' said Beatrice. 'I believe I shall be honoured to assist you.'

'I will not pretend for a moment that it is easy,' Ida told her. 'Some of these girls are veritable savages when we first take them in. They are used to drinking gin and smoking and their everyday language would make Satan shrivel. They have been used by men ever since they can remember, sometimes by their own fathers and brothers, so they think nothing of virtue or virginity. In some cases, their own mothers have sold their maidenheads to the highest bidder to make ends meet.'

'But surely they must be grateful that you have saved them.'

Ida shrugged. 'A fair number learn to be thankful, I'll grant you. But some regard us as pious busybodies and cannot wait to return to their life on the streets. They relish the flattery they are given by licentious men, and the money. They enjoy the orgies, and the drink. They have never been used to discipline or decorum, and they cannot understand that they are not only destroying themselves here on Earth but abnegating any chance they might have had of going to heaven.'

'So what do you do about them?'

Ida reached across and laid a claw-like hand on Beatrice's knee. She was wearing three gold rings – one with turquoise, one with garnet and one with amethyst. Close up, Beatrice could smell how foetid her breath was, in spite of the cinnamon. But that was nothing exceptional – some of her very dearest friends in Sutton had decaying and missing teeth, and Major General Holyoke had been fitted with wooden dentures, which he would take out from time to time and wipe on his cravat.

'This is where I shall be relying on *you*, my dear Beatrice,' said Ida. 'You are younger than me, and I am counting on you to build a rapport with our most difficult girls, and show them that that modesty and abstinence are their own rewards. I am *sure* that you can do it!'

She stared at Beatrice intently, and gripped her knee tight – so tight that she felt as if a hawk had settled on it. Beatrice looked back into her eyes and saw how puffy and inflamed they were. She remembered all those ailing customers who had come in to her father's shop riddled with mercury poisoning, and she reckoned that Ida would probably be dead in three years, if not sooner.

The Reverend Parsons returned, and soon afterwards the girl with the scrubbed-looking face brought in a tea tray, with a glass of milk for Florence. While Beatrice and Ida and the Reverend Parsons talked further about St Mary Magdalene's, little Florence dipped her fingers into her milk so that the cat could lick it off.

Beatrice looked down at her and smiled sadly and thought, *Yes – if I can give even one wretched girl a life of purity and love such as Florence will enjoy, then I will.*

8

After they had finished their tea, the Reverend Parsons guided Beatrice around the Foundery so that she could visit the apothecary and the children's classroom.

The apothecary was a long, gloomy room with a high, tiny window and shelves that were crowded with green, brown and clear glass bottles, as well as mahogany boxes of powders and pipes of pills. At the far end stood an oak bench where a young, balding man with spectacles and a very large nose was stirring a sticky mixture in a china bowl.

'Godfrey!' said the Reverend Parsons. 'Allow me to introduce you to Widow Scarlet, who has come to assist Mistress Smollett at St Mary Magdalene's. Beatrice, this is Godfrey Minchin, our resident apothecary, who will be happy to provide you with any medicines or salves that you require.'

Godfrey bowed his head in greeting, and wiped his nose with the back of his cuff.

'Welcome to the Foundery, Widow Scarlet. You are the daughter of the late and very lamented Clement Bannister, are you not? While I was studying, I found several of his papers on the pox to be of great assistance, not leastly those preparations on corrosive sublimate.'

By corrosive sublimate, Godfrey meant mercuric chloride. Mercury had commonly been used to treat venereal disease for many years but its side effects had been almost as destructive as the disease itself, so Beatrice's father had reduced its potency and combined it with chlorine.

'My father was a wonderful apothecary, and most inventive,' said Beatrice. 'What are you mixing there, may I ask?'

'Sacred bitters, Widow Scarlet, or *hiera picra* to give them their proper name. I am preparing it for the warden, Mr Jewkes, who has been suffering lately from all manner of ill humours – in particular, gripes of the stomach and blockage of the bowels.'

'Ah, yes… aloes and canella bark. And honey?'

'I'm impressed, Widow Scarlet.'

'I spent many hours in my father's laboratory when I was a girl, Mr Minchin. And I remember when he devised his new treatment for the pox, calomel and corrosive sublimate. He heated the sublimate and almost blew both of us up to kingdom come. My apron was torn to tatters and we had to replace the window glass.'

'Well, it is still the best treatment for syphilis,' said the Reverend Parsons. 'You know what they say… one night with Venus and the rest of your life with Mercury.'

Next, they went across the brick-paved yard to the schoolroom. This was high-ceilinged and airy, with tall windows overlooking the lime trees and lawns of Moorfields. About fifty children of varying ages were sitting at six rows of long tables, each with a slate and some broken sticks of chalk. They were laboriously copying a list of words that had been written on the large blackboard that stood on an easel in the corner of the classroom: *cough, plough, rough, though, brought.*

Their teacher was standing at the blackboard with his back to the door as the Reverend Parsons ushered Beatrice inside. She could see that he was tall and slim and straight-backed, with wavy dark-brown hair flowing over his collar. He was wearing a moth-eaten rust-coloured frock coat with a thick green velvet collar, which looked a little moth-eaten too.

'James!' exclaimed the Reverend Parsons, and the teacher turned around. Beatrice didn't know what she was expecting a teacher of ragged children to look like – pale and bespectacled and spotty, perhaps, like Godfrey the apothecary. But this young man was remarkably handsome. In some ways she reminded her of Francis, but if anything he was better-looking, with a strong, squarish face, and a short, straight nose, and large, compelling blue eyes.

He tossed his stick of chalk onto his desk, smacked his hands together to get rid of the chalk-dust and came up to Beatrice with an expression on his face that she could only think of as mischievous.

'Reverend Parsons,' he said. 'And who is this you have brought to visit to me this morning? Whoever you are, madam, it is the greatest honour.'

With that, he bent his arm across his long green waistcoat, and bowed. Beatrice couldn't help blushing.

'Beatrice, this is one of our two teachers, Mr James Treadgold,' said the Reverend Parsons. 'James, may I present Beatrice Scarlet, widow of the late Reverend Francis Scarlet, returned only this very morning from America.'

'I heard about the sad demise of your late husband, Widow Scarlet,' said James. 'It has been some time since his passing, I know, but may I offer you my belated condolences.' All the time his eyes were focused intently on hers, as if he could see a shadow-show behind them of what she was thinking.

'You're very kind,' said Beatrice. She didn't mention that she had also lost Noah. Since setting sail for England she had been trying hard not to think about either Francis or Noah, because it always tightened her throat and brought her so close to tears. She had found that the most effective way of coping with their loss was by concentrating her mind on Florence's welfare, and what the future years might bring them.

'James is the youngest son of Sir Walter Treadgold, who in our early days was one of our most generous benefactors,' said the Reverend Parsons. 'Regrettably, Sir Walter's business was a victim of the war with Spain, but he and his family have remained to this day some of our staunchest supporters. What they can no longer give us in gold they give us in service.'

'I teach the children writing and grammar, and my colleague Timothy French comes on alternate days to teach them their sums,' James explained.

'If these children are ever to overcome the dragon of misfortune, then their two sharpest swords will be words and numbers,' put in the Reverend Parsons. 'Their breastplates, of course, will be a thorough acquaintance with the scriptures.'

James continued to stare at Beatrice with such concentration that she was beginning to feel quite light-headed. She thought that he was extremely attractive, yet she wondered if he were staring at her because he felt the same about her, or if he was simply showing sympathy for her.

One of the older boys at the back of the classroom put up his hand and said, 'Do you say it "*cow*", sir, or "*cog*"?'

James kept his eyes on Beatrice and raised his hand to indicate that he would answer the boy in a moment.

'You must be overwhelmingly weary, Widow Scarlet,' he said. 'However, perhaps when you have rested, we could meet, and you could tell me all about your experiences in America. I have long considered going there myself and I would be fascinated to hear what you made of it.'

'Of course,' said Beatrice. 'I have to caution you, though, that not all of my experiences were happy, and there were times when they were fearful. It is still a savage land with many unexpected dangers, not the least of which are some of the colonists themselves.'

James said, 'I can't wait to hear all about it! I'll take you to the Three Cranes in the Vintry, if you have never eaten there before. They serve a delicious roasted dotterel, and excellent wines.'

Beatrice smiled. 'You've reminded me, James, that I'm hungry as well as tired. I'd better collect my daughter and allow Mrs Smollett to take us to St Mary Magdalene's. It's been a pleasure to make your acquaintance.'

James bowed again. 'The pleasure was all mine, Mrs Scarlet. Rest well.'

The Reverend Parsons took Beatrice back to the drawing room, where Ida Smollett and Florence were waiting for them. Ida was teaching Florence to sing 'London Bridge Is Falling Down' and clapping hands with her.

'If you are not too tired, we can make our way on foot to Maidenhead Court,' said Ida. 'It is only five minutes away.'

'The minute our factotum, Henry, returns from running an errand to Cheapside I will have him wheel around your trunks on his barrow,' said the Reverend Parsons.

'We have more items of luggage to be delivered here when the ship is fully unloaded,' Beatrice told him. 'Perhaps he could be kind enough to bring that, too, when it arrives.'

The Reverend Parsons laid his hand on her shoulder and said, 'I know what pain you have suffered, Beatrice, and that you continue to suffer, and may never completely overcome. May the Lord God give you solace and peace of mind and reward you in the fullness of time for your faith and your endurance.

But do not grieve too bitterly for your Francis. He drew his prize early, and you should wish him joy.'

Beatrice was unable to reply. She simply nodded, with tears in her eyes.

They made their way across the rutted City Road and past the Bunhill burial grounds. They could see a wagon with a plain coffin on it, although there were no mourners around it. The only people in sight were two gravediggers, one of whom was digging in a desultory fashion while the other was leaning on his spade and smoking a pipe.

Next they crossed Bunhill Row into Blue Anchor Alley. The houses and workshops that lined both sides of the alley were rickety old wooden buildings that had survived the Great Fire, and their tilting upper stories overhung the alley so far that their eaves almost touched. They shielded the alley from the wind, so that it was not only gloomy along here, and reeking of sewage, but eerily silent.

They had nearly reached the end of the alley when Beatrice heard the quick patter of footsteps behind her. She turned around and saw that three rough-looking men were running towards them – one in a cocked hat, another in a ratty-looking wig, and the third with a blue-shaven head. The one with the blue-shaven head was carrying a knife, almost as long as a sword, while the one in the cocked hat was swinging a cudgel.

'Hey, ladies!' shouted the one in the cocked hat. 'A moment of your time, if you please!'

Beatrice was already holding Florence's hand, but now she gripped it even tighter and said, 'Run, Florrie!'

Ida turned around, too, and like Beatrice, she gathered up her skirts and tried to break into a run.

It was too late. The alley was as badly churned up as the main road, and Beatrice caught her shoe and stumbled. The man with the blue-shaven head pushed his way past Ida and barred their way into Whitecross Street, waving his knife from side to side and lasciviously licking his gums around his single walnut-coloured tooth.

'We don't mean you no harm, you rum-doxies,' said the man in the cocked hat. He was wearing a filthy red frock coat with frayed shoulders, and his buff-coloured breeches were stained dark with urine. 'All we're after is some chink, and maybe a bit of rantum-scantum.'

'You can take yourselves off to hell!' snapped Ida. 'You'll get neither! Be off before I scream for a constable!'

The man with the blue-shaven head came up to her and held the point of his knife close to her cheek.

'You wouldn't want my chum to fake you, would you, Madam Van?' said the man in the cocked hat. 'Come along, be obliging! There's a doorway back there, and we can go inside and blow off the groundsels on the staircase, where nobody will see us. You can give the young titter here some education in the art of relish!'

Beatrice saw her chance. She pushed the man with the blue-shaven head as hard as she could on the shoulder, so that he lost his balance and fell against the rough plastered wall. Then she started to run towards Whitecross Street, tugging Florence after her. She could only hope that Ida would take her cue and follow her.

As she ran out of the alley, the man in the cocked hat caught up with her and knocked her on the back of her head with the end of his cudgel. He managed only a glancing blow, but it was enough to send her tumbling forward onto the muddy roadway, bringing Florence down beside her. Florence's coat was spattered with horse manure and she screamed in panic.

Winded and bruised, Beatrice twisted herself around and looked up. Her vision was blurred from the blow on the head but she could see the man in the cocked hat glaring down at her. He was swinging his cudgel as if he were preparing himself to hit her again, and harder this time. His face was crimson with drink and exertion and anger, like a huge bloody boil about to burst.

'You *punk*!' he snarled at her. 'Just for that we'll give the titter a prigging, too!' he snarled at her.

Beatrice was so breathless that her voice was reduced to a high, hoarse screech. 'Don't you dare to lay one finger on her, or I will kill you myself!'

'Oh, yes?' the man mocked her, slapping his cudgel into the palm of his filthy hand. 'You and the King's Own Regiment of Foot, I suppose?'

The man with the ratty-looking wig came up to her and caught hold of her sleeve. 'Come along, up you get, my darling!' he said, and she could feel his spit flying against her forehead. Back in the alley, she could see that the man with the blue-shaven head had crooked one arm around Ida's neck, and was holding his knife up only an inch from her face.

Still sobbing with fright, Florence climbed onto her feet, and the man with the cocked hat gripped her arm.

Whitecross Street was quite busy, with shoppers and messenger boys and street sellers. One of the sellers was ringing a bell and shouting, 'A pudding-a-pudding a hot pudding!' and another was crying out, 'Turnips and carrots, ho!' At least six or seven carriages and hackneys and drays went rattling past, but none of the coaches stopped, and as soon as the shoppers saw that the three ruffians were armed with a knife and a cudgel, they crossed over to the other side. It was more than possible that one them might have a pistol, too, and in recent months several passers-by who had tried to intervene in street robberies had been shot dead.

Beatrice kept struggling to get herself free, but she had to allow the man with the ratty wig to pull her up, so that she could protect Florence.

'Come along, then, darling!' the man spat at her, tugging her back into the alley. As soon as he had said that, though, Beatrice heard a clattering of hooves close behind her, and the jingling of harness, and the squeaking sound of a carriage being drawn to a halt.

A man's voice bellowed out, 'Ho there! What do you think you're playing at, you scum?' And then, 'Ida! God in heaven!'

9

The man in the ratty wig tried to drag Beatrice further into the alley, but she twisted and wrenched her sleeve away from him, not just once, but twice, so that it tore. He made a half-hearted attempt to snatch at her again, but then he started to run. The man with the cocked hat started to run, too, and the two of them went pelting off along the alley. Halfway back to Bunhill Row, the man's wig flew off and landed in the mud. He stopped for a second, one hand clamped on top of his scabby head, but then he carried on running, and both he and the man in the cocked hat disappeared around the corner.

Although both of his partners in crime had vanished, the man with the blue-shaven head continued to hold on to Ida, his forearm pressed so tightly against her neck that she was squeaking for breath.

The man who had stopped his carriage came up close to Beatrice and said, 'Are you hurt at all, my dear? What about your little girl? Is she all right?'

He was not a tall man, but he was broad-shouldered, and he had a strong, rugged face, with a broken nose and a deeply cleft chin. There was something rough-hewn about his looks, as if his cheeks had been sandpapered, but his yellow frock coat and his cream-coloured waistcoat were finely tailored, and he had gold buttons and silver shoe buckles. He was wearing a light-brown wig which was tied with a yellow ribbon at the back.

His carriage was painted shiny yellow, and it was drawn by four glossy black Friesians.

Immediately after he had made sure that Beatrice and Florence were uninjured, he crossed the alley to confront the man with the blue-shaven head. At the same time, he drew out his sword and held it up high.

'You – you dromedary!' he barked. 'I order you to drop your blade and release this good lady at once!'

The man shook his blue-shaven head, and twisted his lips into a sneer, but uttered only a gargling sound. It was obvious that he was not only almost completely toothless but also mute. He began to shuffle backwards along the alley, pulling Ida after him.

The man in the yellow frock coat looked around, frowning, as if he were thinking of something quite different. Then he slid his sword back into its scabbard, unbuttoned one of his coat pockets and took out a brown leather wallet. He produced half a guinea, which he held up in his left hand, between finger and thumb.

'I realize by the desperation of what you have tried to do that you must be sorely in need of the King's picture,' he said, and Beatrice was amazed how calmly he spoke. Florence had stopped crying but she was still trembling and now and again she let out a little shivering sob.

'If you release this lady, this half-guinea shall be yours, and no more said,' the man in the yellow frock coat continued. 'I shall call no watchman, nor make any complaint against you.'

The man with the blue-shaven head was staring at the half-guinea, mesmerized. This was enough money to get drunk for a month, or have a harlot.

The man in the yellow frock coat waited patiently, still holding up the gold coin. Behind him, his black horses were shuffling and snorting between their shafts, eager to get moving again, but he ignored them, and he also ignored the curious stares of passers-by, some of whom had stopped on the corner and were cautiously peering into the alley to see what was going on.

After what seemed to Beatrice like a whole long minute of indecision, the man with the blue-shaven head released his grip on Ida's neck and pushed her roughly to one side. Beatrice went across and took hold of her hand, pulling her well away from him, so that he wouldn't be able to lash out and cut her.

'You must drop your knife,' said the man in the yellow frock coat. 'Then this half-bean shall be yours for the taking.'

The man with the blue-shaven head gave a snorting catarrhal sniff, and then he tossed his knife onto the ground. He came forward with a slight limp, holding out of his hand for the half-guinea. Beatrice had a terrible feeling about what was going to happen next, and she held Florence close to her and turned her head away. Ida looked at her and Beatrice had never seen a woman appear so relieved and yet still so frightened.

As the man with the blue-shaven head reached out for the coin, the man in the yellow frock coat slid his sword out of its sheath with a slippery, ringing sound, whirled it around with a flick of his wrist and thrust it straight into the crotch of the ruffian's grubby grey breeches. It made a sharp, sickening crunch. The point must have pierced him at the root of his penis, almost castrating him, because it caused his breeches to flood instantly with blood.

He uttered a weird, distorted scream, like some of the eerie cries that Beatrice used to hear coming from the woods in New Hampshire at night. The man in the yellow frock coat twisted his sword around and then drew it out, his expression still as calm as it had been before. The man with the blue-shaven head staggered backwards, falling against the wall and then dropping to his knees. He was clutching himself between his thighs with both hands but blood was dripping quickly between his fingers. He had stopped screaming but he was making a thin, whining sound, like a hungry cat.

'You had best find yourself a surgeon as quick as you can,' said the man in the yellow frock coat. 'I promised not to call a watchman, and I will be true to my word. Bart's Hospital is less than a mile off, if you can manage to walk there. Otherwise God help you. At least if you bleed to death you won't have to polish the King's iron with your eyebrows.'

He sheathed his sword and held up the half-guinea again, almost under the man's nose. 'I said this would be yours for the taking, did I not? But since you failed to take it, I shall regrettably have to keep it for myself.'

With that, he took out his wallet again, and dropped the coin into it.

'George,' said Ida, tearfully. 'I cannot find sufficient words to thank you. I was certain that he was going to cut my throat.'

'Come on, let us leave here instanter,' said George. 'I could scarcely believe my own eyes when I saw those vagabonds manhandling you and your companions here.'

He ushered them over to his carriage. His liveried coachman was about to climb down and help them but the door was still hanging wide open and he called up, 'Stay where you are, Michael! Let us just quit this place as quick as maybe!'

They climbed inside and George folded up the steps and closed the door. The interior was upholstered in the softest tan leather and Beatrice thought she had never sat in a carriage so comfortable. However, when Michael geed up the horses and they started to trundle southwards on Whitecross Street, the furrows and potholes in the roadway set the carriage swaying and jostling and lurching so much that Beatrice had to cling on to the hand-strap, and keep her arm tightly around Florence to stop her from sliding across the seat.

'You must have been sent by the Lord himself, George,' said Ida. 'I am quite certain that those varlets would have robbed us and had their way with us and then murdered us for sure.'

'It was hardly miraculous,' said George. 'I had agreed to meet you in any event at two o'clock but I went to the Foundery because your blackamoor girl told me that you were still there. By the time I arrived, though, the Reverend Parsons said that you had already left, so I was returning to Maidenhead Court.'

'All the same, I can only believe that it was divine intervention,' Ida told him. 'You won't face any retribution for having pronged that fellow, will you?'

George shook his head. 'No – no, God, no, absolutely not. He appeared to be speechless, and I doubt if he can write, either, so how can he possibly make a complaint to the constables? Besides which, he would have to admit that I wounded him because he was attempting to rob you and worse, and we have witnesses to prove it.'

The coach jolted so violently that Ida had to cling on tightly to one of the straps. But she managed to lay one hand on George's shoulder and say to Beatrice, 'This gentleman who appeared at such a fortuitous moment is Mr George Hazzard. George – this is Beatrice Scarlet, widow of the Reverend Francis Scarlet, who tragically lost his life in New Hampshire. And of course her daughter Florence.'

'I'm delighted to make your acquaintance, Mrs Scarlet,' said George. 'And you, too, Florence. I wish only that we could have met under less exciting circumstances.'

'George is the owner of Hazzard & Son, the tobacco factory in Hackney,' Ida explained. 'Sadly there is no longer a son, but George continues to prosper, and he has used his prosperity to give my girls gainful employment. At the present time, eleven of them are working for him – eleven, isn't it, George? But over the years there have been more than fifty, all of whom eventually found well-paid domestic positions, or husbands – or both, some of them – and so have been rescued from squalor and degradation and moral turpitude.'

'I have been a supporter of the Nonconformist church from the very beginning,' said George. 'Its works of Christian charity are second to none. There is so much desperate poverty in London, and, in particular, so many young girls have been forced onto the streets or into nunneries.'

He was obviously using the euphemism for bawdy house for Florence's sake, for which Beatrice was grateful. She began to think that if St Mary Magdalene's benefactors were all as sensitive and brave and well-mannered as George Hazzard there was no limit to what good work she might be able to achieve. It would be her loving tribute to Francis – her own way of carrying on the charitable mission to which he had devoted himself ever since he was a boy.

His grave might be in New Hampshire, but his memorial would be here in London.

10

They arrived at Maidenhead Court, which was a handsome square on the east side of Aldersgate Street, of four-storey terraced houses with lawns and plane trees all around. The court even had its own gate, which could be locked at night to keep out cracksmen and budges and other riff-raff.

The carriage stopped outside No. 14, and Michael the coachman jumped down to open the door for them and fold down the steps. As Beatrice climbed down, George Hazzard offered his hand to help her. She could see the pale faces of several young women crowded together in the windows of the house, watching them.

'We seem to be the objects of some considerable curiosity, Ida,' said George, with a smile.

'Well, George, you know that your visits are always a cause for great excitement,' Ida replied, as she adjusted her petticoats. 'The girls are always anxious to find out which of them you will choose to work for you. After all, it is their first step towards a happy and a prosperous future.'

Florence said, 'I'm hungry, Mama!'

'Don't fret,' Ida told her. 'We have bread and cheese and cold mutton aplenty. And you shall have some bergamot bomboons too, for being such a brave young girl.'

They went up the steps to the teal-painted front door, which was opened for them before they had knocked, by a strikingly pretty black girl in a mob cap and a long striped apron.

'Thank you, Grace,' said Ida. 'This is Widow Scarlet, who I was telling you about last week, and this is her daughter Florence. Would you take them up to their rooms, please, so that they can rinse their hands and rest for a little while? Their luggage will be arriving shortly.

'Beatrice, after you have seen your room, perhaps you would care to come downstairs to the drawing room to meet some of our young residents, and for refreshment.'

The hallway was narrow and the stairs were steep and uncarpeted, with creaking treads. As they started to climb up behind Grace, Beatrice heard giggling coming from the half-open drawing room door. A girl with curly blonde hair popped her head out to stare at them, and just as quickly popped it back again, followed by even more giggling.

Ida looked up and said, 'You must take no notice, Beatrice. They tend to be highly excitable, our girls. They are used to leading very robustious lives and, by comparison, they sometimes find the routine at St Mary Magdalene's to be rather restrictive. But it is only through routine that they will find fulfilment in this world and salvation in the next. Not to mention cleanliness of body and mind, and constant prayer.'

'Well said, Ida,' George told her, and patted her approvingly on the shoulder.

Ida and George went into the drawing room, while Grace and Florence and Beatrice continued to climb. 'Where are you from, Grace?' Beatrice asked her, as they reached the first-floor landing.

'I was bringed here from Barbadoes by my master when I was seven years old, to be trained in service,' said Grace. She had a slight West Indian accent, but she spoke very clearly and sweetly, almost as if she were singing in chapel.

'And then?' asked Beatrice.

'My master's wife, she died of the spotted fever. She was a good woman and always kind to me. My master married again but his new wife beat me and treated me harsh. In the end I could stand it no longer so I ranned away.'

She paused for a moment, and then she said, 'I was took in by this woman Mrs Starling in Chick Lane. She took the best care of me but of course I had to please all the men who came calling. That was before I was saved by Mrs Smollett, who brung me here, God bless her.'

They had reached the third-floor landing now, and Grace led them down to the end of the corridor. She opened the door of the very last room, and Beatrice stepped inside.

It was so much less spacious than she was used to – an oak-panelled room no more than twelve feet by ten, with a two-seater sofa and a single armchair. A small toilet stood under the window, with a view overlooking the treetops of Maidenhead Court; and less than a mile away, rising behind the cluttered rooftops of St Martin's Le Grand and Newgate Street, the great grey dome of St Paul's Cathedral, the tallest building in London, if not the world.

Off to the left there was another door which led to an even smaller room, with a wardrobe and a washstand and a double bed with hardly three inches to walk around it. The bed was covered with a thick maroon bedspread and over the washstand hung a print of Jesus with one hand raised in blessing and a radiant halo shining behind his head. Beatrice found it disturbing because this depiction of Jesus looked so much like Jeremy.

'I will see you downstairs in a little while, Mrs Scarlet,' said Grace. 'There is fresh water in your jug, and you will find towels in your wardrobe. I hope you have a happy time living here with us. The girls here, they laugh and they seem to be merry, but most of them are so sad, and they need a person like you to talk to. It was only two weeks ago that a girl called Anna hunged herself. She never told nobody that she wanted to kill herself.'

'Well, I hope that I can make a difference,' said Beatrice. 'To you, too – Grace. If there is anything that troubles you, anything at all, you can always come and tell me what it is.'

Grace rolled her eyes as if there was something on her mind, but said nothing.

When she was gone, Florence tugged at Beatrice's sleeve and said, 'Quick! I need a wee-wee!'

Beatrice bent down and lifted the bedspread. Underneath the bed was a large white chamber pot emblazoned with the coat of arms of the Worshipful Company of Tobacco Pipe Makers and Tobacco Blenders – two black men standing either side of a tobacco plant, with the motto *Producat Terra*: Out of the Earth.

Florence lifted her petticoats and sat down on it while Beatrice went to the window and looked out over the view of St Paul's. She still felt weak and shaky after being attacked. More than that, she missed New Hampshire sorely, although she knew that her life in Sutton had been even more dangerous in different way. She almost wished that she hadn't agreed to return to London, yet what else could she have done?

Florence came out of the bedroom and said, 'Finished. And I put it back under the bed.'

'Good girl,' said Beatrice, and picked her up and held her close. 'Now let's have a quick wash and go down and meet our new family, shall we?'

*

The drawing room was large, with tall windows at either end, and a high ceiling from which a two-tier brass chandelier hung like a monstrous spider. As large as it was, the room was crowded with over twenty young girls, some of them wedged onto three gondola sofas or sitting two to an armchair, or on each other's laps.

Ida was sitting in an armchair by the white marble fireplace, and George was standing close behind her with one forearm resting on the mantelshelf. It was plain from the proprietary expression on his face that he considered himself to be the master of this house, and the patron of all of these girls. Beatrice supposed that if he was largely responsible for paying the rent and subsidizing the girls' food and clothing and education, he had every right to feel like that. After all, he had even supplied their chamber pots.

He looked at Beatrice as she came in, and gave her a smile and a nod, almost as if they shared some secret between them. Beatrice nodded in return. She was already beginning to feel that he was the kind of man with whom she could form a warm and lasting friendship.

Ida clapped her hands for silence and then introduced Beatrice and Florence to the assembled girls. Meanwhile, Grace brought over a rosewood armchair so that Beatrice could sit next to her. Florence sat cross-legged on the floor in front of her.

George said, 'I'm delighted to tell you that in the past few months, trade at my tobacco factory has been thriving to such an extent that I have vacancies now for seven more girls. The purpose of my visit today is to choose which seven can start work with me on Monday morning.'

The girls whispered and tittered behind their hands. Beatrice couldn't help noticing that most of them were pretty, with one or two exceptions, and that three or four of them could well be described as beautiful. There was one girl in particular, who wasn't sitting on the sofas with the rest of them, but standing by the window at the end of the room. She was staring out over the small back courtyard, where a life-size stone statue of some Greek goddess was raised on a pedestal.

This girl looked about eighteen or nineteen years old, although she could have been younger. She had loose, tawny curls tied with scarlet ribbons, and she was wearing a pink robe d'anglaise with a low, square neckline which emphasised her very full breasts. Her neckline was decorated with a trailing scarlet knot, and so were each of her elbow-length sleeves.

Beatrice thought her face was extraordinary. She had huge green eyes, and high cheekbones, and a small upturned nose. Her lips were pink and slightly pouting as if she were just about to blow a kiss.

Beatrice leaned towards Ida and said, 'Who is that girl in the pink?'

'Oh, *her*,' said Ida, and flapped her hand, as if she were exasperated. 'She's quite new here. We took her in after the constables carried out a sweep at night of the bawdy houses all along Hedge Lane. They brought in twenty-five girls altogether, some as young as thirteen. This one was given the choice of coming here to St Mary Magdalene's or of being charged at the Old Bailey with prostitution. Jane Webb is her name, and as you can probably judge by her expression, she is less than overjoyed at being here. Sometimes I think she would have preferred to be sent to the Clerkenwell House of Correction with the other molls.'

'How sad,' said Beatrice. 'Her mien is lovely.'

'It's the same with so many of our girls,' said Ida. 'They have no homes, they have no schooling, they have no skills. Their only currency is their appearance and their willingness to lie on their backs.'

George was circling around the drawing room now, jovially talking to several of the girls. They were giggling again, and nodding, and Beatrice could easily tell which ones he was inviting to come and work for him. Jane remained by the window, looking out, as if she had no interest in what was going on. Another girl was sitting on a sewing-stool in the corner, a plump, big-bottomed girl in a brown taffeta–satin dress. She had scraggly black hair and a black star-shaped patch on her cheek which she had probably stuck on to conceal a mole.

Florence went to the front window to look out at the carriages making their way around the court, and, while she did so, Beatrice went up to this girl and smiled at her.

'May I ask your name?' she said. 'It's a pleasure to meet you, although I doubt if we'll be acquainted for very long if you're chosen to go and work for Mr Hazzard at his tobacco factory.'

'Judith,' said the girl. 'But he won't be picking *me*, Mr Hazzard. He never does. This is the third time he's come a-calling since I've been here, and he's never picked me.'

'Perhaps Mrs Smollett has told him that she enjoys your company and would prefer it if you stayed.'

Judith shifted herself on her stool and tugged at the gilt-beaded stomacher which she wore at the front of her dress. Apart from being decorative, this allowed her to adjust her bodice size in the event of putting on weight, without altering her dress.

'It's not that at all,' said Judith, dolefully. She had a strong country accent, Sussex or Kent. 'He only ever picks the pretty ones.'

'I'm sure that can't be true,' Beatrice told her. 'You don't need to be pretty to roll tobacco. Besides, you're as fair as any other girl here.'

'You don't have to flatter me, ma'am. I know that I'm fat and plain. And there are other girls here in the house who won't even trouble themselves to come downstairs to meet Mr Hazzard. They know that he would never want them, because they are so lacking in looks.'

'So what are you going to do? You won't be able to stay here at St Mary Magdalene's forever, will you?'

'I know that, but there's a seamstress who calls here twice a week, and she is learning me to sew and embroider, and Martha is learning me to make pies and pastries. I'm hoping that I'll soon be fit to take up employment in some prosperous house. If I can't find such employment – well… there is still money to be made in one of the bagnios. The gentlemen in the bagnios like their girls bouncing.'

'You wouldn't go back to that life, would you?'

'Only if I need to, Widow Scarlet. But it's easy to be righteous when you're well-dressed and warm and your stomach is full.'

Beatrice laid a reassuring hand on Judith's shoulder. She couldn't think what to say to her, but Judith had given her some idea of how much support and encouragement she would have to give these girls. Why should they work for a pittance as domestic servants when they could be streetwalking every evening on Covent Garden or the Strand, making a guinea or even more from every drunken man they met, and sometimes helping themselves to his handkerchief and his pocket watch and any loose change he had in his pockets? Not only that, there was always a chance that some wealthy man might take a particular fancy to them. Beatrice had heard of several famous prostitutes who had done well for themselves, like Lavinia Fenton, whose mother had sold her virginity for £200 plus £200 a year, but who had eventually married the Duke of Bolton, and died rich; and Nancy Parsons, a ballerina who had earned an extra hundred guineas a week as a prostitute, but had become the wife of Viscount Maynard.

When she had finished talking to Judith, Beatrice crossed the room to Jane. She stood close beside her for a few moments but Jane continued to stare out of the window and didn't acknowledge her.

'Jane,' she said, at last, very gently.

Jane turned to look at her but didn't speak. Close to, Beatrice could see that her eyes were variegated shades of green, with a few small orange flecks, like the eyes of a vixen or a predatory cat. She was wearing a tarnished crucifix around her neck, probably silver-plated, but Beatrice was interested to notice that the figure of Christ had his head turned to the left, instead of the right, as he usually did.

'That's an interesting crucifix. I've never seen Jesus facing that way before.'

Jane lifted up the crucifix so that Beatrice could examine it more closely.

'Me gran give it to me. She said that it's a sinner's cross. On all the other ones, 'e's looking to the right, where 'is mum is, and all the good people. On this one, 'e's lookin' to the left, at all the thieves and the murderers and the merry-arsed Christians. You know – sheep to the right, goats to the left.'

'Has Mr Hazzard spoken to you yet?' asked Beatrice. 'Will he be taking you on at the tobacco factory?'

'I fuckin' well 'ope so,' Jane retorted. 'I've 'ad it up to me tits in this place.'

'You're not happy here, then?'

'What do you think? Nothin' but bleedin' prayin' and washin'. My mother was a washerwoman up at Tower 'Ill, and that's all *she* ever bleedin' did – prayed and washed, prayed and washed – save that '*er* prayers weren't nothin' like the prayers they say 'ere.'

'Jane – Mrs Smollett has only been trying to show you that

there's another way that you could live, safer and more moral, and preparing you for it. She's been teaching you to read and write, hasn't she, and to sew, and other skills?'

'Pff!' said Jane. 'All I ever needed to know was 'ow to count guineas, and 'ow to make sure that every cove puts a cundum on.'

'What if I told you that you could lead a very much happier life? What if you could find yourself a husband who would cherish you and take good care of you? What if you could have children of your own one day, and you could bring them up to be equally happy as you? What would you say to that?'

'I'd say you was talkin' the same gammon that Mrs Smollett cracks on about. I've been livin' on me wits since I was eleven years old, and I know what men wants from me, and 'ow much they'll cough up for it, and that's all that matters. Maybe I'll go to heaven when I die, or maybe I'll go to hell, but the way I see it I don't have no choice in the matter, and I can wash and pray until I'm black in the face but it won't make one splinter of difference.'

Beatrice thought for a moment and then nodded. 'Yes. I can understand why you feel like that.'

Jane stared at her suspiciously, as if she had been expecting the usual disapproving sermon, but said nothing.

'Sometimes I'm led to suspect that praying is of very little purpose,' Beatrice went on. 'My husband was cruelly killed two years ago in New Hampshire, and now I've lost my little boy, too. Most likely he was taken away by Indians, and I will never see him again. I prayed for his return, and when he didn't return I prayed for his safekeeping, but I may never discover for the rest of my life is he alive or dead, or if my prayer had any effect.'

'*Indians* took 'im?' said Jane. 'Like, Red Indians?'

'That's right. They were mainly given to kid-nabbing women, but sometimes they stole children too. And almost always – unless by some miracle they managed to escape – they disappeared forever.'

Jane said, 'I'm sorry for you, ma'am, truly.'

'Well, I thank you for your sympathy, Jane, but please try to understand what I'm saying to you. Your life has been appalling beyond measure – worse than you realize, because you have never known anything else. My late husband, Francis, would be outraged if he could hear me saying this, but I now believe that prayer on its own has no effect. God is our maker but he has given us free will and choices, and if we choose to destroy ourselves, he is not going to intervene, because that would be a denial of the freedom that he has granted us.'

'What do you mean?' asked Jane. There was still an aggressive tone in her question, but Beatrice could tell that she was really interested to find out the answer.

'If I gave you a beautiful silk dress, and you besmirched it and tore it, whose fault would that be? Not mine, because I freely gave you such a gift. If you came back to me and prayed for me to give you a new one, would I be cruel if I refused, and told you to clean and mend the fine dress that I had already given you?'

Jane continued to stare at her, saying nothing, but Beatrice could tell that she had grasped what she meant.

'Some people seem to think that once your virginity has been taken, it is gone and lost forever,' Beatrice told her. 'But if you turn towards a pure and faithful life, you be will be as much a virgin then as you were before. Your beautiful silk dress will be cleaned and sewn, and nobody will ever realize that it isn't brand new.'

Jane was about to reply to her then when George came up to them, and laid his hands on both of their shoulders.

'Now *this* young lady will be ideal for Hazzard's tobacco factory!' he exclaimed. 'You have the look of a hard worker, my dear, and a dutiful employee, and apart from that, you will enhance the premises considerably with your beauty, if I may say so. I can offer you twelve shillings and sixpence per week, as well as comfortable accommodation above the factory, so there will be no need for you to risk walking to and from Hackney every morning and every night.'

Jane looked at Beatrice and Beatrice gave her a little smile, as if to say, well, it's a new start, and even if stripping tobacco leaves and rolling cigars isn't the most glamorous of occupations, it's safer, and more moral, and who knows how God might reward you for turning your back on prostitution?

'All right, then, Mr 'Azzard,' said Jane. 'You're on.'

'What's your name, young lady? I'm giving you and your companions the week's end to pack your things together, and then you can all start on Monday morning, six o'clock sharp.'

'Jane Rose Webb, that's my full name.'

'It suits you, my dear! It suits you! And when you come and work with me, you will blossom like a rose, I assure you.'

11

George said goodbye and left. All the girls that he had chosen to work in his tobacco factory were flustered and excited, and couldn't stop chattering. They would now have more freedom, and be making their own money. Not only that, a job at Hazzard's frequently led to meeting an eligible man of means, and marriage.

George had repeatedly told them that the reason he needed to pay such frequent visits to St Mary Magdalene's to recruit new staff was because so many of his girls caught the eye of the gentlemen customers who came in to order plug or cake tobacco, or cigars, or snuff. These customers would invite the girls out dancing, he said, or for an evening at the theatre, and before he knew it, he had lost another cigar-roller to wedlock.

The only girl who didn't join in the excitement was Jane. She remained by the window, seated now, staring out at the statue of the Greek goddess in the courtyard. Beatrice wondered if she ought to talk to her further, because it seemed as if she were suffering from some deep sadness. She was exhausted, though, and Florence came up to her again and tugged at her dress and said that she was 'hungry, Mama!' so she left Jane where she was, and followed Ida into the dining room on the opposite side of the hallway. The cook and the kitchen maid had laid out a spread of cold mutton and pickles and brawn, as well as macaroni cheese and fish custard, with a dessert of puff-pastry pease-pods filled with cherries.

Beatrice had never been offered fish custard before. It was made with ground almonds, dates and pike roe and eggs, sweetened with rosewater, and after one spoonful she thought that she had never tasted anything so repulsive in her life. Florence loved it, though, and sat on the window seat kicking her legs and eating a whole bowl.

After this luncheon, Beatrice and Florence went upstairs to their rooms to rest. Beatrice eased off her shoes and lay on the bedcover and Florence climbed up and lay beside her.

'Can we go home now?' she asked.

'No, Florrie. We have to stay here in London. Mama has to take care of all of the girls who live here. And you, too, of course.'

'I don't like it here. I want to go home and look for No-noh.'

'Well, I do, too, sweetheart. But God has a laid out a path for us and we should be obedient and follow it.'

'I don't like God.'

Beatrice didn't answer that, but gently stroked Florence's cheek and twisted her hair around her finger. If she and Florence were feeling as sad as this, she couldn't imagine how wretched Noah must be, if he were still alive. What made losing Noah even more painful was that she could see herself in Florence's face, her forehead and her eyes, but no trace of Francis at all.

As she stroked her, Florence felt deeply asleep, and soon afterwards, Beatrice fell asleep, too. She dreamed that she was back at the parsonage in Sutton, walking between the rows of beans, and that she could hear Noah laughing and calling out to her. She tried to make her way to the end of a row, but every time she did so, the ground heaved violently up and down, which made her stagger and cling on to the beanpoles to stop herself from falling over. That, of course, was her residual response to the motion of the waves, after an ocean crossing that had taken more than three weeks.

When she opened her eyes, the bedroom was totally dark, and outside, she could hear that it was raining, and raining hard. She was feeling nauseous, with the taste of bile and fish custard in her mouth, but even in the darkness she knew where the chamber pot was, so she wouldn't have to vomit out of the window. After a while, though, her stomach settled, and she lay back, panting slightly, and perspiring, while Florence continued to sleep. Her period was due in three days from now, and she was already feeling bloated.

Once her eyes had become accustomed to the darkness, she climbed off the bed and groped her way through to her little sitting room. A brass candlestick was standing on the toilet, and beside it a circular tinderbox. It took her several seconds to strike a spark, but eventually she lit the candle and the room was illuminated. She lifted the small silver watch on the end of her equipage and saw that it was only half past seven. She should have time to change and go downstairs again and make a closer acquaintance with some of the girls.

She looked at herself in the oval mirror beside the candle and said, out loud, 'You will not feel miserable any more. For Florrie's sake, you are going to be as cheerful and bright as this flame.'

She didn't know if she could really manage to be happy, but she had told Jane that it was possible for her to put her past behind her, and perhaps she could do the same. She was sure that she would meet Francis and Noah in heaven, and until then she would just have to make the best of what life was left to her. You never knew when you might be stricken by consumption or diphtheria or scarlatina, or any one of the scores of diseases that thrived in London because of the fleas and the lice and the rats and the piles of untreated sewage and animal guts in the kennels.

Beatrice was still staring at her reflection, when she heard a timid knock. She didn't call out because she didn't want to wake Florence, so she went over to the door and said softly, 'Yes? Who is it?'

'Jane. Somethin's 'appened, Widow Scarlet. Somethin' – I don't know – 'onest, it's like a miracle. Can I talk to you?'

Beatrice opened the door. 'Come in,' she said, and Jane stepped inside. She was still wearing her pink dress, although it was speckled with raindrops, and her hair was wet, too.

'It must have been *you*, Widow Scarlet, what you said about prayers what don't work and grubshiteing my dress and all that.'

'What are you talking about?'

'It's like a sign, do you know what I mean? You know like Moses and the burning bush that Mrs Smollett keeps spouting on about? Or the stick that turned into a snake?'

'Are you telling me you've seen a sign from God?'

'Well, it *must* be God. I mean, 'oo else could it be? But I think it was *you* and what you said to me that made 'im do it. 'E give me the nod that you was square.'

Jane was so agitated that Beatrice took hold of both of her hands and said, 'Ssh, and calm, and sit down here on the sofa. Now, tell me exactly what you've seen.'

Jane took a deep breath and looked up at Beatrice with her huge green eyes. There were sparkling tears clinging to her eyelashes.

'After I'd ate me supper I went upstairs but when I was taking off me dress I found that me pocket was gone. I went back down to the drawing room because I thought I must have dropped it in there when Mr 'Azzard come to call. I didn't take no glim because there was plenty of light in the 'all.

'I found me pocket under the sofa and I was dead relieved because it 'ad a fore-coach-wheel in it and me charm bracelet. But as I was getting up – I don't know what it was – but somethin' give me cause to take a butcher's out the window. And I swear to you, Widow Scarlet, without a word of a lie, *I see that statue turn its 'ead around and stare at me*.'

'You mean that statue of a Greek goddess in the courtyard?'

Jane nodded furiously. 'I know you'll think I'm ready for Bedlam. But I see it with my own two eyes, turnin' its 'ead around like it's alive.'

'Jane, that statue is made of marble or somesuch stone. Statues can't move. They're inanimate. They have no more life in them than a brick.'

'That's why I'm askin' if you would come down and take a look for yourself. I need to know that I'm not goin' distracted.'

Beatrice looked into the bedroom and saw that Florence was still asleep.

'Very well,' she said. 'But quickly, before my daughter wakes up.'

'I *know* it's a sign,' said Jane. 'You said to me, didn't you, God's given you a gift, but it's up to you to take care of that gift – like clean it and mend it. And I thought – p'raps you're right, p'raps I *could* start all over again, and go back to being a virgin, of sorts. And I was still thinkin' about it when I went down to look for my pocket.'

'Come along, then, let's go and look,' said Beatrice.

She quietly left the door on the latch and followed Jane downstairs. As they descended, the flickering light from the candelabrum in the hallway cast their distorted shadows on the walls behind them, so that it looked as if they were being followed downstairs by tall, attenuated phantoms.

They went into the drawing room and made their way around

the sofas to the window at the back. It was raining so hard in the darkened courtyard outside that it had flooded. The statue of the Greek goddess had one arm raised, and rain was dripping from her fingers.

'I swear blind that she turned to look at me,' said Jane. 'If she knows you're 'ere now, p'raps she'll do it again.'

'It could have been nothing more than a trick of the light,' Beatrice suggested. 'The candles in the hall – look – they keep dipping in the draught, don't they? They might simply have lit up the raindrops, and made it appear as if she were turning her head.'

'No,' said Jane, emphatically. 'She looked at me, Widow Scarlet, no question about it.'

Beatrice didn't know what to say. It was clear that Jane was desperate for some affirmation that she could change, and perhaps that was why she had imagined that the statue had come alive. She couldn't smell wine on her breath, so she wasn't drunk, but even in the gloomy drawing room she could see that her eyes were watering even more copiously than before. She kept sniffing, too, as if she had some nasal irritation.

Beatrice was about to ask her if she had taken any medication when the drawing-room door opened wider and Ida came in, carrying a triple-branched candlestick with three tall candles.

'Ah, Beatrice, my dear,' she said. 'And Jane, too. My goodness! What are you two doing in the dark?'

'Oh, just talking,' said Beatrice. 'Jane has been telling me about her hopes for the future, now that Mr Hazzard has chosen her for his tobacco factory.'

'And I was showing Widow Scarlet the statue,' said Jane. 'You're not going to believe this, but—'

'Do you happen to have hot chocolate, Ida, or some other nightcap?' Beatrice interrupted her, giving Jane a sharp look to caution her not to say any more.

'Of course,' said Ida. 'But would you not care for some supper? There is a little brawn left, I believe, and plenty of fish custard.'

'Hot chocolate will suffice, thank you. One for me and one for little Florrie.'

'You won't believe this,' Jane persisted. 'I mean, if I 'adn't seen it for meself—'

'It's the statue,' said Beatrice, interrupting her again. 'Jane thinks it's amazingly lifelike.'

'Oh, well, yes,' said Ida. 'It was brought back from Greece by another of our benefactors, Sir Humphrey Nevins. He thought it would be appropriate for St Mary Magdalene's because it represents Astraea, the goddess of purity and justice. She was once holding up a pair of bronze scales, apparently, although those have long since been lost. The legend is that Astraea was so repulsed by the depravity in this world that she flew up to the skies and became the constellation Virgo.'

'So she turned herself into a virgin,' said Jane.

'Yes, you could say that.'

Jane reached out and tugged repeatedly at Beatrice's wrist. '*There*,' she said, '*told* you! She 'eard what you said and that was the sign she was givin' me. *I* did it, and so can you!'

Ida frowned and said, 'I beg your pardon, Jane. Who are you talking about?'

'Don't matter, Mrs Smollett,' Jane told her. 'Not no more it don't. Goodnight.'

With that, she left the drawing room and went upstairs. When she had gone, Ida turned to Beatrice and said, 'I have to confess that I am somewhat bewildered.'

'Don't be concerned,' said Beatrice. 'I believe I managed to show Jane today that she doesn't have to spend the rest of her life in a bawdy house. It was something of a Damascene moment for her.'

She was about to leave the room herself when she saw that Jane had left her pocket on one of the sofas. She picked it up and said, 'Look – she left this behind, and it was what she came down for! Which room is she in? I'll take it up to her.'

The pocket's ribbon was loose and she could see what was inside. A half-crown, as Jane had said, as well as a silver charm bracelet. But there was also a small bottle with a brown-paper label with the word *Anodyne* printed on it.

· Beatrice knew immediately what it contained – ether. Some people drank it and others sniffed its fumes. Whichever way Jane had been taking it, that would account for her watery eyes and her belief that the statue of Astraea had turned and looked at her.

She had learned from her father that it didn't make much difference if ether was drunk or inhaled: it was highly addictive, and eventually it caused the skin to crack and the lungs to seize up, to all kinds of debilitating nervous ailments, and premature death.

She said nothing to Ida, but tied the pocket tight and trudged upstairs to Jane's room, on the second floor. She had a heavy heart, though, as she knocked at Jane's door. Jane was stunningly beautiful, but it looked now as if Beatrice would have to rescue her not only from the temptations of her sordid past, but from the ravages of her drug-dependent future.

12

Early on Monday, the seven girls who had been chosen by George to work in his factory were collected by two hansom carriages from the front door, with a small pony cart for what little luggage they possessed.

Beatrice and Florence and Ida stood outside to wave them goodbye, while the other girls gathered at the windows. It was a sharp, sunny morning and the first leaves were beginning to whirl off the trees. Even though it was only just past six o'clock, they could smell sausages frying, and hear the street sellers walking up and down Aldersgate Street, shouting and singing and ringing handbells.

'I'm hungry,' said Florence.

Beatrice laughed and said, 'You're always hungry! You're a little gannet!' But she was glad that Florence was eating well, and seemed to be less homesick for Sutton.

Once they had gone back in, Ida took them through to the large north-facing room behind the dining room, which she called the 'atelier'. It was light and airy, although still a little smoky from the fire having just been lit, and furnished with chairs and small tables arranged in a semi-circle for the girls to sit and sew, as well as three easels where they could paint.

The girls followed them into the atelier in twos and threes, most of them simply dressed in day gowns and aprons. Ida explained that they would have prayers, and she would read a lesson from the Bible, and then the girls would sew and sing hymns such as 'O, For a Thousand Tongues to Sing' and 'Soldiers of Christ, Arise!' until it was time for breakfast.

Before Ida read her lesson, she introduced Beatrice to the twenty-nine remaining girls one by one. Some of them were shy; some of them were sullen; some of them she judged to be as sharp as knives, while others wouldn't have known a B from a bull's foot. Most of them were tolerably pretty, but there were a few plain ones, like Judith, and at least three of them had disfiguring smallpox scars on their cheeks, and rotten teeth.

They spoke in a variety of rural accents – West Country, Suffolk, Sussex and even Yorkshire – but they all shared a similar tittering laugh. They reminded Beatrice of the warbling vireos that used to cluster in the bush outside her kitchen.

'Please be patient with me, ladies,' she begged them. 'It will take a little while for me to remember all of your names. But you can be patient in another way, too. My main purpose here is to assist Mrs Smollett in helping you all to make a new life for yourselves, but I am also an apothecary. So if you are troubled by any sickness at all – any headache or tissick or fever – please come to me and I should be able to prescribe some treatment to make you feel better.'

She could see that one or two girls were now looking at her with renewed interest. But then she stepped back and allowed Ida to lead them in prayers, and then to read them a lesson from the Bible.

'Let us walk honestly, as in the day,' said Ida, her face plaster-white but her voice warm and encouraging. 'Not in rioting and drunkenness, not in chambering and wantonness, not in strife and envying. But put ye on the Lord Jesus Christ, and make not provision for the flesh, to fulfil the lusts thereof.'

Sitting behind her and observing the expressions on the faces of Ida's girls, Beatrice wondered how many of them really felt in any way uplifted, and inspired to be pure. Some were clearly bored, and yawning, some were glassy-eyed, some were picking their noses and staring out of the window. How many of them heard the words 'chambering and wantonness' and thought instead about the freedom they used to have, and all the guineas they used to make in the brothels of St-Mary-Le-Strand and Covent Garden?

Beatrice was just about to go upstairs and dress when one of the girls came out of the dining room door and whispered, 'Widow Scarlet!'

Inside the dining room, the rest of the girls were clearing up after a breakfast of porridge and soft-boiled eggs and toasted bread, and they were chattering, and clattering plates and one of them was singing 'The Trees They Grow High' in a clear and penetrating tone, which led Beatrice to assume that Ida was out of earshot.

> *'And so early in the morning*
> *At the dawning of the day*
> *They went out into the hayfield*
> *To have some sport and play;*
> *And what they did there,*
> *She never would declare*
> *But she never more complained of his growing.'*

The girl who came up to Beatrice was small, with tangled carroty hair and a pale freckled face. She couldn't have been more than fifteen years old. She was wearing a bottle-green dress with tattered lace cuffs which she tugged at nervously while she was talking.

'You said you could 'elp with sickness, ma'am.'

'That's right. Are you not feeling well?'

The girl grimaced. 'Every time I 'ave my flowers I have such agonies I can barely stand up straight, and when I eat anything I can't stop myself from shooting the cat. Last time Mrs Smollett gave me laudanum which eased the pain but it made me so sleepy that I 'ad to spend three days in my dab, and it made me so dull and mopish.'

'What's your name again?' asked Beatrice. 'Katharine, is that right?'

The girl nodded.

'Katharine, I suffer myself from the cramps, like you. Laudanum has much to recommend it, if you take it in small doses, but, as you say, it deadens the pain without easing the spasms that cause us so much distress.'

'So what do you do?' asked Katharine, quickly turning around to make sure that nobody else was listening to them.

'When I was living in America, I discovered a shrub whose bark has a wonderfully soothing effect during menstruation. The Indians have used a decoction of this bark for countless centuries to prevent their squaws from miscarrying. It's called black haw, and it grows in Europe as well as America.'

'And does it really work?'

Beatrice nodded. 'I tried many different receipts, but eventually I found that if I mixed black haw bark with licorice and camomile and pleurisy root, as well as raspberry leaves, the relief it gave me was almost instant. It worked so well that I used to bottle it and sell it to the goodwives in New Hampshire under the name of "Scarlet's Monthly Easement". Look – I was intending in any event to go to the Foundery as soon as

I'm dressed, to see if the apothecary there can find some black haw for me. I was going to prepare a bottle for myself and of course I'll mix up a special bottle for you.'

Katharine burst into tears. Beatrice put her arms around her and said, 'Ssh, don't be distressed. I know your life has been hard up until now, but things are going to change.'

'I never knew my mother,' Katharine sobbed. 'She died when I was born, and then my father got the typhus and 'e went mad and died.'

Looking down at Katharine's carroty hair, Beatrice saw that it was thickly speckled with lice and nits. It was common for women to have lice in their hair, and in their wigs, too, but Katharine had one of the densest infestations that she had ever seen. There must have been thousands of them, and the back of Katharine's neck was spotted with crimson bites. Her eyelids looked sore and crusty, too, which told Beatrice that she probably had tiny pubic lice in her eyelashes.

'Goodness, Katharine, you have so many uninvited visitors in your hair!' she said. 'The itching must drive you to distraction! I shall mix you up another preparation, too, to get rid of them. Meanwhile, I'll see if I can find you a fine-tooth comb, so that you can rake them all out.'

'Thank you,' said Katharine, hugging her tight. She was so overcome with emotion that she was gasping. 'You're like an angel, come to save us.'

Beatrice closed her eyes for a moment. She could hear the girl in the dining room still singing and she wondered if this was the destiny that God had chosen for her ever since she was very young, sitting next to her father while he told her stories and stirred up vials of pungent chemicals that had made her eyes water.

*

That afternoon, she left Florence to play with Judith and walked to the Foundery to talk to Godfrey, the apothecary. This time she went by London Wall, and Finsbury, past the open gardens of Bethlem Hospital, so that she would avoid any of the narrow, stinking alleys between Whitecross Street and Bunhill Row.

She found Godfrey in his gloomy laboratory, brewing up a large glass flask of liquid the colour of dark urine. It smelled vile.

'A tonic for the Reverend Parsons's gout,' he explained. 'It's my own formula of wild mint, aniseed, ipecacuanha and opium.'

Beatrice tugged out her pocket handkerchief to cover her nose. '*Godfrey* – that smells appalling! Thank God *I'm* not suffering from gout! And what you've mixed up, it's only glorified Dover's Powders!'

'Oh,' said Godfrey.

'My father used to make pills of autumn crocus, which were much less pungent, and easy to swallow. *And* they were really effective, too.'

Godfrey stirred his mixture one more time, but looked dejected. 'I wish I'd known that before I started mixing this. It does stink, doesn't it?'

Beatrice said, 'I came to ask if you have any black haw bark. Or if can you find me some.'

Godfrey frowned up at the bottles and boxes on his shelves, but before he could answer, the door opened again and James Treadgold, the teacher, came in. He was wearing the same red frock coat as before, and his sleeves were smudged with white chalk dust. There was chalk dust in his hair, too.

'Widow Scarlet!' he said, and bowed. 'I saw you arrive, and I had to come to ask how you have been faring. I heard that you and Ida and your little daughter were the victims of a very unpleasant assault.'

He paused, and turned, and wrinkled up his nose. 'Godfrey,

what the devil is that you're cooking up? It reeks like a whore's left armpit!'

Immediately, though, he turned back to Beatrice and said, 'A simile only, Widow Scarlet. I don't speak from personal experience.'

Beatrice gave him the faintest of smiles. 'I'm sure not, James. But thank you for enquiring about our attack. We were all badly shaken, I must admit, but not hurt. I expect you know that we were rescued by Mr Hazzard. He was very brave indeed, and impaled one of those rascals with his sword.'

'So I heard, and thank merciful heaven that you weren't robbed, or injured, or worse.' He paused again, and looked down at the floor, and then he lifted his eyes again and said, more softly, 'My invitation for you to have supper with me one evening... I was wondering if I might ask you afresh. I mentioned the Three Cranes in the Vintry before, because they have a snug where ladies may enjoy a drink and some supper in private, but if you have another preference, I would be happy to take you there.'

'James, I'm sorry, but I'm desperately engaged at the moment,' said Beatrice. 'I'm having to acquaint myself with all of the twenty-nine girls at St Mary Magdalene's, and their anxieties. On top of that I'm already having to devise several preparations to deal with their physical ailments. Having said that, Godfrey, do you happen to have any stavesacre, and perhaps some ground mistletoe seeds?'

'Ah,' said Godfrey, knowingly. 'One of your girls is lousy.'

James said, 'I quite understand how overwhelmed you must be, Beatrice, and I must return to my classroom before my children start to strangle each other and throw their slates around. But if and when you find the time, I would consider it both a pleasure and an honour to spend some time with you, and discover more about you.'

When he had left, Godfrey looked across his workbench at Beatrice and raised his eyebrows. 'Here's your stavesacre and your mistletoe seeds,' he told her, passing over two small wooden boxes. 'I have no black haw bark on my shelves at present, but I will get you some from Collin's in Covent Garden. You don't also require a potion to suppress a young teacher's rampant desire, by any chance? I do believe he is smitten!'

The days seemed to pass faster and faster, as if the pages of the calendar were being stripped away by the rising autumn wind. By the end of the week Beatrice could remember every girl's name, and she spent hours talking to each of them alone so that she could find out how they had come to be prostitutes.

Their stories were depressingly similar. Some of their parents had been too poor to take care of them, and in some cases had even been reduced to selling their clothes and their bedding, and eventually their virginity. Other parents had died of typhus or strangury or rising of the lights, and left the girls as orphans, to make their own way in the world.

Most of them were country girls who had believed they could find their fortune in London, one way or another. Some of them had thought that they would be able to survive by singing or dancing or working as milliners or ladies' maids.

They had quickly discovered the reality of life for penniless but pretty young women in the City. Some of them had been taken in by bawdy houses, and they had been reasonably well cared for, although a few of them had been obliged to hand their bawds every guinea that they made from their clients, which was slavery in all but name. Others had rented rooms in brothels, or resorted to the streets, where they had offered five-shilling frock-lifting wappings in one of the many courts and back alleys off the Strand.

As desperate as their lives had seemed to be, Beatrice had guessed from her very first morning here at St Mary Magdalene's that many of the girls had preferred working as prostitutes to more moral employment. Of course it could be a dangerous life, and there was always a high risk of venereal disease and pregnancy. But mostly they had been complimented and treated well by their gentlemen patrons, and they had been well paid, too, especially the very pretty ones, so that some had saved and done tolerably well for themselves. Others, of course, had wasted all their money and spent their days in a blurry haze of alcohol or opium or ether. But what was the attraction of a life of virtue and sobriety? You might outlive your friends for a few more years, but how dull were those years going to be, and who wanted to live to be old and ugly?

'It's frightful, Widow Scarlet!' Annie told her, as they were sitting by the fire on Friday evening. 'If I live to be twice the age I am now, I'll be *forty*!'

Annie was a voluptuous, creamy-skinned brunette from Devon, quite attractive except for a profuse speckling of moles on her breasts and an alarming cast in her eyes, so that Beatrice was never sure who she was looking at.

'Can you *imagine*?' Annie went on. 'If I ever grow that ancient, I'm going to tie myself to a bag of bricks and kittens and throw myself off the Old Swan Stairs.'

Beatrice patted her knee and said, 'Tell me that again when you reach forty. If you still feel the same way then, I will buy the bricks and kittens for you myself.'

13

On Saturday morning Beatrice was sitting at her toilet writing letters to her dear friends in Sutton, Goody Rust and Goody Greene, who had both attended her when Florence was born, when Katharine knocked at her door. Before Beatrice could call out to her to come in, she opened it and stuck her head round it.

'I hope I'm not disturbing you, Widow Scarlet.'

'Not at all, Katharine. Come in. How are you? How is the monthly easement working?'

'The cramp is so much relieved, thanks to you, Widow Scarlet. But I'm still feeling a terrible itching in my hair. I have combed and combed it, and rubbed on that lotion you gave me, but the lice are still giving me such fierce irritation. On my eyelids, too.'

Beatrice beckoned her to come nearer to the window. 'Bend your head down,' she said, and carefully parted Katharine's hair so that she could see if any lice and nits were still clinging on.

'You're still bathing your eyelids in warm water?' she asked.

'Yes, twice a day, as you said, and I do think they're better than they were.'

'Good – but it seems as if the visitors in your hair are still reluctant to pack their bags and go. I think I shall have to prescribe you something stronger than stavesacre. My father used to swear by tobacco leaves and vinegar, so we might try that. The juice from tobacco kills any insects you have ever heard of!'

'Anything, Widow Scarlet. I have been scratching myself to distraction.'

Beatrice stood up. 'Well, this will give me the opportunity to kill two birds with one stone. I was considering a visit next week to Mr Hazzard's tobacco factory so that I could see how Jane and the other girls were settling in. I could go this afternoon and bring back some tobacco leaves for your hair.'

Katharine said, 'You're so kind to me. I wish there was something I could do for you. I could bake you some queen's cakes, couldn't I? Martha has shown me how, with raisins and mace and orange-flower water.'

'Perhaps when you're all cured,' said Beatrice. She wasn't squeamish. Ever since she was young she had treated people with boils and suppurating pustules and thickly furred tongues that needed scraping. All the same, she preferred not think about eating queen's cakes into which lice had accidentally dropped.

After Beatrice and Florence had finished breakfast, about eleven o'clock, Grace went out to hail a hackney coach for them.

When it drew up outside, Grace opened the door for them and said, 'Tell Jane that I send her my best wishes. She is beautiful, that poor girl, but she has such troubles.'

'She talked to you too?'

'Not when she first come here. She is rude to me at first and call me a Hottentot. But later on the same day she change, like a different person. She tell me how unhappy she is, and weep.'

'I'll let her know that you're thinking of her. You have a kind heart, Grace.'

'I see so many girls in pain, Widow Scarlet. Some have good

fortune and find themself a husband, or some gentleman to keep them as their mistress, anyway. But most have nothing in the days to come but growing old. That's if luck and God is with them, and they don't die young from the typhus, or the Venus curse.'

Beatrice and Florence waved goodbye to Grace and then their coach rattled off at a brisk pace north-eastwards up Shoreditch, past the lofty spire of Shoreditch Church, and out to the countryside towards Hackney. A few ramshackle clusters of cottages lined the sides of Kingsland Road, but out here it was mostly farms and open fields, with cows grazing and trees that were beginning to turn brown. After about two miles they turned a bend and arrived at Silvester Row. Half-hidden by a row of mature elms, a large grey-brick factory building with a tall, smoking chimney stood beside a stream.

When the coach driver opened the door and Beatrice stepped down, she found herself confronted by a sign outside, announcing that this was Geo. Hazzard & Son, Tobacco Blenders, with the same crest that was emblazoned on the chamber pot under her bed, two black men and a large leafy tobacco plant.

It was a chilly morning, but the air out here in Hackney was bracing and fresh, and after the coach had turned around and trundled off, Beatrice stood for a moment holding Florence's hand and breathing it in. It reminded her so much of the cool, clean wind that used to blow down from the White Mountains in New Hampshire. Florence looked up at her with a serious expression and Beatrice wondered if she were thinking the same.

They walked in through an archway that led to a cobbled courtyard, where two wagons were being loaded up with boxes of tobacco and cigars, and several men were standing around smoking.

Beatrice approached one of the men, who was wearing a long, leathery apron and had a long, leathery face to match, with two tufts of white hair behind his ears, like puffs of smoke. 'I have come to visit Mr Hazzard, if he is here,' she told him.

'Of course, ma'am. I'll take you to him directly,' said the leathery-faced man. He bent over to Florence and held out his clay pipe to her. 'How would you fancy a sup of my baccy, young lady? It's capital for clearing out the lungs, and it will save you from catching the consumption!'

Florence hid behind Beatrice's coat. Beatrice smiled and said, 'Thank you for the offer. She has a bubble-pipe already, and she's a little young to start drinking smoke.'

The leathery-faced man led them through a wide pair of black-painted doors and onto the main factory floor. As soon as he opened the doors, the noise and the smell were overwhelming. There must have been more than fifty or sixty women in there, sitting at two long rows of desks, facing each other, stripping the mid-ribs out of heaps of tobacco leaves by hand. At the far end of the factory, tobacco leaves were being soaked in tanks of fresh water to render them more pliant for the strippers, while off to the right, behind a row of brick pillars, machine-men were chopping up tobacco, and stovers were stirring it in steam pans to separate the fibres and then drying it in fire pans to make it fit for smoking.

The clatter of cutting machinery and the hissing of steam and the shrill shouting between the women was deafening; and the pungency of tobacco was so strong that Beatrice felt as if she had been smoking a pipe herself, or taking snuff.

Some of the girls looked up and smiled as Beatrice and Florence passed, but Beatrice was puzzled that she couldn't see Jane among them, nor any of the other girls from St Mary Magdalene's.

The leathery-faced man led them through to a smaller

room where another ten girls were sitting at tables and rolling and cutting cigars by hand. None of the girls from St Mary Magdalene's was there, either.

'Where's Jane?' asked Florence.

'I don't know, darling. We'll have to ask Mr Hazzard.'

George's office was at the rear of the building, and its door was wide open, with billows of cigar smoke drifting out. The leathery-faced man knocked and said, 'You 'ave yourself a wisitor, Mr 'Azzard, sir!'

George was sitting at a massive mahogany desk which was heaped with letters and bills of lading and empty cigar boxes. He was wearing his usual yellow frock coat and a yellow cravat. The walls behind him were lined with rows of bookshelves, all stacked with hundreds of oddly assorted books, and beside him stood a huge tobacco-brown globe.

Out of the window Beatrice could see a large, unkempt garden where a white goat was tethered, and in the distance she could make out the rooftops of Hackney village and the square tower of St Augustine's church.

George stood up, took his cigar out of his mouth and blew a long column of smoke.

'Beatrice! What a delightful surprise! And your charming daughter too. Come in! Have a seat.'

He came around his desk and cleared a stack of accounts books off one of the two leather chairs. 'May I offer you some refreshment? Coffee, perhaps? Or cider? Or a glass of wine?'

'This is only a fleeting visit, George,' said Beatrice. 'I came principally to see how Jane and the other girls were settling in.'

George sucked at his cigar and when he blew out smoke again his face was serious.

'Beatrice – I am grieved to tell you that all seven girls from St Mary Magdalene's have succumbed to a raging fever.'

'What? *All* of them?'

'All of them – every one – without exception. I don't know if the girls remaining in the home have shown any symptoms of it, but it has certainly spread like the plague of Egypt among these seven. For the time being they are all confined to their dormitory upstairs, in case they communicate it on to any of my other employees. I couldn't afford to have my entire work force sick in bed. I would be out of business and bankrupt in a week.'

'They showed no signs of it at all before they left St Mary Magdalene's, and none of our other girls is at all unwell.'

George shrugged. 'They all have the purples, and are hot and chilled alternately, and have no appetite whatsoever. They have been visited by our local doctor, who has prescribed them cold baths and clysters. At my own expense I have also employed a nurse to care for them – a woman of some experience in tending to the sick. But we can only wait and pray and hope that they soon recover.'

'Perhaps I can see them for myself,' said Beatrice. 'My father trained me as an apothecary, and I'm sure that I can prescribe them something more effective than cold baths and clysters. If they have no appetite, why would they need to purge their bowels?'

George shook his head. 'I'm sorry, Beatrice. I'm sure you mean well, but I believe that would be unwise in the extreme. The fever appears to be highly contagious and if you were to succumb to it, you can imagine how mortally guilty I would feel. Why – if I were to allow you to expose yourself to an illness like that, I would almost be committing a criminal act. More than that, think of your precious little daughter here. What if you passed it on to her?'

'George, I have tended to the sick all my life, and I have never been seriously ill myself.'

George shook his head again and continued shaking it. 'I cannot take the responsibility, Beatrice. If you wish, I will keep you informed daily of their progress, but even though I have only recently made your acquaintance, I think of you already with the greatest affection. I would rather cut off my own arm than be responsible for you coming to any harm.'

'Very well,' said Beatrice. 'But – yes – if you could keep me apprised of their condition.'

'I will send word to you daily, I promise.'

Beatrice hesitated, and then she said, 'There was a favour I was going to ask you, although it seems petty now, compared with these poor girls being so ill.'

'Anything at all, Beatrice.'

'One of our girls is suffering badly from head lice, and I wondered if you could let me have a few tobacco leaves so that I can use them to treat her. Tobacco leaves soaked in vinegar are excellent for killing lice.'

'My dearest Beatrice, you shall have a hundred tobacco leaves if that is what you need. Come with me.'

George stood up, and Beatrice stood, too, and he laid his hand on her shoulder and guided her back onto the factory floor. She felt deeply anxious about Jane and the rest of the girls, but her common sense told her that he was right to be cautious. The City was teeming with fevers and agues and poxes, and who could guess what contagion a client might have passed on to one of the girls. The last thing she wanted was for Florence to be left an orphan.

14

On the following Tuesday morning, Grace came into the atelier, where Beatrice was showing a small circle of five girls how to sew a flat-felled seam.

'There's a gentleman called to see you, Widow Scarlet.'

'A gentleman? I'm not expecting anyone. Did he give his name?'

'Mr James Treadgold. He says that he's brung you something you was asking for.'

Beatrice turned to the girls and said, 'I shan't be long. Please carry on stitching and remember that these seams should be almost invisible from the outside.'

She found James standing in the drawing room in front of the fireplace. Instead of his usual rusty-coloured frock coat, he was wearing a grey three-piece suit with waistcoat and knee-breeches to match, and his shirt had a ruffled collar. His wavy brown hair was drawn back and tied with a large black-velvet bow.

'Beatrice,' he said, and bowed, as he had before.

'James. This is a surprise.'

'I know, and I apologise for that, but I have the day free from teaching, and Godfrey told me that you had asked him for some prunella and nightshade water, so I have brought it for you.'

He handed Beatrice a beige cotton bag fastened with a drawstring.

'That's kind of you, James. And you are dressed extremely smartly today, if I may say so. Do you have a rencounter?'

'I was hoping so. Do you have an hour or so to spare?'

'Me? I'm sorry, James. I'm the middle of a sewing class, and then I have to help with the luncheon, and after that I will be spending the afternoon treating whatever ailments our girls have been suffering from. I appreciate your bringing over this prunella and nightshade water. Several girls have blackworms in the face, and if you mix these two with red wine vinegar, you have the very best treatment there is.'

'Oh,' said James. 'It's such a fine day, and I thought that I might persuade you to come out for something to eat by the river, and perhaps a glass of wine.'

Beatrice could see how disappointed he was, so she said, 'I can give you a few minutes. Why don't you sit down?'

James sat on one of the sofas, and Beatrice sat next to him. The door to the hallway was open, and three or four of the girls went past on their way to the kitchen, looked in quickly, and then started tittering.

'They'll be gossiping now,' said Beatrice.

'Well, let them,' said James. 'Perhaps we should give them something to gossip about.'

Beatrice frowned at him in mock-disapproval. 'You're very bold.'

'So what would be the alternative? For me to pretend that I did not immediately find you to be one of the most striking women that I have ever met?'

'James! You barely know me!'

'That is why I came here today – to deepen our acquaintance. Surely you must have had similar experiences yourself, in the past.'

'I'm not sure I follow you what you mean.'

'I'm talking about those times when you've been introduced to some stranger, and you've known in the very first instant that you could be the closest of friends – if not more than friends.'

'James—'

'I can't help myself, Beatrice. I would be deceiving you if I said otherwise, and worse than that, I would be deceiving myself. I invited you to come to the Three Cranes with me, and perhaps you might have accepted. Perhaps not. Whichever you eventually decided, I would have had to wait in a ferment while you made up your mind.'

'Of course I haven't forgotten your invitation, James,' said Beatrice. 'But I've been so busy getting to know the girls here I haven't even had time to unpack my own belongings, let alone think about meeting you for supper.'

'I understand, Beatrice. But I've thought of nothing else but you since I last saw you. I haven't been able to sleep for thinking about you! So when Godfrey told me this morning that he needed to send over some medication for you, I decided that I would have to take the bull by the horns.'

Beatrice looked at him for a long time without speaking. There was no question that he was attractive, and the expression in his amethyst-blue eyes was one of almost laughable sincerity. It was hard to tell how old he was, but she guessed that he must be two or three years younger than her. He was so youthful and good-looking that it was surprising that he wasn't already married, or at least had an entourage of pretty young women. Perhaps he was, and he did.

She was so used to caring for the needs of others that she hadn't thought once that she might be in need of somebody herself – somebody to love her and comfort her and help her come to terms with her grief. But could it be James?

'You must give me a little time, James,' she told him, at last. 'I lost my beloved husband only three years since, and my dearest young son not two months ago. Apart from that, I had to uproot myself at short notice from my home in New Hampshire, and it was a home that was filled with so many memories, both happy and sad. I am not spurning you, believe me. I am greatly flattered that you feel about me the way that you do. But I am in no condition yet to think about returning your affection. My heart is like a mirror that has been smashed into pieces, and at the moment it can reflect nothing but fragments.'

James reached over and gently laid his hand on top of hers. 'The Reverend Parsons told me that your son had been taken from you. I sympathise with your pain completely, for I lost the girl I was betrothed to marry.'

'I'm so sorry,' said Beatrice. 'When did this happen?'

'A year ago this Michaelmas. Without any warning at all she became infected with dropsy in the brain. One evening we were out dancing and the next morning she was dead. Her name was Sophie and she was only nineteen.'

'Dropsy can be very sudden,' Beatrice told him. 'What a tragedy.'

James had tears in his eyes. 'You must not take this amiss,' he said, 'but when the Reverend Parsons brought you into my classroom I thought for one thunderstruck moment that Sophie had come alive again and that he had brought her back to me. You are so much like her.'

'James – I cannot take her place. I may resemble her, but I am not her.'

'I understand that completely, Beatrice, and I would not think of insulting you or Sophie's memory by treating you so. But you cannot blame me for finding you so spellbinding. All I ask is that you consider spending some time with me, to see if our attraction could be mutual. If you tire of me, then all you have to do is tell me, and I will leave you in peace.'

Beatrice was about to answer when she heard screaming coming from the atelier. She stood up just as Ida came bustling into the drawing room.

'Oh, there you are, Beatrice! Your sewing class are fighting like cats! And— Oh, James! To what do we owe this visit?'

James stood up, too, and bowed. 'I was making a delivery of physic from Godfrey Minchin, Mrs Smollett. Widow Scarlet and I were merely exchanging a few pleasantries.'

'Well, you had best curtail your pleasantries before your girls tear each other's hair out! And the bear-garden language!'

Beatrice said, 'Please thank Godfrey for the physic, James. I will be coming over to the Foundery tomorrow or the day after, so I may see you again then.'

Ida left the room and Beatrice followed her. Grace was waiting in the hall to see James to the front door. He stepped outside, but before he put on his black tricorn hat, he turned to Beatrice and blew her a kiss.

15

After her visit to his tobacco factory, George had kept his promise and sent Beatrice a letter every morning, keeping her informed about Jane and the other girls. From what he wrote, though, it seemed as if their fever was daily growing worse rather than better, in spite of the cold baths and clysters that the doctor in Hackney had recommended.

On Wednesday morning, the postboy delivered a letter just before breakfast, which Grace gave to Beatrice while she was sitting in the atelier drinking tea. Some of the girls sitting around her were sewing, while others were copying out 'The Agony', a sacred poem about the crucifixion, to improve their handwriting.

> *Wouldst thou know Love? Behold the GOD,*
> *The Man, who for thy Ransom dy'd;*
> *Go taste the sacred Fount that flow'd*
> *Fast-streaming from his wounded Side!*
> *Love, is that Liquor most divine,*
> *GOD feels as Blood, but I as Wine.*

Two of the girls who had quarrelled the previous day were still glaring at each other, and although Beatrice had admonished them for being so hostile, they kept hissing *'buttock and file!'*

and '*drab!*' at each other. Before she broke the seal on her letter, she said, sharply, 'That's quite enough, you two! If this was a coffee house, the owner would demand that you pay twelve pence every time you uttered a word like that, by law, so be thankful that I don't do the same.'

George had written, 'The girls' fever shows no sign of abating at all, and they are much spotted and scarce able to take more than a few sips of fair water. I fear they may be very close to meeting their maker.'

Beatrice warned the girls not to fight or swear while she was away, and then she went to talk to Ida. She found her in the large basement kitchen with Martha, their cook, teaching three of her girls how to bake a skirret pie. One of the girls was Katharine. The tobacco-leaf-and-vinegar treatment had worked on her hair within a day, and now she was free from lice and nits – at least until she caught them again.

Ida was wearing no rouge today, so her face looked even chalkier and more mask-like than usual. After she had read the letter from George, Beatrice said, 'I must go to Hackney and see what I can do to save them.'

Ida handed the letter back. 'Do you think that's wise?'

'Ida – I know that this fever must be highly contagious, but there has to be a more effective treatment than cold baths and enemas. We had a similar fever in our village in America, and I used Jesuit's powder and antimony stirred with plenty of wine. I was able to cure all save one elderly woman and one sickly child.'

'I admire your intentions, Beatrice, believe me. But what if you contract it, and die? How will I cope here without you to assist me, and what will become of your Florence? What if you bring the fever back here with you, and spread it among the girls here?'

'I cannot remain here and do nothing while those poor girls are so close to death,' said Beatrice. 'I will observe the strictest precautions when I visit them, and cover my face so as not to breathe in any sputum or tainted air.'

Ida shook her head. 'I am still set against it, Beatrice. I'm sorry.'

'Are we not Christians, Ida? Were we not chosen by God to help others – you to rescue girls from prostitution and me to save lives with my knowledge of physic?'

'Yes, but, Beatrice—'

'My husband sacrificed his life in the cause of saving others, Ida, and if God wills that I should share the same fate, then so be it. Whatever you say, I'm determined to go.'

Ida looked away for a moment, to the kitchen table. Katharine was forming a funnel called a haystack in the pastry lid of the skirret pie, so that once it was baked, she could pour in a warm caudle of white wine, sugar and egg yolks.

At last Ida turned back and said, 'I really cannot dissuade you?'

'No,' said Beatrice, quietly but very firmly.

'When were you thinking of going? I'm intending to hold a celebratory hour of hymns this afternoon.'

'Before I can do anything I'll have to find some Jesuit's powder. I believe Godfrey has some at the Foundery, although I don't know that he has it in sufficient quantity. But so soon as I've gathered together all the ingredients, and mixed them, I'll go to Hackney at once. The sooner the better, for the girls' sake.'

Ida raised her eyes towards the clock on the kitchen wall.

'Very well,' she said. 'I cannot forbid you, especially if you believe that you are carrying out God's will. But if any harm comes to you, I shall find it hard to forgive you.'

Beatrice put on her cape and her bonnet and walked over to the Foundery. Florence had started teething, and was asleep, so she left Grace to look after her. It was a grey, overcast day and the rattling of coach wheels and the cries of street sellers sounded muffled, as if the clouds were a thick, suffocating blanket.

As it turned out, a merchant ship had docked from South America only three days ago, and Godfrey had taken delivery of a large box of Peruvian tree bark, which Beatrice could grind into Jesuit's powder. Her father had taught her that it was easily the best remedy for malaria, and for other fevers, too.

She ground up the bark in a bell-metal pestle and mortar, and then she stirred the powder into a large bowl of red wine. She added antimony to purge the girls' stomachs and spoonfuls of honey for sweetness and nourishment. Once all the evil influences had been purged out of them, they would need every ounce of strength to recover.

Godfrey helped her to pour the physic into four green-glass bottles. 'I'll be praying for the girls' recovery,' he said, as he pushed in the stoppers. 'And I'll be praying, too, that God will protect *you*, Beatrice, from whatever fever it is that ails them.'

Beatrice walked back to Maidenhead Court, and the Foundery's grey-haired factotum, Henry, came with her to carry the bottles. Once they had reached the front door of St Mary Magdalene's, Beatrice gave Henry tuppence and thanked him for his help, and Henry mumbled something unintelligible in reply and waddled off.

Ida was coming down the stairs as Beatrice stepped into the hallway, her wide panniers brushing against the banisters.

'You have your mixture?' she asked.

'Yes, Ida. I'll be leaving as soon as Grace can call me a hackney.'

'We're about to commence the hymn-singing. Can you not stay for just one? The Reverend Parsons sent us a newly written hymn last week, "Lord, Before Thy Throne We Bend." You must hear it.'

'Very well,' said Beatrice. She knew that Ida was upset about her going to the tobacco factory, and she didn't want to appear ungrateful or defiant.

All twenty-nine girls were already gathered into the atelier, tittering and shuffling and nudging each other. The singing was to be led by Hephzibah Carmen, a dour, wan, painfully thin young woman dressed in black, who visited St Mary Magdalene's twice weekly to teach music. Although her demeanour was so miserable, her classes were always crowded. Many of the girls had ambitions to sing on the stage, which would greatly improve their chances of attracting a husband, or at least a well-off gentleman to keep them as a convenient.

Hephzibah sang each line of the hymns solo, one line at a time, in a shrill, wavering voice. After each line, the girls repeated what she had sung – not only because they were unfamiliar with the tunes of the newer hymns, but because only five or six of them could read.

Beatrice stayed to hear the new hymn, and then quietly excused herself to Ida and left. Ida nodded to her and seemed less concerned now about her going. Grace had called for a hackney coach and it was waiting outside for her.

'May the angels be taking good care of you, Widow Scarlet,' said Grace.

16

It was starting to spit with rain when Beatrice arrived at the tobacco factory. The hackney coachman helped her to carry the basket containing the physic bottles into the courtyard, and for that she gave him an extra penny on top of his shilling-and-sixpenny fare.

As she paid him he said, gloomily, 'You won't be thinking of buying yourself one of those Hanway things, will you?'

'Oh, you mean an umbrella?'

'Whatever you calls 'em, they'll be the death of the jarvis trade, if you axes me.'

'I doubt it. I wouldn't have cared to walk all the way here, raining or not.'

'There's plenty who would, though, if they had a Hanway. They was invented by the Devil. Who do you think the Lord God created rain for? For the jarvis trade, that's who.'

Before she could knock, both factory doors swung open, and one of George's carters came out, all but his legs and his hands hidden behind the stack of cigar boxes that he was carrying.

'Is Mr Hazzard in?' she asked him.

'Just let me load these onto my wagon, ma'am, and I'll take you to him directly.'

The carter led her through the factory, carrying her basket for her. The factory was busy, but she noticed that neither

Jane nor any of the other girls from St Mary Magdalene's was stripping tobacco leaves or rolling cigars. She assumed that they must still be sick.

George was sitting at his desk talking to a bald-headed man with bushy side-whiskers. He stood up at once when Beatrice came in, putting down his cigar and raising both hands in surprise. The bald-headed man popped up, too, like a jack-in-the-box. Although he had a paunch, he was thin and surprisingly tall.

'My dear Beatrice!' said George. 'What a surprise!'

'I'm sorry to call on you so unexpectedly, George,' Beatrice told him. 'I suppose I could have sent you a letter to warn you that I was coming, but I thought it better if I wasted no time. In these bottles I've brought a physic for the girls to reduce their fever, and with God's grace to cure them completely.'

George came around his desk, looking serious. 'I regret to say that I have some painful news for you, Beatrice. Oh, by the way, this is Mr Veal, my accountant. Edward, allow me to introduce Widow Scarlet.'

The bald-headed man said, 'Charmed, madam! Charmed! George has told me much about the good work that you have been doing at the home for refractory young women.'

'George, tell me, what's happened?' said Beatrice. 'Please don't tell me that some of the girls have already died!'

'It's worse than that, in a way,' said George. 'But please sit down. This will come as a great shock to you, I'm sure.'

Beatrice remained standing. 'What could be worse than death? Please – tell me!'

'I regret to confess that I've been deceiving you, Beatrice. I've been doing it for the sake of the girls themselves, but above all to protect your feelings. You've had to bear quite enough distress and disturbance in your life recently without a calamity like this.'

'Go on,' said Beatrice. She was beginning to feel impatient now, as well as anxious.

'When you came here on Saturday I told you only half the truth. The girls had indeed been stricken by a fever. But it was not a common contagion. It was a fever that they had conjured up themselves.'

'I don't understand what you mean.'

'On their very first night here in Hackney, at the very stroke of midnight, they started chanting and wailing and uttering the most extraordinary screams. When our housekeeper Margaret Lidiard went to their dormitory to investigate, she found all the girls naked and dancing around their beds. Not only that, they had daubed a huge symbol on the wall, a pentagram, in what appears to be blood.'

'*What?*' said Beatrice. She couldn't believe what George had just said, but his expression was so grave that she found it hard to imagine that he was lying to her.

'Margaret remonstrated with them, of course, and told them all to dress and take to their beds, but she had not stepped more than a few feet into the dormitory before she was flung bodily backwards by some invisible force. She said that it was like being blown over in a storm, except that it smelled foetid – akin to the breath of some foul beast. She was thrown so forcibly against the door frame behind her that several ribs were broken and she was knocked almost unconscious.

'She managed somehow to crawl out of the dormitory, but as soon as she had done so, the door slammed shut, even though none of the girls was anywhere near it. Once she had reported what had happened, I went up there myself with several of my staff. We tried again and again to open it, but we were unsuccessful, and so we tried to break it down by force. I had some of my strongest men attack it with post

114

mauls, but to no avail. The mauls shattered as if they had been made of glass.'

Beatrice slowly sat down. 'You must forgive me, George, but I am finding this very difficult to accept.'

'You don't need my forgiveness, Beatrice. It's more than difficult to accept – it's well-nigh impossible. All of us here have scarcely been able to credit what we've been seeing and hearing. After we first failed to open the door, my men erected ladders outside the dormitory windows so that we might see what was happening inside, but all the curtains were drawn together tight, and remained drawn.'

'And the girls have stayed in there ever since they first arrived? With no food or drink or sanitation?'

'We knocked at the door repeatedly and pleaded with them to come out, or at least to let us in to talk to them, but there was no response whatsoever. They were as silent as the dead during the day, but as soon as midnight chimed again, they started singing and screaming once more, and we could also hear some strange, discordant music like flutes playing. This went on every night for at least an hour, although afterwards they fell silent.'

'I heard it for myself, and it was enough to curdle my very blood,' said Edward Veal. 'If what remains of my hair had not already been grey, it surely would have turned that way overnight.'

'Perhaps I should try to talk to the girls myself,' said Beatrice. 'I had some encounters with people performing satanic rituals when I was in America. It was all fakery, but there was a motive for what they were doing, and in the end I discovered what it was.'

'I can't think of any reason at all why these girls should have been pretending that they were summoning Satan,' said George. 'But – you're a day too late, I'm afraid. Early this morning I noticed as soon as I came here into my office that our goat had gone.'

'Your goat?' Beatrice looked out of the window and she could see that the goat's tether was still hanging from the post to which it was fastened, but it had been cut, and there was no sign of the goat itself.

'I went immediately upstairs to the dormitory and I saw at once that the door was wide open,' George continued. 'There was no sign of the girls, any of them, but when I went inside and drew back the curtains – well, I hesitate to tell you what I found.'

'Please, George, I'm not at all squeamish.'

'Our goat was nailed to the wall, its legs widespread, and its belly cut wide open so that its bowels had fallen to the floor. Candles had been planted on the floor all around it, so I can only assume that the girls had been carrying out some kind of ritual sacrifice.'

'How did they manage to cut the goat free and carry it upstairs to their dormitory without anybody seeing them or hearing them?' asked Beatrice. 'Surely it must have bleated or its hoofs made a clatter on the stairs?'

George shook his head. 'I have absolutely no idea, Beatrice. But there were seven of them, weren't there? Perhaps they managed to knock the poor beast senseless and carry it upstairs between them. Or perhaps they had some other way – some supernatural means of lifting it into the air. After all, they had managed to fling Margaret across the room without touching her, and slam the door behind her when none of them were near it. I'm quite prepared to think that they could have levitated the goat by some black magic.'

'But the girls have gone now? Do you have any idea where they went?'

'None. I asked the postboy who came this morning if he had passed them on his way here, but he said that he hadn't. I sent one of my lads to stand at the Bethnal Hamlet crossroads to inquire of coach drivers and any other travellers if they have seen them, and another lad to Jeremy's Ferry past Dalston. So far all seven of them seem to have melted away into nothingness.'

'Spirited away!' put in Edward Veal, clapping his hands. '*Piff!* As if they never existed!'

'I'm totally confounded,' said Beatrice. 'And I must admit that I feel wounded, too. I talked to one of those girls, Jane, and it seemed to me that she was right on the brink of conversion. I don't mean religious conversion. I mean she seemed to have a genuine desire to give up prostitution and change her life for the better. It's really hard to imagine her calling up Satan.'

George puffed at his cigar, and picked a shred of tobacco from his lower lip. 'Beatrice, my dear – I doubt if she had even the slightest intention of giving up being a blower. She was only telling you what she thought you wanted to hear. You know what these girls are like. She probably believes that Satan will give her everything she wants. Fortune and fame and with any luck some rum cull to take good care of her when she loses her looks. All the things that God wouldn't give her, but maybe his satanic majesty will.'

'You don't believe in witchcraft, do you?' asked Beatrice.

'I don't *dis*believe in it, let's put it that way. I have a cousin in Bedford who argued with the old woman next door because her dog broke into his yard and killed five of his chickens. When it broke in a second time he caught it and beat it to death with his cane. The next night he heard the sound of breaking glass from somewhere upstairs. When he ran up to see what it was, he saw the old woman outside, hovering in the air, ten feet clear of the ground, unsupported, smashing his bedroom windows with a brass poker.'

'*There!*' said Edward Veal, as if this were incontrovertible proof of witchery. 'Had she been apprehended for such mischief not twenty-five years before, she could have been hung for it!'

Beatrice raised her eyebrows but said nothing. She believed that there could well be supernatural influences in the world. After all, she believed in God. But she had come across too many fake mediums and too many charlatans not to be sceptical about Satanism. Her father had always taught her to test any evidence first with science; and even if science couldn't yet explain what had happened, he had cautioned her to keep an open mind. 'Our knowledge of chemistry advances by the hour,' he used to say. 'That which seemed to be magic this morning might well be completely mundane by the same afternoon.'

'If those seven girls are in the thrall of the Devil, then I very much doubt that we will ever hear from them again,' said George. 'It's a tragedy – a great, great tragedy – and you have no idea how wracked with remorse I am that this happened while they were under my care. But – they are all disappeared off the face of the Earth, and that's all there is to it.'

'*Piff!*' Edward Veal repeated. And then, '*Piff!*' yet again.

'I presume that you haven't yet told the Reverend Parsons of this? Or Mrs Smollett? She seemed to have no inkling of it this morning.'

George shook his head. 'I've informed neither of them yet, although now of course I will be obliged to. I didn't want to say anything to Ida because it will break her heart. She devotes so much of her soul and her spirit into converting those girls to a Christian way of life. She is certain to feel that she has failed them somehow.'

'Would you like me to tell her?'

'No, Beatrice, no. I have known Ida for many years and it will be better coming from me. Let me tell her in my own way. I shall be down to the City tomorrow and I will call at St Mary Magdalene's and the Foundery before I go to my lodge meeting.'

Beatrice stood up. 'If you'll allow it, George, I would like to see the girls' dormitory for myself.'

'Are you sure? It has not yet been cleaned since this morning, and neither has the goat been disposed of. I was considering that I might ask a watchman to come to inspect it, in the event of the girls later committing some felony, and being arrested for it. The condition of their room would be proof, would it not, that they had forged a pact with Satan? Quite apart from their theft of our unfortunate goat, and its wanton slaughter.'

'Yes... please show me,' said Beatrice. 'They might have left behind them some evidence as to where they are now.'

'Come with me, then,' said George. 'I have to tell you that I'm taking you to see the carnage they've caused with the greatest of reluctance – but, since you insist.'

'As I said, George, I am not at all squeamish. In America I boiled live lobsters and I slaughtered and butchered my own pigs.'

At the rear of the factory stood a two-storey brick annexe with rustling ivy growing up its south-facing wall. The ground floor was taken up with storerooms for tobacco and wooden boxes, and with a large kitchen where meals were prepared for the factory hands. A wide staircase led upstairs to the dormitories for both men and women.

Beatrice went up the stairs first, with George behind her still puffing at his cigar. By the time they reached the landing he sounded out of breath, and he stopped for a moment to cough and punch himself on the chest with his fist.

They walked down to the girls' dormitory at the far end of the corridor. The door was closed, and George took out a key to unlock it.

'You're quite certain about this?' he asked her.

Beatrice said, 'Yes, George. I accepted the responsibility for saving those girls from sin, and even though I knew them for such a short time, I still hope that I might be able to rescue them now.'

'As you wish,' said George, and pushed the door open.

The dormitory had whitewashed walls, and was lined with eight plain iron bedsteads, four on either side. The sheets and blankets on seven of the beds were in wild disarray, and some of them were speckled with what looked like dried blood. Dark brown loops and spots were spattered all the way across the oak floor, and they looked like dried blood, too. The air was swarming with hundreds of flies.

On the end wall a huge pentagram had been smeared, reaching almost from floor to ceiling, and around it had been drawn the mystical symbols for earth, fire, air and water. The white goat had been nailed up against the pentagram with its back to the wall, its legs stretched out so that they were aligned with the pentagram's diagonal lines. Its eyes were yellow slits, its teeth were bared in a snarl and its dry pink tongue was lolling out sideways. Its shaggy beard and its knobbly curved horns made it look even more satanic.

'Now if *that* isn't proof of a ritual to call up the Devil, then I don't know what it is,' said George, and coughed again. He was about to say something else, but he went into another coughing fit and all he could do was wave his hand.

Beatrice stepped into the room and made her way slowly down between the beds. Even though she wasn't squeamish, the ripe, sweet stench made her feel as if she could easily be sick. The goat had been sliced open from its beard down to its testicles, so that all its intestines had slid out onto the floor. They were lying in a glistening, putrid heap, surrounded by a semi-circle of at least a dozen half-burned candles. Flies were crawling all over them, and in and out of the goat's red body cavity, like looters ransacking an abandoned building.

Beatrice took her handkerchief out of her pocket and held it against her nose and mouth as she walked right up to the dead goat. George stayed outside the door, smoking.

There is something amiss here, thought Beatrice. *In fact, there are several things amiss.* George had clearly told her that the dormitory had remained untouched since they had discovered that the girls had disappeared. Yet where were all their clothes? Where was all of their luggage, their drawstring bags and their leather cases? They had needed a wagon to bring them here to Hackney – surely they hadn't been able to conjure up sufficient black magic to spirit them all away. She could also see chamber pots under two of the beds, and both were empty. If the girls had been shut in here since the first night of their arrival, how had they relieved themselves?

She was tempted for a moment to mention these discrepancies to George, but one of his factory foremen had come upstairs to see him, and between coughs he was engaged in conversation, so she decided to say nothing. She had already questioned his belief that the girls had summoned up Satan, and raised her eyebrows at his cousin's story of a flying witch, and she didn't want to antagonise him. After all, he was the principal benefactor of St Mary Magdalene's, and Ida would be less than delighted with her if she aroused his displeasure.

Something else caught her attention. Scores of flies were crawling all over the disembowelled goat, but not a single one of them seemed to be attracted to the blood on the sheets or the floor or the blood with which the pentagram had been painted.

She glanced over her shoulder. George was still talking to his foreman, his head hidden in a cloud of blue cigar smoke, so while he wasn't looking she folded her pocket handkerchief and wiped it against one arm of the pentagram. The blood was stiff and sticky, and she wiped it again, harder, just to make sure that she had a reasonable sample. That's if it actually *was* blood. If it had been painted on the first night that the girls had arrived here, surely it would have dried out completely by now.

She tucked her handkerchief back into her pocket and walked back to join George on the landing.

'Did you ever see a sight so grisly in the whole of your life?' asked George.

Beatrice said, 'Never, George, never. It's perfectly hellish.'

She didn't like lying, because she had seen sights far more stomach-churning when she was in America, the worst of which had been her own husband's solidified body, but again she decided that it would be wiser to humour George than to upset him. If he believed in Satan and witchcraft there was no real harm in it, after all. She knew plenty of other people who were just as superstitious as he was, and she had her own superstitious rituals. If ever she spilled some salt, she always threw two pinches over her left shoulder, in case the Devil was standing close behind her.

'Once I have called for a watchman as a witness, I will have the dormitory thoroughly scoured,' said George, as they went back downstairs. 'I have a good mind, too, to bring in the vicar from St Augustine's to bless it.'

'You might also ask him to say some prayers for our missing girls,' said Beatrice.

'Well, yes, I suppose I could,' George told her. 'In my opinion, though, they are all far beyond salvation.'

17

Beatrice returned first to Maidenhead Court, mostly to reassure Florence that she hadn't disappeared forever.

She was hanging up her rain-spotted cape in the hallway when Ida came out of the drawing room.

'Well?' she asked. 'How are they? Did you give them your physic?'

'As a matter of fact I didn't see them,' said Beatrice. 'Mr Hazzard told me that they were up and about, and I thought that if that was the case, there was no need for me take the risk of exposing myself to their contagion.'

Ida stared at her but said nothing for almost ten seconds, as if she were trying to decide if what she had said had some hidden meaning. Then she momentarily closed her eyes in acknowledgement, and said, 'Very well. That was wise of you.'

Beatrice went to find Florence and took her into the kitchen to give her a bowl of cheese soup with fried sippets. Grace came too. Florence obviously adored Grace, and Grace was already treating her as if she were her younger sister. The two of them giggled together all the way through their supper, and Florence laughed so much she almost spat out her soup.

Beatrice had no appetite. She couldn't stop herself from picturing that split-open goat nailed to the wall of the girls' dormitory, with its fly-clustered bowels hanging out. Florence playfully tried to feed her some sippets, but she pursed her lips.

Even though Grace had been only seven when she had been brought here to London and probably couldn't remember them very distinctly, Beatrice had the feeling that she still sorely missed her family in Barbadoes. All the same, she decided that she would wait until she was better acquainted with Grace before she asked her any more about them. From her own painful experience she knew that some memories, like some poisons, are best kept bottled up.

After supper, at about half past five, the sky grew black and thunder started to bellow directly overhead. Rain gushed from a broken gutter at the back of the house, and in less than ten minutes the back yard was flooded and the statue of Astraea was standing in what looked like an ornamental lake.

Beatrice went through to the atelier where Ida was reading inspirational Bible stories to some of the girls.

'I have to go out for an hour or so,' she told her.

'In this rain? Whatever for?'

'Judith is suffering badly with her dyspnea, and I have no more nightshade to give her. I shall have to go over to the Foundery and see if Godfrey has some.'

'Can't you send one of the girls, with a message?'

'I need to see for myself what he has in stock. My preference for Judith is solanaceae, but he may have only belladonna. Besides, I will have to prepare it as a tonic, and I doubt if Godfrey will know precisely how to do that.'

Beatrice found herself lying for the second time that day, but what she was telling Ida was mostly true. Young Judith was gasping for air so painfully that she had taken to her bed, and Beatrice had run out of nightshade, although she usually preferred to give her patients ipecacuanha or opium if they were desperately short of breath.

She reassured herself that she was only trying to spare Ida's feelings, after all. If she had explained why she really wanted to go over to the apothecary, she would have had to tell her all about the pentagram and the goat and the missing girls.

'Very well,' said Ida. 'But please be careful on an evening like this. Take a hackney.'

Godfrey was shrugging on his coat and was about to lock up when Beatrice arrived.

'Beatrice! I'm afraid I've finished for the day.'

'Please, Godfrey. I know this is an imposition, but I have to analyse one small sample. I can't explain why, but it's a matter of great urgency.'

'Is one of your girls ill?'

'No, it's nothing like that, thank God. But in its way it could be much worse.'

'Look – I'm meeting some friends at the Green Dragon in less than half an hour. Can I ask you to lock up for me when you've finished, and hand the keys to the Reverend Parsons, or Henry if the Reverend Parsons is already at dinner?'

'Of course.'

'And, please, don't forget to snuff out the candles. I would hate to come back in the morning to find the Foundery burned to the ground!'

Once he had left, Beatrice took off her cape and went over to the workbench. There were two large candles burning, one at each end. They gave more than enough light to illuminate the whole apothecary, but she filled two clear Florence flasks with water and placed one in front of each candle flame, so that their light was brightened and focused more sharply on the centre of the bench.

Now she took out her pocket handkerchief and unfolded it, so that she could look closely at the red stain which she had wiped from the pentagram. It was dry now, but unlike blood, which darkened when it dried, this stain had remained the same strong shade of red. She sniffed it, and sniffed it again, and she was sure that she could faintly smell linseed oil.

'As I suspected,' she whispered to herself. 'It's *paint*.'

She took a scalpel from the tray of instruments at the side of the workbench and carefully cut her pocket handkerchief in two. She then set two glass dishes side by side and placed a half of the stained white cotton muslin into each one. Into the left-hand dish she shook two drips of spirit veneris, and into the right-hand dish she spooned a solution of mineral alkali.

The stain in the left-hand dish was unaffected, and stayed red. The stain in the right-hand dish immediately turned a dark violet colour. Although there were several other tests that she could do, Beatrice was now reasonably sure that the pentagram had been smeared on the wall not with blood but with carmine oil paint.

Carmine oil paint was coloured with the ground-up bodies of female coccus cacti insects, or cochineal. She could see the pigment that had coloured this paint had been very finely ground indeed, to give it extra brightness, so that she guessed it had been made by Emerton & Manby. This particular paint company boasted that they used a horse mill to grind their pigments, which meant that their colours were more not only more vivid but could be diluted to make many more gallons of paint than other manufacturers', and so were considerably cheaper.

Beatrice stood at the workbench looking at the results of her tests and wondering what she should do. The paint had still been sticky when she wiped off her sample, and that meant that the pentagram must have been applied to the wall only a few hours before she had arrived at the tobacco factory.

She wished now that she had also taken samples of the spots on the bed sheets and the stains on the floor. They may have been blood, either arterial or menstrual or goat's blood, but she strongly suspected now that they, too, had been splashes of paint.

That could only mean that George Hazzard had been warned in advance about her visit, and had set up the whole scenario in the dormitory for the purpose of deceiving her. Otherwise, why would he have gone to all the trouble of doing it? The spattered sheets, the pentagram, the sacrificed goat, the candles – they had all been arranged to make her believe that the girls had formed themselves into a coven of witches. But why? And where had the girls actually gone? And who had told him that she was on her way?

She was still standing thinking when the door suddenly opened. For a brief moment, the two candle-flames burned blue. Beatrice's father had told her that this was a sign that a friend of the Devil had entered the room; but it was James.

'Beatrice!' said James, coming into the apothecary. He was wearing a sweeping black watch cloak and carrying his tricorn hat. 'What a surprise to see you here! I was looking for Godfrey.'

'Godfrey has gone to meet some friends at the Green Dragon,' Beatrice told him. 'He kindly allowed me to use some of his chemicals.'

'Oh. I hope I haven't disturbed you.'

'No, not at all,' said Beatrice, and began tidying up the workbench. 'I've done what I came to do.'

'You're leaving?' James asked her. He picked up her cape and held it out for her. 'I was going to ask Godfrey if he would care to join me for a draft. Perhaps you would care to join me instead.'

'I'm afraid not, James. I have to get back to Maidenhead Court. Besides, I've a great deal weighing on my mind just now. I don't think that I would be very enjoyable company.'

'Well, at least let me escort you.'

'Isn't it still raining?'

'No, the storm's passed over, and even if you choose not to utter a single word I would consider it a pleasure to walk with you.'

Beatrice remembered the excuse she had given to Ida and took a small bottle of ipecacuanha syrup from the shelf beside her. Then she came around the workbench and allowed James to lift her cape over her shoulders. 'Thank you,' she said. 'You can tell me more about yourself as we go.'

18

James had brought along a lanthorn, although most of their walk back to Maidenhead Court was brightly lit by the convex glass lamps fixed to many of the houses. In some of the narrower streets the lamps were much further apart, or no lamps had been lit at all, and the shadows were as black as the ankle-length cloak that he was wearing.

As they walked, he told Beatrice how his father had come to lose almost all of his fortune, and how the family had been reduced to moving from a mansion in the countryside at Edgware to renting a terraced town house in Henrietta Street.

'My father was broken, but I don't see it as such a comedown. I like living in the centre of the City. It's much more lively, and we have some very interesting neighbours. Kitty Clive lives only three doors away.'

'*The* Kitty Clive? The actress?'

'Yes, *the* Kitty Clive. I see her quite often, coming back from the theatre late at night.'

Beatrice found James such pleasant company that she was tempted to tell him more about herself, and her life in New Hampshire, but she decided she would leave that for another time, when she had found out what had happened to the missing girls. At the moment that was all she could think about.

They reached the gate of Maidenhead Court and the grizzled old nightwatchman unlocked it for them. James took hold of

Beatrice's hand and said, 'We must walk like this again, but in the daylight, and somewhere more amusing. Perhaps I could take you to Ranelagh Gardens, if you could fancy a journey out to Chelsea.'

'I'll have to see,' said Beatrice, with a smile. 'I seem to be occupied every minute from morning till night. If I'm not teaching the girls their letters, or how to sew, or bake cakes, I'm reading them Bible stories and conducting prayers. Even when I was a parson's wife I don't think I prayed as much as I have since I came to St Mary Magdalene's.'

'You're a very rare woman, Beatrice,' said James. 'If *I* pray for anything, it's that you find somebody who will make you happy again.'

He continued to hold her hand and she could feel that he wanted to draw her closer and kiss her, but eventually he said, 'I'm teaching tomorrow, but perhaps I'll see you the day after, if you have any time free. Goodnight, Beatrice. Have wondrous dreams.'

He stood by the gate and watched her until she had climbed the steps of St Mary Magdalene's. After she had knocked, he waved his lanthorn to her like a sailor signalling from a passing ship.

Ida opened the front door for her. She was wearing a nightcap and a long nightgown with an embroidered bedjacket over it, and she was carrying a lighted candle, since the chandelier in the hallway had now been extinguished.

'Ah, Beatrice. I was just going up to bed. Did Godfrey have what you wanted?'

Beatrice held up the bottle of ipecacuanha syrup. 'He had no nightshade, but this should be equally effective.'

'I must tell you that you've been doing exceptionally well here at St Mary Magdalene's,' said Ida. 'I've grown to value your assistance greatly, and I know that the girls feel most affectionate towards you.'

'It's very kind of you to say so,' said Beatrice. 'I've grown fond of them, too.'

A draught from the dining room made Ida's candle flicker, and so she cupped her hand around the flame.

'That pleases me,' she said. 'However, I feel that I must repeat the caution that I gave you when you first arrived.'

Beatrice frowned to show Ida that she wasn't sure what she was talking about.

Ida said, 'I warned you that some of the girls may lead you to believe that they have mended their ways, when they have not. From the way they talk, and the earnestness with which they pray, you would think that they have almost become nuns. Behind their seeming piety, though, they still hanker for the life they lived in the bawdy houses and brothels. They are only professing to have been saved from sin because it has allowed them to escape from being punished by the law.'

'Well, yes, I'm aware of that,' said Beatrice. 'But if only half of their number give up prostitution, surely that's better than none at all.'

'Of course. But if we lose some after they have left here – if they go back to the squalor and the immorality from which we tried to rescue them – you mustn't feel in any way to blame. They are old enough and experienced enough to decide what course they want their lives to take, and what they choose to believe in. They may turn their backs on you, and turn their backs on God, but you have done everything humanly possible to rescue them.'

'Yes,' said Beatrice. She didn't know what else to say.

Ida bade her goodnight and climbed the stairs, holding up the hem of her nightgown so that she wouldn't trip. For some irrational reason, Beatrice almost expected to see that she had a goat's hooves, instead of feet. Those blue candle flames in the apothecary had reminded her of that book about the Devil by Daniel Defoe, and he had written at length about Satan having goat-like feet, although he was sceptical about it himself.

Whenever Satan has Occasion to dress himself in any humane Shape, be it of a fine lady or of an old Woman, *yet still he not only must have this* Cloven-Foot *about him, but he is oblig'd to show it too; they will not so much as allow him an artificial* Shoe *or a* Jack-Boot, *such as we often see contriv'd to conceal a* Club-Foot *or a* Wooden-Leg; *but that the Devil may be known wherever he goes, he is bound to shew his* Foot; *they might as well oblige him to set a Bill upon his Cap, as Folks do upon a House to be let, and have it written in capital Letters, I AM THE DEVIL.*

Beatrice followed Ida upstairs, for she had no candle of her own. Once Ida had gone into her bedroom and closed the door, she would be plunged into total darkness, and she didn't want that to happen while she was thinking about the Devil.

She entered her rooms very quietly, so as not to wake Florence, and quickly undressed, folding her clothes over the back of her chair. Once she had climbed into bed she gave Florence a kiss on her hot little forehead, and then lay back and thought about Ida's words of warning.

If she hadn't known otherwise, she could almost have believed that Ida knew already about the seven girls disappearing, and the pentagram, and the slaughtered goat. *They may turn their backs on God*, she had said, and what more emphatic way could there be to turn your back on God than to make a sacrifice to Satan?

It took her nearly an hour to fall asleep, and when she did, she didn't have the 'wondrous' dreams that James had wished for her. She dreamed instead that her late mother was sitting on the end of the bed, looking sad and singing 'Stript of Their Green'.

The next morning was gloomy again, with a steady drizzle. Beatrice spent the morning teaching the girls tapestry and reading from *The Pilgrim's Progress*. Not long after one o'clock she heard a knock at the front door, and when it was opened, she heard George's voice. Ida said something to him, but she couldn't make out what it was. They both went into the drawing room and the door was closed.

After about twenty minutes, Grace came into the atelier.

'Mrs Smollett asks if you could join her,' she said.

Beatrice told the girls to carry on with their stitching and followed Grace through to the drawing room. George was leaning against the fireplace with his usual proprietary air. Ida was sitting beside him with her lips pursed, looking tense. She had painted two spots of vermilion on her cheeks today, so she looked clown-like rather than deathly.

'Hallo, Beatrice,' said George. 'I've told Ida all about the girls and their witchcraft. I've also explained that I requested you to stay silent about it until I myself had the opportunity to tell her what happened.'

'I'm deeply, deeply shocked,' said Ida. 'I can't tell you how wounding this is. All seven girls! I thought that all of them had truly changed and found God. Instead they might as well have torn the pages out of the Bible and spat on them.'

Beatrice said, 'Have you had no word of their whereabouts yet?'

'I've put word out, but none whatsoever,' said George. 'Since they've clearly acquired magical powers for themselves, they could be anywhere by now. They could have flown to Scotland for all we know, or over the Channel to France. I doubt if we will ever hear from them, ever again.'

'Seven of them,' put in Ida. 'The right number to form a coven, and to summon Satan. You have no idea how guilty and ashamed I feel. I have let them down completely.'

Beatrice said, 'Ida, you told me only yesterday evening that if any of our girls should go back to a life of sin, I shouldn't blame myself. By the same token, neither should you.'

'Yes, but these girls didn't simply return to prostitution – they called on the Devil to give them supernatural abilities. God only knows what terrible crimes they are going to carry out. How can I *not* feel guilty? I should scourge myself for my failings.'

'No, Ida,' said George. 'Each of those girls was born into wretched poverty and brought up to know nothing but immorality. They were steeped in sin from the days when they were suckled at their mothers' breasts. You did everything you could to show them the light, but it was almost inevitable that they would turn back to the darkness.'

Beatrice said nothing. She could have challenged George with her chemical analysis of the carmine paint, but she felt that she needed more conclusive evidence. Supposing the girls had originally drawn the pentagram in blood, and painted over it themselves before they left? Supposing they had arranged for an outside accomplice to bring a wagon to the tobacco factory during the night, and take them all away, along with their luggage?

Of course, both scenarios were highly unlikely. Where would they have found the paint, and a brush to apply it? How would they have been able to get in touch with an accomplice when they were isolated inside their dormitory? And how could they have left the factory with all their possessions without anybody seeing them?

It was also questionable that George had known nothing about the girls' disappearance until he had realized that the factory's goat was missing. But Beatrice sensed that she should tread very carefully. If he had been prepared to kill the goat and deface the dormitory simply to delude her into believing that the girls had summoned up the Devil and flown away like witches, then who could guess what he might do to keep the truth concealed?

She found it more than a little uncomfortable to be thinking this way. Her first impression of George had been of a warm, generous and charitable man. In New Hampshire, though, she had known men like Henry Mendum, a prosperous and seemingly community-spirited farmer. Beneath Henry Mendum's bluff exterior, he had turned out to be cruel, greedy and rapacious.

'Are you going to inform the Reverend Parsons about the girls going missing?' she asked.

'I have already, my dear,' said George. 'I called in at the Foundery on my way here.'

'And what did he have to say about it?'

'He was shocked and horrified, naturally, like poor Ida here. But, like Ida, he recognizes that some of the girls you take in to St Mary Magdalene's will always remain beyond redemption.'

'Did a watchman come to the factory?'

'Yes, early this morning after he had finished his night's duties. However, he was not optimistic about being able to find the girls. He said that since they were given the ability to vanish by the Devil, the Devil will undoubtedly keep them one step ahead of the watch for the rest of their lives.'

'What about placing a notice in the *Gazetteer*? Surely somebody in London must know at least one of them, or have some inkling of where they might be.'

George shrugged and pulled a face. 'I think that would be fruitless, my dear. As I say, they have probably flown far away, to the north of England or Scotland or even abroad, where nobody will recognize them, and where they can carry on their careers as prostitutes without any fear of being apprehended.'

'Well, I'd best get back to my tapestry class,' said Beatrice. 'The girls are quiet at the moment but I don't like to leave them unsupervised for too long. If they start quarrelling, they have a tendency to stick needles in each other.'

'It was a great pleasure as always to see you, Beatrice,' said George. 'It is a pity that we are meeting again under such a black cloud.'

'We'll be saying a special prayer for the girls this evening,' said Ida. 'The Devil may have them in his thrall for now, but there's always hope that God might be able to show them the error of their ways, and return them to us.'

Beatrice gave George a quick, small curtsey, and went back to the atelier, just in time to stop Hannah Bennett from prodding Mary Cox in the back with a crewel needle.

19

That afternoon, Beatrice borrowed Ida's green silk umbrella and a pair of wooden pattens to fit over her shoes so that she and Florence could walk over to the Foundery. Because of the rain the streets were unusually quiet, except for the clopping of horses' hooves and the grinding of coach wheels. The long-song sellers and the hot spiced gingerbread vendors were mostly sheltering in doorways, although a clarinet player with a dancing dog stood in the open on the corner of Fore Street, both of them drenched. The dog kept stopping and looking miserably up at his master as if he were asking him when they were going to call it a day and go home.

Florence didn't mind the rain. She sang, 'Ring around the rosy! *Ashes! Ashes!*' and kept jumping into puddles.

'Florrie! You'll be soaking wet before we even get there!' Beatrice scolded her.

Beatrice had run out of sugar of lead to stop uterine bleeding, and she also needed to ask Gerald for aloe gel so that she could roll some more pills for those girls suffering from constipation or colic. Most importantly, though, she wanted to talk to the Reverend Parsons about the satanic ritual at George Hazzard's tobacco factory.

Once she had collected her physics from Gerald, she went around and knocked at the Foundery's front door. The Reverend

Parsons' smiling young maid let them in and led them through to his study. He was writing a sermon, and Florence was thrilled to see his tortoiseshell cat lying on his cluttered desk, its eyes following every twitch of his quill pen as if it were tensing itself to spring on it and catch it.

'Beatrice, my dear!' the Reverend Parsons exclaimed, pushing back his chair and standing up. 'What a pleasure to see you! How have you been faring at St Mary Magdalene's? Ida has given me an excellent report of your work there – *ex optimis optimus*!'

'Well, I'm grateful for that,' said Beatrice. 'But I came to discuss something else with you – those seven young girls who have gone missing from Mr Hazzard's tobacco factory.'

'Ah, yes. George called here earlier to tell me that they had disappeared, and under what dreadful circumstances. I have to say that it chilled me – *chilled* me – froze me to my very marrow!'

Beatrice said, 'I saw for myself the pentagram that the girls were supposed to have painted on the wall, and of course the dead goat.'

'Horror upon horror, Beatrice! We do everything we can to save those refractory girls, and to guide their feet onto the path of righteousness, but sadly a number of them will always be beyond redemption. I must say, though, that this is one of the most appalling cases that I have ever encountered. To form a coven, and to summon Satan to give them the power to escape – *quod animo fingi non potest* – it defies one's belief!'

'I agree with you,' said Beatrice. 'But I think it unbelievable only because it didn't actually happen. At least, not in the way that George says that it did.'

'I'm sorry, I don't understand. Did you not see the evidence with your very own eyes? The pentagram? The goat?'

'George told me that the pentagram was painted on the wall on the very first evening that the girls arrived at his factory, and that he believed that it was painted in blood.'

'That's right, yes. He told me that, too.'

'I took a sample of the pentagram on my handkerchief. If it had been blood, it would have dried within a very short time of being painted, and its colour would have darkened almost to brown. But it was still viscous, and it was still a vivid red.'

'Yes, but they sacrificed the goat only on the same morning that they disappeared,' said the Reverend Parsons. 'Perhaps they painted over the pentagram a second time with fresh goat's blood, as a way of renewing their homage to Satan.'

Beatrice shook her head. 'Even if they had done that, it was mid-afternoon before I visited the factory, so it would have dried by the time I saw it. Quite apart from which, I analysed my sample here in Gerald's apothecary, and there was no question at all what it was – *paint*, in a strong shade of carmine. It had a base of linseed oil, coloured with cochineal.'

The Reverend Parsons frowned, and said, 'Paint? Are you certain of that?'

'As I said, Reverend, there was no question at all. Not only did it smell of linseed oil, it held its colour when mixed with spirit veneris, and changed its colour to violet when tested with a few drops of mineral alkali.'

'Please, have a seat,' said the Reverend Parsons. 'This is more worrying than I thought.'

Beatrice sat down next to the Reverend Parsons' desk, and he sat down again too. The cat had jumped down onto the floor now, and Florence was teasing it by trailing one of her ribbons along the rug in front of it.

Beatrice said, 'I am loth to suggest that it was George who arranged for the pentagram to be painted on the wall and for the goat to be slaughtered. But I believe it was done so that any witnesses would be led to believe that the girls really *had* summoned the Devil. When I say witnesses, I mean me and the watchman he called. Or *says* he called, anyway.'

'But, my dear, what *possible* motive could he have for such an imposture?' asked the Reverend Parsons. 'He told me that he urgently needed those girls to work in his factory, because he's so pressed for staff. Surely the very last thing he would have wanted would be to lose all seven of them.'

'Perhaps not. But there were several other indications that they didn't disappear in the way he described. All of their clothing and possessions had disappeared, too, and the chamber pots in the dormitory were empty. Even if they had locked themselves in for several days without food or drink, they would have needed to relieve themselves.'

The Reverend Parsons laid his hand on the large leather-bound Bible from which he had been copying quotations for his sermon.

'George Hazzard is one of the most honourable men I have ever had the privilege to know – *ever*. Let me tell you, Beatrice, his contribution to the charitable work of this ministry has been unstinting. Without his financial support and without his influence with the bench at the Old Bailey, we could never have saved so many wanton girls from a life of crime and prostitution.'

'I'm not making any accusations against him,' said Beatrice. 'I don't have sufficient evidence for that. Until we discover where the girls have gone, there's no conclusive proof of how they escaped, or when; or who painted the pentagram and killed the goat; or why. But the indisputable fact remains that the pentagram was described in oil paint, and not blood, and that the lack of luggage and the empty chamber pots suggest that the girls may have disappeared some days earlier than George claims they did.'

'I think it's all perfectly clear,' said the Reverend Parsons. 'The Devil was still present when you went to see the dormitory, albeit invisibly. In order to confuse you and to raise doubts in your mind about George's explanation of the girls' disappearance, he altered the composition of the blood on the wall to that of paint. As for the empty chamber pots, if the girls had locked themselves in for several days, with nothing to drink, it would have been necessary for them to imbibe their own urine to survive.'

Beatrice stared at him. 'You seriously think that the Devil changed the blood into paint?'

'What other explanation can there be? Jesus can change water into wine, and equally the Devil can change any liquid he chooses into any other liquid – coffee into poison, poison into blood, blood into paint – whatever suits his own mischievous purpose.'

'So you believe that the girls really summoned Satan, and that he gave them the power to disappear?'

'Yes, I do, because I believe George implicitly, and I know from my own experience what heinous trickery the Devil can get up to.'

'Very well, then,' said Beatrice. 'If that is your belief, then who am I to argue?'

The Reverend Parsons stood up. 'One day we may discover where those girls went, but I must say that I am not at all hopeful. All we can do is pray for their misguided souls, and that they might someday see the error of their ways. There is no point in castigating ourselves for what they have chosen to do.'

'No, I suppose not,' said Beatrice. 'Florrie, say goodbye to the pussycat now. We have to go back for supper.'

The Reverend Parsons showed them to the front door. He waited while Beatrice fastened the pattens over her shoes and raised her umbrella. Then he said, 'A word of caution, Beatrice. You need to be constantly alert for the faintest whiff of Satan's presence. It may suit his purpose to tamper with more of your analyses, and the consequences could be tragic. Think of it – if the evidence of that paint was presented in court, and George was erroneously found to be responsible for those girls' disappearance, he could be transported or hung.'

'Don't worry, Reverend,' said Beatrice. 'I have an acute sense of smell for all kinds of different vapours – and for the smell of evil most of all.'

Beatrice and Florence had walked no more than a few yards along Windmill Hill when Beatrice heard James calling out to her.

'Beatrice! Wait just a moment!'

He caught up with her. He was wearing no coat, only his shirtsleeves and his waistcoat, so he must have come running straight out of his classroom as soon as he saw her.

'James, you'll catch your death!' said Beatrice.

'I wanted only to ask you again if you might be free for a few hours tomorrow, in the afternoon. If you are, and the weather is better, I would love to take you and Florence to the Ranelagh Gardens, or perhaps to the gardens at Marybone if Chelsea's too far for you.'

'Why, thank you, James. That would be a pleasant diversion. I'll have to ask Mrs Smollett, though. I know we have a visit from a Scots preacher in the morning, to talk to the girls about missionary work among the poor, and then a prayer meeting, but I may have time to myself after that.'

James smiled. There were raindrops sparkling in his long, brown hair and Beatrice thought he looked more appealing than ever. Being a teacher, he was obviously very knowledgeable and worldly wise; and she had seen how firmly he could control a class of ragged and wayward children. All the same, he had an innocence about him which she found extremely attractive. It reminded her so much of Francis, who had always thought the best of people until they proved him wrong.

When she returned to St Mary Magdalene's, she went upstairs first of all to see if Judith was breathing any more easily. Because her gasping and wheezing had been keeping the other girls awake, they had moved her to a tiny bedroom at the back of the house. It was even smaller than Beatrice's bedroom, with only enough space for a single iron-framed bed, a bedside cabinet and an upright rush-bottomed chair. Above the head of the bed hung a bronze effigy of Christ on the cross.

Judith was sitting propped up with two pillows, looking flushed and sweaty, but she was no longer struggling for breath. Beatrice had been dosing her regularly for the past twenty-four hours with elderberry wine and with the nightshade physic that her father had taught her how to mix, and which he had labelled 'Bannister's Aerating Lung Balm'.

A jug and a basin stood on top of the cabinet, and Beatrice poured out some cold water so that she could soak a flannel cloth and press it against Judith's forehead.

'How are you feeling?' she asked her.

'So much better, thank you, Widow Scarlet. It was like my lungs was all stuffed up with thistles before, but I can breathe proper now.'

'You need to rest for another day, but after that you should be fine. All being well, you should be able to get out of bed and get dressed by Sunday.'

Judith was silent for a while, but then she said, 'I heard about the girls who went to Mr Hazzard's tobacco factory.'

'Oh, yes? Who told you?'

'Mrs Smollett told all of us. She said we should take it as a lesson.'

'What exactly did Mrs Smollett say?'

'She said that they prayed to the Devil, those seven girls, because they wanted him to turn them into witches. They killed a goat for him, and lit candles, and because of that the Devil gave them the power to fly. They flew away and nobody knows where they've gone.'

Beatrice sat down on the side of the bed and held Judith's hand. 'Do you believe that?'

'What?'

'Do you really believe that they called on the Devil? Do you really believe that he enabled them to fly?'

Judith blinked. 'I don't know. Mrs Smollett said they did. But I did think it was wonderful.'

'Wonderful in what way?'

'The night before they left to go and work for Mr Hazzard, I was talking to Jane, and Jane was weeping something bitter because she said she'd seen a miracle.'

'She told you about the statue in the back yard, is that it? Did she say that she'd seen it moving?'

Judith sniffed, and nodded. 'She said you'd promised her that she could be like a virgin again, purest-pure, if only she mended her ways.'

'I did, yes. I didn't say that it would be easy, but I did tell her that it was possible, if she put her mind to it, and trusted in God.'

'She didn't believe it when you first told her. She thought you was coming out with one of those old preachy clankers.

But then she saw the statue turn its head and look at her, and when Mrs Smollett told her that the statue was a goddess – a goddess what had left the dirty world behind her and become like a virgin again, just the same as you was telling her to do – she knew that what you was telling her was square.'

Judith's nose was dripping now so Beatrice took out her handkerchief and handed it to her. When she had blown her nose, Judith said, 'She said that after she saw that miracle, she trusted you more than anybody she'd ever known, and that she was dead set on making you proud of her, and that she would never let you down.'

'And she told you that on the night before she left to go to work at Mr Hazzard's factory?'

'The very night. So what was she doing, the next night, calling up the Devil? She wasn't easy, Jane, but if there's one thing she wasn't, she wasn't a wrinkler.'

'Well, Judith, we'll have to find out the truth, won't we?' said Beatrice. 'No – no, please keep the handkerchief. You can give it back to me after it's been laundered.'

20

The Scots preacher who visited St Mary Magdalene's the next morning was even more miserable and dour than Hephzibah Carmen, the singing teacher. He was clothed entirely in black and had one hunched shoulder. His face was thin, with chiselled cheekbones and a long jaw, and his grey wig was perched on top of his head like a filthy, overfed cat.

He spoke of helping the poor, such as those orphans who roamed the streets and had to seek warmth in winter by sleeping close to brick kilns or even in dunghills, and those families so impoverished that they had no furniture and were sleeping on straw because everything else had been pawned or sold to pay for food and rent. He spoke of the mother he had found in a state of putrefaction in an upstairs room, dead for over a month, with her three children naked and starving beside her bed, so weak that they were unable to stand. He described all this with a kind of dry relish, but his voice rose to an impassioned quaver when he started to describe the consequences of sin, and what would happen to the girls of St Mary Magdalene's if they were tempted to return to prostitution or crime.

'Both God and Man have many ways of punishing the woman who strays from the path of righteousness,' he told them, raising his hunched-up shoulder as if he expected a bird of prey to fly down and settle on it. 'Disease is God's way. Be advised that thirty thousand Londoners were buried last year, and that you are blessed if the Lord spares you beyond the age of twenty-one. Man's way, however, is execution... and if a woman is found guilty of a capital crime she can be taken to Tyburn and publicly burned to death. Can you imagine the agony?'

Beatrice found this all deeply depressing, rather than inspirational. It had been desperately difficult to survive in New Hampshire, especially in the early days. The winters had been stunningly cold, and the Indians had raided them again and again, and the crops had repeatedly failed until they had discovered what grew best. But she had always felt optimistic that, year by year, their life would improve; and that God would reward their devotion and their hard work with plentiful food and good health and a simple kind of joy that she had never experienced in England.

Of course London boasted every conceivable amusement, from dancing to street theatre to masquerades to whores, as well as every variety of food and drink that could be thought of, from oysters to wild duck to larks, from gin to rum fustian to flip. But she couldn't help feeling that this self-indulgence was all being enjoyed in a state of panic, as if everybody was frantic to cram in as much pleasure as they could because they were always acutely aware that Death already had his bony fingers curled around their door handle, prepared to step in at any moment.

Death could always be smelled around London's streets, mingling with the smell of hot pies and horse manure.

'Now let us pray,' said the Scots preacher, after talking with unremitting bleakness for over an hour. 'O, heavenly Father, look down upon us sinners in our abject misery, and find it in thy heart to relieve us of our suffering, even if we have brought it upon ourselves. But do not offer us redemption unless we are truly sorry for our misdeeds, and if our belief in thee has wavered. Amen.'

So it was that Beatrice was both pleased and relieved when she heard a knock at the front door and James's voice asking if she were at home. By now the Scots preacher was taking tea in the drawing room with Ida, and talking of his plans to recruit the girls from St Mary Magdalene's to visit the destitute families of Houndsditch and Cheapside and the alleys east of Tower Hill – 'to bring them blankets, and food, and an offer of a place in the workhouse'.

Beatrice could see the sense of that. Most of the girls at St Mary Magdalene's had been born into families like that, and had only gone 'on the town' because they had little or no money. They would treat the poor with understanding, even the thieves and the hopelessly drunk.

'James Treadgold has called for me,' she told Ida. 'Are you still agreeable for me to spend the afternoon with him?'

'Of course,' smiled Ida. 'After all your hard work you deserve a few hours of leisure. But please be back by six o'clock for evening prayers.'

James was smartly dressed in a dark-brown coat, with a long beige waistcoat underneath, and beige breeches, and he was wearing a sword. He bowed as Beatrice came out to greet him, and said, 'Beatrice, are you able to come out with me?'

'I'm looking forward to it, James. I'll just go and find Florence.'

'There's very little sunshine outside, I'm afraid. But who needs sunshine when they have you?'

'James, behave yourself!'

'I promise to try. But if that means I can't pay you any compliments, then I shan't find it easy.'

Beatrice found Florence in the kitchen, cutting out biscuits with Grace. Once she had dressed her, and tied on her own bonnet and fastened her long red cloak, James led them out to a navy-blue one-horse chaise. A barefooted boy with a runny nose was holding the bridle of the chestnut horse for him, and James flicked him a penny.

'Is this gig yours?' asked Beatrice, after they had climbed up into their seats. There was room only for two sitting side by side, and no fold-down seat at the front, so Florence had to sit on her lap.

'Mine? I wish it were,' said James. 'I borrowed it from my cousin Joseph. He runs a very prosperous print shop in Pall Mall. I'll take you to see it one day, if you'd care to. He has some marvellously funny caricatures by Hogarth and other artists like him. Sometimes you can hardly get near to the shop for the crowds outside, laughing at the pictures that he's put on display.'

They rattled out of Maidenhead Court and down towards Newgate Street and St Paul's Cathedral. The paving stones were broken and uneven, but the chaise had cee-springs and leather-strap suspension, and even though they swayed in their seats, they weren't jolted as violently as they sometimes were in hackney coaches.

'Florrie! Keep *still*!' Beatrice admonished her, because Florence kept leaning from side to side to see the street vendors selling fish and carrots and fruit, and the jugglers and dancers and violinists and the men with puppet theatres on their backs.

The streets that took them out of the City and all through Westminster were jam-packed with stagecoaches and phaetons and brewers' drays and slow-moving longwagons, and at times they were barely moving at all.

Beatrice couldn't help noticing that James kept turning his head around to look behind them, and after he had turned around for the third time, she said, 'What's the matter? Is there somebody following us?'

'No, no,' said James. 'I'm just trying to see if I can pull out and overhaul these wagons, so that we can go a little faster, but there isn't the space.'

'We're not in a rush to get there, are we?'

'No, of course not. I don't mind where we are, as long as we're together.'

'*I'm* in a rush,' said Florence. 'I need a wee-wee.'

After less than forty minutes, though, they were trotting alongside the Thames towards Chelsea. The sky was pearl-grey and the river was grey, too, but a south-west breeze was blowing and it was warm for the time of year. The river was crowded with pleasure boats and wherries.

At last they saw the Royal Hospital, with its tall white-pillared portico; and beside the Royal Hospital the trees of Ranelagh Gardens. Behind the trees stood the huge rococo Rotunda, which had been built for concerts and masquerades and dining and simply for promenading around, so that fashionable visitors could display themselves while not-so-fashionable visitors could sit high up in viewing boxes and watch them.

'It's a fairy castle!' said Florence, as they turned into the garden entrance.

'Well, perhaps it is,' said James. 'They say that it casts a spell on everybody who visits it. Apparently more couples have become betrothed here than anywhere else in London.'

An ostler took their horse's reins, and then James helped Florence and Beatrice to climb down. James raised one eyebrow, as if he expected her to reply to what he had just said. She smiled but said nothing. Taking Florence out like this had given her a sudden pang of loss for Noah and she had to swallow hard to suppress the pain.

They strolled around the gardens with Florence running ahead of them. The pathways that led to the Rotunda were crowded with men in finely tailored coats and women in their best dresses and bonnets. Although Ranelagh Gardens was considered to be socially superior to Vauxhall Gardens or Bermondsey Spa or Cuper's Gardens, everybody was so well-dressed that it was difficult to tell the aristocracy from the lower orders, except when they opened their mouths, or started complaining loudly about the 2s 6d entrance fee.

'I used to bring my Sophie here,' said James. 'So you can imagine that this day is somewhat dream-like.'

'James, I told you before, I may resemble your Sophie, but I cannot replace her. I like you, but for the time being I have too many preoccupations of my own.'

They were walking beside a long reflecting pool, over which a Chinese pavilion had been built. A woman in a plumed bonnet was throwing cherries to the orange carp swimming below her.

After a while, James said, 'The Reverend Parsons told me about those seven girls from St Mary Magdalene's... the ones who've disappeared.'

'Oh, yes?' said Beatrice. She didn't really want to talk about it.

'Yes – the ones who formed themselves into a coven, and summoned up the Devil, and flew away. He said that you'd seen for yourself the magical symbols that they'd painted on the wall, and the sacrificed goat. You must have found that truly horrifying.'

'Yes, I did. But mostly because I didn't believe it.'

'The Reverend Parsons told me that you were sceptical about it. But he was hopeful that he had managed to convince you that it really *was* Satan at work.'

Beatrice stopped and looked up at him, frowning. The pale blue ribbons of her bonnet fluttered in the breeze. 'Do *you* believe it?'

'Beatrice, if we don't believe in the Devil, how can we truly say that we believe in God? Goodness and honesty only have any value if they are won against evil and deceit.'

'So you *do* believe it?'

'The Reverend Parsons certainly does. He thinks it's a tragedy, but he doesn't want the Devil duping us into thinking that he doesn't exist. If we let down our guard against him, he will devour our souls like some ravening beast, before any of us have the chance to get to heaven.'

'You sound like some kind of evangelist.'

James laughed, and they continued walking. 'I'm sorry. I didn't mean to get so serious, and I didn't want to distress you. Let's talk about something else. Why don't we go into the Rotunda and have some cinnamon cake and coffee? Florence! Would you like some cake?'

Inside the Rotunda, a violin quartet was scraping out music by Giardini and couples were parading around arm in arm. There was a huge fireplace in the centre, with an elaborate pillared chimney that reached up three stories to the ceiling. A fire was lit here in the winter months, so that visitors could sit around it and keep warm while they took refreshment.

James found them a dining-box on the ground floor, and ordered cake and coffee and apple-juice from the waitress, and cider for himself. Florence stood on her chair to watch all the people promenading around. She waved to them and some of the women smiled and waved back.

'Florrie's having a marvellous time,' said Beatrice.

'But are you?'

'Yes, James, I am. I feel much calmer now. I think I have a

tendency to worry too much about everything and everybody, except myself. It's probably what comes of being a parson's wife.'

'Which, sadly, you are no longer,' said James, reaching across the table and laying his hand on top of hers. 'But yesterday is gone, and there's nothing we can do to bring it back. We can think only of what we're going to do tomorrow.'

'I'm afraid that doesn't help me grieving for what might have been.'

'Let's have one more stroll around the gardens, and then we should think about getting you back to Maidenhead Court. If you can wait here for a moment, I'll find our waitress and pay.'

'Are you sure I can't contribute?' asked Beatrice.

James shook his head. 'A teacher's pay is hardly a king's ransom, but today is my treat.'

He went off in search of the waitress, while Beatrice sat with Florence and watched the circling crowds of people.

'Look at that lady with the funny grey hat!' said Florence. 'It looks – it looks like a *turkey*!'

'Where, Florrie?' Beatrice laughed. But even as she was trying to spot the turkey-hat for herself, she became aware of a darkly dressed figure swiftly crossing the Rotunda towards their dining-box. The figure came up to the pillar on Beatrice's left, less than three feet away from her, and then stopped. After a few seconds, when she realised that it was still standing there, motionless, she turned to see who it was.

He was so tall that he must have been a man, but he was wearing a long black cape with a drooping hood which almost completely covered his face. He looked as if he had dressed up to attend a masquerade as the Grim Reaper, except that he wasn't carrying a scythe.

What Beatrice found unnerving was that he stood there, unmoving, and didn't say a word.

'I beg your pardon, sir, what do you want?' she demanded. 'Can you go away, please?'

The hooded figure remained where he was, still silent.

'I said, "Can you go away, please?" You'll frighten my little girl.'

For almost ten seconds the figure said nothing, but then he reached up with one black-gloved hand and lifted his hood so that Beatrice could see his face. When she saw it, she felt a cold prickling sensation all the way down her back.

It wasn't a face at all, or even a mask. It was a curved oval mirror, so that all Beatrice could see was a distorted reflection of herself, her eyes wide with alarm.

'Go away!' she repeated. 'My friend will be back here in an instant, and *he'll* soon send you packing!'

The figure leaned towards her, so that the image of her own face almost completely filled his hood. She found it deeply eerie, like having a nightmare of being haunted by herself, and then waking up to discover that it was true.

'Beatrice,' he whispered, in a low, croaky voice. 'Do you know what happens to those who don't believe in me?'

Beatrice pushed back her chair and stood up. 'Who *are* you?' she challenged him, although her voice was much shriller than she had intended. Florence had now turned around and was staring up at the figure in bewilderment.

'You know full well who I am, Beatrice,' the figure croaked. 'I am He Who Waits at the Wicket Gate, to prevent sinners like you from passing through, and you know better than to question my existence.'

'Be off with you at once, or I'll call for a constable!' Beatrice told him.

Again, the figure leaned close, and said, 'Do you know what my advice to you is, Beatrice? Leave well enough alone.

She who questions the existence of evil is always the first to be given proof of its reality.'

With that, the figure dropped his hood down over the mirror, swirled around, and strode away. In a few seconds, he had been swallowed up by the crowds. Few people took much notice of him, because masquerades were often held here, with partygoers dressed as chimney sweeps or ghosts or kings or even old Adam, with a pink skintight suit and a green silk fig leaf.

Beatrice turned to Florence. She wasn't crying, but her lower lip was sticking out in distress and her eyes were sparkling with tears.

'Who was that horrible man, Mama?'

'There's nothing for you to worry about, my darling. He was only a silly fellow trying to be funny.'

'He wasn't funny. I didn't like him.'

'Well, I agree with you, Florrie. He wasn't funny at all. That was why I told him to go away.'

James came back. As he stepped up into the dining-box, he saw at once that both Beatrice and Florence were upset. The violin music was scraping ever more discordantly.

'What's wrong, Beatrice? What's happened?'

'Please, James, just take us out of here, and I'll tell you.'

'Beatrice—'

'Please, James. Let's take that stroll. I really need some fresh air, and a little silence.'

Outside, the clouds had cleared and a hazy sun was shining. They walked along the path beside a long line of tall trees, but the trees whispered in the breeze in almost the same threatening whisper as the mirror-faced man.

'He knew my name,' said Beatrice. 'How did he know my

name? And from what he said to me, he seemed to know how suspicious I feel about those seven girls.'

'I don't know what I can do to reassure you,' said James. 'There are several private madhouses around here, so he was probably no more than a lunatic. Either that, or some spoony drunkard. I expect he was close behind us when we were walking towards the Rotunda, and he overheard me saying your name. I don't think that you should feel threatened.'

'How can I *not* feel threatened? He said that he was "He Who Waits at the Wicket Gate", to stop sinners from passing through.'

'The Wicket Gate... that's from *The Pilgrim's Progress*. It represents Jesus. When you pass through the Wicket Gate, you accept faith in Christ.'

'Yes, but who tries to stop sinners from passing through the Wicket Gate? Beelzebub. So this man must have been more than just a drunk or a lunatic. He's the Devil, or at least he thinks he is.'

'Beatrice, please don't be upset. I don't want this to spoil our day out. But – I don't know. Perhaps when you said that you didn't believe that those girls had really succeeded in summoning Satan – perhaps you poked a hornet's nest, spiritually speaking.'

'What do you mean?'

James stopped, and held both of her hands. 'I can understand perfectly well that you don't have the same affection for me that I do for you. I have a hope in my heart that one day, given time, that might change. In the meantime, though, I still want to protect you.'

'From what, James?'

'That man may not have been the Devil in person, but he could well have been an emissary sent by the Devil, even if he *was* a lunatic, or a spoon. You asked me earlier if I believed in Satan, and now I'm asking you the same question.'

'My answer is yes, James. I do believe in Satan. But in my

experience he is often used as an excuse by men who want to perform evil deeds unpunished. "The Devil made me do it."'

'But you still believe in him, don't you?' James asked her. 'And I'm afraid I have to agree with the Reverend Parsons. You tried to prove that it wasn't Satan who gave those girls their magical powers, and because of that the Reverend Parsons thinks that Satan might well feel stung, and wants to show you in no uncertain terms that it *was* him.'

'Why would Satan take such trouble? I'm just one woman, a widow. What influence do I have, either with the law or with the church?'

'You underestimate yourself, Beatrice. You are now a mentor for so many young girls, and whatever you teach them, they will believe, and if you teach them that Satan doesn't exist, his influence will be weakened – just as God's influence is weakened if we turn our backs on him.'

He hesitated, and then he said, 'I'm only saying this, Beatrice, because I want to keep you out of any danger, and so that you're never threatened like this again.'

'But if the pentagram on the wall had been drawn in blood, why would Satan change my sample into paint? That was the mainstay of my proof that the whole witchcraft story was a fraud.'

'The Reverend Parsons believes that Satan did it to discredit you. He wanted to make it appear as if you had invented your evidence. After all, where in the world could those girls have found paint?'

Beatrice twisted her hands away from his, and said, 'Let's just walk. I don't want to talk about this anymore. It's all too confusing, and I've been badly scared, and so has Florrie.'

As they continued along the path, they saw that Florence was squatting down beside a small white pug dog, and patting it. The dog was licking her hand and furiously wagging its tail.

'Florrie!' said Beatrice. 'How many times have I told you not to touch strange dogs? You never know if they have fleas.'

'I think he wants a drink.'

'Well, where is his master, or his mistress?'

'I don't know. He doesn't have a collar.'

Beatrice looked around. Among the promenading crowds, one or two women had small lapdogs with them, either carried in their arms or trotting along behind them on long ribbons, but she couldn't see anybody who looked as if they were searching for their lost pet. The dog was also quite scruffy and dirty, so it was likely that it was a stray. At least it was affectionate, so it wasn't suffering from rabies. Last year in London there had been a widespread panic about rabies, and the order had gone out that every dog roaming the streets should be shot.

'You'll have to leave him, Florrie. We have to go back home now.'

'But I think he wants a drink.'

'Florrie, I'm sorry, but you'll have to leave him.'

They started to walk back to the entrance, where the carriages were parked.

James said, 'I'm sorry, Beatrice. This day has turned out to be a disaster.'

'James – it wasn't your fault. We'll go out another time, perhaps in the evening, without Florrie. We could go to the Three Cranes in the Vintry that you mentioned before.'

She heard Florence giggling, and looked round to see that the little pug was following close behind her.

'Tell him to shoo!' Beatrice told her.

Florence said, 'Shoo! Shoo! *Shoo!*' and waved her arms, but when she started walking again, the pug continued to follow her.

'He won't shoo!' she said.

Beatrice went back and stood over the dog. 'Off you go!' she said sternly. 'Go and find your mistress, or your master, or whoever takes care of you! Go on, be off with you!'

The pug didn't move, but looked up at her and let out a squeaky little yap.

'I don't think it understands English,' said James.

'Oh, well,' said Beatrice, and they all started walking again. When they reached their chaise, though, the pug was still so close to Florence that it was sniffing at her the backs of her shoes.

Florence turned around to it and said, 'I have to go now, doggie. Goodbye.'

The pug let out another yap, and then a thin, pathetic whine. Florence squatted down again to stroke it, and then she looked up at Beatrice and said, 'Can I keep him, Mama?'

'Keep him? No, I don't think so. He's filthy dirty, and I'm not sure if Mrs Smollett would welcome a dog in the house.'

'But I'll wash him and give him a drink and look after him. *Please*, Mama!'

'Florrie, it just wouldn't be practical. What I mean is, no.'

Florence put her arms around the dog, and said, 'We could call him No-noh.'

Beatrice pressed her hand against her mouth. She felt as if she had dropped down a bottomless well.

'Please, Mama, *can* I keep him?' Florence coaxed her.

'Very well. But you must make sure you bathe him as soon as we get home; and before you play with him I will dose him with mercury to make sure that he doesn't have ringworm, although I can't see any bald patches on him. And he must be wormed, too.'

'Oh, Mama! Thank you! Thank you!'

James smiled at her and said, 'That was a sudden change of heart.'

'Well, she has no children of her own age to play with, even though the girls at St Mary Magdalene's adore her.'

'There's an oilskin knee-blanket in the back of the chaise. We can roll the dog up in that while we drive home, to save your cape from being soiled.'

Beatrice and Florence climbed into the chaise, while James folded the blanket around the pug and then handed him up like a badly wrapped parcel.

'Good boy, No-noh, good boy,' Florence cooed at him, as they started off.

Beatrice looked away. She was biting her lip and didn't want James to see how emotional she felt. She could still picture Noah astride his hobby horse, calling out for his soldiers to follow him.

They came out of the gardens onto the embankment. As they passed through the gates, she suddenly caught sight of saw the tall hooded figure standing on the corner, his black cape stirring in the breeze. He lifted his hood as they approached, and she saw a flash of reflected sunlight from his mirrored face.

'James!' she said. 'Look! *There!* That's him! That's the man who threatened me!'

'Hold on, Beatrice! Whoa!'

A four-horse cabriolet was heading towards them at a rattling pace from the direction of the World's End, and James was trying to pull the chestnut horse to a standstill.

'Whoa, whoa, whoa! Whoa, I say! Cock and pie, *whoa*!'

He managed to pull the chaise to a halt, and then look around. By the time he had done so, though, the figure had disappeared into the crowd of pedestrians milling around the entrance.

'Are you sure it was him?'

Beatrice nodded. 'Just take us home, please, James. I think I have had quite enough of the Devil for one day.'

21

Ida agreed that Florence could keep No-noh, provided he was washed and wormed and house-trained.

'I'm very grateful, Ida,' said Beatrice. 'You've just made Florrie very happy.'

'And not only Florrie,' smiled Ida, as if she could sense that in some way that keeping No-noh was important for Beatrice, too, although Beatrice didn't think that she had ever told her Noah's name, or what Florence called him.

She followed Ida into the drawing room.

'There's something I need to tell you about,' she said. 'Something happened today when James Treadgold took us to Ranelagh Gardens.'

'Don't tell me he proposed to you. I can tell that he's perfectly besotted.'

'No, nothing like that. While James went off to pay for our cake, a man all dressed in black came up to me and threatened me. He said that I shouldn't question the existence of the Devil, and he even suggested that he might be the Devil himself.'

'I hope you took no notice of him. London is thronged with idiots like that.'

'That's what James said. But he knew my name, this man, and I'm convinced that he was referring to my belief about our seven missing girls.'

'He knew your name? Perhaps he *was* the Devil. What did he look like?'

'I couldn't say, and I think that's what alarmed me more than anything. His face was nothing but a looking glass.'

'A *looking glass*?'

'Yes. Inside his hood. When I looked at him the only face I could see was my own.'

'Perhaps that in itself was a message. Perhaps he was trying to show you that those who deny his existence only make his work easier. In effect, they become his accomplices.'

'I saw him again, outside the gardens, as we were leaving. He was definitely watching and waiting for me.'

'Well, Beatrice, if you are being warned by the Devil himself, my advice to you is to take serious notice of it.'

'I do take it seriously, especially since he upset Florence, too. And I do believe in the Devil. But I still don't believe that it was the Devil who gave our missing girls the power to spirit themselves away from the tobacco factory; and I refuse to believe that this man with the looking-glass face was the Devil himself, or even the Devil's messenger. If I thought that I could identify him, I would seek to have him arrested, but of course the only face I saw inside his hood was my own reflection.'

The ormolu clock on the mantelpiece whirred and struck six.

Ida stood up and said, 'Anyway, Beatrice, it's time for our evening prayers. I'll add a special prayer today for your protection from the Devil, and with the Lord's help that should ensure that you and Florence are never threatened again. For your own safety, though, I think it would be wise for you to forget about our missing girls, and how they vanished. They are gone and lost forever, I'm sad to say, and no amount of investigation will ever find them. You are simply causing yourself unnecessary anxiety, my dear, and exposing yourself to unnecessary danger. You know from your own experience how prickly Satan can be.'

Beatrice was about to say that, in her experience, men could be far quicker to lash out than Satan, especially if they were caught doing something they shouldn't. At that moment, though, Florence came into the drawing room with Grace, and Grace was carrying No-noh in her arms – a damper No-noh, but much cleaner, with a green silk ribbon around his neck.

'Grace and me washed him with soap,' said Florence, triumphantly.

'Well, I must say he looks a picture,' said Ida. 'If you take him down to the kitchen, cook can feed him some scraps.'

'After that, Florrie, you must go to bed,' said Beatrice.

'Where will No-noh sleep? Can he sleep in our bed?'

'No, Florrie, he can't. I haven't treated him for fleas or ticks or ringworm yet, and we will have to clear his tummy of worms, too.'

'He can sleep in the scullery,' said Grace. 'There's a small laundry basket which we never use, and I can fold an old blanket in it for him. I think somebody teach him already to go outside to do the necessary.'

That night, Beatrice again found it difficult to sleep. Florence was unusually fidgety and kept murmuring and turning over, so that she became tangled in the sheets. Beatrice hoped that she was dreaming about her new pet pug, and not having nightmares about the man with the looking-glass face.

Outside, a bright gibbous moon hung over the dome of St Paul's; and she could hear laughter and shouting and singing in the streets, and what she was sure was a pistol shot. She couldn't stop thinking about their day at Ranelagh Gardens, and about the warning that the man with the looking-glass face had given her, and the seven missing girls. She found it impossible to believe that they had really been turned into witches by Satan and flown away, but their disappearance had still been highly mysterious, like some conjuring trick.

If she had been in George Hazzard's shoes, she would have gone immediately to 4 Bow Street and reported their disappearance to a constable, in case an officer should happen to spot one or more of the girls in the street. She also might have considered placing an advertisement in *Lloyd's Evening Post*, as people often did when they were appealing for stolen property to be returned, or absconding servants to be tracked down.

She was on the verge of sleep when she heard a scratching noise. It started off quite soft and hesitant, like a cat scratching at a table leg. She lifted her head off the pillow and listened. After a moment's pause she heard it again, but it was followed by almost fifteen seconds of total silence.

Then, with no warning at all, there was a crash against the panels of her sitting-room door, followed by a harsh scraping sound as if huge claws were being dragged all the way down it. It happened again, and again, and each time it was louder. It sounded like some monstrous beast trying to rip its way in. Its scraping soon became so violent that the door began to rattle on its hinges.

She climbed quickly out of bed and opened the bedroom door. The curtains were open, and so the sitting room was coldly illuminated by the moon, as if it were frozen. The scraping was growing faster and even more ferocious, and the sitting-room door was creaking. Whatever kind of a creature it was, she was terrified that it was going to come bursting through at any moment.

She picked up the heavy brass candlestick from the toilet and approached the door, holding the candlestick in both hands.

'Who's there?' she called out. 'Who are you? Go away!'

The scraping continued, even louder, and there was an added screeching sound, which set her teeth on edge, as if it were dragging its claws down the door with all its strength.

'*Who are you? What do you want?*' Beatrice shouted, almost screaming; and now Florence woke up and started to cry.

Beatrice went up close to the door, lifted the candlestick in both hands and struck the central mullion as hard as she could.

'*Go away!*' she shrieked. '*Whoever you are –* what*ever you are – go away!*'

She stepped back, and as she did so the scraping abruptly stopped. Florence was wailing now, and calling out, 'Mama! Mama!' Beatrice hesitated for a moment, and when it seemed as if the scraping wasn't going to start again, she went into the bedroom to pick Florence up off the bed and hug her.

'Mama, why were you shouting?'

'Ssh, darling, don't worry. I think some silly person thought that these were his rooms, and was trying to get in. He's gone now.'

'Who was it?'

'I don't know, Florrie. Just some silly man. I expect he'd been drinking too much beer.'

'I was frightened.'

Beatrice stroked her hot, sticky curls and kissed her forehead. 'I know you were, but there's nothing to be frightened of now. Would you like a drink of water?'

Florence nodded, and whispered 'yes'. Beatrice sat her down on the end of the bed and went to pour her a glass of water, but as she did so there was a knock at the sitting-room door, and she heard Ida's voice calling, 'Beatrice? Beatrice? What's happened? Are you all right?'

'Coming, Ida!' she called. She gave Florence her drink and then she went back into the sitting room and unlocked the door. Ida was standing in the corridor in a nightcap and a long damask nightgown, holding a candle. This was the first time that Beatrice had seen her without her white lead make-up. She had puffy bags under her eyes and her cheeks were pitted all over with smallpox scars, like a Cheshire cheese.

'What's happened?' she repeated. 'Are you all right? What in the name of God has happened to this door?'

Beatrice looked at the door and saw that it had been gouged and splintered with deep parallel ruts, all the way down from the top rail to the lock rail.

'Oh, dear Lord,' she said. She still felt breathless and shaky. 'It's worse than I thought.'

'You look dreadfully pale, my dear. You haven't been hurt, though, have you?'

'No. I didn't open the door. I have no idea who could have done this – or *what*.'

'But what happened?'

'I heard something scratching, quite quietly at first, but then it became so furious that I thought it was going to break in and tear us to pieces.'

Ida held the candle closer to the door, and said, 'No man did this, Beatrice. These are the marks of some animal.'

'It must have run downstairs, right past your rooms. Didn't you hear it?'

'I heard only your screams. I was concerned that your bedding or your curtains might have caught alight.'

'But whoever did this – or *what*ever did it – where did they disappear to?'

'Well, as I say, I don't think it was a man who did this. These are *claw* marks, don't you agree?'

'They certainly look like claw marks. But even if it was an animal, where did it go? Whatever kind of a creature did this, it must have been enormous. The size of a bear, at the very least. And where did it come from? There are bears in the bear gardens, aren't there, at Marybone, and Hockley-in-the-Hole, but they're always chained up, aren't they? I've seen no bears roaming wild since I was in America.'

Ida said, 'You ask where it came from, Beatrice, and where it went, but what is much more puzzling is how it could have got in. The doors downstairs are always locked and chained at night, and all the windows are closed and barred.'

'We'd best search the whole house,' Beatrice told her. 'If it's hidden itself somewhere, it could jump out again and attack us. Perhaps we should see if we can find a watchman.'

'No, no, don't worry about the watch. I'll gather some of the girls together – the big strong ones like Hannah Wilkes and Anne Fettle. I have a blunderbuss too that George gave me in case of a burglary. But I have to say that I very much doubt that we'll find anything.'

'Ida – where could it possibly hide itself so that we couldn't find it? I mean, an animal that can cause this much damage?'

Ida lifted her candle to the door again, and with her left hand imitated the action of a clawing beast.

'It clearly wasn't a man... but I'm beginning to doubt if it was an animal, either. And why did it attack *your* door and nobody else's?'

'Sorry, Ida. I don't understand what you're suggesting.'

'Beatrice – many different animals have claws. But no animal is capable of passing through solid doors that are locked and chained. And even if it could, why would it climb all the way up to the top of the house to go after *you*, when there are so many other young women sleeping on the floors below?'

'I still don't understand what you're saying.'

'You've challenged Satan, Beatrice. That's what I'm trying to tell you. It could well have been another warning. If this door wasn't clawed by the Devil himself, he might have sent a demon to do it – Belphegor or Baal.' She sniffed the air, and said, 'Why... you can almost smell the sulphur!'

'I'm flabbergasted,' said Beatrice. 'The Devil – or a demon? I don't know what to say to you.'

'Who else could it have been? Who else but the Devil can materialize himself wherever he wishes, regardless of locks and keys? And who else in this house has questioned that he gave our seven girls the power to spirit themselves away – who else but you?'

'I still think we should search the house,' Beatrice told her. 'I won't be able to sleep unless I'm sure that whoever it was isn't hiding somewhere. I know it will mean waking everybody up, but supposing there *is* somebody here? Or some *thing*?'

Ida laid a hand on Beatrice's shoulder. 'You're quite right, my dear. I still don't believe that we'll find anything, but of course you need reassurance. I'll go downstairs and collect some of the girls together.'

Beatrice went back to see if Florence had settled down. She had finished her water and fallen asleep again, her cheeks flushed and her mouth slightly open. Beatrice thought that she looked like a cherub; but then she thought, *if cherubs can exist in the real world, perhaps demons can too.*

Ida went from one bedroom to the next, waking everybody up, and then she assembled a search party of herself and five of the biggest and strongest girls. Anne Fettle had been a farmgirl from Essex before she came to London, and had fought in several female boxing bouts before she became a prostitute. She was at least six inches taller than Beatrice, with shoulders as broad as a heifer's, with a huge bosom and hips so wide she hardly needed to wear panniers. Hannah Wilkes was smaller and wirier, with a pointed nose and buck-teeth, but all the other girls were careful not to put her back up. According to Ida, she could fight like a cornered cat if you riled her.

The girls grumbled about having their sleep disturbed, but carrying their candles and dressed in their long white nightgowns like novitiate nuns they climbed up and down stairs and searched the house from the basement to the attic, looking into every cupboard and every wardrobe and behind every curtain. They even knelt down and looked under the beds.

After nearly half an hour, Ida came back upstairs to Beatrice's sitting room and declared that they had found nothing and nobody. No man, no beast, no demon.

She stood by the splintery door with the candlelight dipping in the draught so that her expression appeared to be constantly changing, sympathetic one second but sarcastic the next, with her lip curled up.

'Whatever it was, Beatrice, my dear, it's gone now. Just to be doubly sure, I've sprinkled holy water on the front and the back doors, and said a prayer from Ephesians at each door, asking the Lord to dress us in his armour, so that we can stand firm against the schemes of the Devil.'

'You seriously believe it was the Devil?'

'Or one of his minions, yes. But I also believe that the Lord prevented him from breaking into your rooms and doing either of you any harm.'

'It was very frightening, Ida, even if we didn't get hurt.'

'Of course. He was *trying* to frighten you, like the figure you saw at Ranelagh Gardens was trying to frighten you. But in spite of the Lord's intervention, I think it would be wise for you to do what I advised you earlier. Put all your doubts about what happened to our seven girls behind you, and concentrate on saving those girls who remain.'

It was well past two o'clock now. Beatrice said, 'Thank you, Ida. And I shall thank Hannah and Anne and all the rest of the girls tomorrow.'

'Sleep well,' said Ida. 'And may the Angel Gabriel spread his protective wing across you as you sleep.'

22

After breakfast on Monday morning, Beatrice asked Ida if she might be excused for an hour, while she went to Collin's apothecary in Covent Garden to stock up on some of the herbs and powders that Gerald was lacking.

She hated lying, but she wanted to protect herself and Florence and she trusted nobody at the moment, not even Ida. She was reasonably sure that Ida was thinking only of her safety, but what if Ida was being mentally influenced by the Devil in some way, although she didn't realize it, and that was why she was warning Beatrice not to question how the seven girls had disappeared? If this were the case, and if the Devil or one of his demons really *had* entered the house, how could Beatrice be certain that it wasn't Ida who had let him in? Ida, after all, was the only person in the house who had a full set of keys.

Apart from Ida, none of the girls in St Mary Magdalene's was an angel, no matter how much they had looked like young nuns in their nightgowns. Before they had been taken in by Ida, they had mingled with pickpockets and housebreakers and footpads and other assorted scum, and it was possible that one of them had opened a window so that one of their old chums could climb in.

The only problem with this theory was that nothing appeared to have been stolen. All the intruder had done was climb the stairs to Beatrice's door and scrape at it like a ravening beast.

Outside, the day was dry and bright – a little chilly, but Florence was able to play with No-noh in the back yard while Beatrice went out, and Beatrice knew that Grace would keep an eye on her. She had treated No-noh last night for pinworms by pushing a suppository of chopped pork into his rectum, so that the worms would be attracted to burrow into it, and she could pull most of them out in the morning.

She walked quickly eastwards along London Wall, past the Bethlem Hospital, and down Shoemaker Row until she reached the Minories, which was a wide street that ran north from the Tower of London to Houndsditch. Her father had brought her here once, when she was no more than eight years old, to buy the same thing that she intended to buy today.

Halfway down, at No. 154, she reached the bow-fronted shop of Richard Wilson, the gunsmith. Although the windows were glazed, it was gloomy inside, and smelled of gun oil and varnish, and there were rows of shining muskets standing to attention along the walls on either side. Behind the counter stood a thin sallow-faced man in white shirtsleeves and a black waistcoat, who greeted her with a bow of his head.

'Madam? How can I be of assistance?'

'I need a pistol,' said Beatrice. 'A small one, which I can carry with me wherever I go.'

'Has madam any acquaintance with pistols?'

'Oh, yes. I lived in America for some years, and I owned a pistol there. I left it behind when I returned to England. In any event it was much too large.'

'I think I have exactly what madam is looking for,' the gunsmith smiled. He pulled open a drawer underneath the counter and lifted out a small flintlock pistol, only six inches long, and set it down in front of her. 'This is a Queen Anne pistol, the smallest we make. We call it a Toby pistol or a muff pistol, because it can easily be concealed inside a muff or a reticule. This one costs a guinea and a half, and for that I can include both gunpowder and shot.'

Beatrice picked it up and cocked it. She was surprised how light it was.

'I don't know if you're familiar with Queen Anne pistols,' said the gunsmith. 'For a lady like yourself, the great beauty of them is that they are loaded not from the muzzle, but by unscrewing the barrel, pouring the powder directly into the breech and then fitting the ball on top of it before screwing the barrel back into place. Thus, you don't need a ramrod.'

Beatrice handed him the pistol and he demonstrated how the barrel could be twisted off.

'The ball is slightly larger than the barrel so that it remains firmly in place until the pistol is fired. Because it is *forced* out, this makes it unusually accurate, especially at close range.'

'I'll take it,' said Beatrice. 'Would you be so good as to load it for me?'

She paid him, and once he had written her a receipt, she tucked the pistol into her embroidered drawstring purse.

The gunsmith opened the shop door for her, and as she stepped out into the street, he said, 'I trust your purchase will keep you safe, madam, but most of all I hope that you never have occasion to use it.'

She walked back along Shoemaker Row. She had thought long and hard about spending so much money on a pistol, but she had been badly shaken by the threats from the man with the looking-glass face, and the violent attack on her door last night had made up her mind. It was not only her own safety that worried her. Should any harm come to Florence she would never be able to forgive herself.

If the Devil could pass through locked doors, perhaps he couldn't be stopped by a pistol ball, but in spite of what Ida had said, she still found it difficult to believe that it really was the Devil who was warning her off.

She had nearly reached Camomile Street, and was crossing the entrance to the crooked alley that joined Shoemaker Row with Houndsditch, when she caught sight of a portly man standing in the alley about twenty yards away, swaying backwards and forwards as if he were drunk.

She stopped, and then took a step backwards to look at him again, although she wasn't entirely sure why. The man's cheeks were flushed scarlet, but he appeared to be quite respectable, in an olive-green tailcoat and a tricorn hat, and he was carrying a silver-topped walking stick – not the usual type of person that she would have expected to see drunk in an alley at a quarter to twelve in the morning.

When she stepped backwards, she saw that he was talking to a young girl who was standing in a doorway in front of him. The girl couldn't have been older than fourteen or fifteen. She was wearing a crumpled white bonnet over her ratty blonde curls, and her light-blue frock was grubby, but she had a little snub nose and she was reasonably pretty. She was too far away for Beatrice to be able to hear what the man was saying to her, but she kept shaking her head as if she were disagreeing with him.

Beatrice was about to walk on when she saw the girl nodding, and the man reaching into his waistcoat and taking out a coin. He handed it to her, and once she had bitten it and dropped it into her pocket, she hoisted up her frock and her soiled white petticoat underneath and exposed herself to him. Her thighs were skinny and white and blotched with bruises, but that didn't deter the man at all. He dropped his walking stick onto the cobbles with a clatter, and then he unbuttoned his breeches and dropped down the front flap. Leaning against the door jamb, he pried out his lavender-headed penis and gave it three or four vigorous rubs to stiffen it.

Beatrice wasn't sure what to do. She was employed by St Mary Magdalene's to save young women from prostitution, and she was the widow of a parson, but at the same time she was pragmatic enough to know that this young girl was probably impoverished and hungry and had no other way of making enough money to survive. There were thousands of young prostitutes in London and it would be impossible for her to rescue them all, even if they wanted to be rescued.

She stayed beside the entrance to the alley, though, keeping close to the wall so that she wouldn't attract the young girl's attention, and watched as the man in the olive-green tailcoat bent his knees slightly so that he could push his penis up into her. The girl's arms hung loosely over his shoulders while he jerked up and down, and the expression on her face was one of complete disinterest, as if she were wondering if it might rain tomorrow, which would stop her going out on the town.

The man was still thrusting himself into her when two rough-looking men came around the dogleg at the far end of the alley. One was bald with a broken nose and the other had long, greasy hair and a scarf tied around his head like a pirate. They were both wearing filthy coats and baggy breeches. The two of them came up to the man in the olive-green tailcoat and positioned themselves on either side of him. It was clear that he was oblivious at first: he was pumping himself into the girl faster and faster, as if he were about to ejaculate, and he must have had his eyes tight shut. But then one of the men dipped into his pocket and took out his wallet and his handkerchief, while the other reached around him and tugged at his watch chain.

'Hi!' he shouted out, and tried to twist himself around, but now the girl clung on to him tight. 'Give those back to me, you blackguards!'

The bald man smacked the hat off his head, while the other man punched his right ear, so that he lost his balance and staggered sideways. The girl dropped her frock down to cover herself and Beatrice heard her say something like, 'Leave him, 'Arry, for fuck's sake! Let's buy a brush!'

But the bald man kicked the man in the olive-green coat hard in the knee, and he fell heavily onto his back, rolling over and knocking his head against the doorstep. The bald man seized his left wrist and started to tug at the gold ring that he was wearing on his wedding finger. 'Come on, lobcock, let's have that glim star off of you!'

Beatrice was aware that she should simply walk away, as fast as she could, and forget the robbery that she was witnessing. But she had a pistol, and neither of these two ruffians appeared to be armed, and Francis wouldn't have walked away, whether he had a pistol or not.

She took the Toby pistol out of her purse, cocked it, and approached the two men, holding it in both hands, pointing it directly at the bald man's head.

'Give him back his property!' she snapped.

The two men and the girl stared at her in amazement.

'Give him back his wallet and his watch!' she demanded. 'Do it now, or I'll shoot the first one of you who moves!'

The bald man stopped trying to pull off the wedding ring, and stood up. The man with the long hair began to back away.

'You heard me!' said Beatrice. 'I'll count up to three and then I'm pulling the trigger, and don't for a second imagine that I won't!'

There was a long pause. None of them spoke. All they could

hear was the sound of carriages clattering and rumbling along Shoemaker Row and some street seller blowing a discordant horn.

Suddenly, the man with the long hair said, '*Scour!*' and he and his bald-headed companion started to run away. The girl gathered up the hem of her frock and tried to run after them, but she lost one of her shoes on a broken paving stone and stumbled.

Beatrice could have shot at one of the men, but they were both weaving and feinting from side to side and she probably would have missed. Instead, she hurried up to the girl and caught her skinny wrist and held her tight.

'*Let me go, you scab!*' the girl screamed at her, trying to wrench herself free. "*Oo told you to stick your fuckin' nozzle in? Let me go!*'

By now the man in the olive-green tailcoat had climbed to his feet and was buttoning up his breeches. His wig was tilted to one side and a red bruise was swelling across his forehead.

'You young *shlut*!' he slurred, spitting as he spoke. '*That* wash what you were up to, washnit? Robbery! And I'll thank you to give me my guinea back!'

'Oh, fuck off,' the girl retorted. 'You 'ad your fun, didn't you, you old buck fitch?'

'I losht my wallet and my watch, you young doxy. If it hadn't been for thish gallant lady here, I would have losht my ring, too. Madam – I have to thank you mosht shincerely. Let me go and find a conshtable and have thish shlut arreshted.'

The girl tried even harder to tug herself away, but Beatrice held on to her. She was underfed and weak, and her wrist was thinner than a broom handle, while Beatrice still had the strength of a well-nourished woman who had been digging her garden and rubbing down her horse and chopping wood for the oven.

'Don't trouble yourself finding a constable, sir,' she told the man in the olive-green tailcoat.

'Why? Why not?'

'Sir – if this young madam were to be arrested, you would be obliged to appear in court as a witness and explain how she came to entrap you. You don't really wish to suffer that embarrassment, do you? Leave her to me.'

'What about my watch? What about my wallet? I had three poundsh in my wallet. Three poundsh, three shillingsh and shixpenshe!'

'I'll see if I can persuade her to tell me who those two friends of hers are.'

'Oh, you think I'm a fuckin' nose, do you?' said the girl. 'I'll swear on the Bible I never ever seen those two cullies in my life!'

The man in the olive-green tailcoat picked up his hat and his walking stick. He came unsteadily up to Beatrice and said, 'If you do happen to elishit any information from thish young shlut, dear lady, my name ish William Newbolt, and I reshide at five Green Arbour Court, by the Old Bailey. I shall be eternally in your debt if you do.'

'Very well,' said Beatrice. She waited until he had teetered away and disappeared around the corner into Shoemaker Row. Then she turned to the girl and said, 'Tell me your name.'

'Fuck off.'

'Tell me your name or I'll take you directly to a runner and give evidence of what you were doing.'

'You wouldn't.'

'You don't think so? I'd have shot one of your friends if I'd thought that either of them was worth the price of the powder.'

The girl remained silent and sulky. After a few moments, Beatrice eased forward the hammer of her pistol and dropped it back into her purse. 'All right, then,' she said, 'if that's how you want it. You realize that you could be hanged for this, or at the very least transported.'

'I didn't do nothing. And like I said, I'll swear that I never knew either of them cullies.'

'Oh, that's how you knew that one of them was called Harry? I could give evidence to that effect, and who do you think the judge would believe?'

The girl said nothing for a few moments more, but then she coughed and Beatrice could hear the phlegm rattling in her lungs. She lowered her eyes and when she spoke again she sounded defeated.

'Eliza,' she said, and coughed again. 'Eliza White.'

'How old are you, Eliza?'

'Fourteen. Fourteen and a half.'

'And where do you live?'

'Black 'Orse Yard.'

'Who with? Your parents?'

Eliza shook her head. 'I never knew my dad and my mum died 'avin' a baby. I live with my aunt and 'er three daughters and some nocky boy called Dick. You ain't goin' to 'and me in, are you?'

'That depends entirely on you, Eliza. I work with some kind and generous people who help girls like you to get off the streets and live very much happier lives. Perhaps you've heard of St Mary Magdalene's Refuge.'

Eliza shook her head again.

'You could come back with me now and join us,' said Beatrice. 'We'd teach you to read and write, if you don't know already, and train you for some useful occupation, like sewing, or music, or cookery.'

Eliza coughed and looked up at her. 'What if I don't want to?'

'Then, yes, I'll hand you in, because you're a thief. But think about it, Eliza. If you come back with me now, you'll be given a hot meal, and clean clothes, and a bed of your own to sleep in. You won't be in danger of catching the pox any longer, or some other horrible sickness like the King's Evil. You won't find yourself with child, so that you risk an abortion. As it is, you don't sound at all well, and I could give you some physic for that.'

'What will my aunt think, if I don't come back, and she never sees me again?'

'We can get word to her and tell her where you are, and she can come and visit you if she wishes. But listen to me, Eliza – this is an opportunity you may never be given again, ever. Even if the court doesn't find you guilty, what will you do? Go back to selling your body, until you're too old and too ugly, or dead of syphilis? Have you seen women with syphilis, all covered in blisters, with their noses all fallen in? Or will you go back to your thieving, with the strongest chance that you'll be caught again, and hung?'

Eliza's eyes filled up with tears, which ran down her dirty cheeks and dripped off her chin. She didn't sob, but she coughed again, and had to wipe the phlegm from her lips with the back of her hand.

Beatrice said, 'Come on, Eliza, what's it to be?' as sternly as she could, although she knew that she wouldn't really hand her to a constable, or give evidence against her in court. If she absolutely refused to come to St Mary Magdalene's with her, she would simply let her go. In Beatrice's eyes, the life of prostitution and pickpocketing that she was leading was punishment enough. She would probably be dead in two or three years from venereal disease or scrofula or puerperal fever.

Eliza looked around. An elderly woman in a stringy grey shawl appeared around the corner of the alley, her back stooped, one eye covered with a black eyepatch. She stared at them both as she shuffled past, and for no reason at all said, '*Hah!*'

Perhaps Eliza saw that as a warning of how she might look in the future, because she said, 'All right, then. I'll come. Is it far?'

'In distance? Not even ten minutes. But from this life – it's about as far away as you could imagine.'

Beatrice released her hold on Eliza's skinny wrist and started to walk back towards Shoemaker Row. Eliza could have run away, but after a moment's hesitation she followed her.

23

Ida welcomed Eliza as warmly as she welcomed all her 'stray lambs', as she called them. Eliza's frock was torn and stained, her cheeks were smudged with street dirt and her nose was running, but Ida hugged her like a long-lost daughter.

'You must think of this house as your new home, my dear, and everybody in it as your friends!'

Eliza looked over Ida's shoulder at Beatrice, slightly bewildered, but Beatrice gave her a reassuring smile.

'She's very hungry, and she's thirsty, too,' she told Ida. 'Before we do anything else, let's give her something to eat.'

She led her through to the kitchen where Katharine and three other girls were making mutton pies and a celery ragout. Martha the cook was there, too, stirring up a saucepan of lentil soup with carrots and parsnips and ham. Beatrice sat Eliza down at the table and Katharine brought her a bowl of soup and the crusty end of a fresh-baked loaf.

'All my nits have gone now, Beatrice!' said Katharine, cheerfully. She peered closely at Eliza and said, 'You've got 'em, though, ain't you, love? Nits! But don't you worry, Beatrice 'ere will soon get rid of 'em for you!'

It was then that Eliza covered her face with her hands and started to sob. She cried so sadly that she could hardly breathe, and every sob ended in a bout of coughing. Beatrice put her arm around her shoulders and shushed her.

'I know,' she said. 'I know. Sometimes it's hard to understand that strangers can want to take care of you. But that's what the Bible tells us to do, and that's what this refuge is for.'

Eliza managed to stop sobbing. She wiped her nose on her sleeve, and looked up at Beatrice with her eyelashes stuck together with tears.

At that moment, Florence came into the kitchen carrying her doll, Minnie, with No-noh trotting close behind her.

'Why is that girl crying?' she said.

'That's Eliza,' said Beatrice. 'She's come to stay here, and she's crying because she's happy.'

Florence dragged out the chair next to Eliza and climbed up to sit on it. 'Hallo, Eliza. This is Minnie and this is my doggy. His name's No-noh like my brother who got lost.'

'Your brother got lost?'

Florence nodded, with a serious expression on her face. 'The Indians took him away.'

Beatrice laid her hand on Eliza's shoulder again. 'Just eat your soup,' she said. 'I'll tell you all about it later.'

Eliza picked up her spoon and looked at her upside-down reflection in it. 'I think *I* was lost, too,' she said. ''Ow the fuck did you manage to find me?'

After Eliza had scraped up the last spoonful of soup and wolfed down her bread, Grace took her upstairs to change her clothes and wash. To begin with, she would be given the small bedroom at the back where Judith had been quarantined – at least until Beatrice had deloused her and cleared her lungs and made sure that she had no venereal disease or tapeworms.

Before she followed them upstairs, Beatrice went through to the atelier, where Ida was supervising a millinery class, teaching the girls to weave straw-work flowers into the brims and crowns of wide summer hats.

'You don't mind that I brought young Eliza back with me?' Beatrice asked her.

'Not at all, my dear. It is our divine mission to rescue young girls like her. Where did you find her?'

'In an alleyway off Shoemaker Row. I caught her giving herself to some drunken old fellow who should have known better.'

Beatrice decided not to mention the two rascals who had robbed the man in the olive-green tailcoat. There was no need for Ida to know that Eliza was a thief as well as a prostitute, and she would only have to explain how she had managed to chase them away.

As it was, Ida said, 'Shoemaker Row? I thought you were going to Covent Garden.'

'Oh, I did, but Collin's didn't have the oils and the powders I needed, so I tried Culpeper's in Aldgate.'

Beatrice could feel herself blushing. She had never lied so blatantly in her life, to anyone. Yet how could she now tell Ida that she had lied to her to begin with, and had gone out to buy herself a pistol?

But Ida appeared to accept this explanation, because she smiled and said, 'For Eliza's sake, it is just as well that you did. Sometimes we are led in unexpected directions, but I do believe that when this happens, the Lord is guiding our footsteps to carry out his own benevolent purpose.'

She turned to one of the girls in the class and said, 'No, no, Josephine, dear – under and *then* over and *then* tie it into a knot.'

'I must attend to Eliza now,' said Beatrice. 'She has a very troublesome cough and I don't want it to get any worse.'

Ida said, 'By the bye, Mr Hazzard has sent word that he will be visiting us again tomorrow, and the Reverend Parsons, too. I trust that you have accepted that it really *was* Satan who gave our girls the wherewithal to escape, and that George knew nothing of it until they had gone.'

'It's one possibility, I grant you,' said Beatrice. 'But I am still inclined to believe that their disappearance was contrived by man, rather than Satan.'

'In spite of the man with the looking-glass face, and the demon that clawed at your door?'

'I'm simply reserving judgment, Ida, until I have more evidence.'

'But what evidence could you possibly hope to find?'

'I have no idea yet, but in my experience even the cleverest tricksters usually make mistakes. If that trickster turns out to be Satan, then yes, I'll accept that it was him. But I am a long way from coming to that conclusion just yet.'

Ida laid her hand on Beatrice's arm. 'Please say nothing about your misgivings to George, will you? He is the most generous of men but he doesn't take kindly to being doubted. We depend almost entirely on his benevolence to keep St Mary Magdalene's open.'

'I promise, Ida. Now, I really must go and see to Eliza. I don't want her coming down with the phthisis.'

Eliza kept coughing until well after midnight. Beatrice had given her three spoonsful of her own cold remedy, which was a mixture of red roses, balsam of sulphur, oil of vitriol and syrup of coltsfoot. It loosened the phlegm in her lungs a little, but eventually Beatrice dosed her with a tincture of opium so that both of them could get some sleep.

It was nearly eight o'clock before Beatrice woke up. It was a dark and gloomy morning, so dark that if Florence hadn't left the bed she could have believed it was still night-time. Florence had probably gone downstairs to give No-noh his breakfast. She had become so fond of him that Minnie had almost been forgotten.

Beatrice climbed out of bed herself and quickly dressed in her favourite Prussian-blue gown. She had so many chores to do today. Her period had almost finished, but her pads had been soaking in cold water in the scullery and she needed to boil them.

Ida had told her that the periods of nearly all the girls in the house had synchronised now, and she wondered if she would soon be joining them.

'Starting with the new moon, we always have a few days of weeping and argument and disorder,' Ida had told her. 'I call it the "fretful moon".'

As she closed the deeply scratched sitting-room door behind her, Beatrice heard the clattering of a carriage outside. She went along the landing to the window that overlooked Maidenhead Court, and saw a young lad climbing down from a two-horse calash. Once he was down, the driver handed him a large brown hatbox. The young lad came up the steps of the house and Beatrice heard him knocking at the front door.

At first she thought that Ida must be having a new hat delivered, but then spots of rain started to fall, and the calash driver took off his black wide-brimmed hat to look up at the sky. Beatrice recognized him at once as the leathery-faced man from George Hazzard's tobacco factory, the one who had first led her through the factory to his office, and had offered Florence a puff of his pipe.

She went across to the banisters and looked down to the hallway below. She could hear Ida and the young lad talking, although she couldn't make out what they were saying. Then the front door closed, and when she went back to the window she saw the young lad climbing back into the calash. The leathery-faced man flicked his whip and the calash drove off.

Beatrice thought: *Well, that's strange – or perhaps it isn't. Perhaps George Hazzard has made Ida the gift of a hat, or perhaps one of the girls has a birthday coming, and he has arranged for her to be given a hat as a present.* That didn't seem likely, though, because the girls had been learning millinery for over a week now, and they were all busy making their own hats.

She went in to see if Eliza was any better. She was still sleeping, but her cheeks were rosy pink and although she was breathing through her mouth she sounded much less clogged up than she had yesterday. Beatrice quietly closed her bedroom door and went downstairs.

She found Ida in the kitchen, talking to Martha, but there was no sign of the hatbox. Florence was kneeling on a chair at the kitchen table, still in her nightdress, spooning up a bowl of gruel with a lump of melted butter in it. No-noh the pug was sitting on the chair next to her, occasionally licking his lips as if he had just eaten.

'Good morning, Beatrice,' Ida smiled. 'How is our new stray lamb this morning?'

'I gave her opium last night and she's still fast asleep. But her lungs sound much clearer, and I'm sure that having a good supper and a warm bed will have worked wonders.'

'For that young girl, Beatrice, the real wonder was being rescued by you. I must tell George this afternoon what you did. He's coming here about two o'clock, and Martha is going to lay on a splendid lunch for him and the Reverend Parsons. We'll be having oyster soup and sweetbreads and stuffed cabbage and partridge and roasted pork – complete with the pig's head with its ears baked crisp! Then jellies and meringues for dessert.'

'That all sounds delicious, Martha,' said Beatrice.

'Doesn't it just?' said Ida. 'And after we've eaten, the girls will entertain us with songs. Not *all* sacred, mind you – "Country Gardens" and "The Raggle-Taggle Gypsies" and "Fare Thee Well". For their finale, though, they'll be singing John Wesley's new hymn, "Come Thou, Almighty King". You haven't heard it yet, have you? It's so stirring it brings tears to the eyes.'

Beatrice wondered if she ought to ask about the hatbox, but she decided not to. Ida had been nothing but supportive, almost motherly, but after her experiences in New Hampshire, Beatrice had learned to be wary of any incidence of ill-fortune that was claimed to be the work of Satan, whether it be cattle disease or bouts of madness or babies struck dead in their cribs.

If Ida believed that the looking-glass man and the beast at her door really had been the Devil, or one of his emissaries, then let her believe it. But Beatrice was still highly suspicious about both visitations, and until she knew for certain who was behind them, she was beginning to think that she and Florence might be safer if she kept her thoughts to herself.

Ida clapped her hands. 'Now, girls, we have much to do this morning!' she announced. 'The floors need sweeping and all the chamber pots need to be thoroughly washed out. We want the house to smell sweet for Mr Hazzard now, don't we?'

24

The Reverend Parsons arrived first. He was in a jolly mood, his cheeks flushed, breathing out the small beer that he had drunk for breakfast and the pipe that he had smoked soon afterwards. He embraced Ida and nodded to Beatrice and then let out a squeaky fart.

'I so much enjoy my visits here, Ida! It is so heart-warming to see the charitable aspirations that we have put into practice, and all these young girls saved from a life of turpitude!'

'Having Beatrice join me has been such a boon,' said Ida. 'Only yesterday she rescued some poor young girl from the streets and brought her here to find God.'

'I trust the Devil has now left you in peace, Beatrice,' smiled the Reverend Parsons, as he eased himself into an armchair. 'There are times when we have to leave the administration of justice to the Lord, and I believe this is one of those occasions. I have prayed for those seven young witches, that they will see the error of their ways, and repent, and seek to return to Christ's bosom. I expect that you have, too. Apart from that, there is little else that we can do.'

Beatrice said nothing, but nodded, and gave him the ghost of a smile.

Ida said, 'Would you care for some cider, Reverend Parsons? Or a glass of spruce ale?'

The Reverend Parsons didn't answer at first, but continued to stare at Beatrice, as if he were still expecting some response – some word that she agreed with him, and that the girls *had* been possessed by Satan.

'Or a lemon cordial?' Ida persisted. 'Or a posset, with honey and wine?'

Still without taking his eyes off Beatrice, the Reverend Parsons said, 'A posset sounds tempting, Ida. It will help to clear my head.'

'Let me fetch it,' said Beatrice, and stood up. She was beginning to feel more and more that she had been cast without her knowledge in some mysterious religious play – a play in which everybody knew their lines except her.

Four tables had been arranged end-to-end in the atelier and laid with a long white linen cloth, and places had been set for sixteen. The Reverend Parsons sat at the head of the table with Beatrice on his left while Ida sat at the opposite end with George on her right. The remaining places were taken by the girls who had been resident at St Mary Magdalene's the longest. None of them was pretty, which was probably why George hadn't picked them for his tobacco factory; but they could be counted on to make at least some attempt at polite conversation, and not to swear or take the name of the Lord in vain. They were all dressed in their best and had sprinkled themselves with rose water and rouged their cheeks, and they chattered and giggled as soon as they had sat down. All the other girls would be fed later, in the kitchen.

Because the afternoon was so dark, two three-branched candelabra had been set on the table, as well as the centrepiece, which was a crystal vase crowded with pink and yellow alstroemeria. Raindrops pattered against the window, and every now and then from over the river they heard the distant grumbling of thunder, as if Southwark were at war.

Beatrice couldn't help noticing that George was oddly distracted, and that Ida had to keep patting his arm to keep his attention. When he did speak, it wasn't in his usual rich, measured tones, but in a series of abbreviated blurts, and he kept turning his head around and looking towards the door, as if he were worried that the Devil himself might walk in.

The Reverend Parsons went into a long self-congratulatory discourse about the charitable work that the Foundery had been doing since Francis and Beatrice had left for America; and in return Beatrice told him about the hardships of life in New Hampshire, creating her vegetable garden out of a wilderness, and rearing her own pigs.

'But we never felt that God had abandoned us there,' she told him. 'In fact, we felt that he was closer than ever, watching over us, and doing everything he could to give us strength.'

'I can only offer you my condolences again about the loss of your little son,' said the Reverend Parsons. He paused, and belched softly into his fist. 'It only goes to show that you can never trust a heathen. We have been planning to send missionaries to Africa, you know. Yes, Africa! If any continent is crying out for the light of the Lord, in every respect, it is Africa. Some of the natives believe that humans were created by a so-called god fashioning figurines out of mud, and breathing over them. I ask you! Others believe that their deities send them messages of life or death through the sound of the wind, or the cries of passing animals. It is going to take much dedicated work to convince them of the truth.'

'The American Indians have their own gods, too,' said Beatrice. 'They also believe that everything has a spirit – animals, rocks, rivers – everything.'

'Sometimes I wonder why God created people who could think such nonsense,' said the Reverend Parsons. He looked down at his empty bowl and said, 'That was a capital oyster soup, I have to say. At least I know why God created oysters.'

Three girls came in from the kitchen to clear away the plates from the first course. One of them was Grace, who smiled across the table at Beatrice, but Beatrice noticed that as soon as George saw her, he leaned towards Ida and held up his hand to shield his face, as if he were saying something confidential, and didn't want to risk anyone reading his lips.

Grace was beautiful, with skin the colour of melted chocolate and a full-breasted figure, and she walked with an engaging sway of her hips. Beatrice could understand why George might be taking notice of her. All the same, she doubted if Ida would let him take her away to work at his tobacco factory. Grace helped to run the household by shopping and cleaning and organizing the laundry and answering the door to visitors, and she also acted as Ida's personal maid. She dressed Ida in the morning and took care of her clothes and quilled her wigs.

If she were to leave, Florence would be devastated, because she adored her. Whenever Grace had a few spare moments in her busy day, she would always find Florence and play with her and No-noh, and sing Florence some of the songs that her mother had taught her in Barbadoes, like 'Da Little Cat' and 'Da Cocoa Tea'.

Now the girls carried in the main course, on four trays with silver dish-covers on them. They placed one of the dishes in front of Ida and George, and lifted the lid to reveal two roasted partridges. In the centre of the table they set down four more dishes, with stuffed cabbage and slices of roasted pork and a boiled leg of mutton with capers. Katharine came in last with a covered silver dish which she put down in front of the Reverend Parsons and Beatrice.

'The pig's head,' she smiled.

She took off the lid, but as soon as she did so she let out a shrill scream and dropped it on the floor. Instead of a pig's head sitting on the plate, there was the goat's head from the dormitory at George's tobacco factory. Its eyes were opaque and its white hair was matted, and what made it appear all the more grotesque was that it had a red apple stuffed in its mouth, as the pig's head would have done, and strands of watercress wound around its curly horns.

The Reverend Parsons stood up immediately, so that his chair tipped over backwards. Beatrice stood up, too, feeling numb with shock. As soon as the girls at the table saw the goat's head, they let out cries of disgust, although two or three of them giggled, as if it were nothing more than a practical joke.

'What in the name of God is the meaning of this?' demanded the Reverend Parsons. Then, to Katharine, 'Did you not know what you were carrying on this plate, girl? Surely you must have seen it in the kitchen!'

Katharine was sobbing and wringing her hands. 'It *was* a pig's head, I swear it. I saw Martha taking it out of the oven, and dressing it.'

Ida left her seat and came up to join them, closely followed by George.

'That is *my* goat!' said George, in a blustery voice. 'That is the very same goat that the seven girls sacrificed to Satan! I had it buried in the back yard! How could it have appeared on this plate? And look at it! It has not decayed in the slightest. It is in the same condition as the day it was killed.'

Ida looked at Beatrice and slowly shook her head. 'Black, black magic,' she said. 'This can only be another warning from Satan.'

Beatrice didn't know what to say. It was clear from Katharine's distress that she hadn't known what was under the dish-cover, but Martha must have known, even if she hadn't decorated the goat's head herself and put it on the plate instead of the pig's head.

Was this what George had sent down from Hackney this morning, in the hatbox? If it had been a hat, surely Ida or one of the girls would have shown it off before now. And George was right. It *was* the same goat that had been disembowelled and nailed to the wall of the dormitory, even though it didn't smell of rotting flesh, as Beatrice would have expected it to. When her pigs had died in New Hampshire, they had started to stink after only a few hours, although it had been summer then, and very hot.

Ida said, 'I'm afraid we'll have to abandon this meal. I don't think any of us have much of an appetite now, do you? I'll go to the kitchen and ask Martha how this could have happened, although I'm sure that it was Satan's work, and that he transformed the pig's head between the kitchen and here. He is more than capable of such mischief, after all.'

Ida left the room, and most of the girls followed her. The Reverend Parsons and George started to talk to each other, with the Reverend Parsons telling George about other satanic miracles, or 'lying wonders' – especially those mentioned in the Bible in Matthew and Thessalonians.

'This goat's head, surely this one of the Devil's false enchantments. It was done for no other reason except to demonstrate that he exists, lest any of us should still doubt it.'

'Well, Reverend, I have to agree with you,' said George. 'It's a great pity that he should have ruined such an excellent dinner just to prove a point.'

The Reverend Parsons looked mournfully at the pork and the partridges and the stuffed cabbage. 'We could stay for supper, couldn't we, and have it served cold?'

'Not me, I'm afraid,' said George. 'I have to be back at the factory by five. We're expecting a large shipment of tobacco leaves from the Carolinas.'

While they were talking, with their backs half-turned, Beatrice picked up a small pair of sewing scissors from the shelf at the side of the atelier, went across to the dinner table and quickly snipped a tuft of hair from the goat's wiry beard. She folded it into a napkin and pushed the napkin into her pocket.

As she passed him on her way to the door, the Reverend Parsons said, 'You mustn't blame yourself too severely for this unfortunate enchantment, Beatrice. But there seems to be no question at all that Satan is making sure that you recognize how influential he is, and how much power he invested in those seven unfortunate girls.'

Beatrice didn't look at him, but at George instead. 'Yes, Reverend. I believe I know now what kind of a demon I'm up against. After today, I certainly can't question that he's real, can I?'

George raised his eyebrows slightly, as if he caught the inference in what she was saying. 'That's very wise of you, Beatrice. It's sad but true that those who challenge his satanic majesty often come to an unfortunate end.'

Although Beatrice realized that he was making a thinly veiled threat, she resisted the temptation to tell him not to try to intimidate her. She wanted him to think that while she suspected him of hiding the truth about the coven's disappearance, or at least of misleading her, she was going to take no further action to discover what had really happened to them, or voice her suspicions to anybody else.

She left George and the Reverend Parsons and went along the corridor to the kitchen, where Ida was questioning Martha. Most of the girls were gathered around, and even Florence was there, holding No-noh in her arms, even though No-noh was almost as big as she was, his face crumpled and his back legs hanging down.

Martha was sitting at the kitchen table looking defiant rather than upset. When Beatrice came in, she stood up immediately and said, 'Widow Scarlet – I was just a-tellin' Mrs Smollett 'ere that I don't 'ave even the faintest notion 'ow a goat's 'ead could have turned up on that there plate. I swear on my dead 'usband's grave that it was a pig's 'ead I put on it, with an apple in its mouth and cress around its ears. 'Ow it got to be a *goat's* 'ead between 'ere and the dinner table I 'ave no idea at all. Witchcraft, I calls it. Witchcraft!'

Beatrice looked around the kitchen. 'If the pig's head was somehow removed from the plate and the goat's head put in its place, then where is the pig's head now?'

'It ain't nowhere,' said Martha. 'It's not like one 'ead was swapped for another. It was like, 'ocus-pocus.'

'There's a strong smell of burned pork in here now,' said Beatrice.

'Well, of course. I roasted 'alf the pig and 'eated up the 'ead really 'ot, so the ears would be crisp.'

Florence said, 'I'm *'ungry*! And No-noh's 'ungry, too!'

Beatrice was about to admonish for dropping her aitches, but thought it more diplomatic to wait until they were alone – just as it was more circumspect to agree that the pig's head had been transmogrified into a goat's head by Satan.

I believe in Satan, she thought. *I believe in Satan as much as I believe in God.* Her dear dead Francis had felt so threatened by Satan in his work as a parson that he always wore a medal of St Benedict around his neck, with the initials VRSNSMV around the rim – *Vade retro Satana; nunquam suade mihi vana*: Begone Satan, suggest not to me vain things.

But she also thought: *Surely Satan must have his hands full stirring up wars and mass murders and terrible catastrophes, like cities burning and passenger ships sinking with all on board. Why would he take the time to frighten me – one young widow, who is no threat to him at all?*

George came into the kitchen and said, 'I'll be off now, Ida. I'm sorry this hugely pleasant occasion had to end so abruptly. But we must arrange another dinner very soon. I'm extremely partial to a crisp pig's ear.'

'What about the goat's head?' asked Ida.

'Don't worry. Giles my coachman has taken it, and we'll bury it in our cesspit. That's the only place that Satan deserves to be buried, don't you agree, Beatrice? The cesspit?'

Beatrice smiled wanly. The kitchen was still filled with the smell of burned pork and she was beginning to feel as if her clothes and her hair were permeated with it. She could hear Florence crying in the atelier, so she gave George a curtsey and said, 'You'll have to excuse me. I don't think Satan has succeeded in dulling my Florrie's appetite, even if he's made the rest of us feel queasy.'

25

They spent the rest of the afternoon in prayers and hymn-singing, led by the Reverend Parsons. At six o'clock, they all sat down to a supper of cold meats, with the Reverend Parsons managing to eat almost the whole boiled leg of mutton by himself, cutting slice after slice, and calling on Martha to bring him another boatful of caper sauce.

Nobody mentioned the goat's head, but Beatrice couldn't stop thinking about it, and after the Reverend Parsons had left she excused herself and took Florence upstairs to their rooms. She didn't know what Francis would have said, but she couldn't bring herself to believe that at some point between the kitchen and the dinner table, underneath a silver dish-cover, Satan had managed to work one of his 'lying wonders'.

'Grace was funny at supper,' said Florence.

Beatrice was sitting at her toilet, writing her diary. 'Funny? What do you mean?'

'She wouldn't talk to me. But she kept hugging me. She hugged me so tight I was nearly *sick*.'

'I wonder what the matter was.'

Florence picked Minnie up from the floor and climbed up into her chair, cuddling the doll close. She hadn't shown such affection for Minnie since No-noh had come into her life. 'I don't know. But when I took No-noh into the garden for his poo-poo, Grace was there, and I think she was crying.'

'Oh,' said Beatrice, and recalled the way that George had been looking at Grace at dinner, and talking to Ida behind his hand.

'I said, "Are you crying, Grace?" but she wiped her eyes with her apron and said no.'

'I'll have to ask her if she's worried about something, or not feeling very well,' said Beatrice.

'I love Grace,' said Florence. 'I love Grace and I love No-noh and I love Minnie.'

'What about me?'

Florence jumped down from her chair, came across the room and stood on tiptoe to give Beatrice a kiss.

'I love you best of all, Mama. And I love my brother Noah, and I love Papa in heaven.'

Beatrice looked down at what she had already written in her diary.

Dear God, I pray that my suspicions are unfounded.

She couldn't sleep. It had stopped raining and the clouds must have cleared away, because when she turned over in bed she could see stars. Just visible over the window ledge towards the south-east was the bright star Fomalhaut. Her father had told it was always called the Lonely Star of Autumn.

Florence was deeply in dreamland with Minnie lying next to her, although Minnie was wide awake and staring provocatively at Beatrice as if to say, *Go on then, have the courage of your convictions, Widow Scarlet.*

Strangely, she thought that she could still smell burned pork, and quite strongly, too. After she had undressed for bed, she had sprinkled her dress and her petticoats with bergamot and rose blossom water to mask the odour that was still clinging to them. This smell must be drifting upstairs from the kitchen, even up here to the top floor.

After she had heard the clock downstairs chiming one, she climbed out of bed, went to the wardrobe, and took out her long white day gown. Her heart was beating fast, and although she knew what she was intending to do, she didn't feel as if she were the person doing it.

This is another Beatrice, bolder and much more irrational than the usual Beatrice.

Quietly, she opened the sitting-room door and went out onto the landing. The house was silent, and dark, although there was just enough light from the moon to be able to see where she was going. She waited for a few seconds to make sure that nobody was awake, and then, barefoot, she went downstairs, keeping close to the panelled wall so that she wouldn't make the treads creak.

The smell of burned pork had almost faded away now. Perhaps Martha had been telling the truth, and it had been caused by her roasting the pig's head at high temperature, so that its ears became crisp. But why should it smell as if it had been *charred*? Beatrice could remember a house fire on the corner of Giltspur Street, where she used to live when she was a young girl. Three adults and five children had been trapped in one of the bedrooms, and she had walked past not long after the first floor had collapsed, and their incinerated bodies had dropped down into the chandler's shop below. She had never forgotten the smell and this smell was almost the same.

She tiptoed along the hallway and eased open the kitchen door. The hinges groaned, and again she paused and listened to make sure that nobody had heard her.

Inside the kitchen, it was still warm from the day's cooking, although the wood fire in the hearth had died down now into a mound of white ash, with only a few spots still glowing red. Unlike the cast-iron metal Franklin stove in Beatrice's kitchen in New Hampshire, this was an open brick fireplace, with big-bellied pots hanging down on hooks for boiling, and a gridiron in front of the fire for roasting joints of meat and poultry on a spit.

She made her way around the kitchen table until she reached the hearth. It was so dark at this end of the kitchen that she could hardly see, but she found three candles on the shelf beside the cookery books, and she lit one by bending down and holding its wick against the red-hot ashes.

The cooking pots were still hot so she put on a thick padded mitt so that she could lift up their lids and peer inside. They were all empty. There was nothing on the gridiron, either, except for a few blackened shreds of meat, and these wouldn't have been enough to account for the smell which had pervaded the whole house.

Beatrice was about to take off the mitt when the ashes in the grate gave a sudden lurch. She picked up the poker from the fire iron stand, and gave the ashes a tentative prod. She felt something underneath them, something curved and hard. She prodded again, and then again, and as the ashes dropped away she could see what it was. A pig's skull, most of its snout and its cheeks burned away and its bone scorched dark brown. Its ash-filled teeth grinned at her as if it had been hiding here in the hearth with the deliberate intention of scaring her.

She hung up the poker, took off the mitt, and stood for a while staring at it. So Martha had been lying. Either she or one of the other girls had arranged the goat's head on the dish, for no other purpose than to frighten her. They had obviously supposed that they could cremate the pig's head in the hearth overnight, and then crush the skull into unrecognizable fragments, so that she would never know that they had been trying to deceive her.

In one way, she felt a sense of relief, because she was sure now that it wasn't Satan who was warning her off. In another way, she felt even more disturbed, because she no longer knew who to trust. Had Ida been party to what Martha had done, or had she been taken in too? And what about George? How could he be so benevolent and caring, and at the same time seem to be so threatening? *Had* he threatened her, she asked herself, or had she simply been reading too much into his insistence that the seven girls had summoned up the Devil? Even the Reverend Parsons agreed with him, and the Reverend Parsons was one of the kindliest and most tolerant clerics she had ever met, even if he was the greediest. He believed that every young woman who went astray should be given a second chance to avoid hanging or transportation and ultimately hell. Without his inspiration and George's money, St Mary Magdalene's would never have been founded.

Beatrice blew out the candle, replaced it on the shelf and left the kitchen, closing the door behind her. She climbed the stairs in the same way that she had come down, keeping close to the side-panelling.

Florence stirred when she climbed back into bed, and murmured, '*Ashes, ashes…*'

Beatrice lay beside her without sleeping, watching the Lonely Star of Autumn rise to its apogee and then disappear behind the dome of St Paul's.

26

Before breakfast the next morning Beatrice dressed herself and Florence in their capes and their bonnets and walked over to the Foundery. No-noh came trotting beside them, with a collar and a lead that Judith had made for him out of an old brown leather knee boot that she had found lying in the street. She had no idea what had become of its fellow knee boot, or the owner of either.

Beatrice took Florence into James's classroom, where he was teaching the children an alphabet song. 'E is for Egg and F is for Frog – G is for Goat, you know, and H is for Hog!'

He stopped singing and smiled at her and called out, 'Just a moment, class! We have a very beautiful visitor this morning!'

Two or three of the older children came out with a mocking 'Woooo!' and made loud kissing noises when he said that, but he took no notice and came over to Beatrice and bowed.

'Beatrice. You've brightened my day a hundred times over.'

'Thank you, James. You flatter me. I have to prepare some tonics in the apothecary and I was wondering if Florrie could sit with you while I do that. It shouldn't take me long.'

'Florence is more than welcome,' said James. 'And so is No-noh. Eustace, would you fetch a bowl of water, please, for this little fellow?

One of the boys got up and went off to the kitchen. James turned to Beatrice and said, 'You seem a little subdued, Beatrice, if you don't mind my saying so. There's nothing troubling you, is there?'

'I think you and I should talk,' said Beatrice.

'About?'

'I can't discuss it now. But I am troubled, yes, and I have nobody else to confide in but you.'

'Very well. My offer of a supper at the Three Cranes still stands. Would you be free to come out this evening?'

'I believe so, unless one of the girls falls sick with the whooping cough or tumbles downstairs.'

'I look forward to it, Beatrice. I will come by at six o'clock if that suits you.'

He brought over a chair for Florence so that she could sit at the front of the class with No-noh sitting beside her, and then he started up the alphabet song again.

'I is for Ink and J is for Jam – K is for Kitchen and L is for Lamb!'

Beatrice gave Florence a little finger-wave and then went through to the apothecary. Godfrey was talking to an elderly woman with wild white hair and a dusty black cape who was trembling and jolting as if she were sitting outside in a freezing gale. She was toothless, and as soon as Beatrice entered the apothecary she could smell her poisonous breath. Her skirts were draggled with horse manure which made the atmosphere even more offensive.

'Ah, Beatrice!' Godfrey greeted her. 'Is there anything I can help you with? Did you manage to find that pleurisy root at Collin's?'

'I wondered if I might use your equipment to test a sample.'

'By all means. I'll be attending to this unfortunate woman for a while yet. As you can see she's suffering from severe tremors, and I've recommended that she be rubbed all over with warm ashes and brandy, and then has a tobacco-smoke clyster. Our nurse will treat her, and with luck and God's help her symptoms should subside.'

'Thank you, Godfrey,' said Beatrice. She hung up her coat and went over to the workbench. She lit the whale-oil lamp that Godfrey used for heating chemicals, and then she went over to the shelves and took down a large glass flask and some U-shaped glass tubing, as well as a ceramic dish.

She felt slightly guilty about waiting until Godfrey's back was turned before she took out her handkerchief and carefully shook the sample of the goat's beard into the ceramic dish. She was sure that Godfrey wasn't party to any conspiracy to frighten her, but she thought it sensible not to let him know what she was testing.

First of all, she lifted the dish to her nose and sniffed the hair. She had an acute sense of smell, and her father had often asked her to smell samples that he was analysing because he couldn't detect any odour himself. The hair didn't smell of turpentine, which she had suspected it might, but when she closed her eyes and sniffed it a second time, and held her breath, she was sure that she could faintly smell almonds.

She dropped the hair into the flask, and added a spoonful of zinc powder and a measure of sulphuric acid, and gently shook them. Then she stoppered the flask and connected it to the U-shaped glass tube. After only a few seconds she could smell a garlicky gas, so she lit the end of the tube and held the cold ceramic dish over the flame. It took less than a minute for the dish to be stained with a patch of silvery-black.

'Everything going well?' asked Godfrey. He had finished preparing the long-stemmed tobacco pipe which the Foundery's nurse would insert into his trembling patient's anus. 'What precisely is it you're testing for?'

'Antimony,' said Beatrice. And please, dear God, forgive me for lying again.

'Ah! You're thinking of making kohl for the girls' eyes, are you?' said Godfrey. It was a good guess: antimony had been used by women to darken their eyes since the days of Cleopatra, and when it was tested in the same way as arsenic it left a similar black stain.

'Nothing so flippant, I'm afraid,' said Beatrice, forcing herself to smile. 'I'm merely thinking of mixing up a purgative.' She had often mixed antimony in her tonics because it brought on sweating, vomiting and diarrhoea. It was a drastic remedy, because antimony was so poisonous, but it was less drastic than bloodletting.

She snuffed out the lamp, and then she dismantled the flask and the tubing, washing them out so that no trace of the goat's hair remained. The ceramic dish she wrapped in her handkerchief and when Godfrey turned his back again she dropped it into her purse. On its own, the silvery-black stain proved nothing, but together with other samples it might make convincing circumstantial evidence.

Most importantly, though, it confirmed her suspicions about the goat's head, and why it hadn't started to decay. The gas given off by the hairs from its beard was arsine, which oxidised when burned into water and arsenic. Arsenic was commonly used by morticians to embalm dead bodies, so that they could display them to grieving relatives who had been obliged to travel for several days to pay their respects. Surgeons used it too, to keep corpses reasonably intact for anatomical dissection.

Satan, with his great supernatural powers, would have had no need for it.

*

They walked back to Maidenhead Court, with Florence skipping along, singing the alphabet song.

'What will you be doing today, Florrie?' Beatrice asked her. 'You can come and join my drawing class this afternoon, if you like.'

'Grace is going to take me and No-noh for a walk and buy some cakes to eat.'

'That's very kind of her. I'll give her some money for the cakes.'

'I love Grace. I wish I was brown too. Then we could be sisters.'

Beatrice said, 'The colour of your skin doesn't matter, Florrie. You can be sisters on the inside, even if you don't look like sisters on the outside.'

'Do you think Papa in heaven likes Grace?'

'I'm sure he loves her just as much as you do,' said Beatrice, although she felt a dull sense of sadness because she still suspected that Francis wasn't Florence's real father. She knew that she shouldn't let it disturb her, because Florence was a gift from God whoever had caused her conception, but she wished there were some scientific test which could prove her paternity beyond doubt.

When they reached St Mary Magdalene's and knocked at the door, it was Judith who opened it for them. Once they had taken off their coats, Florence ran into the kitchen to find Grace. Beatrice went through to the atelier to take out all the tapestry frames and coloured silks the girls would need for the cross-stitch class that she would be holding after breakfast.

She was still opening and closing the drawers in the sewing cabinet when Florence came in, looking upset.

'I can't find Grace.'

'Perhaps she went out shopping,' said Beatrice.

'I asked Molly but Molly said she was gone.'

'She can't be gone for long, Florrie. She'll be back in time for breakfast. Why don't you ask Martha if you can help in the kitchen?'

When she had laid out everything ready for her sewing class, Beatrice went into the drawing room, where Ida was sitting stiffly at her small walnut escritoire, writing a letter. Ida was dressed today in spinach-green silk, and her face looked whiter than ever. If her quill hadn't been twitching as she wrote, a casual observer might have thought that she was dead.

'Ah, Beatrice, my dear. How is everything? Is Eliza making a recovery?'

'I'm going up to see her now,' said Beatrice. 'Florence was looking for Grace. Have you sent her out on an errand?'

Ida stopped writing but didn't turn to look at her.

'Grace has left us,' she said.

'Oh. That's very unexpected. Poor Florence is going to be so disappointed! Grace had promised to take her out for a walk today and buy her some cakes.'

'Well, sometimes life can take unexpected turns, as well you know.'

'So where has she gone?'

'To a far better life, I hope. George Hazzard has taken her to work at his tobacco factory. He's been interested in employing her for quite some time, because he believes that darkie women have a natural gift for cigar-rolling. Barbadoes, after all, is where tobacco first came from, before it was all planted for sugar.'

'Grace was seven years old when she was brought here from Barbadoes. I hardly think that she would have had any experience making cigars at that age.'

Ida pursed her vivid red lips. 'I'm sorry to lose her, I have to admit. She's a sweet girl, very hard-working, and it wasn't her fault that she fell into such bad company. But... he who pays the piper. What George Hazzard wants, George Hazzard must have.'

'Don't tell Florence just yet, please, Ida. I'll tell her myself after breakfast. If she finds out now, I know that she'll be too upset to eat anything, and she needs her strength.'

'Very well,' said Ida. She looked at her hand holding her quill pen as if she had forgotten how to make it write. Beatrice sensed that she was more disturbed about George Hazzard taking Grace away than she had admitted. She could have questioned her further, but she decided that it would be wiser to say nothing, at least for the time being.

'I'm going up to give Eliza some more tonic,' she said. 'I'll see you at breakfast.'

'Yes,' said Ida, and Beatrice had never heard a single 'yes' sound so bleak.

27

Before she went upstairs, Beatrice went into the kitchen to see what Florence was doing. She found her kneeling on a chair with a large apron tied around her and her cheeks smudged with flour, rolling out pastry. Martha the cook was standing by the hearth, stirring porridge, and she gave Beatrice a quick, beady look when she came in, but then immediately turned her back.

You served up that goat's head, Martha, thought Beatrice. *And it was you who cremated the pig's head in the fire to try and hide what you'd done.*

'Did you find out where Grace is?' asked Florence.

'Not yet. I have to give Eliza her medicine first.'

'She probably went to buy some bacon. Martha said she's used up all the bacon because the girls are so greedy. She said they're greedy pigs!'

'Yes… perhaps Grace did go shopping,' said Beatrice, and again she thought, *I'm telling another white lie. What is it about St Mary Magdalene's that has made me so devious?*

She kissed Florence on top of the head and then she climbed the stairs to Eliza's small room at the back of the house. She knocked at the door but there was no reply, so she guessed that Eliza must still be asleep. When she went inside, though, she found that Eliza's bed was empty. The sheets were twisted like a rope, and the room smelled of stale sweat, but there was no sign of Eliza.

Beatrice went back out onto the landing. As she did so, three girls came down the stairs, giggling.

'Good morning, Widow Scarlet!' they chorused.

'Good morning to you, too,' said Beatrice. 'You haven't seen Eliza, have you?'

''Oo's Eliza?' asked Hettie, a short bosomy girl with a mass of blonde hair who had already made friends with Florence by teaching her to dance a very bouncy version of the gigue.

'That girl I brought her here yesterday. She had a bad cough so we put here in this room, in case any of you caught it.'

All three girls shook their curls. 'No,' said Hettie. 'Ain't seen her. But she ain't upstairs, I can tell you that for nothin'.'

The girls carried on downstairs and Beatrice was left on the landing, wondering where in the world Eliza could have gone to. Perhaps she had decided that she wanted to return to her life of prostitution, and sneaked out of St Mary Magdalene's when nobody was looking. Beatrice wouldn't have been surprised if she had. Even if she followed a pious and moral life, she would probably die before she was thirty-five, as most women did, so why not enjoy the years she had left?

Beatrice was about to go downstairs herself when she heard coughing from inside Eliza's bedroom. She went back inside, stood perfectly still, and listened; and then she heard two more spluttering coughs, and a wheezing sound. She picked up her skirts and knelt down beside the bed. Eliza was lying underneath, staring at her wide-eyed like a cornered rabbit.

'Eliza,' she said. 'What in the Lord's name are you doing under your bed?'

'I don't want 'im to take me.'

'Who are you talking about?'

''Im. That George 'Azzard. Is 'e still 'ere or 'as 'e gone?'

'He's gone, Eliza. You can come on out. You shouldn't be lying under your bed with a chest infection like yours. It's too dusty.'

Eliza crawled out from under the bed and stood up, shivering. Beatrice straightened her sheets and her blankets for her, and plumped up her pillows.

'There,' she said. 'Get back into bed. I'll give you some more tonic and I'll ask Martha to warm you up some milk and honey.'

Eliza climbed into bed, still coughing.

Beatrice sat on the bed beside her and said, 'You know George Hazzard?'

Eliza nodded.

'How do you know him? And why were you hiding from him?'

'It was 'im what took me into Leda Sheridan's 'ouse.'

'I'm sorry, Eliza. I've been away from London for quite some time. Who's Leda Sheridan?'

'She runs this knockin' shop in Drury Lane, by the Theatre Royal. Well, it ain't really what you'd call a knockin' shop. It's rank civil. All dukes and nibs and swells and such.'

'And it was George Hazzard who took you there? How did that happen?'

'I was standin' on a corner in 'Oundsditch sellin' the pincushions what my aunt makes, and this yellow carriage stops and out steps George 'Azzard. 'E says I'm a real dimber-mort and would I like to come and 'ave a good time.'

'So you said yes?'

''Course I did. I was cold and I was flippin' soaked because it was rainin' and I was banded, too. 'E took me in his carriage to Drury Lane and into Mrs Sheridan's case. I'd never seen nowhere like it in the 'ole of my life. There was carpets and fires burnin' and girls in beautiful frocks all smellin' like flower baskets.'

Eliza started another coughing fit, but Beatrice waited patiently until she had managed to get her breath back. She decided that she would make a bolus of rose and powdered frankincense for Eliza to swallow, and before she went to sleep tonight she would massage her stomach with sweet almond oil and syrup of violets, mixed with candlewax, saffron and nutmeg. That should allow her to breathe more easily.

'What happened when you went to Mrs Sheridan's?' Beatrice asked her.

Eliza took a deep breath. 'A couple of the girls give me a bath, and orange perfume, and a pretty lace gown to wear. They curled my 'air for me, and tied it up in ribbons, and dabbed rouge on my cheeks. When I see myself in a looking glass, I can't even believe it's me.'

'You must have thought that you were in heaven,' said Beatrice.

'I did. I did. That's exactly what I thought. They takes me down to the kitchen, don't they, these two girls, and they gives me soup and bread and an apple, and after that they lets me sit in front of the fire and 'ave a snooze.'

'Did they tell you why they were being so kind to you?'

Eliza shook her head. 'I thought they was doin' it out of charity. You know, like sometimes people tip you a mopus in the street for no reason except they feel sorry for you.'

'But of course they wanted something in return?'

Eliza looked directly into Beatrice's eyes, and Beatrice could see that as young as she was, there was no innocence there.

'I falls asleep in front of the fire, don't I? But when I wakes up, I says I have to go back home to my aunt's. But Mrs Sheridan she says oh no, love, you're stayin' right 'ere tonight, there's a gentleman 'oo's got 'imself a taste for young girls like you.'

'How old were you then?' Beatrice asked her.

'Twelve. Six days past my birthday.'

Beatrice took hold of her hand. 'You don't have to tell me any more. I can imagine how terrible it must have been for you.'

'It 'urt, all right,' said Eliza. ''E did it to me front and back, three times that night. But I'd seen my aunt at it with 'er fancy-man so it weren't no great mystery, like. And 'e was ever so good to me. 'E told me 'ow pretty I was – like a little angel, 'e said – and 'e give me a jogue and a glass of 'is wine.'

'So what happened after that? Did you go back home, or did you stay there?'

'I stays there. Mrs Sheridan says I'm a money-spinner. She takes good care of me, and she buys me all nice clothes. Every night there's another gentleman I 'as to be good to, or some nights there's two or even three, and I 'as to let them do whatever they pleases, but I soon gets used to it. There's only one thing that Mrs Sheridan makes me do, on pain of a whippin', like, and that's to tell every gentleman that my pipkin 'asn't been cracked yet, and I was never with any other man before them.'

'How long did you stay there, at Mrs Sheridan's?'

'I don't know, ma'am. George 'Azzard takes me there in September, and I'm still there at Christmas, and the New Year, and at least until spring. But I loses count of the days, don't I? One day's just like the next, and one night's just like the next, and one gentleman's just like the next. After about an 'undred of 'em you start losin' count, and you don't give moonshine what they does to you. Some of them even likes pissin' in your gob but 'oo cares.'

'Did you see George Hazzard at Mrs Sheridan's very often?'

'Oh, yes, what? 'E was there loads. Always comin' in and out, bringin' new girls in with 'im.'

'Did he ever spend the night there?'

'No, never. Not that I ever sees 'im there, any'ow.'

'Did your aunt know where you were?'

''Course. Mrs Sheridan sends a boy to tell 'er, and my aunt sends the word back that it's all plummy by 'er.'

'When did you leave?'

'Like I say, I never knows the day or the month, do I, but it's spring, because the trees is all blossom. Up to then, all you can 'ear in the case for most of the night is laughin', and the girls goin' ooh-ooh-ooh! because they're pretendin' they're enjoyin' it, do you know what I mean? But then one night I can 'ear three or four girls screamin' like the Devil's walked in through the door, but then the screamin' suddenly stops. I asks Mrs Sheridan in the mornin' what it was but she won't tell me. She just says mind your own work.'

'Didn't any of the other girls tell you what the screaming was all about?'

'No. And my best friend there, Juliet, she cautions me not to be askin' 'er a second time, and to stick my fingers in my lug'oles if ever I 'ears it again. Two nights later, though, I 'ears it again, screamin' and screamin', and the gentleman in bed with me, 'e 'ears it, too, but 'e don't say nothin'. In fact it makes 'im 'ard again, 'ard like a constable's truncheon, and 'e starts bangin' away at me like 'e's ridin' all the way to Stepney and back.'

'And you still couldn't find out who was screaming, or why?'

Eliza shook her head again, and coughed. 'All I knows is, Juliet ain't around the next morning, and when I asks where she is, nobody tells me. One girl puts her finger to 'er lips, like ssh! it's a secret. That's when I makes up my mind to run away. I don't care what the screamin' is, but it makes me feel like Satan's in the case, and I just wants to get the 'ell out of there.'

'How did you get away?'

'The front jigger was always locked so I climbed out the back-jump and never stopped runnin' till I got back to Black 'Orse Yard.'

'And ever since then you've been selling your favours on the streets?'

'I couldn't do nothin' else, could I? My pipkin was well and truly cracked and I didn't make 'ardly no wedge at all sellin' them pincushions. Some days them two clinkers comes with me and they always gives me a fair share of the winnings, like, after they've braced them up.'

Beatrice smiled and said, 'Let me get you some more tonic. If that stops you coughing, perhaps you can come down and join the rest of the girls for breakfast.'

'Does George 'Azzard come here often?' asked Eliza, anxiously.

'About once a week, I'd say. I haven't been here long enough to tell you for certain. He's the home's main benefactor, although there are several others.'

'Whenever 'e comes, you won't be lettin' on that I'm 'ere, will you? I don't want to go back to Leda Sheridan's, not never.'

'Of course I won't tell him you're here, Eliza. I doubt if he would even remember you, anyway.'

'P'raps 'e would and p'raps 'e wouldn't, but I don't want to chance it. I don't wit what goes on at Leda Sheridan's and I don't want to wit, neither.'

'Don't you fret, Eliza. That world is behind you now, and you don't ever have to go back. We'll send somebody today to tell your aunt where you are, and that you're safe. If she was happy for you to stay at Leda Sheridan's, I'm sure she won't worry about your living here.'

28

As soon as the clock in the hallway had chimed six, Beatrice heard James knocking at the front door. Judith let him in, and he came through to the drawing room, smiling. He was wearing the same dark-brown coat that he had worn when he had taken Beatrice and Florence to Ranelagh Gardens, and the same beige waistcoat and breeches. There was a small razor cut on his left cheek and he smelled strongly of some musky perfume.

Beatrice was sitting by the fire with Ida, sewing. She had dressed herself in a pale-blue silk gown which had been made for her in Sutton for a visit by the Governor of New Hampshire, Benning Wentworth, and her hair was tied up with pale-blue silk ribbons. Her own perfume was rosewater, and she had hung a silver scent pendant around her neck because they would be walking along streets that stank of sewage.

'A very good evening, Beatrice,' said James, with a bow. 'There isn't a picture in the Foundling Hospital to match you.'

Beatrice looked at Ida and Ida smiled and shook her head.

'You are an incorrigible flatterer, James,' said Beatrice. 'Let me get my coat and my bonnet.'

It was a chilly night, but clear, and as they left St Mary Magdalene's Beatrice could see the moon over St Paul's. Although it wasn't far to the Three Cranes in the Vintry, down through Cheapside to New Queen Street, by the river, James had a hackney coach waiting outside.

As they rattled and swayed through the darkened streets, he reached across and laid his hand on top of hers, and she didn't push him away. She needed somebody like James, not only because of his learning and his masculinity, but because she had nobody else to confide in.

When she stepped down from the hackney, Beatrice could hear raucous laughter and shouting from the tavern. After he had paid the jarvis, though, James took hold of her arm, and said, 'It sounds rough, I know, but we'll be dining in a private room where ladies are welcome, and won't be choked by pipe smoke or deafened by profanity.'

He pushed open the front door and they went inside. The main room was crowded and smoky, with more than seventy or eighty men drinking and chaffing and laughing uproariously. A barmaid came forward, though, and led them through to a small oak-panelled room at the side of the tavern where there were five tables, and a fire burning. There were only two other couples in the room – a very fresh-faced young man and his wife – and the other quite elderly, a bespectacled man of at least fifty years old, with a tilted wig and a worn-out frock coat, and a bosomy companion with a gravelly voice, who turned out to be his sister.

James asked for two glasses of Portuguese wine, and both he and Beatrice chose the roasted widgeon, with parsnips and cardoons and cabbage and roasted potatoes. Once the barmaid had taken their order, James lifted his glass to Beatrice and said, 'Here we are then, Beatrice. Alone at last.'

'This wine is lovely,' said Beatrice. 'The last glass of wine I drank was the communion wine that we used to give our parishioners in New Hampshire. It tasted so sour that it almost made me wish that transubstantiation was true, and that it really *did* become the blood of Christ.'

'Well, we're in Vintry Ward, home of the vintners, after all,' said James.

Beatrice was silent for a few moments, looking at him. The firelight was dancing in his eyes and she wondered if that was romantic, or a warning. His wavy brown hair made him look like a poet, or an artist, or a cultured pirate.

'I'm confused,' she said at last.

James said nothing, but waited for her to continue.

'I'm more convinced than ever that those seven girls didn't really summon up Satan, and that they didn't become witches and fly away. In fact I'm sure of it now.'

'All right,' said James. 'But what has convinced you? I thought you'd agreed that Satan is just as real as God.'

'I believe he is. But I don't believe that he had anything to do with those girls disappearing.'

'You realize what a risk you're taking. Next time it won't be a man with a looking-glass face, or some beast scratching at your door. It'll be someone or something far more dangerous. I'm desperately worried, Beatrice, that you're going to come to serious harm.'

'Well, there's already been another threat,' said Beatrice, and she told him about the goat's head being served up at dinner.

'There you are, then,' said James, leaning back in his chair, as if that proved his case conclusively. 'How could the goat's head have magically appeared on that platter unless Satan put it there?'

'Very simply. Martha the cook put it there, and dropped the pig's head into the kitchen fire. I went down during the night and found it in the hearth, burned right down to the bone.'

'You didn't actually witness Martha dropping it into the fire, though, did you? Satan could still have done it.'

'Oh, come on, James! Satan would have made it vanish altogether. He would have flung it into the middle of the Atlantic Ocean, or made it fly to the moon, where I never could have found it. He wouldn't have needed to cremate it in the kitchen. But not only that, I took a sample from the goat's beard and tested it in Godfrey's laboratory.'

'And what was the result of that?'

'The goat's head was almost certainly preserved with arsenic, to stop it from decomposing. Again, Satan wouldn't have needed to do that.'

'But again, Beatrice, he could have altered your sample so that it *appeared* to show you the evidence of arsenic, even when it actually didn't.'

'Why would he do that?'

'I don't know. To discredit you, I imagine. To confuse you. You said, didn't you, that you're confused.'

The barmaid brought their plates of roasted widgeon, and all their vegetables in separate china dishes. The widgeon was glossy and brown as if it had been varnished, and smelled of honey, sherry and mustard. Beatrice wished only that she had more of an appetite.

She was in two minds whether to tell James about Eliza or not, and what Eliza had said about George Hazzard picking her up off the street and taking her to Leda Sheridan's brothel, but she decided not to. She had promised Eliza that she would keep her past a secret, and that she would make sure that George didn't find out where she was. Apart from that, she wasn't sure how well James knew George, and if he might accidentally or deliberately let it slip that Eliza was now being cared for at St Mary Magdalene's.

'You're a jingle-brains, that's what you are!' the bosomy sister at the next table suddenly exploded. She leaned forward so that her breasts were pressing into her plate of half-eaten carp and cabbage and she was spitting bits of fish into her elderly brother's face. 'You haven't an ounce of sense in you, have you? You're a maggot-pated, bird-witted, hare-brained cod's head! You're a *clunch*!'

'Sorry about that,' smiled James. 'It's usually quiet in this room, and very civil.'

Following that outburst, Beatrice and James spoke no more about Satan, or the coven. They talked instead about Beatrice's life in America, and art, and the latest plays that would be showing at Henry Gifford's theatre or the Theatre Royal.

James told her that the last time he had been to a play at the Little Theatre, four ladies had entered a box with such fantastical hats on their heads that the entire audience had burst out laughing at them, and they had hurriedly left.

Beatrice managed to eat most of her widgeon's breast, and some cardoons, and drink another glass of wine. They finished their supper by sharing an orange cream.

After they had left the tavern, they walked hand-in-hand down New Queen Street to the Three Cranes stairs. The tide was coming in fast, and the river was black and gurgling with only the moon and a few reflected lights on its surface. It was here that the three wooden cranes stood. They had been built for lifting casks of wine from lighters moored beside the stairs, but to Beatrice they looked like strange abandoned catapults from some mediaeval war.

They stood by the water's edge for a while in silence. Eventually James said, 'You know that I want only to protect you.'

'From what? From Satan?'

'If it *is* Satan who's been warning you off, then yes.'

'But what if it isn't?'

'Then whoever it is, I want only to protect you from them. I'm asking you, Beatrice – no, more than that, I'm *begging* you – please forget about those seven girls altogether. They're gone, and nothing that you do or say is going to bring them back from wherever they are.'

'Do you know something that you're not telling me?' asked Beatrice. She looked up at him and she could see his eyes glittering in the darkness.

'I know that I was thunderstruck when I first set eyes on you, because of how much you resembled my poor lost Sophie. But now I see you only for you – *yourself* – and I freely confess that I'm falling in love with you, Beatrice. Your beauty, your grace, your spirit, your determination. I fully understand that you're still mourning your late husband as much as I still mourn my Sophie. But my affection for you has grown every single minute of every single day, and if I can help you to put back the broken pieces of your heart, then you will certainly help me to mend mine.'

Beatrice laid her hand on James's left shoulder, and lifted herself up a little so that she could kiss him on the cheek.

'We'll see,' she said, very softly.

They began to walk back up New Queen Street so that they could hail a hackney on the corner of Thames Street. After only a few steps, though, Beatrice tripped over something that made a clanking noise, and if James hadn't been holding her hand she might well have fallen over.

He bent down and picked it up, and held it up in the light from the tavern windows. It was an iron bar, a little over a foot long, with three curved prongs on the end of it.

'A grappling hook,' he said, and tossed it over to the side of the street so that it jangled as it bounced off the cobbles. 'The dockers use them for shifting the wine barrels, but they're always leaving them lying about. It didn't hurt you, did it?'

'No,' said Beatrice. 'But I'd best be getting back now. I've an early start tomorrow.'

James took hold of both of her hands. 'You *will* think about what I've said, won't you? About keeping yourself safe... and also about me, and the way I feel about you.'

Beatrice said, 'Of course. And thank you for this evening. You've managed to make me feel like a woman again, instead of a widow, and a mother, and an apothecary, and a shoulder for distraught young girls to weep on.'

29

The following day Beatrice had several hours of free time, for which she was grateful, because she wasn't used to drinking so much alcohol and last night's Portuguese wine had given her a nagging headache. Hephzibah Carmen was coming in the morning to give one of her twice-weekly singing lessons, and in the afternoon, the girls were being taken on a special visit to Bethlem Hospital to see the lunatics.

The Reverend Parsons believed that if the girls saw first-hand the madness that was brought on by venereal diseases, they would be encouraged to choose the straight and narrow path towards the Wicket Gate.

Beatrice had little appetite at breakfast and ate only a small bowl of porridge. She couldn't stop herself from staring across the kitchen at Martha, unsmiling, with the deliberate intention of making Martha uneasy. She wanted Martha to think that she didn't believe her story about the pig's head, and that she wasn't going to let the matter rest. She knew it was vindictive to stare at her like that, but she was beginning to feel vindictive after the clawing at her door, and the appearance of the man with the looking-glass face, and the goat's head – especially since her head was hurting.

Whenever Martha turned away from the hearth and saw her staring at her, she quickly turned away again and busied herself with stirring the large pot of chicken broth that was suspended over the fire, or briskly chopping onions and carrots.

Florence said, '*Finished!*' and dropped her spoon into her empty bowl. She had eaten twice as much as Beatrice, although she had been helped by her doll, Minnie, who had ended up with her mouth and chin and the front of her grey dress plastered in porridge.

'I wish Grace was still here,' said Florence, sadly, as she watched Beatrice wiping the lumps of porridge from Minnie's face.

'Well, I don't have any classes this afternoon, and it's a nice bright day. Why don't we go to Hackney and see her?'

'Can No-noh come?'

'Of course he can. We can take him for a walk by the marshes.'

They cleared away their bowls and then they climbed back upstairs, with Florence singing the alphabet song again. Beatrice was about to open the door to their rooms when she suddenly stopped, and touched the scars and furrows in the woodwork with her fingertips.

'Aren't we going in?' asked Florence.

'Yes, Florrie, we are...' said Beatrice, but for a few seconds more she continued to stroke the damaged door as if she were a blind woman feeling the face of a stranger for the very first time. If she had learned only one thing as the wife of a parson, it was that God is continually giving us hints and clues and messages, prompting us to discover who we are and where our lives are taking us, although we rarely notice them, and even when we do, we rarely act on them.

She opened the door and she and Florence went into their sitting room. 'Do you need to use the potty?' she asked Florence. 'If not, we're going out directly for a walk by the river. And, yes, No-noh can come.'

They put on their overcoats, but before they went out, Beatrice went out into the yard at the back of the house, and looked inside the small wooden shed where the man who came to tidy the flowerbeds kept his tools. She had seen him at work, stuffing all of his weeds and bush-cuttings into an old flour sack. The sack was hanging over his spade handle, and she picked it up, folded it, and tucked it under her arm beneath her overcoat.

Florence was waiting for her at the back door with No-noh. 'What's *that* for?' she asked.

Beatrice smiled and said, 'You never know what you're going to find when you go for a walk, do you? It might be another dog like No-noh, or a cat, or a big pile of golden guineas. It's always wise to take a sack with you, so that you can carry it home.'

They left Maidenhead Court and walked down through Wood Street and along Cheapside until they reached New Queen Street. A beggar with one leg hopped after them almost all the way, calling out, 'Give us thrums, lady! Give us thrums!'

Beatrice felt sorry for him, but if she gave threepence to every beggar along the way, she would have no money left by the time she reached the river.

They walked down the cobbled street, past the Three Cranes tavern where James had taken her last night, until they reached the Three Cranes stairs. This morning the river was crowded with ships and lighters, their flags all fluttering in the stiff south-east breeze. The stairs were busy, too, with one of the cranes lifting barrels out of a barge and loading them onto two large wagons. The crane was creaking and the dockers were swearing because one of the barrels had come loose and was swaying dangerously overhead, and Beatrice had to hope that Florence wasn't really listening to what they were shouting to each other.

A few yards further down from the tavern, beside a peeling black-painted door, she saw the three-pronged grappling hook which she had tripped over, and which James had tossed across the street. She walked across to it and picked it up, dropping it into the flour sack. It was much heavier than she had thought it would be, and its prongs protruded from the neck of the sack, but nobody seemed to take any notice of what she had done except for Florence, who frowned at her and demanded, 'What's *that*? What do you want that for?'

'It's a hook,' said Beatrice. 'You never know when you might need a hook. What if we both got too hot in our coats, and we had nowhere to hang them up?'

Florence thought about that as they walked back up towards Thames Street. No-noh had seen a scruffy mongrel sitting next to a beggar and she was having to drag him along behind her with his claws scraping on the cobbles.

'But what will you hang the hook on?' she asked, at last. 'You can't hang it on the sky.'

'You're a clever girl, Florrie,' said Beatrice. 'I think you take after your mother.'

When they got back to Maidenhead Court, Beatrice hid the sack behind one of the spindle bushes that grew on either side of the front steps. She didn't want anybody to see her carrying it inside.

'Why have you put it there?' asked Florence, but Beatrice touched her finger to her lips and said, 'Ssh! It's a secret. You mustn't tell anybody, or they'll all want it.'

Judith let them in, and while Florence took No-noh through to the back yard, Beatrice waited in the drawing room until Judith had gone back to join Hephzibah Carmen's singing class. They were all singing 'Jesus, Lover of My Soul', much higher than Beatrice had ever heard it sung before, so that some of them were shrill and off-key, and others could barely catch their breath.

'Jesus, lover of my soul,
Let me to Thy bosom fly,
While the nearer waters roll,
While the tempest still is high!'

Looking quickly down the corridor to make sure that nobody else was around, Beatrice opened the front door and went back down the front steps to retrieve the grappling hook from behind the bush. Then she carried it upstairs to her room.

She lifted it out of the sack and held it up against her deeply furrowed door. She had been concerned that she might be making a ridiculous mistake, but she felt strongly that God was taking care of her now, in the absence of anybody else. Even if it wasn't Satan who had been warning her off, it was some person or persons with malicious intent, and she needed guidance and protection more than she had ever done in the whole of her life – even when she had been threatened by a witch in New Hampshire.

And she hadn't made a mistake. The prongs of the grappling hook matched the furrows in her door almost exactly. It was clear that the marks were in threes, and apart from their size, she didn't know of a single bird or beast on God's earth that had only three claws. Although the bald eagles she had seen in New Hampshire had three long talons, they had a fourth opposing talon, too. She was in no doubt at all that her door had been attacked by a man or a very strong woman wielding a grappling hook like this one, or some similar implement.

Hephzibah Carmen's singing lesson must have finished, because Beatrice heard voices in the hallway, and footsteps coming up the stairs. She went into her sitting room and closed the door behind her. She couldn't let Ida or any of the girls see her carrying the grappling hook, so she went through to her bedroom and hid it under the bed, behind the chamber pot.

She had only just dropped the bedcover back down when she heard a knock at her door. It was Ida, already wearing her coat and bonnet, ready to go out.

'Are you quite sure you don't want to come with us to the Bethlem?' said Ida. 'I'm told that some of their new patients are highly amusing. One man believes that he's a cannon, and makes tremendous booming noises; and another is convinced that he's a dog, and walks around everywhere on all fours.'

'I don't think so,' said Beatrice. 'I promised Florence that I would take her for a walk in the country.'

'How was your evening with James?' Ida asked her.

'Very pleasant, thank you. And the supper was excellent.'

'He's a steadfast young man, James. What he lacks in wealth he makes up for in looks, and personality. You could do worse.'

'Are you matchmaking, Ida?'

'This church is a family, Beatrice. We are all related in spirit, and we all owe each other our affection and our trust. Most of all, our trust. We never challenge each other's beliefs.'

'You've all made me very welcome,' said Beatrice, but she was sure that Ida was hinting yet again that she shouldn't question the disappearance of the seven girls any further.

Ida ran her grey suede-gloved fingers down the splintered furrows in the sitting-room door panels.

'I've arranged for a carpenter to come next week and replace this for you. It must be extremely disturbing for you to be constantly reminded that Satan is displeased with you. One really *dreads* to think in what way he might threaten you next.'

'He's quite a conjuror, I'll grant him that,' said Beatrice. 'If he could perform that goat's head trick in a theatre, I'm sure he'd make a fortune.'

Beatrice gave her one of her a puckered rosebud smiles, and said, 'Enjoy your walk. I'll make your excuses to the lunatics, shall I? – and give them your best regards.'

Beatrice hailed a carriage on the corner of Aldersgate Street. When they had climbed aboard, with Beatrice holding No-noh on her lap, they rattled and bumped through Shoreditch and out between the fields and farms to Hackney. Florence was so excited to be seeing Grace that she couldn't stop singing one of the songs that Grace had taught her, 'Sally Go Round de Sun'. She had brought some honey gingerbread for her, too, wrapped up in brown paper, because that was one of Grace's favourite cakes.

'Sally go round de sun, Sally go round de moon, Sally go round de chimbly pots on a Sunday afternoon!'

When they arrived at the tobacco factory, Beatrice lifted Florence down from her seat and paid the jarvis only his one-and-sixpenny fare, even though he had asked for an extra twopence 'to drink madam's health'. Inside the factory yard, they found the man with the leathery face and the leathery apron. He was standing on the back of a wagon stacking boxes of cigars, and he greeted Beatrice and Florence by cheerfully lifting his floppy leather hat.

'Come to see Mr 'Azzard, 'as you?' he asked, jumping down from the back of the wagon.

'Well, no, actually. We've come to see Grace.'

'Grace? You got me there.'

'The new girl he's brought from St Mary Magdalene's. You must have noticed her. She's very pretty and she has dark skin.'

The leathery-faced man shook his head. 'Wooh, no. Ain't seen no girls of that description, ma'am. Why don't you come inside and ask Mr 'Azzard 'isself?'

He led them through to George Hazzard's study. George was sitting behind his desk smoking a cigar and talking to a scarlet-faced man with an over-powdered wig and a sizeable belly which strained at his black soup-stained waistcoat. The cigar smoke was thicker than an autumn fog and it made Florence sneeze.

'Beatrice, how good to see you!' said George. 'I must introduce you to John Bellflower, my lawyer. John – this is the Widow Scarlet I was telling you about. One of the very few women in this world who combines beauty with intelligence!'

'It's a considerable honour to meet you, madam,' said John Bellflower. 'You will forgive me if I don't rise... I've been suffering a devilish attack of the gout these past few days.'

'I'm sorry to hear that,' said Beatrice. 'What have you been taking for it?'

'My physician recommended that I roast a fat old goose, stuffed with chopped kittens, lard, incense, wax and flour of rye; and that I consume the goose and then rub the cooking fat on my feet.'

Florence said, 'Urrrghh, that's horrible!' and pulled a face.

'So did you do it?' asked Beatrice.

'No. My cook is absurdly sensitive, and she refused to chop the kittens. I would have dismissed her, but she makes an incomparable oyster stew.'

'I don't think in any case that treatment would have given you much relief,' said Beatrice. 'My late father made a preparation of autumn crocus, which was most effective in cases of gout. I will mix you some, if you wish, and have it sent to you, if you let me know your address.'

'Most generous of you, Widow Scarlet,' said John Bellflower. 'No wonder George admires your intelligence, as well as your aspect.'

George puffed at his cigar, and then he said, 'May I ask what brings you here today, Beatrice? I'm delighted to see you and young Florence, but I wasn't expecting you.'

'We've come to see Grace,' said Beatrice. 'She and Florence formed a most affectionate friendship, and Florence was distraught when you took her from St Mary Magdalene's to come and work here. She's brought her some gingerbread.'

'Oh, Grace!' said George. 'I'm mortified to disappoint you, young Florence, but I'm afraid that Grace is not with us now. I happened to be talking to the Earl of Coventry at Joshua Reynolds' studio in St Martin's Lane last week. Mr Reynolds has a black footman himself who has appeared in several of his paintings, and I mentioned that Ida had in her care a most attractive dark-skinned girl. I'd been intending for some time to take Grace on here in Hackney, but the earl asked me if I might lend her to him, so to speak, to impress a number of important guests that he's expecting. I think he wants to make his household appear more exotic.'

'So where is she now?' asked Beatrice. She was upset that George seemed to regard Grace as property that could be lent and borrowed. She was not a slave, after all. Several of the farmers that she had known in New Hampshire had owned slaves, but mostly they had treated them with reasonable humanity, feeding them well and caring for them if they fell sick.

'I dispatched her to the earl's house on Grosvenor Square,' said George. 'I've no idea how long he'll want to keep her. Perhaps for only a few weeks, perhaps for years. She's a most alluring young woman, I have to say, despite her colour.'

'Isn't Grace here?' asked Florence, pushing out her bottom lip in disappointment.

'No, sweetheart, I'm afraid not,' Beatrice told her. 'But she's been taken to a very grand house and I'm sure she's being well looked after. Come on – let's take No-noh for a walk by the marshes and get some fresh air.'

'But I brought Grace some gingerbread.'

'I know, Florrie. We'll just have to eat it ourselves.'

George stood up and bowed his head. 'It's always a great pleasure to see you, Beatrice. I'll be coming back down to St Mary Magdalene's in a few weeks' time, and I look forward to seeing you again. Perhaps we'll be able to enjoy a dinner without any satanic surprises.'

Beatrice said, 'Goodbye, then, George. Goodbye, Mr Bellflower,' but nothing more. She ushered Florence out of George's study, through the noisy factory with its steam pipes hissing and its cutting machines clanking, and out across the yard.

Behind the poplar trees that surrounded the factory lay a wide pond, with ducks on it, and she took Florence down to the water's edge and stood there for a while, so that the breeze would blow the smell of cigar smoke from her coat.

'I'm sad,' said Florence. 'I wanted to see Grace and sing a song with her.'

'I expect Grace misses you, too, Florrie. But never mind. I expect she's happy where she is.'

That evening, as she sat sewing by the fire in the drawing room, Ida came in, her chalk-white face making her look like a ghost. She sat down opposite Beatrice with a rustle of her silky gown and said, 'I almost wish that I hadn't visited the madhouse today.'

'Why is that, Ida?'

'I'm sure that it will give me the most terrible nightmares. There was a man who kept hitting his head against the wall so hard that you could hear his skull crack, and woman who had to have a leather mask buckled to her face because she wouldn't stop screaming and trying to tear her own eyes out.'

'In that case I'm glad that Florence and I went for a walk instead.'

'Where did you go?'

'As a matter of fact, we went to Hackney, not only for a walk but to see Grace at George's factory. Florence misses Grace so much.'

'Well, I miss Grace, too, I must say. She was so good at caring for my wardrobe, and applying my cosmetics. Judith almost cut my thumb off today when she was trimming my nails. How was Grace, anyway?'

'She wasn't there.'

'Oh. I see. Wasn't she?'

Beatrice thought: *You don't sound very surprised. Did you know that she wouldn't be there?*

She lowered her sewing and said, 'George told me that he'd met the Earl of Coventry last week, at some artist's studio.'

'That would have been Joshua Reynolds, that's right, in St Martin's Lane,' said Ida. 'George wants to have his portrait painted. I went with him, because I've been acquainted for some years with Mr Reynolds, and George was hoping that I would persuade him to lower his fee somewhat. He charges thirty-five guineas these days simply for a head, and one hundred and fifty for a full-length. Can you imagine!'

'Well, I suppose George can afford it.'

'I'm sure he can. But the Earl of Coventry wasn't there. Not in the flesh, anyway. His *portrait* was there, yes, because Mr Reynolds had completed the head some weeks ago and was finishing off the drapery and the background. That was probably what George meant.'

'Yes, he must have done,' said Beatrice, and after a moment she picked up her plain-work again. She didn't say any more about Grace, partly because she suspected that Ida might have some idea what had really happened to her, and partly because it was clear that George had been lying, or at least disingenuous. Grace may well have been taken into service at the Earl of Coventry's house, but George couldn't have arranged it with him at Joshua Reynold's studio.

There's only one way to find out for certain, and that's for me to go to Grosvenor Square and see for myself if she's there. But I must make sure that they don't find out who I am. If George discovers that I've been questioning the truth of his story, the Lord only knows who might come tearing at my door with a grappling hook next time, or what strange men with looking-glass faces might come seeking me out, or what severed heads might be served up to me on the dinner table?

30

She waited until the following afternoon, when Ida and most of the girls had arranged to go over to the Foundery to attend a celebration of the birthday of the Virgin Mary, with hymns and Bible readings.

About an hour before they were due to leave she told Ida that she was suffering from a blinding headache. She said that she would take sulphate of quinine, and if that gave her any relief she would join them all later. As she was saying this to Ida she could see herself reflected in the gilt-framed drawing-room mirror, and she thought, *I should really call it* guilt-*framed… it's a living portrait of me telling yet another lie.*

Florence went with Judith to the Foundery, while Beatrice put No-noh out into the back yard. He yapped plaintively for a while, but then he settled down. Beatrice couldn't help thinking about Noah, and wondering what kind of life he was living with the Ossipee, assuming that he was still alive. Had he forgotten her altogether, or was he grieving for her as sorely as she was grieving for him?

She went through to the atelier and picked up a box of willow charcoal sticks that the girls used for drawing. Then she went into the kitchen. There was nobody there because Martha and the girls who usually helped her had gone to the Foundery too. Martha may have pretended to do the Devil's work by swapping the pig's head for the goat's head, but she was devoutly religious, and if any of the girls ever spoke the Lord's name in vain she would smack them hard on the knuckles with a wooden spoon.

Beatrice opened the larder door and went inside to pick out the ingredients that she needed to prepare her disguise – arrowroot powder, cornflour and honey. She set them out on the kitchen table and started by snapping the charcoal sticks into small pieces and grinding them into dust with the pestle and mortar that Martha usually used for crushing peppers.

In a china bowl, she stirred all of the ingredients together with water until she had a smooth, black, shiny cream. She carried the bowl upstairs to her sitting room, as well as two more tablespoonfuls of arrowroot powder which she had wrapped up in a poke of baking paper.

She locked her door. She didn't think that she would be interrupted, but if any of the three or four girls who had stayed behind in the house came knocking, she wanted to make sure that they didn't come bursting in and see her.

She listened for a moment. On the floor below she could hear Eliza coughing, and in the next room Emma was singing a coarse comical ballad called 'My Thing Is My Own'. Beatrice couldn't help thinking how sad a song that was for a girl who had been a prostitute since she was thirteen and a half years old.

She took off her primrose-yellow gown, hanging it over the back of her chair, and sat down in front of the mirror on her toilet.

Very carefully, she dipped the corner of a handkerchief into the bowl of black cream and smeared it all over her nose and her cheeks. She took great care wiping it around her eyelids and her eyes, because she didn't want any pink showing.

After she had painted her face and her ears and her neck, she painted her chest, too, as far down as her corset. She would wear long black gloves, so there was no need for her to paint her hands, but as a precaution she painted her wrists.

When she had finished, she sat and stared at herself and she could hardly believe that it was her. Although the black make-up was shiny because of the cornflour, she could have been an African. Her father had originally devised the formula for Walter Blake, an actor who had been employed by David Garrick to play Othello at the Theatre Royal, and who had wanted to surprise his audience by looking as much like a real Moor as possible, and not just a white man blacked up.

To finish off her disguise, she lightly dusted her face and cleavage with arrowroot powder, which took off the gloss and gave her skin a more natural appearance. She had a small pot of beeswax coloured with carmine which had been given to her in New Hampshire, and she blended a little of this with the black make-up to darken it, and applied it to her lips.

She dressed herself in her black satin gown and put on the high black bonnet which she had worn to Francis's funeral, tucking her hair out of sight and lowering the lacy veil over her face.

She opened her sitting-room door a few inches to make sure that there was nobody on the landing outside. Emma was still singing, and she thought she could hear Juliet laughing because 'My Thing Is My Own' was so bawdy. Beatrice had heard it sung in the street by beggars but Emma wouldn't have dared to sing it if Ida had been in the house.

'A *Master of Musick came with an intent,*
To give me a lesson on my instrument,
I thank'd him for nothing, but bid him be gone,
For my little fiddle should not be played on.'

Beatrice held up her petticoats so that she could run quickly and quietly downstairs, across the hallway and out of the front door. It was beginning to spit with rain so when she reached the corner of Newgate Street she hailed a hackney.

As she climbed in, the jarvis said, 'Fearful sorry for your loss, ma'am.' He obviously thought that she was veiled and wearing black because she was in mourning, and a word of condolence might earn him a twopenny tip. If he could have seen that her face was black, too, he might have been less solicitous. Beatrice had seen that black men and women were not uncommon in London these days, but with some exceptions most of them were servants or slaves brought over from the West Indies with visiting businessmen, and any black person who strutted about and put on airs would be openly jeered at.

'Do you know the Earl of Coventry's house on Grosvenor Square?' asked Beatrice.

'Of course, ma'am. And a wery grand 'ouse it is, too – *wery* grand. Right gentry-cove-ken.'

The streets were crowded with carriages and wagons and pedestrians spilling out across the roadway, and it took them nearly twenty minutes to reach Grosvenor Square. Because it was raining, the circular ornamental gardens in the centre of the square were almost deserted this afternoon, except for a sodden man in a coalman's hat with a back flap who was scraping out a mournful melody on a violin.

The Earl of Coventry's house had steep steps and a pillared portico. Beatrice wondered if she ought to go down to the basement and knock at the servants' entrance, but she decided that she would like to hear about Grace from the earl himself, or at least from a member of his family, so that she could be certain that she was being well cared for.

She rang the bell-pull at the double front doors and she could hear the bell echoing inside the hallway. After a few moments the door opened and a young footman in a blue-powdered wig and a braided navy-blue uniform appeared.

'Good afternoon, madam,' he greeted her. 'Is madam expected?'

'No, I have no appointment,' said Beatrice, trying to imitate Grace's accent. 'But I am making inquiries about a young woman who has recently been employed here. Her name is Grace, and I am told that she was sent here by Mr George Hazzard.'

'May I trouble you for your name, madam?'

Beatrice lifted her veil to show her black face, and the footman blinked at her furiously, although he tried hard not to show how surprised he was.

'I am Grace's older sister, from Barbadoes. I wanted to inform her that I have arrived in London, and I wanted also to make sure that she is in good health and good spirits.'

'Grace?' said the footman. 'We have nobody here by that name. You must have been given this address in error. Good day to you.'

He began to close the door, but Beatrice said, 'Wait! Perhaps your master is calling her by a different name. She has dark skin, like me, and she is eighteen years old, and very comely.'

The footman shook his head. 'The earl has only one blackamoor in his employ, and that is his positilion Limbrick.'

'You're sure? Is it possible that you haven't yet seen her, or that your master has installed her in a different house?'

'I'm quite certain. All of the earl's household were assembled only this morning to be given instructions on this evening's banquet, and there was no black person amongst them.'

Beatrice saw a movement in the window next to the porch, and behind the glass she saw a pale-faced woman in a tall grey wig and a red dress staring out at her, with one hand shading her eyes. As soon as she saw that Beatrice was looking at her, she stepped away from the window and disappeared.

Beatrice turned back to the footman. 'Is there somebody at home I can ask about this further?'

'Not to you,' said the footman. Beatrice had noticed that as soon as she had lifted her veil he had stopped addressing her as 'madam' and his tone had become increasingly dismissive.

'No, please, listen – I *have* to know where she's gone,' she said, forgetting to talk with a Barbadoes accent. The footman gave her an almost imperceptible shrug and closed the door.

She rang the doorbell again, and then again, but nobody came to answer it. After a few minutes she went down the steps to the basement, and knocked at the door there, but again nobody came to see what she wanted.

She could have gone around to Adam's Mews at the rear of the house to see if she could find the black postilion, but it was raining much harder now and she guessed that the footman had probably been telling her the truth, and that Grace really hadn't been taken in by the Earl of Coventry. After all, what would be the purpose of him lying?

She lowered her veil again and walked to the corner of Charles Street, where she managed to hail a hackney just after a big-bellied man in a huge periwig had climbed unsteadily down from it, loudly breaking wind as he did so.

'Awful thundery weather, what?' he remarked, before staggering away.

When Beatrice returned to St Mary Magdalene's, Juliet opened the door for her, holding up a half-eaten apple in her hand like Holbein's painting of Eve.

'Yes?' said Juliet, frowning. 'There ain't nobody at 'ome at the moment – sorry. They've all gone churchifyin'. 'Oo did you want?'

'For goodness' sake, Juliet, it's me,' said Beatrice, without lifting her veil.

'Be-*ah*-trice?' said Juliet, but by then Beatrice was already climbing the stairs back up to her rooms.

It took her nearly half an hour to wipe and wash off all of her make-up, and by the time she had finished, the water in her basin was black, and so was her towel. She changed back into her primrose-yellow gown and as she laced herself up she wondered whether her disguise had been worth all the effort. At least she had managed to confirm that George Hazzard had lied about sending Grace to Grosvenor Square, while the Earl of Coventry's footman would only be able to tell him that 'some black woman' had come asking for her. But if Grace wasn't there, where was she?

She went down to the next floor to see Eliza. She tapped on her door but there was no response, so she opened it and went in. Eliza was asleep, looking peaceful and breathing easily. Beatrice had seen several of the other girls in the reformatory when they were sleeping, and she had always thought how young and innocent they looked, like orphaned children rather than hardened gigglers, as they sometimes called themselves.

She drew the plain wooden chair across to the bed and sat beside Eliza, watching her sleep. After about ten minutes, Eliza must have sensed that there was somebody else in the room, because she opened her eyes and lifted her head off the pillow.

'Beatrice! What you doin' 'ere? You didn't 'alf give me a fright!'

'I came to see how you were feeling, that's all.'

'Not too bad, thanks. I ain't coughed all day. And I can breathe through me nozzle now, even if it whistles now and again.'

'That's good. I'll give you some more physic in a minute. But listen, I've just been out looking for Grace.'

'What for? I thought you said you knew where she was. George 'Azzard borrowed 'er to some nib, didn't 'e?'

'That's what he told me. He said he'd sent her to work for the Earl of Coventry at his house in Grosvenor Square. But I had reason to doubt what he'd said, and so I went to Grosvenor Square to find out for myself.'

'And? Did you find 'er?' asked Eliza, sticking one finger up her left nostril and twisting it around.

'Eliza, you mustn't say a word about this to anyone. Not to Ida and not to any of the other girls – especially not to Ida.'

''Ere – what do you think I am? I ain't a snitch. I never turned a split on no one, not never.'

'All right. I went to the house but she wasn't there, and from what the footman said I don't think they'd even heard of her. So she's not working at the tobacco factory and she's not working for the Earl of Coventry.'

'If you asks me, Beatrice, I reckon I know where she is. In fact I'll post the pony on it. Old 'Azzard's sent 'er off Leda Sheridan's. That's what 'e's done. 'E wouldn't 'ave 'er workin' in 'is fogus factory – a dimber-mort like 'er? She's black, too, and some coves'll pay more than double for black.'

'Oh, dear Lord, I pray not,' said Beatrice.

'Well, you can pray as much as you like, but prayin' ain't goin' to 'elp poor Grace – not one whit. I don't know what 'orrible things they was doin' to them other girls when I was there, but if I 'adn't cleared off when I did, I'd 'ave gone to Peg Trantum's long ago. I'm sure of it. I still 'ave 'orrible dreams about them screams. You never 'eard the like of it. Ugh!'

Beatrice said nothing for almost half a minute, thinking, while Eliza finished picking her nose, studying what she had excavated, and then rolling it up and flicking it across the room.

'You know exactly where Leda Sheridan's house is, and what it's like inside, don't you?'

''Course I do. I could draw it for you. I'm a dab 'and at drawin'.'

'What I'm thinking is, perhaps I could go there in some sort of disguise, and see if I could find Grace, and help her to get away. That's if she's there.'

'I'll bet you a stranger that's where she is – well, I would if I weren't so seedy, and I 'ad one. But you know, thinkin' about it, you wouldn't 'ave no trouble with a disguise. Leda makes most of the girls wear them fancy masks when she's puttin' on one of 'er orgies.' She pronounced 'orgies' with a hard 'g', like 'ogres'.

'Oh, yes? You mean the sort of masks that women might wear to a ball?'

'That's it. I seen them in Vauxhall Gardens, too, in the evenin's sometimes when they're 'avin' a bit of a dance. Leda makes the girls wear 'em so that 'er customers can't tell one girl from another, and which ones 'ave been prigged and which ones 'aven't, so she can sell them as virgins twenty times over.'

Beatrice sat back. In her mind she was already working out a plan for finding out if Grace had been sent to Leda Sheridan's brothel, and how she could safely rescue her. She would also have to consider the possibility that Grace might not wish to be rescued. Life at Leda Sheridan's might be dangerous but it would be exciting and lively, and she might well prefer it to a life of piety and prayer and acting as Ida's unpaid maid-of-all-work.

But what Eliza had told her about the screaming had disturbed her. She knew very well that there were men who would pay handsomely to see girls bound and whipped and penetrated with all manner of objects, and even have congress with dogs and donkeys. Several of them had visited her father's apothecary when she was younger, asking for liniments to soothe their injuries, and although her father had always spoken to them in private, she had often hidden behind the door and listened to them. One girl had been hysterical because she thought that she might give birth to puppies, and begged her father for pennyroyal oil to abort them.

'I'll bring you some more tonic,' she told Eliza. 'Now that you're breathing so much better, I think a little syrup of coltsfoot should be sufficient to soothe you.'

'Are you goin' to do that?' asked Eliza. 'Are you really goin' to go and find Grace? She's a lovely girl. You ought to.'

Beatrice nodded. 'Yes... I'll try my very best.'

'Could you bring us up some paper and pencils, then, and I'll do you a drawin' of Leda Sheridan's case. It's all big rooms downstairs, but upstairs it's like a rat's nest.'

'Thank you, Eliza. But let's hope that you lose your bet, and that Grace is somewhere else, and safe.'

She heard the front door opening downstairs, and voices. Ida and the rest of the girls were back from their service at the Foundery.

'Remember,' said Beatrice, standing up and touching her finger to her lips.

31

Once she had tucked Florence into bed that night, she sat at her toilet and wrote five letters to her friends and former parishioners in Sutton, including Major General Holyoke, William Tandridge and the Widow Belknap. She also wrote to Goody Rust and Goody Greene, who had both attended her when Florence was born.

She asked them to send her news of life in the village, and to place flowers on Francis's grave for her, although she expected that they did that anyway, because he had been very well loved. When she had put down her quill, she realised how much she missed New Hampshire, and wondered if she would ever find a way of going back. She could almost hear the whippoorwills warbling in the forest.

Completely unexpectedly, she started to cry, and sat there with her hands clasped tightly together and tears rolling down her cheeks. After Florence had been born, Goody Greene had sat on her bed beside her and said that 'the tears of grief water the garden of happiness', but this evening she felt only misery. She missed Francis so much that it felt like a physical pain.

After a few minutes she took out her handkerchief and wiped her eyes. Francis was gone, but she would need a male companion if she were to enter Leda Sheridan's brothel looking for Grace. She wouldn't be able to ring the doorbell and simply ask if Grace were there, and say that she wanted to take her back to St Mary Magdalene's. From what Eliza had told her, Leda Sheridan was a termagant – domineering and bad-tempered and obsessed with making money. She wouldn't allow Grace to go easily, especially if Eliza was right and her customers were paying double for her.

Beatrice thought briefly about enlisting Godfrey to come with her, because he was so watery and mild-mannered and she felt that he would probably do anything she asked of him. But Godfrey didn't really look like the kind of man who had the money or the style or even the inclination to spend the evening in a high-class brothel in Drury Lane. She would have to ask James.

She knelt beside the bed while Florence slept and said a prayer in memory of Francis, and for all the desperate girls and women in the world who had to sell themselves simply to survive. She had been an obedient wife, but Francis had been a caring and reasonable husband, and that was rare among men, particularly here in London.

She climbed into bed and lay there for almost an hour, unable to sleep. It was cloudy tonight, although it wasn't raining, so there was no moon. Beatrice could only hope that God could see her.

James said, 'You want me to do *what*?'

They were sitting in a dark corner of Whitney's coffee house in Threadneedle Street. Although it was early, it was crowded with men buying and selling stocks, and reading newspapers, and having loud conversations, and laughing, and smoking. Beatrice was the only woman in there, and she had dressed herself discreetly in her dark-brown cape and hood.

'I need you to pretend that you're interested in having a party for some of your men friends before you get married, and that you've heard that Leda Sheridan's is the best brothel in which to hold it.'

'I'm speechless, Beatrice.'

'I know that I'm taking a liberty in asking you, but I don't know any other man who could carry it off. The Reverend Parsons is far too old, and Godfrey doesn't look as if he has a licentious bone in his body.'

'And I do? Well, thank you for that!'

'Oh, you know what I mean. But I can't go to Leda Sheridan's unescorted, and I couldn't think of any other way to persuade her to admit us, and to show us around. You should wear your very best clothes, and so will I, but I will be playing the part of your peculiar, and wear a mask, so that Mrs Sheridan won't be able to describe me to George Hazzard afterwards.'

James reached across the table and laid his hand on top of hers. 'I have to allow you this, Beatrice. You have the most devious mind I have ever come across, in any woman. But don't take that badly – I admire you for it. In fact I envy you.'

Beatrice sipped her cup of coffee, and then she said, 'What you must do is ask Mrs Sheridan if she has any unusual girls in her house – Chinese, perhaps, or mulattos, or Africans. I pray that Grace is not there, but if she is, that should encourage Mrs Sheridan to bring her out and show her to us.'

'And if she is? Then what?'

'While you engage Mrs Sheridan in conversation, I'll take Grace aside on the pretext of asking her what unusual tricks she could perform for your party. I'll let her know who I really am – that's if she hasn't recognized me already by my voice. I'll ask her if she wants to leave Leda Sheridan's and come back to St Mary Magdalene's.'

'And if she says no?'

'If she says no, we wind up our fakery as quickly as we can, and make our excuses, and leave. If there is one thing I learned as a parson's wife, it's that you can never help those who have no desire to be helped, no matter how much you try to persuade them.'

'And if she says yes, but Mrs Sheridan can call a flashman or two who won't permit us to take her away? I was taught boxing at school, but I doubt that I could best some brothel bully.'

'In that case, we call for a constable.'

James took out his watch and flipped open the lid. 'Look, it's nearly nine, and I have to be back in time for my class. What time were you thinking of going to Leda Sheridan's?'

'Not until this evening, at nine o'clock perhaps, after supper and after Mrs Smollett has retired.'

'I don't know, Beatrice. This sounds like a very dubious enterprise, to say the least. We could both end up in the river.'

'I know it could be dangerous, James. But I can't leave Grace at the mercy of some bawd like Leda Sheridan.'

James stared down at his cup of coffee. He picked it up and sipped it, but it had gone cold, and so he pushed it away. Beatrice could tell that he was deeply troubled.

'James, say no if you really don't want to do this.'

He grunted in bitter amusement. 'You sound exactly like my poor late Sophie. She always gave me a choice, and that was the way in which she persuaded me to do anything she wanted.'

Beatrice was greatly relieved that evening when Ida rose from the table after finishing her supper and declared that she was going to retire early. She said that she was feeling exhausted after a long day teaching the girls how to comport themselves in refined company. Apart from that, she had drunk three large glasses of burgundy with her pork chop and parsnips, on top of the cider which she had drunk with dinner, and she had been mixing up her words when she had been saying after-supper grace.

'Lord, you have fled us – *fed* us – from your gifts and flavours. Favours. Fill us with your mercy, for you live and live and live forever and ever. Amen.'

As soon as Beatrice had heard Ida close her bedroom door, she hurried upstairs to her rooms to change. It was only yesterday that she had opened the last of the five trunks which she had brought with her from America, and inside this trunk was the dark-blue silk dress which had been made for her to attend a celebratory ball in Concord. It was cut low with a ruffled white lace collar and ruffled white lace cuffs.

For a few seconds she held it to her face and breathed in. It still smelled of the perfume she had worn that night, when she had danced with Francis.

Once she had laced up the gown, she took out its matching bonnet of artificial blue roses and white gardenias, with dangling blue ribbons. It had been slightly squashed inside the trunk, but she managed to straighten it.

That afternoon, in Tompkins in Gracechurch Street, she had bought a papier mâché masquerade mask covered with pale-blue silk and decorated with silver sequins. She tried it on in front of the looking glass and thought she looked extremely elegant and mysterious, exactly as the mistress of a fashionable and wealthy young man might look. But her heart was beating hard and she was beginning to wonder if her plan to rescue Grace was far too dangerous.

But then she thought: *What can they do to me, even if they unmask me? And the risk must be worth it, if I can manage to save Grace from a life of depravity.*

She had told Judith that she was going to Snow Hill to visit some old friends who had known her father when he had first opened his apothecary shop in Giltspur Street. Judith promised to look in on Florence from time to time during the evening, in case she was woken up by a bad dream, or needed a drink.

Beatrice was ashamed that she was finding it easier to tell lies, but she knew that she had to protect herself and Florence. Although she had her suspicions, she wasn't yet certain who she could trust, and who was behind the elaborate satanic warnings that she had been given. Whoever it was, it wasn't Satan.

She had asked James not to come and knock at the door, but to be waiting outside with a hackney coach at nine o'clock sharp; and when she went across the landing and looked out of the window, there he was, five minutes early. She took down her cloak from the peg on the back of the door and then she went downstairs as quietly as she could, her slippers pattering and her silk dress whispering against the banisters.

It was cold outside, with an easterly breeze blowing, but dry. James helped her up into the hackney and said, 'Brydges Street, please, by the Theatre Royal.'

'I have to admit that I'm very nervous,' said Beatrice, as they jolted down Ludgate Hill towards Fleet Street.

James took hold of her hand and said, 'Do you want to change your mind? We could always go somewhere else for a drink, perhaps. Or we can simply turn around and go back.'

'No, James. I can't abandon Grace now.'

They went up Fleet Street and along Butcher Row into Wych Street, and then into Drury Lane. Brydges Street was at the back of the Theatre Royal, and a performance must have been coming to a close, because it was lined with hackney coaches and crowded with street musicians and link boys and beggars and prostitutes old and young. The evening was filled with a cacophony of fiddles and flutes and hoarse-voiced singing and laughter. Two prostitutes were having a violent fight and screaming at each other and scratching each other's faces, while people stood around them cheering them on and clapping.

Leda Sheridan's house was a tall narrow four-storey building at the end of Brydges Street, on the corner of York Street. Its front door was painted glossy red, and there were two oil lamps burning either side of it, but there was nothing to indicate that this was one of the most celebrated brothels in London. Beatrice and James climbed the front steps and James rang the bell.

The door was opened immediately by a burly flashman in a scarlet military coat and white buttoned-up leggings which resembled the uniform of the Grenadier Guards, although a ratty white wig was perched on top of his head instead of a guardsman's mitre. His nose was broken into an S-shape and most of his front teeth were missing.

'Be of *service* to you, sir?' he said, in a tone that was halfway between obsequious and sarcastic.

'I wish to speak to Mrs Sheridan,' said James, clearing his throat. 'I'm hoping to arrange a party here for my friends.'

'And your *name*, sir?'

'Do you not know me? Viscount Wolstenholme, of Wolstenholme Hall.'

'I do beg your pardon, your lordship. Please come in. I'll advise Mrs Sheridan that you're here.'

Beatrice and James entered the hallway. It smelled strongly of musky perfume, and the walls were papered in lurid pink with scenes of naked nymphs and well-endowed shepherds and fauns playing pan pipes, as well as being hung with swags of crimson velvet drapery. Beatrice could hear laughter coming from upstairs, and running feet, and a girl crying out, 'No, you duddering rake! How *dare* you!' although it was obvious that she was teasing rather than angry.

The burly flashman ushered them into the drawing room, which was also wallpapered, this time in mustard yellow, with pictures of Romans in togas surrounded by naked dancing girls. Over the fireplace hung a huge oil painting of a satyr and a large-bottomed woman making love, and a log fire was burning in the grate. The room was furnished with two immense camelback sofas upholstered in purple velvet, and four matching armchairs.

'My first time in a house of ill repute,' said James, looking around. 'I have to say that I'm quite impressed.' Then, nodding towards the painting over the fireplace, 'You're not offended, are you?'

Beatrice smiled and said, 'Life in New Hampshire could be very basic at times, James, and I have seen women's posteriors before.'

A few moments later, a small woman in a red-and-black dress came into the room. Her dress was cut so low that her ample breasts were forced upward and it looked as if she would only have to sneeze and they might both tumble out. A lacy black shawl was draped around her shoulders and she wore a sparkling hat with three huge black ostrich plumes on top, which almost doubled her height.

Beatrice thought that she must have been very attractive when she was younger, because she had high cheekbones and a small curved nose and sensual heart-shaped lips, but her eyes were so puffy now that they were nearly closed, and she had three black-velvet patches attached to her face, two stars and a crescent. Sticking a patch next to her left eye was supposed to indicate passion, while the patch on her upper lip suggested coquettishness, and the patch on her cheek meant pride. They also probably meant that she was hiding sores caused by syphilis.

'You're most welcome, your lordship,' she said. 'Leda Sheridan at your disposal. May I ask what brings you here this evening?'

'Of course,' said James. 'And may I introduce Miss Pandora Stevens, my companion?'

'Miss Stevens,' said Leda Sheridan, nodding her ostrich plumes, although she gave Beatrice only the briefest of glances. It was plain that she had little respect for mistresses, no matter how eminent their keepers might be.

'A good friend of mine is about to be wed, and I would like to arrange a jolly pre-nuptial celebration here for him and sixteen other gentlemen,' said James. 'I was thinking about the ninth day of next month, if that is convenient.'

'I think I should be able to accommodate you and your party, your lordship,' said Leda Sheridan. 'Is there any particular theme you had in mind?'

'Exotic, that's what I'm looking for,' said James. 'A variety of girls of differing nationality, if it's possible. Say a Chinee or two, and an Arab, and a Hottentot, if you have any such girls available.'

'I have two Chinese girls... well, one Chinese and one Japanese,' said Leda Sheridan. 'I can also provide you with a dark-skinned Berber girl from Morocco and one from Spain who has a very dusky appearance.'

'No black girls at all?'

'I may be able to acquire one or two for you. Won't you be seated, your lordship, and I will tell you exactly what manner of entertainment I am able to provide, and what refreshment, and what the cost is likely to be.'

'Very well,' said James, and he sat down on one of the camelback sofas. Leda Sheridan sat next to him, very close.

'May I please use your lavatory?' asked Beatrice.

Leda Sheridan glanced at her quickly and tutted. 'It's at the very end of the hall, on the right.'

Beatrice said thank you, and left the room. She knew she had very little time, and from what Leda Sheridan had said about black girls, it didn't seem likely that Grace was here. In spite of that, she crossed over to the staircase, where a bronze statuette of a voluptuous naked woman stood on top of the newel post. She could still hear laughing and footsteps running around on the first-floor landing, so she turned back towards the drawing room to make sure that Leda Sheridan couldn't see her, and then she quickly began to climb up the stairs.

As she reached the landing, a door opened on her left and two girls came bursting out, a redhead and a brunette, both laughing. The brunette was wearing only a short linen chemise and the red-haired girl was bare-breasted and had nothing on except her petticoats.

A coarse man's voice from inside the room shouted, 'I'll spank the both of you for that!' He sounded as if he were drunk, or drugged.

''Allo, lovey!' said the redhead, when she saw Beatrice. 'Are you new 'ere?'

'Oh – yes, yes I am,' said Beatrice. 'But I'm looking for a friend of mine. A black girl called Grace.'

'Come back here or I'm coming out after you!' the man shouted. 'Pissing all over me like that!'

'Oh, shut your trap!' the brunette called back. 'You loved it, you cully! I'll come back and give you Sir Reverence next!'

'There's a blacky girl 'ere but 'er name ain't Grace,' said the redhead. 'Mrs Sheridan calls 'er YaYa.'

'Where is she?' asked Beatrice.

''Ere, I'll take you to 'er. She's 'avin' a bit of a Bo-Peep, I expect. There's goin' to be a big party at midnight and she's the main attraction, ain't she, Ellie?'

'Rather 'er than me,' said the brunette, and gave an exaggerated shiver.

The redhead led Beatrice along the landing to the last door. The carpet was rumpled up so Beatrice had to be careful not to trip.

'She only come yesterday and she's been sleeping most of the time so I ain't 'ad the chance to talk to 'er,' said the redhead. She opened the door without knocking and went inside.

The room was small and dark and smelled of musk and sweat and some apple aroma like tansy. There was a large brass-framed bed in the middle, with heaps of cushions but no blankets, even though the room was chilly. A black girl was lying asleep on the horsehair mattress, dressed in nothing but a white cotton nightgown which had ridden right up to her waist.

'Is this your friend?' asked the redhead.

Beatrice entered the room and edged her way around the end of the bed. The black girl had one hand in front of her face, so she knelt down on the bedside mat and gently lifted it away, and it was Grace.

'Grace,' she said, shaking her shoulder. '*Grace.*'

The redhead said, 'I'd best get back. 'Is nibs is goin' to start 'ollerin' for Mrs Sheridan and wantin' 'is money back. I'll see you later, lovey, all right?'

'Yes,' said Beatrice, but immediately turned back to Grace and shook her again.

'Grace, can you hear me? Grace, this is Beatrice. *Grace!*'

She shook her three or four times more, and then Grace opened her eyes. She stared at Beatrice for a long time without saying anything, and then licked her lips.

'Grace, please try to wake up. I've come to take you away from this place.'

Grace's eyes were filmy and unfocused, and Beatrice

wondered if she could see her at all. She licked her lips a second time and then said, in a croaky whisper, 'Where am I?'

'Grace, you're in a brothel. George Hazzard took you away from St Mary Magdalene's and brought you here. Please, Grace, try to wake up. We need to get you out of here quickly.'

'Who are you?' said Grace.

'It's Beatrice, Grace – Beatrice. Little Florence's mother. Please, Grace, we have very little time. Do you think you can stand up?'

Grace didn't answer her, and after four or five seconds she closed her eyes again and started to breathe deeply and steadily.

There's no question, she's been drugged. What with, God alone knows – probably laudanum. But if they've had to drug her, that almost certainly means that she didn't come here to Leda Sheridan's because she wanted to.

Beatrice stood up, uncertain what to do next. She could go out and call for a watchman, but she would then have to prove to him that Grace had been abducted. Leda Sheridan would only have to deny it and it was unlikely that the watchman would take any further action. From what the girls at St Mary Magdalene's had told Beatrice about brothel-keepers, Leda Sheridan would either be bribing the watch to turn a blind eye to whatever happened behind her front door, or granting the watchmen free usage of her girls, or both.

Even if Grace had woken up by the time he arrived, and told him herself that she had been brought here against her will, Grace was black, and a prostitute, so no matter what she said she wouldn't be believed.

Beatrice could go downstairs and tell James that Grace was here, and James was probably strong enough to carry her out in his arms, but she seriously doubted that he would be able to force his way past Leda Sheridan's flashman.

The red-headed girl had said that Grace was going to be the main attraction at a midnight party, so presumably she was expected to have woken up by then. Beatrice thought that if she could manage to hide in the house until Grace had fully recovered consciousness, it might be possible to find a way for both of them to escape.

She went hurriedly back down the staircase and into the drawing room. James and Leda Sheridan had finished their discussion about the party that 'Viscount Wolstenholme' was keen to arrange, and James said, 'Ah! Pandora! I think everything has been worked out to our mutual satisfaction. Are we ready to leave?'

The front doorbell jangled, and the scarlet-uniformed flashman passed by the drawing room on his way to answer it. Beatrice heard the door open, and then raucous men's laughter, and the sound of women chattering like a flock of chaffinches. Thirty or forty people came crowding into the hallway, and some of them peered into the drawing room and raised their hands to Leda Sheridan in salute.

Leda Sheridan said, 'In any event, your lordship, I must bid you good evening. I have to entertain my guests.'

'Of course,' said James. 'And I thank you for all your inventive ideas for my party. Dalmatians? That's going to be extraordinary! Five virgins deflowered by Dalmatians! It's going to be the talk of the town for years!'

Leda Sheridan left them and went out into the hallway, where she was greeted with loud shouts of 'Mrs Sheridan!' and '*Bravissima!*'

Beatrice leaned close to James, and said, in a low voice, 'She's here, James. Grace. I found her in a bedroom upstairs, but she's been drugged and I can't wake her up.'

'My Lord,' said James. 'But what can we do? I don't think

there's much chance of them standing aside and allowing us take her out of here, is there?'

'I considered calling a watchman, but I think that would be futile. Don't tell me that Mrs Sheridan doesn't have the Drury Lane watch in her pocket.'

'Well... we could rescue her by force,' said James, looking round to make sure that Leda Sheridan couldn't hear him. 'Some of my pupils have fathers and brothers who are right hackums, believe me. I could muster some of them together tomorrow morning and we could break down the door and carry her off, whether her ladyship liked it or not.'

'My idea is to conceal myself somewhere in the house until later,' Beatrice told him. 'One of the girls said that Grace was going to be tonight's star attraction, whatever that means. After that, perhaps, and when everybody else has retired to bed, I could manage to sneak her away.'

The doorbell rang again, and even more people came pushing their way into the house. Some of them had to back into the drawing room as the hallway overflowed. All of them were wearing masquerade masks, like Beatrice – the men with black masks like highwaymen or pirates or demons, and the women with silk masks decorated with feathers and sequins and pearls. They were all finely dressed, both men and women, and several women wore filmy lace or organdy bodices through which their bare breasts were visible. They were all laughing and shouting as if they were highly excited, and drunk, too.

'I don't think I'll have to find anywhere to hide,' said Beatrice. 'I'm sure I can mingle with all of these and Mrs Sheridan won't notice me.'

'Are you sure?' said James. 'If she does recognize you, there could be the Devil to pay.'

'I don't think I need to be concerned about the Devil himself, James – only about people who behave like the Devil. But what is the worst that they could do to me? Throw me out into the street?'

'I'll wait for you,' James told her. 'The Denmark coffee house is only a few doors away, and they don't close until their last customer has fallen flat on his back.'

He took hold of her hand, and briefly squeezed it, and then he kissed her on the cheek. 'All I ask is, take the utmost care, won't you?'

32

The front door was still wide open, and the hallway was now packed with shouting, jostling revellers, so James was able to elbow his way out and leave the house without Leda Sheridan noticing that he was leaving on his own. In any event, she had now mounted halfway up the stairs, so that she could turn around to the crowd below her and raise both hands for their attention.

'Lend me your ears, please, all of you! Welcome – welcome and good evening! Tonight you are going to witness the most shocking and extraordinary performance that you have ever seen – *ever!* – and I promise on my honour that none of you will forget it for the rest of your natural lives!'

A great cheer went from the revellers, followed by applause. Beatrice was standing among them, but close to the wall, so that she was half-hidden from Leda Sheridan's sight behind one of the red velvet swags that hung down from the ceiling.

'For your refreshment, you shall have a choice of wines of all kinds as well as geneva and brandy,' Leda Sheridan continued. 'You will also be served oysters and scotched collops and quails and chickens, as well as biscuits and tarts and various sweetmeats. And to whet your appetite even more, you will be presented with our principal entertainment for this evening – the delectable black virgin from darkest Africa, YaYa!'

There was another cheer, even louder than the first. Then Leda Sheridan descended the stairs and led the way along the corridor to the back of the house, her black ostrich feathers swaying like the black plumes on a funeral horse. Her guests all followed, still talking loudly and laughing, with Beatrice in their midst. She stayed close to a very tall man with a long-nosed Venetian carnival mask. He had four or five young women clustered around him, so she thought that she might simply be mistaken for one of his entourage. He was wearing an expensive orange frock coat with gold braid and gold-plated buttons, and he spoke with a loud, commanding boom, so she imagined that he must be a man of some importance.

The guests filed through double doors into a large room where a coal fire was burning in a large, blue-tiled fireplace. The walls were papered in blue, and featured scenes of voluptuous naked women having congress with minotaurs and centaurs. As the guests entered, four musicians seated in the far corner struck up with 'Lady of Pleasure' – a violinist, a cellist, a flautist and a curtal player, all dressed in white with elaborate white periwigs.

Against the left-hand wall a long table had been laid with a white damask cloth on which silver tureens and bowls and plates and cake stands were set out, as well as red and green and orange jellies and dozens of bottles of wine and spirits, and crystal glassware.

On the right-hand side there was a low semi-circular stage, its edge decorated with white silk roses and chrysanthemums and white silk ribbons tied into bows. In the centre of the stage stood an oval table, about seven feet in diameter at its widest point, and this was also spread with a white damask cloth.

About thirty gilt chairs had been arranged around the stage, even though Beatrice guessed that the revellers gradually filling up the room must number close to a hundred. The only lighting came from six silver candelabra standing on the table, while the main chandelier that hung from the ceiling remained unlit. This filled the room with constantly moving shadows, as if it were filled not only with living people, but with memories of living people, and ghosts.

Beatrice found a chair at the far end of the stage, where the shadows were at their deepest, although she could see that Leda Sheridan was too busy taking care of her guests to notice her. Even if she had, she had paid so little attention to her when she had been talking to James that she probably wouldn't recognize her.

Once all the revellers had entered the room, Leda Sheridan stepped up onto the stage and clapped her hands. Immediately a door beside the back of the stage opened up and five naked girls came tripping in. Like the revellers, they all wore masquerade masks, as well as red agate necklaces and bracelets. All their pubic hair had been shaved off, and each girl's right buttock had been tattooed with a swan, presumably to show that they belonged to Leda. One of the girls was Chinese or Japanese, and another was dark-skinned, with tightly curled black hair, but Grace wasn't among them.

The girls tiptoed quickly across to the tables and began to pour out glasses of wine and hand around plates of oysters and slices of game pie. The shouting and laughter in the room was almost deafening, especially when the girls gave out drinks to the men, because they gave each man's crotch a quick fondle as they did so.

Leda Sheridan opened the door at the back of the stage, and beckoned, and two more girls came out. They were wearing pink silk day gowns and high pink wigs, and both of them wore pink silk masks with fluffy pink feathers on them. As they mounted the stage, the musicians began to play 'The Frolic', and the revellers clapped in time to the music.

The girls' day gowns were fastened at the front, and they untied their ribbons and opened them up – first to the left and then to the right – giving the audience a quick glimpse of their naked bodies underneath. Then they gradually let the day gowns slip from their shoulders, baring their breasts; and after twirling around and around, they let them drop to the floor. Their pubic hair wasn't completely shaved, but it was trimmed to a heart shape and bleached white.

They wrapped their arms around each other and gave each other a long, lascivious kiss. After that, they stood side by side facing the audience and stretched their vulvas open as wide as they could with their fingers. The audience cheered and clapped, both men and women.

Now one of them climbed onto the oval table, lying back and parting her thighs. The other reached under the table and produced a huge ebony phallus, highly polished. She positioned the head of it against her partner's anus, and then slowly pushed it inside her, rotating it as she did so, until less than an inch of it was showing. The musicians were playing 'The Frolic' faster and faster, and the audience were stamping their feet now, as well as clapping.

The girl standing beside the table leaned forward, stuck out her tongue, and started to lick the prone girl's clitoris, tipping the velvet as fast as the music. After two or three minutes, the girl on the table let out a little scream, and shuddered, and kicked her feet, and this brought even the seated revellers to their feet, knocking some of the chairs backwards.

The two girls left the stage, but three more performances followed. In the first, two fat, hairy men wearing miserable clown masks had simultaneous sex with a naked girl in a smiling fairy mask. Beatrice couldn't guess the girl's age, but her breasts were still budding, so she was probably no older than thirteen or fourteen.

In the second performance, a bare-breasted young brunette in a white ball gown fellated two naked men, her head ducking frantically from one to the other until both of them climaxed on her face and left semen dripping from her lips and the end of her turned-up nose.

'Oh, heavens above!' exclaimed one of the young women in the orange-coated man's entourage, pressing her hand to her mouth. 'I think I'm going to cast up my accounts!'

The orange-coated man was standing behind her and patted her on the shoulder. 'You know what they say, my dear Gemma?' he bellowed. 'Better fellate than never!'

Next, three men and three women with strapped-on dildoes made a daisy chain, performing a rippling thrust that went from one end of the chain to the other, all to the sound of 'The Jolly Brown Turd', with deep suggestive farting notes from the curtal.

Yet where is Grace? That redheaded girl said that she was going to be tonight's main attraction, and Leda Sheridan announced her as YaYa, but so far there's no sign of her. Perhaps she's still too drugged to perform.

The five naked girls flitted around, filling up the revellers' glasses and passing round sugar-cakes and jellies, and then Leda Sheridan climbed up onto the stage again.

'And now, the very highlight of tonight's entertainment! An act which I guarantee will give my gentlemen clients the hardest pego they have ever known, and which will flood Eve's custom house of every lady here!'

The three musicians started to play a slow version of 'Lady Lie Near Me'. The door at the back of the stage opened again, and Grace appeared, wrapped in a long white silk cloak trimmed with white feathers, and supported by two of the men who had appeared in the previous performances, both bare-chested but now wearing tight white breeches.

Beatrice could see that Grace's eyes were open, but she still looked glazed, and her knees appeared to buckle as she came through the door, so that the two men had to lift her up onto the stage. She was the only person in the room not wearing a mask, and she stared at the assembled crowd of masked faces as if she couldn't understand where she was or what she was doing.

While the two men held her up, two of the naked girls who had been serving drinks climbed onto the stage and stood either side of her. Leda Sheridan clapped her hands and the musicians played a dramatic chord. As they did so, the girls dragged off Grace's cloak and tossed it off the stage, so that she was naked, too. She was full-breasted, with crinkled nipples as dark as prunes, but otherwise she was very thin, with prominent pelvic bones and a wide gap between her thighs.

Between them, the two men heaved Grace onto the table and lay her down on her back. The girls then bound her wrists and ankles with white silk ribbons. They lifted the tablecloth to reveal four brass rings attached to the underside of the table, and they ran the ribbons through these rings and knotted them, so that Grace was pinned down and unable to move. She didn't struggle: she only lifted her head a little, and then let it drop back down again, as if she were still half-comatose.

The two men and the two girls left the stage, and then the musicians played another chord. The door opened and out stepped a muscular young man with tousled black hair and tattoos on his chest and his forearms. Beatrice thought that he was handsome in a brutish way, with deep-set eyes and thick, rubbery lips. From his physique, she guessed that he could have been a chairman or more likely a lighterman – a keel-bully as they were called. He was completely naked, with a tangled rug of black hair on his chest, and legs as hairy as an ape's. He was holding his purple-headed penis in his left fist and it was already half-erect.

The hubbub in the room grew even louder, and as the hairy man stepped up onto the stage, some of the women let out little screams of delight. He turned to face the revellers, and grinned, and licked his rubbery lips, and gave his penis four or five hard rubs, as if he were pumping the handle of a butter churn.

Dearest Lord, thought Beatrice, *what is he going to do to poor Grace?* Although the room was crowded and hot, she felt as if her blood had turned to ice water, and she couldn't stop herself from shivering.

The hairy man climbed up onto the table, and hunched over Grace on his hands and knees. Grace lifted her head again, and stared up at him, and let out a thin, pathetic mewling sound as if she knew what he intended to do to her.

He lowered himself between her skinny black thighs, and opened her up with his thumb and forefinger so that he could force his penis into her, as far as it would go. Then he began slowly and rhythmically to move his buttocks up and down, grunting under his breath with every thrust.

The revellers were hushed to begin with, but when he pushed harder and harder – so hard that Grace's hips were jolted up off the tablecloth with every thrust – one of the men started to count each thrust out loud.

'*One*-a-penny! *Two*-a-penny! *Three*-a-penny! *Four!*'

Two of his friends joined in, and soon all the revellers were chanting. The hairy man turned his head and gave them a grin, licking his lips lasciviously to show them how much he was enjoying himself. He was sweating now, with his sweat dropping onto Grace's breasts, and his face was as red as a freshly boiled crab, but he kept on pushing himself faster and harder, and grunting louder and louder as he did so. Grace's eyes were closed, and she might just as well have been unconscious. Beatrice hoped that she was.

When the counting reached a hundred, some of the revellers started shouting, 'Where is he? Where's the nim gimmer? That's what you promised us, Mrs Sheridan! Where's the nim gimmer?'

Beatrice looked around at the crowd, bewildered and frightened. Nim gimmer was slang for a surgeon, she knew that, but why should these revellers be calling out for a surgeon?

'Nim gimmer! Nim gimmer!' they chorused, the men hoarse with drink and excitement, and the women shrill, and all of them clapping in time to the hairy man's grunting.

The door beside the stage suddenly opened again, and the revellers all cheered. Out came the tall figure of a man wearing a floor-length white robe and a white pointed hood, like a phantom, or a Nazarene penitent in a capirole, with only two small holes for his eyes. Without hesitation he climbed up onto the stage, and stood beside the oval table.

'Nim gimmer! Nim gimmer!' chanted the crowd.

The man in the white robe looked at the hairy man, and Beatrice could just make out his eyes glittering. He seemed to be aroused, or anxious, because the front of his hood was being sucked in and out very quickly as he breathed. The hairy man nodded, and said something to the man in the white robe, although the shouting all around her was so loud that Beatrice couldn't make out what it was. He slowed down his thrusting, though, and before each thrust he drew his penis completely out of Grace's vagina, and then paused for a few seconds before he slid it back in again.

'Come on, then, sir!' shouted the man in the orange coat. 'Give us what we paid good money for!'

The man in the white robe reached into the folds of his garment and drew out a short curved sword, like a scimitar. He raised it up above his head and circled it around and the revellers roared their approval.

Beatrice thought: *No! He's not going to hurt her, is he? Oh, dear God, don't let him hurt her!*

The man in the white robe stepped up closer to the table and held the sword above Grace's neck. He looked again at the hairy man, and they nodded in unison as if they were two musicians about to play the same piece of music together.

Beatrice stood up and screamed out, 'No! You can't! Stop it! Stop it! You can't!'

She tried to push her way up to the stage, but she couldn't force her way past the rows of chairs in front of her, and now more and more of the revellers were standing up, and blocking her way through.

She kept on screaming, 'No! You can't! In the name of God, you mustn't!' but her voice was drowned out by the shouting and the stamping and the clamour all around her.

Grace still had her eyes closed. If she were conscious, she would have heard the pandemonium in the room, but she wouldn't have realized what was about to happen to her.

The hairy man nodded, and the man in the white robe leaned forward and sliced Grace's neck from side to side, so that dark red blood flooded out and sprayed all over the tablecloth. Grace opened her eyes in shock, but then the man in the white robe sliced her neck again, separating her vertebrae with a forceful twist of his wrist like a Smithfield butcher.

Grace's head rolled sideways and tumbled off the table, onto the stage. At the same time, the hairy man let out an exultant shout and climaxed into her decapitated body, his buttocks tense, his leg muscles rigid, and both of his feet curled up.

The whole room was in chaos. The men were shouting and groping the women, hauling up their petticoats and feeling up between their legs, as well as tugging down their bodices and baring their breasts, while the women were busy unbuttoning the front of the men's breeches and plunging their hands inside so that they could prise out their erections.

Beatrice's heart was beating hard and she felt as if she couldn't breathe. She sat down on her chair again and lowered her head, but the room began to grow dark and the shouting and laughter sounded muffled and distant and she knew that she was close to fainting.

A man in a blue frock coat came up to her and said, 'Hey there, my darling, how about some rantum-scantum?'

She couldn't even raise her eyes to look at him. All she could see was his frock coat and his breeches.

'No,' she said, and her voice didn't even sound like her own.

She managed to stand up. She didn't turn towards the stage, although she could see that the hairy man had now jumped down from the table and was lifting his arms up like a champion boxer. She steadied herself by holding on to the back of the chair, and then she weaved her way through the over-excited crowd.

Out in the hallway she saw Leda Sheridan talking to two men in black pirate masks, and laughing. She walked straight past her but Leda Sheridan didn't even turn to acknowledge her. She went to the front door, where the scarlet-uniformed flashman was standing, looking bored. He opened the door for her, and said, 'A very good night to you, miss. You're leaving early. You did enjoy yourself, I hope.'

Never in her life before had Beatrice been tempted to tell anyone that they should be damned, and burn in hellfire forever, but she was close to saying it then. She said nothing, though, and stepped out into the night, to go and find James.

33

James was sitting in the smoky back room of the Denmark coffee house with a pewter mug of ale and a copy of the *London Chronicle* spread out on the table in front of him. A drunken rabble of men standing at the bar gave Beatrice whistles and shouts of approval as she walked past them, obviously thinking that she was a pretty prostitute who had come into the tavern to find herself a gentleman client.

As soon as he saw her, James folded up his newspaper and stood up.

'Beatrice!' he said. 'What's happened? You look white as a ghost! And – my God – you've been crying!'

He came around the table and held her in his arms. She still felt cold, as if she would never know what it was like to be warm ever again, and she couldn't stop herself from shivering.

'Sit down,' James said. 'Would you care for something to drink? A glass of brandy, perhaps? Please, tell me why you're so distressed.'

It took her almost half a minute and several deep breaths before she was able to explain how Grace had been beheaded for the entertainment of Leda Sheridan's braying crowd of revellers. James sat still and listened, his face grave, holding her hand.

'I can hardly believe it,' he said, when she had finished. 'I've heard stories about wealthy men who are willing to pay hundreds of guineas to watch girls being murdered, but I always believed that they were nothing more than figments of somebody's depraved imagination. You must have been shocked to the very core! Are you sure I can't order you a brandy?'

'We should go the justice house in Bow Street,' said Beatrice. 'The evidence will still be there. How will Leda Sheridan be able to deny that she had Grace killed when her poor young body is lying there for all to see? Oh, and all the blood! The blood was everywhere!'

James thought for a moment, still holding her hand. Then he said, 'I realize how barbarous this was, Beatrice, and those responsible should be arrested and sent for trial. But you need to be extremely careful. You will be the only witness who is prepared to give evidence against Mrs Sheridan and the men who perpetrated this crime. Nobody else in that audience is going to admit that they paid money in the expectation of seeing Grace having her head cut off in the heat of a carnal act. To admit that would make them accessories to her murder in the eyes of the law, and even if they weren't hung or gaoled or transported for their participation, it would have a most toxic effect on their reputation.'

'In the name of everything holy, James – don't you think they deserve it?'

'You're missing my point, Beatrice. You will be the only hostile witness and without your testimony the case will have little chance of success.'

'But isn't her body proof enough?'

'Proof that she's dead, yes, of course. But who was it who gave her the cuts that killed her? You saw only a figure in a white hood. It could have been anybody. Leda Sheridan might well say that he rushed in without her knowledge and approval and cut off her head before anybody had a chance to stop him.

And how is he to be identified? For all you know, Beatrice, it was Satan himself.'

'Of course it wasn't Satan. It was a man. Nim gimmer, they called him – a surgeon.'

'How do you know for certain that he was a man if you didn't see his face? You know from your own experiences that Satan is abroad in London at the moment.'

'James, it was a man, I'm certain of it.'

'Who killed Grace is not really relevant, Beatrice. What *is* relevant is that Leda Sheridan has many close connections in high places, and that there were probably members of her audience who would take any steps to prevent it being public knowledge that they had paid her to stage such an atrocity. If they had no compunction about murdering Grace for their own sexual entertainment, they would surely have no compunction in doing the same to you in order to preserve their reputations.'

'So what am I supposed to do, James? Nothing? I saw an innocent young woman beheaded in front of my eyes and I should ignore it, as if her life was worth nothing?'

'I'm not saying that, Beatrice. I'm saying that you need to think seriously about your own safety, and Florence's too. Grace was a former prostitute, and she was black, and the courts may well consider that her life was of very little value.'

'What about you? Do *you* think her life was of very little value?'

'Not as valuable as yours, or Florence's. Like all of those girls at St Mary Magdalene's, she chose a career which was always going to put her at risk.'

'She was trying to redeem herself. God forgives those who show true repentance, or have you forgotten that?'

James said, 'Now you're talking like the widow of a parson. Come on, let me take you back to Maidenhead Court. You need a warm drink and a warm bed and a good night's sleep. The shock of this will have worn off by the morning.'

Beatrice was about to say, 'The shock of what I saw tonight will never wear off, not for the rest of my life,' but she knew that James was right, and she needed to get back to her rooms, and to Florence. She wouldn't be able to sleep, but she needed warmth, and comfort, and time to think.

They left the coffee house and stood outside on Drury Lane to hail a hackney. The night was cold now, although there was fresh horse manure steaming in the middle of the street. James looked down at her, and gave her a rueful smile.

'I shouldn't have agreed to take you to Mrs Sheridan's, should I? Sometimes in life I think we're better not knowing the worst.'

When she returned to St Mary Magdalene's she knocked softly on Judith's door. Judith was sitting up in bed with her hair in rags, stitching a tapestry sampler of vegetables and apple trees with the motto *All Things Grow With Love*.

'Oh, Beatrice, you're back,' she said, with a smile. But then, 'Has something alarmed you? You look deathly pale, if you don't mind my saying so.'

'I'm just a little tired,' said Beatrice. 'How was Florrie?'

'She woke up once and said she'd had a dream about her brother coming into the room. She was upset at first, but I gave her a drink and sang her a song and she soon went back to sleep.'

'Thank you, Judith. I'm very grateful.'

'Are you sure there's nothing wrong?'

'No. I need to get some sleep, that's all.'

'Well, I must, too. This candle's almost burned down and I don't have another.'

Beatrice said goodnight and went to her rooms. Although

she was so exhausted, she doubted if she would be able to sleep. She kept seeing the startled expression on Grace's face as the knife sliced her larynx in half, and hearing the dull thump as her severed head dropped onto the stage.

Once she had lit the candle on her toilet, she looked into the bedroom. Florence was fast asleep, all twisted up in her sheet with her bare feet showing, and sucking her thumb. The poor little girl hardly ever mentioned her brother Noah, but occasionally Beatrice had overheard her talking to him, as if they were still playing together.

She took off her blue silk dress and her corset and her petticoats, and put on her long white nightgown with the wide lace collar. She knew there was no point in her going to bed. She would only disturb Florence, and even if she managed to fall asleep, she would only have terrible nightmares. Instead, she took out her quill and opened her inkstand, and began to write down everything that had happened that evening at Leda Sheridan's whorehouse, in as much detail as she could. Even though they had all been masked, she listed as many of the revellers as she could remember, describing their wigs and their clothes and their jewellery. She was sure that it would be possible for some of them to be identified in a court of law, particularly the man in the orange frock coat with the gold braid and buttons, and the long-nosed Venetian mask.

She thought about the warning that James had given her about reporting Grace's murder to the law officers at Bow Street. She appreciated that he was thinking only of her own safety, but surely such an act of barbarity couldn't be allowed to go unpunished. She also began to suspect that if George Hazzard had sent Grace to be beheaded for the sexual gratification of Leda Sheridan's clients, perhaps a similar fate had befallen Jane Webb and the other six girls that he had called a 'coven'.

And who could tell how many other girls he had spirited away in the past, so that a sadistic crowd of wealthy revellers could delight in seeing them raped and bloodily murdered?

When James had advised her in the coffee house to keep her peace, Beatrice had thought that he was being over-cautious – cowardly, even. She had been threatened several times by corrupt and violent men when she was in New Hampshire, and she had boldly faced up to those threats. But on reflection she had to concede that the situation here in London was different, and potentially far more dangerous. It was one thing to stand up to your enemies, but quite another if you weren't at all sure who your enemies were.

She decided to pretend that she knew nothing at all about Grace's fate – for the time being, anyway. She would also make sure that George Hazzard had no idea that she was still determined to discover what part he might have played in the coven's disappearance. Neither would she voice any of her suspicions to Ida, or the Reverend Parsons, or even to James.

She finished writing her account of Grace's murder, and sifted sand across the paper to dry the ink. Then she blew out her candle and sat for a while in darkness, listening to the sounds of the night – the bells dolefully ringing the hour, the watchmen calling in the streets below, and three or four men weaving their way along Aldersgate Street and drunkenly singing 'Oyster Nan'.

'Poor dear Grace,' she whispered. 'I hope Jesus is holding you in his arms tonight, and soothing you.'

34

Beatrice was just stepping out through her sitting-room door the next morning when Eliza came running upstairs in her white stockinged feet, holding up her petticoats.

''E's turned up again!' she panted. 'Mr 'Azzard! For the love of God don't let 'im know that I'm 'ere!'

'George Hazzard? Of course not, Eliza. I wonder what he's after this time.'

'I don't give a tuppenny toss what 'e's after, so long as 'e ain't after me! 'E's the very Devil, that man!'

Eliza went back to her room while Beatrice continued downstairs. When she reached the hallway, she heard George Hazzard's voice in the drawing room, and Ida laughing. She gave a light knock at the half-closed door and then went in.

George was wearing his usual yellow frock coat and was just about to light a cigar with a taper. When Beatrice walked in, he lowered his cigar and blew out the taper and gave her an exaggerated bow.

'Beatrice! You look charming as ever! That shade of green is most becoming.'

'Good morning, George,' said Beatrice, trying not to sound too cold. 'Ida.'

'George has come to gather up more girls,' said Ida. 'Since those seven disappeared, he has been left gravely short of workers.'

'It's true,' said George. 'I have more orders than my factory can cope with, especially for cigars. My Lord, White's Club alone have ordered twenty-five cases! If I'm forced to turn customers away, I may lose their business for good and all. There are more than seventy other tobacco factories in Hackney and Clerkenwell, and they are all circling like wolves, eager to steal my business.'

'I see,' said Beatrice. 'How many more girls do you need? I'm afraid the ones we have left are not quite as becoming as the seven you took before.'

George came across to Beatrice and looked her directly in the eyes. She noticed for the first time that his left eye was brown and his right eye was greeny-blue.

'Beatrice, I'm well aware of your suspicions. You believe that I failed to take sufficient care of those seven girls, and that their disappearance was somehow my fault. You also believe that I was responsible for the goat's head appearing on the dinner table, and for the scratching at your door, and the demon with the looking-glass face who threatened you at Ranelagh Gardens.'

Beatrice said nothing, but waited for him to continue. Ida stood watching them both, tugging nervously at her lacy cuff.

'I can only apologize to you, Beatrice,' said George. 'Deeply, deeply apologize. I was offended by your suspicions, and I reacted aggressively, which was wrong of me. I confess that I'm the kind of man who doesn't take criticism lightly. I wouldn't be able to run my factory so efficiently if I weren't. But I've been thinking over the way you responded to the coven's disappearance, and I can understand now that it was only natural for you to be sceptical.'

'I believe in Satan, George,' said Beatrice. 'It was just that I found these particular manifestations to be less than credible.'

'But if they weren't the work of the Devil, my dear, what else could they have possibly been?' George asked her. 'How did that goat's head magically appear on that plate? How did that demon with the looking-glass face know that you were visiting Ranelagh Gardens? Whatever beast it was that clawed at your door, how did it manage to enter the house, and how did it know which door was yours?'

'Well, I expect that you're right,' said Beatrice. 'Who else could have done such things but Satan himself?'

She looked back into George's face with his broken nose and his rough dry-skinned cheeks and she could have spat at him. He was standing so close that she could smell the sour tobacco on his breath. She was aching to tell him that he had lied about Grace being sent to the Earl of Coventry's house, and how she had been horribly murdered right in front of her eyes, but she knew that she needed to save that for the time when she had more evidence against him.

George said, 'Beatrice, my dearest – I should like to believe that you and I are good friends again. I should also like to think that if you are ever threatened again by his satanic majesty that you can call on me for protection at any time, day or night.'

'Thank you,' said Beatrice. 'I sincerely hope that I never have to do that.'

'Now, George, you need to select some girls, don't you?' Ida put in, with undisguised impatience. 'How many altogether?'

'Four or five, if that's possible. I can give each of them full-time employment stripping tobacco leaves and rolling cigars. I find that bunters are particularly nimble with their fingers. They will all be fairly paid. As I say, business is booming and I need all the staff that I can recruit.'

'I'll call the girls now,' said Ida. 'In any event, they have to come down for their breakfast.'

When she had left the room, George said to Beatrice, 'I hope you believe that my apology is sincere. And I assure you that I will pay much closer attention to the welfare of these new girls than I did to that coven of witches. I believe now that it must have been one of the seven who persuaded the other six to summon up the Devil, so I doubt if it will happen again. But, all the same, I will alert my staff to keep their eyes and ears open for any sign of satanic symbol, or of chanting, or any kind of ritual sacrifice. Crows, chickens, rabbits. The Reverend Parsons tells me that it isn't important what kind of a creature a Devil-worshipper kills to summon Satan, so long as a life is taken, and there's blood.'

'Very well,' said Beatrice. She was growing desperately anxious to leave now. George's presence was making her feel shivery again, especially since she had proof that his contrition was so blatantly false. He had arranged for Grace to be murdered as surely as if he had cut her head off himself.

George went over and relit his wax taper from the hot coals in the fireplace. He puffed at his cigar for a few moments, and then he said, 'Perhaps it will calm your suspicions if you come out to Hackney to visit these new girls once they've started work. Then you'll be able to see for yourself that they are safe and well-cared-for. Come out tomorrow with Ida, or the day after tomorrow, and bring you delightful little girl with you. You can have a walk in the country, and afterwards we can go to the Cat and Shoulder of Mutton tavern for some lunch. Who knows? We might even see some pig-swinging.'

'I'll see,' said Beatrice, uneasily.

'Beatrice, my dearest, I hope you will. I know that you have faith in your chemistry, but surely our faith in God must be stronger. Chemistry will never defeat Satan, but God will.'

Beatrice could hear the girls clattering downstairs and

making their way through to the atelier. Then Ida appeared and said, 'George? They're ready for you. Come and make your selection.'

George picked five girls altogether, including Judith and Katharine. Ida had tried to find Eliza, too, but there was no sign of her, and in the end she had given up. Beatrice had said nothing, although she guessed that Eliza was hiding under her bed.

The girls went back up to their rooms to pack their clothes and their few belongings. Beatrice was glad that Florence was out in the back garden playing with No-noh and the orange crochet rabbit that Judith had made for her. Florence was still distressed that Grace had disappeared, and she would be inconsolable now that Judith was going, too.

Beatrice was deeply fearful about what was going to become of these five girls, although it was possible that George was telling the truth about his urgent need for more factory hands, and after all he had invited her to come to Hackney with Ida to see them at work. She knew that it was un-Christian of her to think such a thing, but all the girls were fairly plain, and three of them had disfiguring smallpox scars on their cheeks, and she thought it was less likely that George would pass them on to Leda Sheridan.

At last the girls all gathered in the hallway and said their goodbyes. Beatrice went out into the garden where Florence was sitting underneath the statue of Astraea, pretending to feed her rabbit with dandelion leaves.

'Florrie, can you come inside? Judith and some of the girls are leaving us. They have to go and work for Mr Hazzard in his tobacco factory.'

Florence looked up in shock. Then her lower lip turned down and her eyes filled with tears. Beatrice bent down and picked her up and hugged her.

'Why does Judith have to go, Mama? I want her to stay!'

'She has to go, darling, because that's the way life is. We love people but then we lose them. Like your papa. Like your brother. Like Grace. But we should just be thankful that God brought them to us, and that we had such happy times with them. God will bring us new friends, don't worry.'

'But I don't want new friends! I want Judith!'

'Come on, now, don't let Judith see that you're sad. Come inside and wave her goodbye. Mr Hazzard says that we can go to his factory tomorrow or the day after and see her working, and we can take No-noh for a walk by the marshes, too.'

They went inside. The girls were already climbing into George's yellow carriage and a two-horse clarence which he must have hired especially to take them back to Hackney. Florence ran up to the clarence and called out, 'Judith! Judith!' and waved her orange rabbit.

Beatrice stood on the porch and wiped her eyes with her fingertips. Ida was standing close behind her.

'Why are you sad?' Ida asked her. 'They are going to a much better life than they deserve.'

'I'm sad because life can be very cruel sometimes.'

'Only to those who question the will of God.'

'I suppose so. But sometimes the will of God can be very difficult to understand.'

'*Vincit qui patitur*, Beatrice. He conquers who suffers.'

Beatrice turned around. Ida's face was painted with even more white lead than usual, so that she looked as if she were wearing a death mask. There were fine hairline cracks around her eyes and the sides of her mouth. It was impossible to tell what she was really thinking, but Beatrice could sense nothing but pain. Whatever had happened to Ida Smollett in the past, it must have hurt her beyond any hope of recovery.

Beatrice spent the rest of the day giving the girls sewing lessons and reading from the Bible. She was still in shock from seeing Grace being beheaded, and so she tried to keep herself as quiet and as calm as possible. She attempted to eat, but she took only one mouthful of stewed lamb at dinnertime and gagged, and had to run from the kitchen and spit it out into the garden, with her stomach painfully heaving.

As she came back inside, she found Ida standing in the kitchen doorway.

'Is something ailing you, Beatrice?'

'I think Hettie laced my bodice too tight for me, that's all.'

'You're not pining for any illness, I trust.'

If it's an illness to be appalled by the perversity of human pleasure, then yes, I'm critically ill. But I'll recover, with God's help, and make sure that justice is done, not only for Grace, but for every other girl whose life has been treated with contempt by people like you.

35

The following day it rained hard from morning until mid-afternoon, with occasional flickers of lightning and booms of thunder from south of the Thames. The river rose as high as the Three Cranes stairs, and the streets of the City were quickly turned into a quagmire of mud and sewage and floating lumps of horse manure. Underneath St Mary Magdalene's the cellars were flooded knee-deep in foul-smelling tan-coloured water, so that wooden crates of wine bottles began to circle around, and over a month's stock of flour sacks were soaked into a sodden pulp.

There was no question of going to Hackney in this weather, so Beatrice stayed in the atelier for most of the day, giving art lessons. She told the girls to draw their idea of heaven, and she was surprised how many of them drew not only God, and Jesus, and flying angels, but other figures too, in ordinary clothes. When she asked who they were, these ordinary people, almost every girl said, 'My mother, who died giving birth to me,' or, 'My father, who died of drink,' or, 'My three sisters who died of consumption before they reached the age of six.'

Florence knelt at the window looking out at the garden, hugging her orange rabbit and watching the rain trickle down. Beatrice didn't have to ask what she was thinking.

*

Overnight, the skies cleared, and when morning came the sun was blindingly bright.

Ida came into the kitchen when Beatrice and Florence were eating porridge, and said that George had sent a hansom to come and collect them and take them to Hackney. Beatrice had half a mind to say that she didn't want to go, but she knew that George had extended this invitation for the specific purpose of allaying her suspicions about him. It was crucial that he should believe that she had forgiven him, and that she now held him blameless.

They put on their coats and bonnets and wooden pattens over their shoes and climbed up into the hansom. This was a private-hire coach, with shiny leather seats, unlike the filthy, worn-out interiors of most hackney carriages. The coachman was almost lordly, with a tall top hat and a dark-green box coat and a huge walrus moustache.

The journey to Hackney was slow, because the road was still rutted and muddy and flooded in places from yesterday's rain, but Beatrice and Florence sang songs all the way, and Florence sat No-noh up on her lap and clapped his paws together in time to their singing. Ida sat and stared at the passing fields and farms, her face impassive. Beatrice had the feeling that she was only coming on this outing because she had been told to, and not out of choice.

George came out to greet them as soon as they turned into the factory courtyard. He was accompanied by Edward Veal, his bald-headed accountant. Edward Veal was wearing a black frock coat and black breeches, so he resembled a giant stag-beetle standing on its hind legs.

'Welcome, welcome and thrice welcome!' said George, helping Beatrice down from the hansom. 'And welcome to you, too, sweet Florence, and welcome to your pup, as well. What's the little fellow's name?'

'No-noh,' said Florence, solemnly. 'After my brother who was stealed away by Indians.'

'Oh,' said George, and looked at Beatrice sympathetically. 'Forgive me for asking.'

He led them into the factory. Inside, it was as noisy as ever, with steam hissing and cutters clanking and the workers shouting to each other. The five new girls George had taken from St Mary Magdalene's were sitting together at the long rows of desks where heaps of thin, wrinkly tobacco leaves were draped. They were stripping out the mid-ribs with such speed that Beatrice could have believed that they had been doing it all their working lives, instead of being prostitutes and pickpockets.

Florence saw Judith and ran around the desks to fling her arms around her. Judith waved to Beatrice and smiled and mouthed some inaudible words to let her know that she was well. Three of the other girls waved too.

'There,' George breathed in Beatrice's ear. 'See how comfortably they have all settled in. This work makes them feel useful and valued, and it will pay them nearly twice as much money as they could ever make being a seamstress, or a scullery maid. God willing, they'll never again be tempted to sell their bodies to any louse-infested man with a drunken lust and a shilling in his pocket.'

'Most commendable, George,' said Beatrice, stepping away from him so that she wouldn't have to smell his breath.

'Come into my office,' said George. 'There's coffee, or tea, or cider if you prefer, and cakes. Perhaps little Florence would care for sweet lemonade.'

They all went through to George's office and sat down. One of the factory girls came in to pour out drinks, and passed round plates of biscuits and queen cakes scented with rosewater, and then George began to explain how he wanted to invest more money into St Mary Magdalene's so that they could take in even more girls – perhaps as many as a hundred at a time. Edward Veal explained that he had been in consultation with the leaseholders of the property next door in Maidenhead Court, and that they might soon be able to occupy that house too.

'I want us to be known as the greatest saviours of refractory young women in the whole of London's history,' said George, puffing at his cigar so that his head was almost invisible behind a cloud of curling smoke. 'I want scholars and clerics to look back in years to come and say that it was St Mary Magdalene's that changed the morality of this great city forever.'

'Hear, hear,' said Edward Veal, and sniffed.

'I want posterity to recognize that St Mary Magdalene's opened its arms to the lost and the destitute, to the used and abused, when others would only turn their backs,' George continued. 'I want future generations to know that we parted the dark clouds of sinfulness that hung over the heads of these misguided young women and shone down on them the pure dazzling light of Christianity. St Mary Magdalene's will have demonstrated that hard work, chastity and prayer bring far greater rewards both on Earth and in heaven than idleness, sluttishness and thieving.'

Edward Veal banged the desk in approval, and Ida said, 'You should have been an evangelist, George,' although her face remained expressionless.

'Well?' said George. 'What do you think?'

'No-noh needs a wee-wee,' said Florence, with her mouth full of cake.

George slapped his thigh, and laughed and coughed. 'Very well. Agnes! Agnes will show you how to get out into the garden, my dear. Agnes! Can you show this young lady how to get out of the back door?'

'I'll go with her, if you don't mind,' said Beatrice. 'I'm in need of a little fresh air.'

A very thin girl in a long apron and a floppy bonnet showed Beatrice and Florence to the back door, and they stepped out into the narrow grassy garden where the goat had been tied up. The goat's tether was still hanging from its post, frayed at the end.

After the eye-watering fog of George's office, the breeze outside was blissful, even if it was chilly enough to make Beatrice shiver. The trees were gossiping excitedly as the last few leaves of autumn were whipped off their branches, and in the near distance they could hear sheep bleating.

Beatrice held Florence's hand while No-noh ran up and down the garden, sniffing and cocking his leg.

'Judith said she was happy,' said Florence, sadly.

'Well, I know how much you miss her, Florrie, and I'm sure that she misses you, but so long as she's happy, that's the most important thing of all. If you want to, we can come here again in a week or so, and perhaps Mr Hazzard will allow Judith to come out for a walk with us.'

'I don't like Mr Hazzard. He's too smoky.'

'I know. But I think we'd better go back inside. He wants to take us somewhere for dinner.'

No-noh was scratching furiously in the middle of the garden. Beatrice thought at first that he might have done his business and was making a cursory attempt to cover it up, as dogs do, but then she saw that he was actually digging.

'No-noh! Come here, No-noh!' called Florence. But No-noh paid her no attention and kept on tearing at the turf.

'No-noh! I said come here, you naughty, *naughty* puppy!' said Florence, putting on her cross-mama voice. She stalked over and took hold of No-noh's collar, pulling him away. But then she bent down and picked something up from the grass. She came back and held it out in the palm of her hand so that Beatrice could see what it was.

A tarnished silver crucifix, on a broken chain. But this was no ordinary crucifix. The figure of Christ had his head turned to the left, instead of the right. Without a doubt, it was Jane Webb's crucifix.

Beatrice glanced quickly behind her to make sure that neither George nor Edward Veal was watching her out of the office window. Then she walked over to the torn-up spot where No-noh had been digging. He had dug only three or four inches down, but underneath the soil he had ripped through some tattered red cotton and exposed a muddy fan-shaped bone. She recognized immediately what it was. Her father used to have a skeleton hanging in his laboratory, and she could see that this was a human shoulder blade.

She bent forward, and sniffed. In spite of the chilly breeze, she was sure that she could detect the distinctive sweet smell of a decomposing body.

She gave another quick glance behind her. Edward Veal had his back to the window and George was leaning over his desk, and there was no sign of Ida. She kicked the lumps of turf that No-noh had dug up, so that the hole was covered up. Her heart was thumping hard against her ribcage and she felt that she could hardly breathe, but she knew that she had to stay composed.

'Let's go back in, shall we?' she said to Florence.

Florence said. 'All right. But who does that cross belong to?'

Beatrice crouched down and laid her hands on Florence's shoulders so that she could look her directly in the eyes.

'Florrie, this is important. You mustn't tell anybody that you found it. Don't tell Ida. Don't tell Mr Hazzard. Don't tell Mr Veal. There isn't any cross.'

'But there *is*! You've put it in your pocket.'

'I know. But that's our secret. You know what a secret is, don't you?'

Florence nodded. 'It's not telling.'

'Good. So you won't say anything about finding this cross, not to anybody?'

She pretended to sew up her lips with a needle and thread, and Florence dutifully copied her.

'Good girl, Florrie. You're my angel.'

They went back inside and George stood up from behind his desk, coughing and waving the smoke away.

'Has your pup relieved himself, little Florence? Excellent. Let's repair then, shall we, to London Fields, and the Cat and Shoulder of Mutton? They serve the most unctuous game pie that I've ever tasted, and I can heartily recommend their roasted pork, too.'

'I don't want pie,' said Florence, lifting her hand to her chin. 'I'm full right up to *here* with cake.'

George patted her on the head. 'You must eat as much as you can, little Florence. *Num-num-num!* Girls who eat all their dinner grow up to be buxom and healthy and beautiful, and attract all the wealthiest gentlemen!'

And then they end up beheaded, or dead and buried in your factory garden, thought Beatrice.

George grinned and extended his hand towards her to usher her out of his office, but she lifted her elbow and shied away from him. She was so filled with revulsion and fear that she could barely speak, let alone smile. She followed him with mechanical steps as he led the way out of the factory, knowing that she would have to endure the rest of this visit without giving him the slightest indication that she had found a buried body, and that in all likeliehood it was Jane Webb's. For all she knew, the six other girls were buried in the garden too.

She thought about the crucifix in her pocket and remembered what Jane had said about it. *'Jesus is lookin' to the left at all the thieves and the murderers and the merry-arsed Christians. Sheep to the right, goats to the left.'*

After she had climbed up and seated herself in the corner of George's yellow carriage, she turned her head to look out of the window so that she wouldn't have to endure him smiling and winking at her. Her throat was clenched tight and she could have sobbed out loud, remembering how pretty Jane had been, and thinking how her life had been so sinfully wasted.

'Yes, little Florence!' said George. He sat down opposite, so that the carriage's springs creaked and swayed, and then he reached across to squeeze Florence's knee. 'One day soon you're going to be a fair roebuck, believe me, and all the fine gentlemen will be knocking at your door!'

'There's time enough for that, George,' said Beatrice, still without looking at him.

'Maybe so,' said George. 'But time waits for no one, as well as you know.'

How true, thought Beatrice. *But if only you knew how quickly your time is rushing towards you, George Hazzard, you wouldn't be sounding half so merry.*

Because it was a sunny afternoon, the Cat and Shoulder of Mutton was packed, not only with farm workers and wagon-drivers and tinkers, but with lawyers and traders who had come up to London Fields to take a breather from the City and mingle with a rougher and more boisterous crowd than they found in their usual coffee houses.

George ushered them inside the tavern, to a small private room at the back, with a circular oak table and a stained-glass window and a log fire burning. Beatrice sat near to the door, as far away from George and his cigar smoke as she could, and asked only for a mug of cider and a thick slice of bread and Cheshire cheese.

'You'll have some pie, Beatrice!' George shouted at her, from the other side of the table. 'We can't have you dwindling away! You're too comely!'

He ordered a whole game pie, which was brought in after twenty minutes by a burly woman with a scarlet face beaded with perspiration, and forearms like hams. The pie was six inches deep and almost two feet in diameter, and freshly baked. After mopping her face with her upraised apron, the woman announced that underneath its decorated pastry crust the pie was filled with finely minced pork and veal, as well as fillets of chicken, pigeon, partridge, hare, pheasant, grey plovers and grouse, all flavoured with allspice and garlic and cockscombs, and filled up with a thick brown gravy of claret and anchovy and sweet herbs.

On any day before today, Beatrice would have loved a slice, but when George cut it open, she had to press her scented handkerchief over her nose and mouth to stop herself from retching. It smelled far too much like a decomposing human body.

George ordered not only pie, but oysters and sweetbreads and devilled kidneys, with side dishes of endive and salsify and leeks and parsnips and potatoes. Between them, he and Edward Veal ate so much that they barely spoke for nearly an hour. Occasionally they stopped pushing food into their mouths for long enough to take a swallow of wine, or to wipe their chins on the sleeves of their frock coats and their hands on their breeches, but most of the time they were completely absorbed in their eating, and their eyes were focused on nothing at all.

Ida ate greedily, too, tearing the sweetbreads apart with her long, chalky fingernails, although it seemed to Beatrice that she chewed every mouthful over a hundred times before she attempted to swallow it, and even when she did her gorge appeared to rise as if she were going to bring it all back up again.

Inside the crowded main room of the tavern, the singing and raucous laughter was deafening, and outside on Church Path, where most of the drovers and waggoners were gathered, Beatrice could hear shouting and whistling and also the squealing of pigs. The Cat and Shoulder of Mutton was a popular stop for pig-breeders bringing their stock down to Smithfield for slaughter. They could have a few beers and a pie before they went on to drive their herd down through the City streets and into the meat market.

George and Edward Veal and Ida had only just finished eating when Beatrice heard a high-pitched panicky screaming, and a great roar from the men assembled on the path.

'Ha, ha! We're in luck by the sound of it!' said George, slapping the table and rising to his feet. 'Come outside and see the fun!'

'What's going on?' asked Beatrice.

'Pig-swinging! Tremendous sport! And you can lay wagers if you want to.'

They left the table and went to join the circle of spectators who were standing on the grass opposite the tavern.

In the centre of the circle, two drovers were holding down a small struggling pig, while a third man was smearing its tail with butter. Another man was strutting around them – a short, barrel-chested man with curly grey hair tied back with a scarf, and a brown leather waistcoat. Every now and then he beat his chest with his fists and lifted up his arms like a challenging boxer, and every time he did so he was cheered.

'What are they doing with that piggy?' asked Florence.

'I'm not sure, Florrie, but I don't think the piggy likes it much, whatever it is.'

Once the pig's tail was well buttered, the barrel-chested man came over and gripped it with both hands. The pig squealed and kicked, but the two drovers held it still until the tavern's fat landlord stepped forward. He was wearing a wine-stained blue waistcoat with gilt buttons and a ratty white periwig tied with a ribbon.

'Usual rules!' the landlord bellowed, so that he could be heard above the crowd. 'Whosoever swings the pig the fastest, and can keep his grip for the longest, he shall be awarded the golden cap, and free ale for the rest of the day!'

There was another great roar, and then the two men released their hold and the barrel-chested man tilted himself backwards like a shot-putter and started to swing the pig around by its tail. He lifted it clear up into the air and swung it around and around, while the pig shrieked in a voice that was horribly human. After six or seven increasingly fast rotations, the man lost his grip on the pig's tail and it was flung, still screaming, into the crowd. It scrambled to its feet and tried to run towards the open fields, but the two drovers hurried after it and caught it.

'Next contestant!' shouted the landlord. 'But I reckon you'll be hard-pressed to beat that performance!'

Another man stepped forward, a skinny jarvis with a blue chin and a pointed nose and a tricorn hat, rolling up his sleeves as he came. As he did so, though, Beatrice stepped into the circle herself.

'Yes, mistress, how can I help you?' the landlord asked her. 'I'm afraid there's no prize for the fairer sex for pig-swinging, but you're welcome to try your luck!'

Beatrice said, 'Actually, I think that's enough cruelty for one day.'

The landlord bent forward and cupped his hand to his ear. 'I beg your pardon? Did I hear you aright?'

'You did, yes. You should stop this contest right now. I've kept pigs myself and I know how much pain and distress you're causing this poor beast, for nothing else except your own amusement. Isn't it enough that by tomorrow it'll have its throat slit and be cut up for chops?'

The landlord looked around, completely nonplussed. 'My dear lady, pigs have been swung here every week for more than a hundred years. And – up until today – not a single person except for yourself has expressed anything but sheer delight. Neither has a single pig lodged a complaint – either vocally, or in writing.'

Several of the spectators who had overheard their conversation burst out laughing.

Beatrice held her ground. 'Animals have no voice, sir,' she said. 'That's why sometimes we have to speak for them. In the name of God, I am pleading with you to call this contest off, and not to mock and mistreat this unfortunate beast any further.'

The landlord looked around again, as if he were seeking further support from the spectators, and when he spoke he was beginning to sound irritated. 'I appreciate your concern, mistress, and I admire you for being so cockish. However, pigs have no sentiments, and I believe that they were created not only for our dinner, but to amuse us, too. You're right – they do lack voices. But because they cannot speak they cannot pray, and that which cannot pray cannot reasonably expect God's protection.'

It was then that George came up behind Beatrice and took hold of her arm.

'Come along, Beatrice. You won't persuade these good people to give up their sport.'

Beatrice twisted her arm away from him, but after giving the landlord one last hard stare, she followed him back to where Ida was holding Florence's hand, and Edward Veal was sucking the last of the grease from his fingers.

'Perhaps we'd best be getting back to Maidenhead Court,' said Beatrice.

'Of course,' said George. 'But I have to confess that you've been fascinating company. If you were a man, Widow Scarlet, I have to admit that I would tread very softly whenever you came close.'

Beatrice gave him a long look that was half challenging and half curious. 'You're not *afraid* of me, Mr Hazzard?'

George turned around to make sure that nobody else was listening. Then he said, 'Attracted. Afraid. But there has never been a woman in my life who hasn't bent to my will, sooner or later.'

Behind her, Beatrice heard the pig screaming again as it was whirled around the jarvis's head.

'Let's leave before we have to witness any more of this,' she said, taking Florence's hand. 'I thank you for entertaining us today, George. In the end, it was more than I'd hoped for. Much more.'

36

They returned to Maidenhead Court around half past three. As soon as they had climbed down from the hansom, Beatrice told Ida that she had to go over to the Foundery. Three girls who shared a bedroom on the second floor had caught colds and chesty coughs, and she needed to collect some tincture of opium and purple coneflower to mix up some fresh physic for them.

'Very well,' said Ida. 'But please be back in time for this evening's prayers. It's the Feast of the Guardian Angels today, as well you know, and I think we need to give special thanks to the messengers of God who protect us, don't you? Especially since Satan has shown himself to be prowling so close.'

'I promise you that I won't be late,' Beatrice told her. 'I'll ask Hettie to take care of Florence for me.'

She was walking towards the kitchen to find Hettie when Ida called after her, 'You – you haven't *vexed* George in any way, have you?'

'Vexed him?' said Beatrice, turning around. 'What makes you say that?'

'Well, today he invited us to Hackney so that you and he could patch up your differences and be friends again. Yet I thought that you treated him very frostily.'

'It wasn't intentional, Ida, I can assure you.'

'Perhaps not. But you must remember that George is by far our most generous benefactor, and that we can't afford to put his back up. He would only have to withdraw his funding, and we would find it almost impossible to keep St Mary Magdalene's open.'

'I can't imagine that I gave him any reason to be offended,' said Beatrice. 'But I'm still mourning the loss of my husband, Ida, even after all this time, and George does have a way of being over-familiar.'

'You should try to accept his interest in you with good grace. Men can be devilishly worse than over-familiar.'

Beatrice hesitated. She had the feeling that Ida was about to tell her how badly she had been treated by some man in her life, but all she said was, 'You won't be late, will you? Prayers are at six.'

Beatrice reached the Foundery gates just as James's scruffy pupils came tumbling out of their classroom, laughing and shouting and scuffling with each other, so she had to wait at the door until the last one had left – a shy girl, painfully thin, who smiled at her. When she was able to step inside she found that the classroom was empty. She was worried for a moment that James had already left, so she walked quickly along the corridor that led to the apothecary, to see if Godfrey knew where he was.

She was only halfway along the corridor when James came out of the apothecary door, and said, '*Beatrice!*' and opened his arms to her in greeting. As handsome as he was, Beatrice thought he was looking a little waxy, like a sick poet, and his chin was prickly with dark stubble.

'Thank goodness,' she told him. 'I thought you might have gone.'

'No. But I've been suffering an infernal toothache all day, and Godfrey's given me some laudanum for it.'

'You should have asked me. My father devised a most effective cure for the toothache. He made it with pressed garlic and oil of cloves.'

'Not very conducive to kissing, I would have thought. But I didn't expect to see you today. This is not about Grace again, is it? I'm sure you're still fretting about her, but you have to consider your own safety first, and Florence's.'

'I know that,' said Beatrice. 'But today I've discovered something even more dreadful. I've discovered what happened to the seven girls who were supposed to have summoned up Satan – the coven. I believe that I have, anyhow.'

'What? How? My God, Beatrice, you're serious, aren't you?'

'George Hazzard invited us up to Hackney today. He was trying to convince me that he was not responsible for the girls' disappearance. But while we were there—'

'Beatrice, not here,' said James, looking behind him. 'Let me collect my books, and then we can go somewhere private to talk and you can tell me everything. I'm on my way back in your direction anyway, so perhaps we can find ourselves a quiet corner in the Salutation.'

Taking her arm, he led her back to the classroom. He picked up the two books that he had been using for his lessons that afternoon – *A Description of a Great Variety of Animals and Vegetables,* and *Divine Songs Attempted in Easy Language* – and stowed them into a leather hunting bag. Then he ushered her out and locked the door behind him.

'I don't trust those children one inch! If I left the door unlocked they would come back at night with their older siblings and steal all the furniture!'

They walked together down to Newgate Street, saying very little. The streets were unusually deserted, and the breeze was becoming colder and harsher, so that the signs outside the taverns and coffee houses all along the way started swinging and creaking. Beatrice noticed that several signs featured a woman's hand holding a coffee pot, which indicated to knowledgeable Londoners that there was more than coffee available inside.

They went into the smoky Salutation tavern and James led Beatrice past the bar and up the narrow stairs to a room overlooking the street, where women could sit. The only other person in the room was a tired-looking middle-aged woman with bedraggled silk flowers in her bonnet, staring at her empty port-wine glass as if she could mesmerize it into refilling itself.

'Now, tell me what you've discovered,' said James.

Beatrice waited for a moment while a freckly red-haired serving girl came up from the bar to ask them what they wanted to drink, and if they wanted food. James ordered a decanter of sweet white Malmsey for both of them.

After the serving girl had clattered back downstairs, Beatrice said, 'I've no absolute proof of this yet, James, but I believe that all the girls are probably dead, and that they're buried at the back of George Hazzard's factory.'

She took Jane Webb's left-facing crucifix out of her pocket and set it down on the table in front of him.

'So – what's this?' he asked her.

She told him how Florence had found the crucifix, and how No-noh had dug up what looked like the ragged remains of a red linen dress, and a human scapula.

James didn't interrupt her, and even when she had finished he sat back and thoughtfully scratched his stubbled neck and said nothing for almost half a minute.

At last he asked her, 'This Jane Webb girl – you're sure this crucifix is hers?'

'I don't have the shadow of a doubt.'

'So what are your proposing to do now?'

'To go to Bow Street, of course, to Sir John Fielding's justice house, and report it to one of his constables. He can send officers to Hackney to exhume the body – or *bodies*, if all seven of them have met the same fate.'

'My God, Beatrice, you're treading on very dangerous ground here. And what evidence do you have? Only this crucifix, which could have been anybody's, and your glimpse of a human bone – or what you thought was a human bone.'

'I know my anatomy, James. And have you *ever* seen a crucifix with Jesus looking to the left? Have you ever seen any painting or sculpture of the crucifixion with Jesus looking to the left?'

'Well, no, I can't say that I have. But George Hazzard will have only to deny that he knew that there was anybody buried in his factory garden, and what charges can be brought against him?'

'We'll just have to find somebody who's prepared to bear witness against him,' said Beatrice. 'He wouldn't have taken a spade himself and dug Jane's grave, would he? He must have assigned some of his factory workers to do it, or maybe he paid some casual navvies. And somebody must have carried her body to the grave and laid her in it.'

James shook his head. 'I don't know, Beatrice. Any witnesses will have been well bribed to keep their mouths shut, or else they'll be terrified to speak out against him. Don't underestimate what a powerful man he is, and what influential connections he has. He belongs to the same club as Sir Crisp Gascoyne, for goodness' sake.'

'I'm still going to go to Bow Street and tell them what I saw. I'm simply asking that you come with me, to give me moral support. They're far more likely to take me seriously if I have a man with me, especially a teacher like yourself.'

James remained silent while the serving girl brought up their wine. He poured himself a glass, but Beatrice laid her hand on top of her glass to show him that she didn't want any. She needed to have a clear head for what she intended to do. As a woman, it was going to be difficult enough to persuade the officers at Bow Street to investigate what had happened to the coven, without them smelling wine on her breath.

She could see that James was turning something over in his mind, something that was troubling him deeply. He was gnawing at his lip and staring at her with his amethyst-blue eyes, and his fingertips were drumming on the tabletop. She had the feeling that what he was thinking about could change his life forever.

When he still didn't speak, she leaned forward and said, very softly, 'Whether you agree to accompany me to Bow Street or not, James, I still intend to go. I owe it to Jane, and I owe it to Grace, and all of the other girls. They might have been prostitutes, but they were all God's children, and they deserve justice. So do those who so cruelly ended their lives.'

James swallowed some more wine and wiped his mouth with the back of his hand.

'I can't contain myself any longer, Beatrice. I've fallen in love with you. Not because you look so much like my poor lost Sophie, although I freely admit that was the reason I was first attracted to you.'

'James—'

'No, Beatrice – hear me out, please! I think about you constantly, day and night. I think about you when I wake up in the morning and I think about you when I retire to bed at night. I think about you even when I'm teaching. Every moment I spend with you only strengthens the spell that you are holding me under.'

He reached across the table and laid his hand on top of hers. 'It's not only your beauty, and your natural grace. It's your courage, and your determination, and your charity to others, and your Christian sense of fairness. By comparison, you make me feel weak and grubby and despicable.'

'James, don't say that about yourself! You've been caring and you've been solicitous, and you've given me very wise advice when I've been tempted to be rash.'

James shook his head again, much more vigorously this time. 'No, Beatrice. I've been cowardly. The truth is that I've known all along what George Hazzard does with the girls that he takes from St Mary Magdalene's. He says that he's taking them to work at his tobacco factory, but that's a barefaced lie.'

Beatrice slowly withdrew her hand from underneath his, like pulling off a glove. '*What?* You've *known* that they were going to be murdered?'

'No – no – not that! Great heavens, no! I've never had any inkling of that! But I've known that he picks out the prettiest girls and sends them to Leda Sheridan's brothel, and other brothels, too. They pay him a handsome finder's fee for every girl he sends them, and as far as I know, a percentage of their earnings until they're too old or raddled to earn any more.'

He took another drink, almost choked on it, and coughed.

'As you know, Beatrice, most of those girls at St Mary Magdalene's have been arrested in Chick Lane or Covent Garden or thereabouts for whoring or thieving. If the Reverend Parsons didn't regularly go the courts and speak out on their behalf, the magistrates would have sent them to the Clerkenwell House of Correction. Either that, or transported them, or have them hung. But the Reverend Parsons stands up for them and says that if St Mary Magdalene's Refuge is permitted to take them in, their sinful ways will be mended and they will be turned into shining models of Christian morality. I've attended court, and I've heard him say it. He's utterly convincing.'

'But does he know what's *really* going to happen to them? Does he know that they're going to be bathed and brushed up and taught manners, but then sold off to be better-class whores?'

'Dear Lord, Beatrice, I shouldn't be telling you any of this. You're in quite enough peril as it is. But if they're being murdered—'

'James, you're doing the right thing by telling me, believe me. If the Reverend Parsons knows about it, he can't be allowed to escape unpunished, any more than George Hazzard.'

James swallowed hard, and he was close to tears. He clenched his fists and said, 'He does know, yes. Of course he knows! So does Ida Smollett. But these girls bring in so much profit for the church, which finances their missionary work, and he considers their lives to be worthless. As far as the saintly Reverend Parsons is concerned, those girls became less than dirt from the moment they first sold their bodies for money. Do you know what he says? "A woman's virginity belongs to God, and only those husbands of whom God approves should be allowed to deflower them, because they are entering their bodies on God's behalf."'

'And Ida knows about this, too?'

'Oh, certainly. I would say that almost everybody in the church is aware of it, but the whole congregation shares the same belief – that these girls are irredeemable sinners. Once a girl has sold her purity – that's what they think – she can't buy it back. You can't put an eggshell together again once you've cracked it.'

Beatrice reached across and poured herself a small measure of Malmsey, and drank it. Then she said, 'What about you? Have you always known? And do you think the same, that God is never going to forgive them?'

'I never thought that, and I don't think that now. But I looked the other way, to be truthful with you, coward that I am. After my father lost all of his wealth during the Spanish War, it was George Hazzard who lent him sufficient funds to save him from bankruptcy and complete humiliation in society. My father still owes him a fortune, and I doubt if he'll ever be able to repay him before he dies. Not only that, it was George Hazzard who recommended that the Reverend Parsons take me on as the Foundery's teacher.'

'James, if your employment is going to be jeopardized, I can't ask you to come to Bow Street with me. I'll simply have to trust that Sir John Fielding's officers believe me.'

'No, Beatrice, I'll come – I *will* come,' James told her. 'I have to redeem myself somehow. How can I possibly hope that you might find it in your heart to return my affection if I allow you to go and report this crime alone? Very well – if the Reverend Parsons gets to hear that I've supported you, I might lose my teaching position at the Foundery; and if George Hazzard gets to hear of it, I might even be placing myself at considerable risk of my life. But how will I be able to face myself every morning in my looking glass if I show myself to be weaker than a young defenceless widow like yourself? If *you're* not frightened, then neither am I.'

'Ah, but I *am* frightened,' said Beatrice. 'It's just that I prayed last night, and asked God what I should do. And, do you know? – when the sun came up this morning it was reflected in the water of my washbasin, and it hovered like a halo on the ceiling above my head. I knew then that God was blessing my determination to seek justice for Grace. I also believe that when we went to Hackney, he used Florrie's dog No-noh to direct me to Jane Webb's remains. It was God, guiding me. It couldn't have happened by chance.

'No matter how fearful I am, James, the Lord has charged me with this mission, and I will do everything I can to fulfil it.'

At that moment, the middle-aged woman sitting opposite hiccuped, and made a smacking sound with her toothless gums, and then said, to nobody in particular, 'Welladay my poor heart! Welladay!'

37

Beatrice and James hailed a hackney to take them to Bow Street, but it was nearly a quarter to five by the time they arrived outside No. 4, which was a narrow-shouldered five-storey building with a peeling black-painted front door.

A rowdy crowd was gathered outside, mostly unshaven men in ragged coats and soiled breeches and ratty perukes, although there were one or two women as well, whose rouged cheeks and lurid red lips suggested to Beatrice that they were either actresses or prostitutes. They were singing and chanting '*Don't 'ang 'Arry! Don't 'ang 'Arry!*' and some of the men were so drunk that they were hanging on to the railings to keep themselves upright.

Beatrice weaved her way between them and mounted the steps, with James following closely behind her. Once inside, they were met in the hallway by a short swarthy doorman in a tightly buttoned-up navy-blue tunic. His forehead was low and the backs of his hands were hairy and Beatrice couldn't help thinking that he looked like a trained chimpanzee dressed up in uniform.

'Yes, your honour, how can I be of assistance?' he asked.

'I've come here to see a constable and report two crimes, and possibly more,' Beatrice told him.

'Begging your indulgence, ma'am, could you repeat that?' said the doorman. 'Sorry – it's that mob outside! Some fellow's up for burglary but it don't matter how much racket they make, he'll be dancing on nothing unless the Lord intervenes.'

'It's urgent that I speak to someone in authority,' Beatrice told him, raising her voice. 'I know of several murders of young women, and where their remains might be found.'

The doorman looked at James as if he were seeking reassurance that Beatrice wasn't cuckoo.

James said, 'This lady is a qualified apothecary, sir, and the widow of a church minister. I can assure you that what she has to report is not only genuine, but of the utmost gravity.'

'I see, sir,' said the doorman. 'If you will kindly give me your names, and then follow me through to the waiting room, I'll see who I can drum up for you.'

Beatrice and James waited for more than twenty minutes in the small stuffy waiting room. The fire had burned down to ashes, and it was growing increasingly chilly. The sombre portrait of Sir John Fielding on the wall did little to alleviate the gloom: he was paunchy and blind, with a black ribbon tied around his forehead, underneath his wig, and his expression was grim.

'You know what they say about him, don't you?' said James. 'He may be blind, but he can identify three hundred different criminals by their voices alone.'

'He looks exactly how I feel,' said Beatrice. 'Miserable and confused, and completely in the dark.'

'My dearest, you mustn't despair,' said James. 'You've been brave enough to come so far, and I believe that you're right, and that this is what God intends you to do. I'm convinced that you'll soon see the light. It's happened to me today, Beatrice. Because of you, I've seen myself for what I am, a craven coward, and I'm determined to redeem myself. This morning I was Saul. Now I'm Paul.'

They waited a further ten minutes, and then the door opened and a clerk came in, with a quill behind his ear. 'Mr Treadgold? Widow Scarlet? The constable will see you now.'

They followed him into an office at the back of the building. Sitting behind a cluttered desk was a thin, beaky-nosed young man in an olive-green frock coat. He stood up when Beatrice and James came in, and inclined his head, although he didn't hold out his hand. The room was stuffy and hot and smelled strongly of Royal Essence, a perfume made from musk, civet, clove and cinnamon, although it did little to mask the underlying odour of tobacco and stale perspiration.

'Please, take a seat,' said the beaky-nosed young man. 'Jonas Rook is my name. I understand that you have some felony to report.'

'Murder,' Beatrice told him, but as she said that she suddenly had a picture in her mind's eye of Grace's expression as her throat was sliced open, and she had to stop for a moment and take several deep breaths.

Jonas Rook had been idly leafing through some papers on his desk but now he looked up at her with one eyebrow raised. The clerk was sitting in the corner with his quill poised to take down whatever Beatrice said, and he stared across at her too.

'More than one murder,' said Beatrice. 'Two at the very least, and possibly as many as eight.'

'Go on,' said Jonas Rook. He didn't sound at all shocked, but he kept his eyes on her now, and didn't look down at his papers again. The clerk dipped his quill in his inkwell again, to freshen it, and licked his lips.

Beatrice started by telling Jonas Rook how George Hazzard had come to St Mary Magdalene's, and how he had selected the seven prettiest girls to work in his tobacco factory. Then she told him how the girls had disappeared, and how George had claimed that they had summoned Satan, who had given them the power to be witches, and fly away.

'And what evidence did he have for this?' asked Jonas Rook.

'A pentagram, painted on the wall, and the body of a goat, which he claimed the girls had sacrificed. I saw these for myself.'

'But what caused you to doubt that these girls had actually succeeded in raising the Devil?'

Beatrice explained how she had analysed the 'blood' that had been used to paint the pentagram. Then she told him about the goat's head appearing on the dinner table in front of her, and how she had taken a sample of its beard, and analysed that, too.

She went on to tell him about the man with the looking-glass face, and the claw marks in her door, which had exactly matched the three-pronged grappling hook that she had picked up on New Queen Street, down by the river.

James reached across and laid his hand on her arm, because she hadn't told him about the grappling hook, but he didn't try to interrupt her.

In the plainest words that she could, and omitting none of the graphic details, Beatrice described the sexual revelry at Leda Sheridan's brothel, and how Grace had been beheaded. Finally, she produced Jane Webb's crucifix, and leaned forward to place it on top of Jonas Rook's papers, and explained what she had discovered this afternoon in George Hazzard's factory garden.

'A *human* shoulder-bone?' said Jonas Rook. 'You're quite sure about that?'

Beatrice nodded. 'And red dress material, too. And I could smell putrid human flesh. I've no doubt at all that there's a body buried there.'

Jonas Rook sucked in his cheeks. He turned to his clerk, who was still frantically scribbling down Beatrice's description of the hooded executioner who had murdered Grace.

'"Nim gimmer", did you say?' asked his clerk. 'Is that what they were shouting?'

Beatrice nodded. 'They knew what was going to be done to her. That's what they had paid good money for. I have no idea what Mrs Sheridan had charged them to see Grace being violated and murdered, but I imagine it was quite a sizeable sum.'

Jonas Rook picked up the crucifix and turned it around and around between his fingers. 'I had occasion to caution Mrs Sheridan myself last year. One of her clients was complaining that a moidore had been stolen from his fob, and Mrs Sheridan's bullies beat him so hard that they took out his eye. If I remember rightly she was asking fifty guineas to witness a young country girl having her virginity taken by two men at once. I can only guess that she must have charged at least a hundred guineas a head to see your poor blackamoor being despoiled and dispatched.'

Beatrice said, 'You believe me?'

Jonas Rook sat back in his chair and laced his fingers together. 'Yes, Widow Scarlet, I believe you. In fact I've been waiting for a long time for a credible witness such as yourself to come here to Bow Street and report on Mr George Hazzard's activities. It would not be appropriate for me to tell you of all the accusations that have been made against him, but apart from his involvement in prostitution, we've received intelligence about extortion and bribery and evasion of the import tax on tobacco.'

'So what will you do now?' asked James.

Jonas Rook looked up at the clock on the wall above his clerk's head, and said, 'It's dark now, and plainly too late to do anything today. But I'll present your evidence betimes tomorrow to Sir John. If he agrees, I'll arrange for the necessary warrant and organize a party to disinter the remains of these young women – always supposing that they're buried where you believe them to be.'

He stood up, and Beatrice stood up, too.

'Thank you for your courage in coming forward, Widow Scarlet,' he said, and bowed his head again. 'If only more Londoners were as brave as you. But I have to warn you that Mr Hazzard will do anything to discredit you, and may even threaten you with injury or worse. I agree with you that those so-called satanic threats that you received could well have been his doing, and if he was prepared to go to such extraordinary lengths to warn you off, he may try to silence you with even greater finality.'

James was still seated. He said, very quietly, 'It *was* him. It was George Hazzard. At least one incident was, that I know of.'

'Really?' asked Jonas Rook. 'And which incident was that?'

'The man at Ranelagh Gardens with the looking-glass face.'

Beatrice said, 'James! You *knew* about that?'

James nodded. 'I'm ashamed to say that I did. But I sincerely thought that if you were cautioned to stay out of Mr Hazzard's business, it would be safer for you. I had no idea then that those seven girls might be dead. I *did* know, though, that Mr Hazzard is not a man to be trifled with. Three of his employees who tried to make off with a hogshead of his tobacco were found drowned in the Lea with their eyes put out and their legs broken, and other people who have tried to cross him have come to a very sorry end.'

'You *knew* about that man, even on the very morning you took us there?'

'Yes, Beatrice, I did. I admit it. The thing of it was, I told the Reverend Parsons the day before that I was intending to take you to Ranelagh Gardens. I told him in all innocence, believe me, because I was so pleased and excited about it. But the Reverend Parsons dined that day with Mr Hazzard, and must have told him, too. Later that afternoon he came back to say that we would be followed there, and that you would be approached by a man who wouldn't hurt you in any way, but whose appearance would alarm you sufficiently to deter you from prying into his affairs any further. Those were almost his exact words.'

Beatrice couldn't think what to say. She turned to Jonas Rook but all Jonas Rook could do was shrug, as if to indicate that there was nothing he could do, and this was a matter that Beatrice and James would have to resolve between them.

'I'll send word to you at St Mary Magdalene's in the morning,' he said. 'I'll also let you know what we succeed in digging up at Mr Hazzard's factory, if anything.'

'I'm still praying that I'm wrong,' said Beatrice. 'I would far rather those girls were alive and working in a brothel than dead and buried in that garden.'

'Well, amen to that,' said Jonas Rook. James said nothing.

They hailed a hackney and returned to Maidenhead Court. They didn't speak until they were passing St Paul's.

James said, 'I suppose that you find it impossible to forgive me.'

'You could have told me earlier, couldn't you, when you were having your Damascene moment in the Salutation?'

'Yes, I could, and I should. I feel utterly wretched.'

'I'll send you a message tomorrow to let you know what Constable Rook has decided to do, and later, if he finds any bodies,' said Beatrice. 'But you need to heed his warning as much as I do, James. If George Hazzard finds out that you've helped me to give evidence against him, your life will be in jeopardy, too. I've seen him run a man through with his sword, right in front of me.'

'I'm not teaching tomorrow. I could come around to see you.'

'No, James. I'd rather you didn't. I need time to think about our friendship, and so do you. I know you believe that you love me, but there's more to love than romance and physical attraction. There's absolute honesty, too. "A man of words but not of deeds"? I was badly frightened by that man with the looking-glass face, and what's worse, you *knew* that I would be. What else haven't you told me?'

'There's nothing else, Beatrice. I've told you everything now. If only you knew how mortified I feel.'

They turned into Maidenhead Court and the jarvis helped Beatrice to step down.

'Beatrice—' said James.

'Don't say it,' Beatrice told him. Then, much more quietly, 'Please don't say it.'

38

Beatrice was nearly half an hour late for the Feast of the Guardian Angels prayer service. She had missed everything except for an off-key rendition of 'Come, and Let Us Sweetly Join', sung line by line because so few of the girls could read; and then some quotations by Ida from Basil the Great.

'All the angels have likewise among themselves the same nature, even though some of them are set over nations, while others of them are guardians to each one of the faithful.'

After the service, as Beatrice was about to take Florence upstairs to bed, Ida came up to her and said, 'I'm very disappointed, Beatrice. You promised that you would be back here on time.'

'I apologize,' said Beatrice. 'Godfrey didn't have any purple coneflower so we had to send out for it.'

Ida stared at her hard as if she weren't sure that she believed her; but now that Beatrice knew that she was complicit in sending her girls off to work in Drury Lane brothels, and not in George Hazzard's tobacco factory, she found that it was much easier to lie to her.

'There's cold beef for supper, and stuffed tomatoes, and barley soup,' said Ida, still staring at her, and even though she was simply reciting tonight's menu, she made it sound as if it were some kind of indictment.

'I haven't much of an appetite, to be truthful,' said Beatrice. 'I'm going to tuck Florrie up, and then I'll probably retire to bed myself.'

'It's likely that some new girls will be arriving here the day after tomorrow,' said Ida. 'The Reverend Parsons has told me that five of them at least will be up in front of the Old Bailey, all from Black Boy Alley, charged with lewdness and petty theft. He'll be attending in person to speak up on their behalf.'

More grist for the reverend's financial mill, thought Beatrice, as Florence hopped upstairs in front of her.

She felt a sense of relief when they reached their rooms and she locked the door behind her. It occurred to her, though, that she and Florence may not be able to stay here at Maidenhead Court for much longer. It would depend on what Constable Rook discovered in George Hazzard's garden. Next time, it might not only be her door that was torn with a grappling hook. The trouble was, where she could go?

She remembered some old friends of her father's from the Worshipful Society of Apothecaries, one of whom had lived in Clerkenwell and another out by Lamb's Conduit Fields, but she hadn't seen them since her father's funeral, and she didn't know if they were still at the same addresses, or even if they were still alive. The only relative she knew was her Cousin Sarah in Birmingham, but she wasn't at all sure if she and Florence could expect to be welcomed if they turned up there.

She had another problem: the church had not yet paid her for the time she had spent helping at St Mary Magdalene's. She had less than thirty pounds left, although she still had a silver-and-topaz ring and two gold necklaces that she could pawn.

She undressed, and washed herself, and put on her nightgown, but she found it impossible to sleep. She couldn't stop thinking about James and the way that he had deceived her about the man with the looking-glass face. Was his contrition genuine, or would he go to George Hazzard and warn him that she had reported him to Bow Street, in order to save his own skin? It gave her a cold empty feeling that she could trust nobody now, and that she had nobody in whom she could safely confide, except perhaps for Jonas Rook. It was like floating in space, in darkness, where it was useless to cry out for help, because nobody would hear her.

'There's a letter for you,' said Hettie, coming into the kitchen. 'The boy's still waiting outside for his penny.'

Beatrice was holding a thick slice of brown bread in front of the fire to toast it. She put down the toasting fork and reached into her pocket. 'Here,' she said. 'Three farthings, that's the only change I have.'

Hettie went to pay the boy and Beatrice sat down at the table to break the red wax seal on her letter. Martha the cook was standing close behind her, so she tilted the letter at an angle so that she wouldn't be able to see who had sent it.

Dear Widow Scarlet, further to yr visit to Bow Street yesterday, I have this morning recounted yr evidence to Sir J. Fielding. He has agreed to issue a general warrant and I am now assembling a party of law officers and labourers to proceed with the excavation of the garden at the Hazzard Tobacco Factory in Hackney. Should we exhume any human remains we will transport them to the mortuary St Bart's for a surgeon to assess the cause of death. Yr obdt servant Jonas Rook, Constable.

'Bad news?' asked Martha, as Beatrice folded the letter and tucked it into the top of her bodice.

'For some, perhaps,' said Beatrice.

She had promised James that she would send him a message when Jonas Rook was ready to start his exhumation, but now she decided against it. She had no way of telling for certain if there was any risk of him alerting George Hazzard, and she felt slightly ashamed of herself for not trusting him. In spite of that, she thought that there was more chance of justice being done if Jonas Rook's arrival at the tobacco factory came as a complete surprise, and George Hazzard had no time to dig up and hide any bodies that might be buried there, or think up some plausible explanation for why they were there.

The day seemed to pass with glutinous slowness. Every time Beatrice looked at the clock the minute hand barely seemed to have moved. She gave a crochet lesson to twelve of the girls, and then read them verses from the Bible about prostitution.

'A foolish woman is clamorous: she is simple, and knoweth nothing. For she sitteth at the door of her house, on a seat in the high places of the city, to call passengers who go right on their ways. Whoso is simple, let him turn in hither: and as for him that wanteth understanding, she saith to him, "Stolen waters are sweet, and bread eaten in secret is pleasant." But he knoweth not that the dead are there; and that her guests are in the depths of hell.'

A girl called Rebecca put up her hand and said, 'Fair do's, Mrs Scarlet, you shouldn't prig water, but what's wrong with eating bread in secret?'

Beatrice couldn't help smiling. 'It doesn't really mean eating bread. It means having secret sexual congress with somebody you shouldn't, such as a prostitute.'

'And that's what they say in the Bible? If that's what they meant, why didn't they fucking say so? "Eating bread in secret" – my arse.'

Beatrice was about to answer when Hettie came into the atelier, with another letter. She said, 'A coachman brung it. He said he was instructed to make sure you read it, and to wait for you.'

Beatrice opened it and it was another letter from Jonas Rook. As she read it, her hands began to tremble, and she tasted bile in her mouth.

Dear Widow Scarlet, I regret to inform you that your surmise was correct, and that we have uncovered the remains of seven females. I have sent conveyance for you, and I ask that you come to Hackney as quickly as you may, in order to identify them. Please inform no one at St Mary Magdalene that you are coming here, and more especially the purpose of your visit. Your obdt servant, J. Rook.

Beatrice stood up. 'Something wrong, Mrs Scarlet?' asked Rebecca. 'I'm ever so sorry, I didn't mean to curse like that. It just kind of slipped out.'

'No, don't worry about that, Rebecca. I've been given some very shocking news and I have to go at once. Please, carry on with your crochet and try to be well-behaved for Mrs Smollett. Hettie – can I prevail upon you again to take care of Florrie for me? I may have to be away for three or four hours, perhaps more.'

'Oh, I don't mind at all, Mrs S. I love looking after 'er. She's a little darlin'.'

Beatrice put on her cape and bonnet and then she went into the drawing room, where Ida was sitting at her desk, writing in her accounts book.

'You're going *out*?' asked Ida, sharply. 'What about this afternoon's reading class?'

'I'm afraid that I've something much more pressing to attend to.'

'Oh, really? Such as what, exactly?'

'I'll tell you when I return.'

'No,' said Ida, dropping her quill and standing up. 'I think you had best tell me now. In recent days you've been absent from your duties here again and again, on various flimsy pretexts. Do I have to remind you that you were given this position here as an act of charity to sustain you in your widowhood? The church could have evicted you from your home in America and left you abandoned and penniless, but we cared for you with due Christian consideration. The least you could do is show some appreciation.'

'Ida – don't think that I'm not grateful. But I'm not at liberty to tell you where I'm going or why.'

'Oh? Who says that you are not at liberty to tell me?'

'I regret that I can't tell you that, either, not yet.'

'Well, I'm… I'm… I'm utterly confounded! I've never heard of such behaviour. You appear to think that you can come and go as you please, regardless of your obligations.'

'Ida, I beg you not be vexed. I would never normally dream of letting you down like this, but this is a matter of the greatest importance.'

Ida came up close to her, sucking her teeth and flaring her nostrils. 'This is not concerned with that coven of witches, is it?'

'I can't say, Ida, and I really have to go. There's a carriage waiting for me outside the door.'

'It is, isn't it? It's that coven of witches! You claim to be a Christian, and yet you deny the reality of Satan! How can we battle against the forces of darkness if you refuse to believe in their prince?'

'I believe in him, Ida, but I also believe that he can appear in many different guises.'

'And what is *that* supposed to mean, pray?'

'It means I have to leave. Hettie is taking care of Florrie for me. I'll be back as soon as I possibly can.'

'Very well. But when you return, Beatrice, we will have to have a serious conversation about your future here.'

'Yes, Ida. I'm sure that we will.'

39

When her hansom drew up outside the tobacco factory, Beatrice saw that there were seven or eight more carriages and wagons lined up under the poplar trees outside, and a crowd of factory workers milling around or sitting on the grass, most of them smoking.

As she was helped down by the coachman, Jonas Rook came striding out of the factory yard to meet her, wearing a long black frock coat and a large black tricorn hat, so that he looked more like a mortician than a constable. His expression was grim.

'Thank you for coming so promptly, Widow Scarlet,' he told her. 'I'm grieved to have brought you here on such a ghastly errand, but it's vital that we identify the remains of these poor girls as soon as we can.'

He crooked his elbow, and she took his arm, so that he could lead her through the crowd. She looked around quickly to see if Judith was among them, but there was no sign of her, nor of any of the other five girls whom George Hazzard had taken only two days ago. She hoped that they were still inside the factory somewhere, or had been told to return to their dormitory.

They walked through the factory. It was deserted and silent except for the hissing of the steam boilers. The door to George Hazzard's office was closed, and a grey-haired, moustachioed constable was standing guard outside it with his arms folded and his bottom lip stuck out as if to show that he wasn't going to tolerate any nonsense.

'Mr Hazzard's here?' asked Beatrice.

'Oh, yes,' said Jonas Rook. 'And not in the best of tempers, I can tell you. He tried to deny us access when we first arrived, but of course we have a general warrant. He's already sworn to sue us for defamation and loss of profit. Oh yes, and cursed us to everlasting doom.'

They stepped out into the garden. Half a dozen labourers with spades were standing around, and as many law officers, including Hackney parish constables. John Bellflower was there, too, George Hazzard's lawyer, sitting on the low brick wall like Humpty Dumpty.

The turf had been lifted in the centre of the lawn, exposing a trench that was less than a foot deep but three yards wide and nearly eight yards long. Lying side by side in the trench were the bodies of the seven girls – three of them wearing dresses and petticoats, two of them wearing nothing but corsets and stockings, and the remaining two naked. Four were lying face up, one on her side, and the others face down. It was clear that they had been buried in a hurry. Once they had been laid down in the trench, soil had been loosely shovelled all over them and then the turf laid roughly on top.

'Dear God in heaven,' said Beatrice. She had slaughtered and disembowelled and butchered her own pigs in Sutton, and often visited the local abattoir while cattle were being bled to death. She had seen men and women hung and a man who was partially dissolved in acid, but she had never seen anything as grotesque as the bodies of these seven dead girls. 'Dear God, I hope they didn't suffer.'

All seven corpses were grossly swollen, and their skin was as grey and shiny as slugs. Their eyes had sunk into their skulls and their teeth were bared in hideous grins. The bellies of the two girls wearing corsets had burst open so that their pale-green intestines had coiled out between their thighs like thick tubes of pasta. Even on this cold breezy day, Beatrice could smell the rotting-chicken stench of death with every breath that she took in.

She clutched Jonas Rook's elbow again, if only for a moment, just to steady herself.

'Are you sure that you have the strength to do this, Widow Scarlet?' he asked her. 'If it's too much for you, please tell me.'

'No,' she said, clearing her throat. 'I have to. I have to – for them.'

She let go of his elbow and stepped forward, taking out her handkerchief to hold up to her face. The girls' bones had pierced through their skin in several places – their hips and their ribcages and their kneecaps – and as Beatrice approached the trench she could see the body in the red gown that she had first discovered, face down, with its shoulder blade still sticking out. She recognised the gown, and of course this was where Florence had picked up Jane Webb's crucifix.

One of the constables rolled the body to one side so that Beatrice could see her face – and in all its blind and grimacing horror, it was Jane.

She walked slowly along the side of the trench. Although they were so badly decomposed, she could put names to four of the girls, and she could remember the faces of the other three, even though she had never known their names.

The constables and the labourers watched her in solemn silence. When she reached the end of the trench and pressed her hands together in prayer, they took off their hats and caps to show their respect.

'You know them?' asked Jonas Rook, who had been following close behind her.

Beatrice nodded. 'Yes. All seven of them. Mr Hazzard's

coven of witches. Witches! They didn't manage to fly very far, did they, poor girls? Poor, wretched girls.'

John Bellflower had climbed off the wall and had been hovering close by, and now he came up to her, briskly rubbing his hands together. 'You remember me, ma'am. John Bellfower. Mr Hazzard's lawyer.'

'Widow Scarlet has nothing to say to you, Mr Bellflower,' said Jonas Rook, stepping in front of him.

But John Bellflower persisted. 'Did I hear aright, that this lady has identified these bodies, and that these are the very same girls who summoned Satan?'

'You will have to wait until this case comes to court,' Jonas Rook told him.

'Case? What case?'

'The case against your client Mr George Hazzard for manslaughter.'

'*What?* Manslaughter? And who will bring such a case?'

'Widow Scarlet, of course, with Mr Fielding's full support.'

'That's preposterous! Mr Hazzard had nothing whatsoever to do with these young women meeting their maker!'

'Oh, no? Then who did?'

'Where's your proof, constable?' John Bellflower blustered. 'Where's your substantive evidence? Why, he's a respectable man of business, Mr Hazzard! He's a highly regarded member of the Worshipful Company of Tobacco Pipe Makers and Tobacco Blenders, and a selfless donor to countless needy charities. A paragon of virtue! Why, some regard him quite rightly as a living saint!'

He paused for breath, and waved his hand towards the seven bodies lying in the trench.

'I grant you that the death of these unhappy young women is terrible beyond belief, but I assure you that Mr Hazzard is just as appalled by their discovery as I am. Yet let's be realistic, constable, look at the condition of these bodies. This can't be the doing of any man. This must the work of Satan himself!'

'You don't really believe that, Mr Bellflower,' said Jonas Rook. 'Neither for a single moment do I. As for evidence, well, you shall hear it if and when we lay it before a judge and jury at the Old Bailey.'

John Bellflower turned to Beatrice. 'I cannot imagine what your motivation is for persecuting Mr Hazzard in this way, madam,' he protested, spitting as he spoke. 'You may take it from me, though, that you will suffer the consequences. Oh, yes!'

'Now then, sir!' said Jonas Rook. 'I advise you not to threaten Widow Scarlet. My general warrant gives me the power not only to detain Mr Hazzard, but to arrest you, too, as an accessory, and anybody else who seeks to obstruct this inquiry.'

Beatrice said, 'I wish to speak to Mr Hazzard. Is that possible?'

'You wish to speak to him *now*?' asked Jonas Rook. He seemed to be surprised by her sudden calmness.

'Yes, if possible. I have at least two questions I wish to ask him.'

'I doubt very much that he'll agree to see you, madam,' said John Bellflower.

'He's in no position to disagree,' said Jonas Rook. 'If you really wish to speak to him, Widow Scarlet, come with me.'

'I protest!' said John Bellflower. 'I protest in the strongest possible terms! I shall advise him not to reply to you, no matter what questions you put.'

Jonas Rook laid his hand on John Bellflower's shoulder and leaned close to his ear. 'Shut your bone box, Mr Bellflower,' he said, so quietly that nobody else but Beatrice could hear him.

John Bellflower let out an explosive *pfff!* with his lips, and flapped one hand dismissively, like a fat Covent Garden Molly, but it was clear that he didn't dare to answer back.

They went back into the factory, and the constable guarding the door of George Hazzard's office stood aside while Jonas Rook knocked and then entered without waiting for George Hazzard to reply.

George was standing behind his desk, smoking the stub of a cigar. His cheeks looked rougher and redder than usual and his eyes were bulging and Beatrice didn't think she had ever seen a man look so comically furious. His accountant, Edward Veal, was sitting opposite him, blowing his nose noisily into his handkerchief.

'What now?' George demanded. 'And what in the name of God is *she* doing here?'

'Widow Scarlet has carried out the valuable service of identifying the deceased for us,' said Jonas Rook. 'Following her identification, Mr Hazzard, and on the basis of certain evidence that she has submitted to the justice office, I may require you to accompany me to Bow Street in a day or two for further questioning. It will depend on what the surgeon has to say about the way in which these unfortunate young women met their end.'

'She has evidence? What tosh! The woman's distracted!'

'Well, sir, that will be for a judge and jury to decide, should the case go before the court.'

George puffed the last quarter-inch of his cigar, and then angrily stubbed it out. He glared at Beatrice as if he were quite prepared to come stalking across his office and slap her, hard.

Jonas Rook said, 'Widow Scarlet has some questions she would like to put to you, if you have no objection, or even if you do.'

'Questions? Questions? This is a woman who can't even see men swinging a pig without sticking her inquisitive nose in!'

Beatrice stepped up close to his desk. 'George, please. It's about those girls you last recruited from St Mary Magdalene's. I'm simply curious to know where they are now. I was hoping I might be able to talk to them today, and offer them some consolation. All of them knew the deceased girls well, and two or three of them were very close. To see their friends' bodies in such a condition must have distressed them dreadfully. Yet I haven't seen a single one of them anywhere.'

George narrowed his eyes, and then looked across at Edward Veal, who was still mopping his nose. Edward Veal shrugged, as if to suggest that he couldn't help.

'Actually, sir, I would be interested to hear your answer to that myself,' said Jonas Rook.

George was silent for a few moments, but then he suddenly barked out, 'If it's any of your business, which it manifestly *isn't*, I suffered them all to take a day's holiday. They haven't even seen the bodies, and of course they won't. By the time they return, you'll have toted them all off to the mortuary, and thank the Lord for that.'

'You gave them a day's holiday?' asked Beatrice. 'Why? They haven't even been working for you a full week yet. It's not a public holiday today, is it?'

'The reason is… listen… the reason is that we'd intended to carry out some routine maintenance work in the factory today. The fire pans and the chopping machines both require attention. That meant we didn't need so many girls stripping leaves. It's – it's the last week of Southwark Fair, so I arranged for them to go down early and spend the day there. I even gave them a shilling each – didn't I, Edward? – to spend however they wished. Am I to be under suspicion for being such a benevolent employer?'

'You sent them down to Southwark Fair?' asked Beatrice. 'But only those five girls? Aren't the rest of your employees a little disgruntled?'

'Not at all, because they've already had treats enough aplenty,' George snapped back. 'I grant them a free day in September each year to go to the Bartlemy Fair, and I always reward them at least a penny an hour if they put in extra hours.'

'But they'll be coming back here this evening, those girls?'

'I don't have to answer that, Beatrice. You're offending me deeply with all these vindictive questions. You can't deny that I went to extraordinary lengths to mollify you after our earlier *contretemps*. Is this how you repay me?'

'George,' said Beatrice. Her bodice was beginning to feel tight now, and her voice sounded high and breathy. 'How is it possible that those poor dead girls were buried in your garden, in full view of your office window, without you being aware of it?'

'I don't have to answer that, either,' said George. 'I've had more than enough of this now. I am innocent of any wrongdoing, and I take the gravest exception to your suggestion that I had anything whatsoever to do with the deaths of these young women. I took them in. I gave them employment, and accommodation, and what did they do in return? They defaced their dormitory wall with satanic symbols, and sacrificed my goat, and now they have falsely implicated me in their own apparent suicide.'

'*Suicide?*' said Beatrice. 'How can you possibly say that they committed suicide?'

George was about to snap back at her when Jonas Rook gently laid his hand on Beatrice's shoulder. 'These are questions for Mr Fielding and myself to ask Mr Hazzard at Bow Street, Widow Scarlet, and all in the fullness of time. Let us leave him for now. I don't want him accusing us of harassment, or of obtaining any admissions under duress. As I said, there is little we can do until the surgeon has had the chance to carry out his post-mortems.'

'You'll get no admissions,' George growled at him. 'Damn your admissions, that's what I say! Damn and double damn your admissions!'

Jonas Rook led Beatrice out of George's office and they walked together back through the empty factory.

'Do you believe that he sent those girls off to Southwark Fair?' asked Beatrice.

'We'll have to have patience,' said Jonas Rook. 'If they return here safely this evening, then we shall know that he was telling us the truth. But I shall ask the Hackney watch to come here tonight to make certain.'

'I don't think George Hazzard would know the truth if it seized him around the neck and hit his head against the wall of St Paul's.'

Jonas Rook led her across to her carriage, which was waiting for her in the factory yard. The crowd of workers was still hanging around, not knowing if they should stay or call it a day and go off to the tavern for a few pints of porter. She caught sight of the man with the leathery apron and the leathery face and he lifted his hand to acknowledge her.

'I'll send word to you later,' said Jonas Rook, as he helped Beatrice to climb up into her seat. 'I doubt if it will be for some days, but you can be assured that I will keep you apprised of every development.'

Beatrice was beginning to like him. He had hawklike features, like a man who worked too hard and forgot to eat regular meals, but he was attractive in a lean and predatory way. She was impressed most of all by his threatening smoothness. She guessed that he could be quick to take dramatic legal action against anybody who crossed him, but mostly he chose to remain courteous and almost eerily calm. She was captivated by his eyes, too. They were silvery grey, and gleaming, like penny coins that the King's head had worn off.

She was reassured by his agreement that in testifying against George Hazzard she was doing what God wanted her to do. In spite of that, she couldn't help feeling a sickly anxiety in the pit of her stomach as the hansom jolted its way back to Maidenhead Court. It began to thunder when they reached Moorfields, and the chestnut trees that lined the road started to thrash around as if they were panicking, and were trying to uproot themselves and run away. She couldn't help taking that as an omen that her life was going to become even more dangerous in the days ahead.

40

Although Ida had promised her that they would need to have a serious conversation about her future at St Mary Magdalene's, she was closeted in her own bedroom when Beatrice returned from Hackney, and she remained there for the rest of the day. She failed to appear even for supper.

'She's says she's got a monstrous pain in the noddle,' said Hettie, when Beatrice asked her where she was. 'Worse than bein' 'it between the eyes with a ball-peen 'ammer, that's what she told me. I 'ad to take 'er plain-work class for 'er, and I can 'ardly thread a blinkin' needle, me.'

'Well, I'm sorry to hear she's not well,' said Beatrice, although she felt more frustrated than sympathetic. She had been rehearsing all the way back how to tell Ida that she had identified the bodies of the seven dead girls, and that she had no doubt whatsoever that neither Satan nor any of his demons had played any part in killing them. Of course she didn't yet know how they had died, but she was quite sure that they had been murdered by men – either by George Hazzard himself, or by others at George Hazzard's behest.

Late in the afternoon, as it grew dark outside, she took a candlelit reading class herself, with seventeen girls. She asked each of them in turn to recite a chapter from John: 'Ye are of your father, the Devil, and the lusts of your father ye will do.

He was a murderer from the beginning, and abode not in the truth, because there is no truth in him. When he speaketh a lie, he speaketh of his own: for he is a liar, and the father of it.'

The girls had no idea why Beatrice had chosen this particular quotation, and most of them didn't understand what it meant, but it condemned not only murder but lying about murder, and it made her feel even more strongly that her action against George Hazzard was vindicated by the Bible.

She ate an early supper with Florence in the kitchen – cold beef and mustard pickles, with an apple cream for dessert. She forced herself to finish her plateful, even though she kept visualizing the grey, puffed-up bodies that she had seen in the tobacco factory garden, and she found it hard to swallow. *But if I allow myself to become weak and faint, I will be of little use to Florence, nor to Jonas Rook, nor to God.*

After she had tucked Florence into bed and sung her a lullaby, she stayed up and wrote in her diary. Then she sat watching the stars appear and disappear as the night wind blew the clouds over St Paul's. She thought about Francis, and what he might have done if he had been faced with a man like George Hazzard. She could almost hear Francis's voice. *'God will forgive him, if he shows repentance. Man, of course, will not, and he will hang. But in each outcome, there is an equal measure of justice. Spiritual mercy, but temporal retribution.'*

Soon after eleven o'clock, she eased herself into bed. She was sure that she would spend another night awake, afraid to close her eyes in case she had nightmares. After only twenty minutes, though, she slid into an ink-dark sleep, and she slept deeply and dreamlessly until the clock in the hallway chimed six.

It was then that she was woken up by a furious knocking at her sitting room door, and a voice shouting, 'Beatrice! Beatrice! Are you awake? *Beatrice!*'

Tying the sash of her day gown around herself, she went through to the sitting room and unlocked the door. When she opened it, she found that James was standing outside on the landing, leaning over the banisters so that he could see all the way down the staircase.

'James! I thought I recognized your voice. What on earth are you doing here? What time is it?'

He came over and said, 'I don't think I've been followed. It's only just gone six so you should have time to dress yourself and get out of here. You and Florrie can come and stay with me at my parents' house in Henrietta Street.'

'James, what *are* you talking about? Look – come inside and tell me what you're doing here.'

She went back into the sitting room and sat down in front of her toilet. James came in after her, although he took a long look back at the staircase before he eventually closed the door.

'My deepest apologies if I've woken you up,' he told her. 'I was terrified I might be too late.'

'Too late for *what*, James?'

At that moment, Florence appeared in the bedroom doorway, rubbing her eyes.

'It's all right, Florrie,' said Beatrice. 'James has just come to tell me something. Why don't you and Minnie start getting yourselves dressed? You can wear your flowery dress with the roses on today, if you like.'

Florence nodded and went back into the bedroom. James leaned forward and spoke in a near-whisper, so that she wouldn't be able to hear.

'I tried to come around here late last night to warn you, but the gate was locked and the gatekeeper was asleep, and even though I threw stones at his window I couldn't rouse him.'

'Warn me about *what*?'

'An old friend of mine from Balliol came around to see me yesterday evening, Barney Thomas, and we went to the Goose and Gridiron and had a few drams. It was nearly midnight by the time we left the tavern, but then it struck me that I'd left my bag in the classroom, with my father's fob watch in it, which I'd collected for him from the jeweller's. I said goodbye to Barney and walked back to the Foundery. But who do you think was there, at that hour?'

'I don't know, James. You've only just woken me up and I'm a little muzzy-headed. Tell me.'

'Here's a clue. There was a carriage waiting outside. A *yellow* carriage.'

'George Hazzard's carriage? What was *he* doing there?'

'I let myself into the schoolroom and then I went along to the Reverend Parsons's rooms to find out. I could hear the Reverend Parsons and George Hazzard talking together, very loudly, as if they'd been drinking, and I was about to knock when the door was flung open. I'm not sure why, but I ducked back and hid myself in the alcove. I suppose I didn't want them to think that I'd been standing outside, eavesdropping on them.'

Beatrice was growing impatient. '*James*,' she said, 'what exactly is it that you've come here to warn me about?'

'That's what I'm coming to. George Hazzard stepped out of the door, but then he stopped and turned around and said, "Have no fear, Reverend! By breakfast-time tomorrow, she won't be able to testify to anybody, not any more. Not for ever and ever – amen!"'

Beatrice felt a cold shiver down her spine. 'Dear God. Do you think he meant *me*?'

'I'm certain of it. Who else is going to give evidence against him?'

Beatrice stood up. Now she felt ashamed that she had doubted James's sincerity.

'Florrie!' she called out. 'Get yourself dressed as quick as you can, darling! We have to go out in a minute!'

Then, to James: 'He didn't see you there, did he, George Hazzard? I mean, he doesn't know that you heard him say that?'

James shook his head. 'I stayed hidden in the alcove until he'd left and the Reverend Parsons had gone off to bed. Then I tiptoed out of the Foundery as quietly as I could.'

'Thank you, James. I think I may owe you my life. If you don't mind waiting here for a few minutes I'll get myself dressed.'

'Don't worry about packing anything,' said James. 'I can always send our maid Bronwen over later to collect the rest of your possessions. Once you're safely ensconced at my parents' house, I'll go to Bow Street and tell Constable Rook that I heard George Hazzard threaten to have you silenced. I'm prepared to swear to it in court, Beatrice.'

'I can't tie my bow, Mama!' Florence called out.

'It's all right,' said Beatrice. 'I'm coming in to help you now.'

James sat down while Beatrice went into the bedroom to finish dressing Florence and hurriedly to dress herself. As she stepped into her petticoats and buttoned up her bodice, she felt almost as if she were still asleep, and dreaming this.

'Aren't you going to plait my hair, Mama?' asked Florence.

'No, Florrie. Not now. Later. We really have to go.'

'What about No-noh?'

'No-noh can come too. We can't leave little No-noh behind, can we?'

She pulled on Florence's brocade slippers and then put on her own shoes.

'Right, Florrie, are you ready?' she said.

'Minnie's not dressed yet.'

'Don't worry about Minnie, we'll dress her later.'

'Are you ready, Beatrice?' James called out.

Almost as soon as he said that, Beatrice heard a loud bang, which sounded as if the sitting-room door had been kicked open. James let out a peculiar cry, and then there was scuffling and thumping and another bang, as a chair was knocked over.

'You – *graah* – unh!' James exclaimed.

Beatrice said to Florence, 'Stay back – don't move!' and then she pulled open the bedroom door. She was horrified to see James struggling with a figure in a black hood and long black cape. James was gripping the side of the figure's hood and trying to wrench it off, and as the figure twisted his head away, she saw the silvery glint of its looking-glass mask. It was the same frightening man who had approached her at Ranelagh Gardens.

'*Get out!*' she screamed. '*Get out before I call a constable!*'

Florence immediately started to cry, so Beatrice turned around and said, 'Florrie, stay there!'

As she turned back, she saw that the man in the black cape had drawn out a sword. She screamed again, '*No! Get out! Go away! James! James, be careful!*'

James snatched at the man's sleeve and attempted to seize his sword-wrist, but the man kicked him hard in the shin and he stumbled backwards against the fallen chair. He lost his balance and fell against Beatrice's toilet, so that her candlestick and her tinder box and her mirror toppled off, and her writing paper was scattered across the floor.

Without hesitation, the man stepped forward and with an audible crunch he thrust the point of his sword underneath James's chin. He hesitated, and then he gripped James's shoulder with his left hand and stuck the blade even further upward, until it was buried up to six inches into James's throat. James gargled, and his eyes stared wide in shock. He tried to grip the blade and pull it out, but in an instant his fingers were sliced to the bone and his hands were smothered in blood.

The man didn't relax his grip on James's shoulder and kept his sword firmly in place until James stopped struggling and his hands dropped slackly down by his sides. James's chest rose and fell slower and slower, and blood was pouring out over the front of his white shirt so that it looked as if he were wearing a wide crimson cravat.

Beatrice remained in the open bedroom doorway, paralyzed with horror. She thought of grabbing Florence's hand and trying to run past the man and out of the door, but he would only have to tug his sword out of James's neck and he could strike them down both before they had even reached the top of the stairs. Her Toby pistol was still in her purse, but her purse was lying on the armchair on the other side of the sitting room.

James gave a final convulsive shudder. His eyes were still open but his head fell back, and now the man drew out his bloodied sword and turned towards Beatrice, and she could see her own distorted reflection in his looking-glass mask.

'Now let's silence *you*, madam, shall we?' he said, in his croaky voice.

For an instant, Beatrice thought of screaming for help. But even if any of the girls heard her, and came running, what could they do against a man with a sword? One of them might run outside and try to find a constable, but by the time they had brought him back here, she and Florence would both be dead.

As the man came towards her, she slammed the bedroom door shut. It had no lock, so all she could do was hold on to the knob as tightly as she could, to try and stop him from twisting it open, and to press herself against it. He rammed it with his shoulder, so that it shook, and then he started to kick it.

'*It's no use!*' he croaked. '*You were warned but you didn't listen, did you? You're a witch, if anybody is, and you know how we punish witches, don't you?'*

Beatrice said nothing, but grimly held on to the doorknob. The man kicked at the bottom door panels again and again, and after the seventh or eighth kick the right-hand panel splintered and cracked. She knew that it could only be a matter of minutes before he broke in.

Florence was standing on the other side of the bed in her rose-patterned dress. She had stopped crying now, although her eyelashes were still glistening wet, and she was staring at Beatrice and anxiously biting at her thumbnail.

The man kicked again, and again. '*Witch!*' he panted. '*You just wait – witch!*'

Beatrice said, 'Florrie... under the bed... where the potty is... there's that big metal hook.'

'What?'

'That *hook*, Florrie – that hook we found down by the river! Can you crawl under the bed and pull it out?'

Florence looked bewildered for a moment, but then Beatrice snapped at her, '*Florrie!* Crawl under the bed and pull that hook out *now*!'

The man kicked again, and this time he split the door panel from top to bottom, so that half of it dropped out, and she could see the black leather toecap of his shoe. '*Ha! Nearly got you now – you and your little witchling!*'

Whimpering, Florence knelt down beside the bed and then crawled underneath it.

'Come on, Florrie, hurry,' Beatrice urged her, as the man began to kick at the left-hand door panel. All she could see of Florence now was her legs.

'It's stuck,' said Florence. 'It won't come out.'

'Pull harder!' Beatrice told her.

'It's still stuck.'

'Try pushing it away from you, and *then* pulling it.'

Seconds passed. The man cracked the left-hand door panel.

'Florrie? Have you got it free?'

More seconds passed.

'Florrie, have you managed to get it free yet?'

'Yes, Mama,' said Florence, and she began to edge her way out backwards from under the bed, dragging the grappling hook after her.

'Bring it over here, darling,' said Beatrice, and Florence carried it across to her, flinching every time the man gave the door another kick.

'Now go and crouch down behind the bed, and close your eyes,' Beatrice told her. 'Make believe that you're back at home in Sutton, and that it's bedtime, and that you're sleeping.'

Florence frowned at her, not really understanding what her mother was trying to tell her, but she made her way around the bed and sat down on the floor, although she didn't close her eyes.

Beatrice kept a tight hold on the doorknob with her left hand but she reached down with her right and picked up the grappling hook. It was much heavier than she remembered.

Please God, give me all the strength you can. Give me my own strength, but give me the spiritual strength that I inherited from Francis, and give me the strength that James sacrificed in trying to save me.

The man kicked again, so hard that his foot smashed completely through the left-hand door panel, up to his ankle. He tried to twist it out again, but his large silver shoe buckle was snagged by the splinters, and Beatrice could tell that he must be off-balance.

'*Bugger!*' he swore. '*Bugger and bloody damnation!*'

Beatrice wrenched the door open as wide as she could, a few inches at a time, with the man hopping on one foot and clinging on to the edge of the door to stop himself from keeling over sideways. His hood had fallen back, and above his looking-glass mask his head was bald and knobbly.

Neither of them spoke, and there was an eerie moment when Beatrice felt that time had stopped altogether and all the laws of reality were suspended, and that they would stay in these improbable postures forever.

But then – with a sharp crackling of splinters – the man pulled his foot out of the door panel, tugging off his shoe as he did so. He swung his sword and lurched towards her, but at the same time she had lifted the grappling hook high above her head. He managed to take only two stumbling steps before she swung it down and struck him with such force in the dead centre of his mask that she shattered the image of her own face.

The man stopped, and staggered, letting out a cry that was more like a high-pitched cough than a scream. His face was a jumble of blood and broken fragments of mirror, and he sank slowly to his knees, dropping his sword and raising his hands to try and pick the sharpened pieces out of his forehead and his eyes.

Beatrice took a short step back, breathing hard. *God give me strength, but please God, forgive me.*

She lifted the grappling hook a second time, paused, and then hit him so hard on top of his bald head that she hurt her hands. The barbed steel prong cracked into his skull, but somehow he still managed to stay upright. He lifted his head as if to show her that no matter what she did to him, she wouldn't be able to kill him.

She tried to pull out the grappling hook so that she could hit him yet again, but it was wedged fast in the top of his head, and no matter how she levered it, it refused to come out. He was kneeling in the doorway like a wounded stag with three-pronged antlers. He didn't speak, or couldn't, because his lips had been cut to ribbons by broken glass. All he could do was sway from side to side, so that the grappling hook kept knocking against the door frame.

Florence started crying again – deep, painful sobs. Beatrice hesitated for a few seconds, to make sure that the man was incapable of standing up and coming after her, but she could see that he was stunned, and that he was probably dying. She made her way around the bed and picked up Florence in her arms and hugged her.

'It's all over, Florrie. The bad man can't hurt us now. But you *must* close your eyes, and pretend that you're not here at all. I don't want you to see him, and I don't want you to see James, either, because the bad man has sent James to heaven.'

Florence's mouth was turned down and tears were dripping down her cheeks, but she nodded, and shut her eyes tight. Beatrice carried her towards the doorway, and as she did so, the man in the black cape toppled backward, his knees still bent and the grappling hook still sticking out of his skull.

As the back of his head struck the sitting-room floor, some of the jagged pieces of his looking-glass mask fell away from his face, like a bloodstained kaleidoscope. Although the point of the grappling hook had crushed the bridge of his nose and his cheeks were so lacerated, Beatrice recognized him immediately. It was Edward Veal, George Hazzard's accountant.

She stared down at him for a moment, her stomach churning, her heart beating painfully hard. When James had told her that George Hazzard was out to silence her, she had believed him, but here was the physical proof. He had sent Edward Veal here to close his account with her forever. If she had eaten breakfast, she would have brought it up all over the carpet. As it was, her mouth was flooded with saliva.

Pressing Florence's face close against her shoulder, she managed to inch sideways past Edward Veal's body. She hadn't wanted to look at James, but she had to step past him to pick up her purse from the sofa, because she knew that she would need it. James was sprawled backwards on top of the tipped-over chair in his blood-soaked shirt, with his sightless eyes staring at the ceiling, but once she had collected her purse she turned her head away. She didn't want to remember him like that, and it hurt too much to think that he had been killed trying to save her.

She had just started to make her way down the stairs when Eliza came climbing up towards her, panting. Her hair was a tangled mess and she was barefoot and still wearing her nightgown.

'What's 'appenin'?' she said. 'I 'eard all this bangin' and crashin' but when I went to Mrs Smollett and asked 'er what it was, she said that it was only the chippies come to mend your door. She said I 'ad to stay in my room till they'd finished, but I thought, sod that.'

Beatrice didn't stop, but continued to carry Florence as quickly as she could down the stairs. Eliza turned around and came down close behind her.

'We have to leave here as quickly as we can,' Beatrice told her. 'A man broke into our rooms and tried to murder us. It was Edward Veal, George Hazzard's accountant. Poor James Treadgold from the Foundery tried to protect us, but Veal killed him first.'

Eliza looked back up the staircase in disbelief. 'You're jokin', ain't you?'

'Not at all, Eliza. We're going directly to Bow Street to report this to the justice office.'

'Fuckin' 'ell. But Mrs Smollett said it was chippies.'

'Oh, no. Mrs Smollett knew exactly who it was.'

'But I don't understand. Why was George 'Azzard trying to do you in?'

'I've offered to go to court and testify against him, that's why. You know those seven missing girls I was telling you about? They were all found dead yesterday at George Hazzard's factory, and I have evidence that he was behind it.'

'So 'Azzard sent this cove around to stow your whids and plant 'em? And Mrs Smollett must 'ave been wise to it, mustn't she? Chippies, I ask you!'

They had reached the hallway now. They could hear voices in the kitchen, and the banging of cooking pots, but the kitchen door was closed and there was nobody else around.

'Let's go and fetch No-noh,' said Beatrice. 'Then we have to leave at once.'

'I'm comin' with you,' said Eliza.

'You're not even dressed,' Beatrice told her.

'I don't care. I'm coming with you. 'Cause after you've been to the runners, where will you go?'

'I hadn't thought about it, Eliza. We just need to get out of here.'

'You can come and stay at Black 'Orse Yard if you like, with me and my aunt. And I'll tell you somethin' else, I'll stand up next to you in court and say what Mr 'Azzard was up to, *and* that Mrs Sheridan. I never saw them killin' no girls, but I knew they was 'urtin' them, and 'urtin' them somethin' dreadful, and there was randy coves what called themselves gentlemen payin' good money to watch them do it.'

'Eliza – you don't even have any shoes on!'

344

'I don't bloody care, I'm comin' with you.'

Beatrice and Florence went to the laundry room beside the back door, where No-noh was still asleep in his basket. Florence picked him up and said, 'Come on, No-noh. We have to run away.'

Beatrice lifted their capes down from the hooks in the hallway, but after she had fastened Florence's cape, she wrapped her own around Eliza's shoulders. 'Don't worry,' she said. 'I'll be warm enough, and it won't take us long to get to Bow Street.'

She opened the front door, but as they stepped outside they heard an ululating wail from upstairs, and then Ida screaming out, '*Murder! Murder! Beatrice, where are you? Beatrice! Anybody! Help! Somebody call for a watchman! It's murder!*'

41

Outside, on Aldersgate Street, they hailed a hackney to take them to Bow Street. Beatrice was feeling so shaken by what she had seen and what she had done that she found herself incapable of talking sense, so Eliza had to tell the moon-faced jarvis where they wanted to go. Once Beatrice had climbed up into her seat she couldn't stop shivering, and so Eliza dragged her cape over her shoulders so that they could share it.

As they set off, Florence was silent at first, but she cuddled No-noh, and kept kissing the top of his head, while Eliza couldn't stop chattering.

'Blimey! I don't know *what* my Auntie Vi's goin' to say when I turns up again. She must 'ave thought that she'd seen the last of me, and good riddance, too, I'll bet she thought that. And my three cousins – what? I can just see them three pullin' faces!'

They were only halfway down Ludgate Hill, though, when Florence let out a long, mournful wail. Her wailing grew louder and increasingly hysterical, and by the time the hackney had started to jostle its way up Fleet Street she was red in the face and she could hardly breathe. Beatrice put No-noh down on the floor of the hackney and picked her up, and it was then that she realized that Florence had wet herself.

'Ssh, Florrie, shh,' she told her, rocking her gently in her arms. 'It's all over now. That bad man is never coming back.'

Then she said to Eliza, 'I can't expect Florrie to come to the justice house in this condition. Do you think we could turn back and go to your aunt's place, and settle her down? Then I can go to Bow Street on my own, if you'll be kind enough to take care of her while I'm gone. You wouldn't mind that, Florrie, would you, if Eliza looked after you for a little while?'

'Poor little scrap,' said Eliza. 'Yes, I'd be 'appy to.'

She stood up and leaned around the hackney's hood so that she could shout up to the jarvis, ''Ere, cully, we've changed our minds! Take us to Black 'Orse Yard, will you?'

'Black 'Orse Yard?'

'Just off of Spittle Market.'

'I know it. But I'll still 'ave to charge you for comin' as far as 'ere.'

It took them another ten minutes to turn around and go back along London Wall to Bishopsgate Street and into the crooked maze that led to Black Horse Yard. Most of the shops and houses here had survived the Great Fire, and were timbered buildings of three and four storeys high, with damp-stained facades and tiny leaded windows. The streets were cobbled but many of the cobbles were loose or broken, and they were never swept, so that the chilly morning air was filled with the pungent smell of horse manure and raw sewage.

Florence had stopped wailing, but every now and then she let out a quivery little moan, and No-noh looked up at her worriedly.

Black Horse Yard was a small, gloomy court with tall lodging houses on three sides and a brown-brick stable on the other. When Beatrice had paid the jarvis a shilling and sixpence, Eliza led them to a narrow doorway and knocked.

'I hope we're going to be welcome,' said Beatrice.

'Oh, she's all right really, my aunt. She's 'ad a 'ard life, though. 'Er first 'usband died of the barrel fever and 'er second disappeared like a conjuring trick and 'er third got twisted for stealin' two glimsticks. But she's always 'ad 'er fair share of fancy men, so I don't think she's that bothered, not these days.'

She knocked again, louder, and then took a step back and shouted out to the first floor, 'Auntie Vi! Auntie Vi! It's me, Eliza! Open the bloody door, will you? It's taters out 'ere!'

She knocked one more time, and after about a minute the door opened and a grey-haired woman in a peach-coloured day gown appeared. She blinked at Eliza and then she blinked at Beatrice and Florence, and then she said, 'I'm dreamin'.'

'No, you ain't,' said Eliza. 'It's me. There's been some rare old trouble at the girls' 'ome and we've 'ad to scarper. This is Beatrice what took me into the 'ome in the first place, and this is 'er little girl, Florrie.'

'So what do you want me to do about it?' the woman asked.

'Oh, come on, Auntie Vi! Some cove breaks into the 'ome and 'e was supposed to top Beatrice, and 'e *did* top 'er friend. So Beatrice ends up toppin' 'im, doesn't she?'

'You're 'avin' a laugh, ain't you?'

'It's true, Auntie Vi. It's that George 'Azzard. Beatrice found out that 'e murdered some girls and now 'e's after 'er, so as she can't say nothin' against 'im in court.'

'Not that same George 'Azzard what took you into Leda's?'

''Ow many fuckin' George 'Azzards do you think there are?'

'And 'e's murdered some girls?'

'Seven all told. Well, eight, because there was another one, a black girl, and they only cut 'er bloody 'ead off.'

'Bloody 'ell!'

Beatrice took a deep breath and said, 'My name's Beatrice Scarlet, madam. What Eliza has told you is absolutely true, otherwise we wouldn't have come to you for some temporary refuge. My little girl Florence here is desperately distressed by what she's seen this morning, and she's cold, and she needs a change of clothing. May I beg you to let us in for a while?'

The woman looked again at Beatrice, and then at Florence, and then shrugged and said, 'All right. Come on in. It ain't St James's Palace, but if you need a ken to stay for a day or two, and you're not too sniffy to share a bedroom, you're welcome.'

She stepped back so that Beatrice and Florence could enter the narrow hallway.

'I'm Violet,' she said. 'Mrs Violet Vickery – as was Thompson, as was Hudnutt, as was White. Widowed now.'

'I'm sorry to hear that,' said Beatrice. 'I'm widowed, too.'

'Oh, *I* ain't sorry to be widowed,' Violet told her. 'Me? Sorry? Not one whit.'

She hesitated and looked at Beatrice keenly, and then she said, '*You,* though, *you're* still grievin' – ain't you, love? You ain't wearin' black, but you miss 'im somethin' rotten, don't you?'

Beatrice gave her a quick, rueful smile but she didn't answer. She guessed that Violet was in her late forties, but although she had fine wrinkles around her eyes, and her neck was becoming stringy, she was still unusually attractive. Her eyes were mint-green, and wide apart, and her nose was short and straight, and her lips had an upward curl to them if she found life endlessly amusing. Cockneys must have called her a fair rum-doxy when she was younger.

They climbed up a creaking flight of dark, narrow stairs. It was smoky inside the lodging-house, and there was a strong smell of burned liver, mingled with tomcats' urine and attar of roses, which Beatrice could only assume that somebody had splashed on themselves to try and overwhelm all the other odours. Violet led them across the bare-boarded landing and opened the door to her apartments. They were gloomy inside, because the thick burlap curtains were still drawn, but she went across to the window and dragged them open.

'I always thought that George 'Azzard was a queer cove,' she said. "E mixes with the nibs, and everybody says what a swell 'e is. But I don't know. 'E gives off the smell of sulphur, that's what I always said. I bet if you lifted his wig off, you'll find 'e's got 'orns stickin' out of 'is bonce.'

Violet's sitting room was airless and cramped, with four sagging armchairs and a footstool and a threadbare rucked-up rug. The fire hadn't yet been lit, and the grate was heaped up with last night's ashes, so the room was chilly, as well as damp. The walls had once been papered with a pale-brown trellis pattern, but they were stained and speckled with black mould and in the far corner the paper had sloughed off the plaster like dead skin.

Violet shouted out, 'Pammy! Maggie! Betsy! Let's be 'avin' you out of your dabs, you lazy slamkins! Eliza's 'ere, and she's brought company! Respectable company, too. You, too, Dick. Get your fat arse out 'ere and make up the fire!'

Beatrice heard groans of protest from a half-open door on the right-hand side of the sitting room.

'Them's my daughters,' Violet explained. 'Why I ever 'ad 'em, I'll never know. The only good they ever do is bring in some chink.'

The bedroom door opened wider and a big-bellied young man appeared, blinking and sniffing and scratching himself. He had scruffed-up black hair and near-together eyes and a snub nose like a Staffordshire terrier. His filthy woollen nightshirt came down only as far as his knees, and the stockings that he was wearing underneath were so full of holes so that Beatrice could see his black-rimmed toenails.

'This is Dick,' said Violet. 'You'll 'ave to make allowances for Dick because 'e's a bit of a ben. Bit of a cod's head, ain't you, Dick? Say 'ow d'you do to the lady and 'er daughter, Dick.'

'I'll put on my breeches,' said Dick, slurring his words, and then snorted.

'No, Dick, you light the fire first because we're all feelin' cold in 'ere and the lady and 'er daughter will be wantin' a cup of somethin' 'ot. Now, come on, Beatrice, you sit yourself down and make yourself at 'ome, and we'll soon 'ave you sorted.'

Beatrice sat down on one of the armchairs and Florence climbed into her lap, sucking her thumb, while No-noh hid underneath the chair behind her skirts. Eliza took off Beatrice's cape and draped it over her shoulders to keep her warm, and then she went into the bedroom to talk to her three cousins. Violet came and sat in the chair next to Beatrice, laying a hand on her arm and speaking to her softly and confidentially as if she had known for her years.

'Like I say, I always thought that George 'Azzard was a sharper. Too full of 'imself by 'alf. But as for 'im bein' a miller, that does surprise me.'

Beatrice told Violet how the so-called coven had disappeared, and how their bodies had been dug up. She also told her about Grace, although she called her 'a certain young lady of our acquaintance' and she was careful to choose her words because she didn't want Florence to realize what she was saying.

'I don't yet know what part George Hazzard might have played in their demise, or exactly how their lives were ended. Their remains were so decomposed that it was impossible to tell at a glance how they passed. But I do have some very strong suspicions about what might have happened to them, and Constable Rook at Bow Street seems to agree with me.'

'So 'ow do you think they was topped, then?'

'Almost as soon as they arrived at his factory I believe he packed them off to Leda Sheridan's – the same as he did with that certain young lady of our acquaintance – and that was where they met their end. I admit that some or all of them might have gone willingly. We hadn't succeeded in converting them all at St Mary Magdalene's, not by any means, and Leda Sheridan's has a very high-class clientele. Before we took them in, most of the girls had been plying their trade in back alleys off the Strand and Chick Lane bawdy houses so you can understand that they might have been tempted.'

'You won't believe this, but I know Leda Sheridan. I've known 'er ever since she was a young girl,' said Violet.

'Really?'

'No word of a lie, Beatrice. You might think she's 'igh-class now, but she was brung up around 'ere, on Fort Street, and she was plain Linda Codd in them days. She used to give gentlemen a stand-up clicket be'ind the market stalls for a shilling. Then when she got a a few years older she used to go and 'ang around Covent Garden, and outside the Theatre Royal, and that was 'ow she met up with some rich old swell what set her up with fancy rooms and whatever she asked for. Captain Something, 'is name was. I forget. But when 'e croaked 'e left 'er enough money to set 'erself up on Brydge Street. She married some lawyer after – a right puzzle-cause 'e was, about twenty years older than 'er – but 'e croaked, too.'

'Eliza told me that George Hazzard came across her selling your pincushions on the street, and he sent *her* to Leda Sheridan's,' said Beatrice. She hesitated. She didn't want to sound as if she were accusing Violet of being careless, or neglectful. 'She said that when you heard about it, you didn't seem to be worried. In fact you gave her your blessing.'

'Yes, I did, but that was before I ever met George 'Azzard and clocked 'im for being a sharper.'

She paused, and took hold of Beatrice's hand, and squeezed it.

'Listen, Beatrice, I know that a parson's widow like yourself will think the worst of me. I don't blame you. But we didn't 'ave 'ardly nothin' to live on in them days. I wasn't makin' more than a few farthings out of pincushions and I was too ill with the quinsy to do nothin' else. My three daughters was all on the streets – what else could they do? – and I was worried sick about 'em night and day in case they got beaten or the watch picked them up or they caught some 'orrible clap. I knew that Leda would take good care of Eliza, and that she'd make a fair bit of wedge, and she might even meet a swell like Captain Something, and live 'appy ever after.'

'But what did you think when Eliza ran away, because she'd heard other girls screaming?'

'I didn't think nothin' much of it, to be truthful with you. There's men what like whippin' women and there's women what like to be whipped, and worse. I took Eliza back because I didn't 'ave no choice, but I told 'er she'd 'ave to pay 'er own way. Which she did, most of the time.'

Beatrice made no comment, and didn't tell Violet that Eliza had been robbing her clients as well as offering them sex, although Violet probably knew that she was. These women were struggling every day simply to survive, and Beatrice didn't feel that she could judge either of them. Instead, she told her about the five new girls George Hazzard had taken from St Mary Magdalene's, and how he had claimed to have sent them to Southwark Fair.

'I was going to go to Bow Street and find out from Constable Rook if they returned to the factory last night. And of course I have to go and tell him about us being attacked, and my poor friend James. I have to explain that I only struck Edward Veal to defend myself.'

Dick was kneeling in front of the fireplace now. He had shovelled out the ashes and relaid the grate with crumpled-up newspaper and kindling sticks and lumps of coal, and he was blowing on it with a mooing noise like a cow that badly needed milking.

Violet said, 'Tell you what – I'll come with you, lovey, seein' as 'ow I know George 'Azzard, and Leda, too. The girls will look after your little darlin' for you, don't you worry. Maggie 'ad a baby boy of her own, Stevie, so she knows all about carin' for kids. Stevie died from the measles when 'e was only six months, poor mite, but 'e was ever so 'appy while 'e was with us.'

'That's kind of you, Violet, thank you,' said Beatrice. 'Florrie, do you mind staying with Eliza and the other girls while Mama goes out for a while? I promise I won't be long.'

'I'll get Betsy to make you some 'ot porridge,' said Violet. 'And we've got plenty of bones for that doggy of yours.'

Florence nodded, very gravely. Beatrice couldn't help thinking that even if Francis hadn't been her father, she had somehow inherited his seriousness, and his sense of duty.

Violet stood up and said, 'I'll just go and get myself dressed. P'raps you'd care for a cup of 'ot chocolate before we go. I always prefer a brandy, myself.'

'Do you know something?' said Beatrice. 'I do believe I might join you.'

42

They arrived outside No. 4 Bow Street a few minutes before eleven o'clock. The pavement was even more crowded than usual, not only with protestors, but with curious spectators and four or five men in dusty frock coats who looked as if they might be journalists.

Beatrice was about to step down from the hackney when she caught sight of a yellow carriage waiting by the corner of Russell Street, at the very end of a row of hansoms and hackneys and other carriages.

She said to Violet, 'Wait. I believe that's George Hazzard's carriage. He must be here already.'

'You ain't afraid to face 'im, are you, after what 'e's been a doin'-of?' asked Violet.

'Violet, he tried to have me and Florrie murdered, and he had James killed. I can't.'

'Yes, but think about it, lovey. From what you told me, them bodies is goin' to speak for themselves, ain't they? 'Ow's George 'Azzard goin' to explain 'is own accountant bein' there, wearin' that lookin'-glass mask and all, and 'ow's 'e goin' to explain your poor friend, stabbed in the throat?'

'I still don't want to face him, Violet. He's sure to have some plausible explanation for what happened, and I can't risk being arrested for killing Edward Veal, even if they only charge me with manslaughter. How can I possibly prove that I was only defending myself, when Florrie and I are the only living witnesses?'

'Well, it's up to you,' said Violet. 'Me – I'd believe a parson's widow against a ratbag like George 'Azzard any day of the week.'

But as if God had stage-managed it to confirm Beatrice's fears, the door to the justice house suddenly opened, and George Hazzard stepped out. He was accompanied by a stout man in a gold-braided frock coat with a black ribbon tied around his forehead, and Beatrice recognized him from his portrait in the waiting room. It was Sir John Fielding, the blind magistrate, and the founder of the Bow Street justice house.

The two of them were talking and nodding and then George Hazzard patted Sir John Fielding on the back and shook his hand.

'Let's go, before he sees me,' said Beatrice. 'Just look at the two of them, chatting like old friends. I need to think what I can do next.'

'You want to talk to that constable, don't you?' said Violet. ''E sounds like 'e'll believe you.'

'Are you two ladies gettin' out 'ere or what?' their jarvis shouted.

'No, we ain't!' Violet shouted back. 'Take us back where we come from!'

'Gor blimey!' he retorted. 'I wish you'd make your bloody minds up!'

'What's it to you, you clunch, so long as you get your fare?'

The jarvis cracked his whip and turned the hackney around in the middle of the street, so that they could rattle their way back to Black Horse Yard.

Beatrice said, 'I know what I'll do. I'll write to Constable Rook and explain exactly how we were attacked, and why we've gone into hiding. I'll also ask him if Judith and the rest of our girls are back at the tobacco factory. We can send a messenger, can't we, and he can wait and bring back an answer, without having to reveal to Constable Rook where I am.'

'What if he writes back and says that the girls *are* there?'

'I shall be thankful, of course. But I really don't believe that they are. Why do you think George Hazzard has come down from Hackney to talk to Sir John? I'm sure that he's pulling strings to get himself out of trouble. Do you know, Violet, if only I could find out how those seven girls were murdered. They couldn't have died of natural causes, not all seven of them, but unless we know how they died, George Hazzard can't be touched – and neither for that matter can your friend, Leda.'

'What about your blacky girl, the one what 'ad 'er 'ead whopped off? They can't deny 'ow she got topped.'

'If we could find her body, then we'd have some proof. But I doubt that we ever will. They probably cut her up into pieces and dropped her into the river, or burned her, or buried her in some plague pit. Who can say?'

They arrived back at Black Horse Yard. When they went back upstairs to Violet's apartments, Beatrice found Florence in her daughters' bedroom. The three girls were all very different: Pammy was petite and flaxen-haired, with a pretty heart-shaped face; Maggie was a plump brunette who wheezed when she breathed; and Betsy was red-haired and freckled and looked Irish. Beatrice didn't ask, but she guessed that all three girls had different fathers, and that one or two of the fathers hadn't been Violet's husbands.

They were all laughing, though, and so was Florence. They had perched her up on the windowsill and they were making her face up: powdering her nose and painting her cheeks with rouge and lining her lips with red beeswax.

'There!' said Eliza, giving Florence's mouth a final dab with a pad of Spanish wool. 'A real gentry-mort! All the nibs will be after *you*, my darling, there's no mistake about that!'

Beatrice forced a smile. She didn't find it comfortable to see Florence being amused by four young prostitutes, but she was grateful that they were taking her mind off her horrifying morning, and she was deeply relieved that Violet had given them somewhere safe to hide from George Hazzard, at least for now.

She went into the sitting room and sat by the fire, where the coals were now glowing hot. She took her travelling penner and inkwell out of her purse and turned to the first blank page in her small brocade-bound diary.

'Dear Constable Rook,' she wrote,

I am desperately hoping that I can rely on your support and also your utmost discretion. You will of course know by now of the tragic incident at St Mary Magdalene's this morning, in which Mr James Treadgold was ruthlessly murdered and Mr George Hazzard's accountant Mr Edward Veal also met his maker. These are the exact circumstances, regardless of what Mr Hazzard might have imparted to Sir John Fielding.

She described James's killing and Edward Veal's death in detail, and then she told him that she and Florence were remaining at a 'confidential address' until they could be guaranteed protection. Finally, she asked him if the Hackney watch had reported that Judith and the other girls had returned to the tobacco factory last night, or if they were still missing.

When she had finished, Violet sent Betsy across the court to fetch the skinny nine-year-old son of one of her neighbours, who supported her five children by taking in washing. Beatrice instructed the boy where to take her letter, and to wait for Constable Rook to write a reply. When he returned, she promised that she would give him sixpence.

'Make sure that nobody follows you on your way back,' she told him. 'If you think that they are, wait in a doorway until they've gone past.'

'I ain't no mopus,' he told her.

'And don't read it,' she said, as she handed him the letter, but he simply stared at her as if she had spoken to him in a foreign language. He had never been to school and never would.

All she could do then was sit and wait, and listen as Violet's daughters played with Florence. After an hour or so, Pammy and Betsy started to dress and put on their own make-up, because it was time for them to be going out on the streets to make what Violet called 'chink'. If they didn't, they wouldn't be able to pay the rent, and there wouldn't be any food on the table.

It was five past one before the boy returned with a letter from Jonas Rook. He looked exhausted. The sole of one of his worn-out brown boots had started to flap loose when he was walking along Butcher Row, and so he had been forced to hop most of the way back. Beatrice gave him an extra threepence as well as his sixpence, so that he could have it mended, but he took it with a scowl, and left the door wide open on his way out.

When she first read Jonas Rook's reply, Beatrice was surprised how pessimistic he seemed to be. Yesterday he had given her so much encouragement, and had appeared so eager to pursue a prosecution, but the tone of this letter was completely negative.

Dear Mrs Scarlet, Wherever you are I must insist that you attend these offices in person so that I may question you more fully about the circumstances in which Mr James Treadgold and Mr Edward Veal both met their deaths.

The remains of the seven young women who were exhumed from Mr Hazzard's factory garden have now all been removed to the mortuary at St Bartholomew's Hospital. They are being examined by no less a surgeon than Mr Percivall Pott. However, we can come to no decisions about court proceedings until he has sent us his completed post-mortem reports, which he warns may take some days, or even weeks.

Even so, I am advised by Sir J. Fielding that without irrefutable evidence the likelihood of successfully prosecuting Mr Hazzard for the young women's murder is remote. It is not in itself an offence to have human remains discovered on your premises. Even if the young women can be shown to have been unlawfully killed in some way, it must be established beyond question who killed them, and should they have been killed on another's instruction, who issued such instruction.

In regard to your inquiry about the five young women from St Mary Magdalene's about whose whereabouts you questioned Mr Hazzard yesterday, the Hackney watch have reported to me this a.m. that they did not return to the factory dormitory yesterday evening, and there is no sign of them at the factory today.

I raised this with Sir J. Fielding, but his view is that their apparent disappearance is a separate matter altogether, unrelated to the discovery of the seven dead girls, and that there is no need for it be pursued any further unless prima facie evidence can be found by <u>concerned parties</u> that they are in jeopardy, or have already come to some harm.

I await your appearance at Bow Street at your earliest convenience.

Yr obdt servant, Jonas Rook, Constable.

It was only when she read the letter a second time that she began to suspect that he was telling her between the lines that he was still determined to charge George Hazzard with murder. He was making it clear, though, that they would have to come up with overwhelming evidence. Whatever George Hazzard and Sir John Fielding had discussed this morning, it sounded as if it had left Sir John strangely reluctant to press any charges against him.

It was the way that Jonas Rook had underlined *concerned parties* that suggested to Beatrice that he was still on her side. By *concerned parties* she was sure that he meant her, and that he was encouraging her to find more evidence that could bring George Hazzard to book.

She read the letter one more time and then she got up and went to knock on Violet's bedroom door. Violet called out, ''Old on a minute!' but after a short while she came to the door and opened it, still straightening her gown.

'Constable Rook has told me that those five girls are still missing,' said Beatrice, holding up his letter. 'What do you think the chances are that he's sent all or some of them to Leda's?'

'I don't know, lovey, but from what you've said, and from what that James fellow told you, I wouldn't say no to layin' a bet on it.'

She paused, and then she said, 'There's only one way to find out, ain't there, and that's to go to Leda's and take a look.'

'I suppose so. But how can we manage to do that?'

'Easy. Go to 'er nunnery on Brydges Street and ring the doorbell. We can say that we was passin' and just dropped in it to say 'ow do you do. She'll be over the moon to see me, Leda, I can promise you.'

'Are you sure?'

''Course I'm sure. We was always close, me and Leda. Like

sisters, almost. I used to mend 'er dresses for 'er whenever they go torn by some cully treatin' 'er rough, because she couldn't sew for nuts.'

'What about me?' asked Beatrice. 'Won't she want to know who I am?'

'You can pretend to be my long-lost friend from when I used to sing at the Spread Eagle in the Strand, after the theatres closed. We used to sing filthy songs and then the customers would bid for which of them was goin' to take us upstairs.'

'Supposing Leda realizes what we're really doing there?'

'She won't. She ain't never seen you before, 'as she?'

'Only that one time I saw Grace being killed, but as I told you, I had James with me then, and I was wearing a mask.'

Violet said, 'Listen to me, lovey. I can understand you bein' shit-scared, after what you went through this mornin', but it seems to me like justice 'as to be done, and you want to see it done, and I think you're braver than what you think you are. Besides, I owe you, for what you done for Eliza. She could've ended up in quod, or even climbin' the ladder.'

Whatever Violet said, Beatrice had never felt less brave in her life. She felt tired, and defeated, and the shock of striking Edward Veal with the grappling hook was only now beginning to wear off. She would have done anything to creep into her bed at St Mary Magdalene's and pull the blankets up to her neck and close her eyes.

'You can do it,' said Violet, looking at her intently with those mint-green eyes. 'What 'appened to you was bad enough, I'll grant you. But think what must 'ave 'appened to them poor girls. And what might 'appen to these other girls, if Leda's got 'em round 'er ken.'

Beatrice nodded. 'You're right, Violet. Can Eliza take care of Florrie for me? I can pay you for any food and milk you give her.'

'Don't you worry about that,' said Violet. 'It don't matter if we're gentry-morts or trugs, sometimes us women 'as to 'old 'ands and stick together, because we're women, and that's all there is to it.'

43

Violet had to jangle the bell twice before the door to Leda Sheridan's brothel was opened. Her scarlet-coated flashman looked down at the two of them, and said, 'Good afternoon, ladies! And what can I do for you? Do you have an appointment?'

'No, we h'aint but we've come to see Mrs Sheridan,' said Violet.

'May I tell her who's calling?'

'Tell 'er it's Vi the Pie from Spittle Street. She'll know 'oo I am.'

'Vi the Pie from Spittle Street?' the flashman repeated, cupping his hand to his ear as if he had misheard her.

'That's right. That was my name, when we was knockin' around together. And 'ers was Coddy the Body.'

'Wait there, will you?' said the flashman, and went back inside, half-closing the door.

'Vi the Pie?' Beatrice asked her, as they waited.

'I was 'ard on the outside, that's what the fellows used to say, but I was fruity on the inside.'

They could hear voices and laughter from inside the house, and somebody playing a spinet. Then suddenly the sound of clattering heels, and a long-drawn-out scream. The door was flung open again, and Leda Sheridan appeared, both of her arms stretched out. She was wearing a headdress of purple ostrich feathers and a plum-coloured gown with a deep décolletage that bared her wrinkled cleavage, and panniers on her hips that made her look almost as wide as she was short.

'Vi! My dear Lord in heaven, it really is you! What a wonderful surprise! I haven't seen you since – when was it?'

'Vauxhall Gardens, five years ago, when it was the King's birthday. What a fuckin' night that was!'

'Come in, Vi, come in. Come and have a glass of sherry. And who's this you've brought with you?'

Violet laid her hand on Beatrice's shoulder and said, 'This is my friend Bea. 'Er and me used to sing together at the Spread Eagle. Strike me blind, them was the days! *And* the nights, God 'elp us! I ain't seen *'er* for years, neither, but she come tappin' at my door this mornin'. Not long back from America, she is, where she was widowed. So I thought, I've met up with Bea again, I should meet up with Coddy, too.'

'Now then, Vi,' said Leda Sheridan, as she led them into her drawing room. 'I don't call myself that any more. Haven't done for years. A quality establishment this is, with a quality clientele. And I *was* Mrs Sheridan, the wife of Henry Sheridan, the lawyer, before the apoplexy took him, so I'm no longer a Codd, not in any respect.'

Beatrice could hear now that Leda Sheridan's upper-class accent was very forced and precise, and that occasional words sounded cockney, such as 'mo-ah' for 'more' and 'wiv' for 'with'.

Leda Sheridan tinkled a small bell, and a pretty young girl in a long apron and a mob cap came in.

'Susan,' she said. 'Pour us three glasses of sherry, will you? And fetch us a plate of those Florentine biscuits.'

Violet looked around the drawing room and said, 'You've really done yourself proud, ain't you, Leda? It's 'ard to believe you was brung up round Spittle Market, same as me.'

'I have my dear late Captain Forrest to thank for that, when I was his peculiar. He paid for me to have all the reading and the writing and the elocution lessons, and he taught me the etiquette, too, such as how to talk to royalty, and how a lady should eat asparagus so that she doesn't look like she's being suggestive. But it was what I learned about the gentry when I was with him that made all the difference.'

'All *I* know about the gentry is that most of them is by-blows,' said Violet.

'Well, I couldn't agree with you more,' said Leda Sheridan. 'They put on a fine show of being moral and upright, don't they? Regular churchgoers and devoted husbands. But underneath those fancy waistcoats they have as much raging lust as your common man, if not more. And what's much more important, they have the money to indulge whatever perversion takes their fancy. That's what I learned, and that's what this house is built on. I give them everything and anything they want. They want flogging, or to watch girls playing with a pig? I can arrange it. But I always make them feel like this is the most respectable establishment in London.'

The maid came in with a silver tray, and poured them each a glass of amontillado.

Leda Sheridan raised her glass and said, 'A toast to happy reunions, Vi.'

''Appy reunions,' said Violet, but almost as soon as they had all taken a sip of their sherry, the clock on the mantelpiece chimed four.

'My stars, look at the time!' said Leda Sheridan. 'I'm afraid that I won't be able to chat to you for too much longer. We're staging a special performance here this evening, and I've so many preparations to make. Vi – perhaps you and I can arrange to meet another day.'

'What sort of performance?' asked Beatrice.

'Aha, I'm afraid that's highly confidential,' said Leda Sheridan. 'We have some very eminent guests attending, and they insist on absolute secrecy. It would be ruinous for many of them if they were known to have been here and witnessed our spectaculars.'

'Don't you worry,' Violet told her. 'We know 'ow to cheese it, don't we, Bea? Some of those coves what used to roll into the old Spread Eagle for some rantum-scantum, they was celebrated, but we never let on to nobody, did we?'

Beatrice nodded. Her cheeks were flushed, not only because the drawing room was so warm, but because she still felt guilty telling lies. She knew that she had to, but she could only hope that God would forgive her if and when her mission was successful.

Leda Sheridan took another sip of her sherry, and then she said, 'What I *can* tell you is that we'll have five girls performing this evening, simultaneous. There won't be another show in London to match it. We've sold over a hundred tickets at a hundred guineas each, and if we'd only had the space to accommodate everybody who wanted to attend, believe me, we could have sold a hundred more.'

'*Five* girls?' said Beatrice.

'Five, yes! All virgins, of course, and all deflowered at once!'

'Oh, of course,' said Violet. 'Just like you and me used to be, Coddy – sorry, Leda. Lost our virginity every night, didn't we, but we always got it back in the morning – over and over and over again. I stayed a virgin until I was nineteen, Bea, until I got poisoned with Maggie. I can tell you, though – it's bloody 'ard pretending you're a virgin when you're three months up the duff.'

A bosomy young woman in a pink silk day gown came into the drawing room and said, 'Mrs Sheridan? Sorry to interrupt you, ma'am, but the 'pothcary said he was ready for them now, so I'm bringing them all downstairs.'

'Very well,' said Leda Sheridan. She stood up and took Violet's hand between both of hers. 'Why don't you call by next week, Vi, perhaps on Wednesday afternoon? I'd love to reminisce about the old days on Fort Street – my goodness! And good day to you, Bea. It was a singular pleasure to meet you.'

They went out into the hall, where the scarlet-coated flashman was waiting to escort them to the front door. But they were less than halfway to the front door when they heard footsteps coming down the staircase behind them, lumpy and irregular, as if a number of people were coming down and they were having difficulty in keeping their balance.

Beatrice turned her head and saw the young woman in the pink day gown. Behind her came the five girls from St Mary Magdalene's, Judith among them, all of them snatching at the banister rail to stop themselves from losing their footing. They were all dressed in long white nightgowns like a procession of novice nuns, and their faces were deathly pale.

Beatrice looked back at Violet, and gave her a quick, almost imperceptible nod. *You were right, Violet. You've won your bet. They are here.*

The flashman opened the front door, and said, 'I bid you good afternoon, ladies.' Before they could step outside, though, Beatrice heard an extraordinary squeal, more like a slide whistle than a young girl's voice, and then, 'Beatrice! Beatrice! It's *me*, Judith!'

Leda Sheridan reappeared from her drawing room door. 'Who's that?' she said, her ostrich plumes nodding. 'Who was that calling?'

Judith lurched to the bottom of the stairs. She staggered and almost fell, but then she pushed her way past the young woman in the pink silk day gown and came stumbling towards Beatrice, flapping her arms.

She collided with her, and gripped her cape to keep herself upright. Her hair was tangled like a bramble bush and her eyes were glassy. She smelled strongly of stale perspiration and some sweet chemical, like ether.

'Beatrice,' she said. 'I'm so glad you've come. I don't know what I'm doin' 'ere. 'Ow's little Florrie? 'Ave you come to take us back to St Mary's? I don't know 'ow I got 'ere. Where am I?'

Leda Sheridan came marching up to them with her panniers bouncing noisily.

'What's the meaning of this?' she demanded. 'How does this girl know your friend, Vi?'

'This is *Beatrice*,' said Judith, emphatically, although she was slurring her words as if she were drunk. 'Beatrice looks after us at St Mary Magdalene's, don't you, Beatrice?'

'What?' snapped Leda Sheridan. 'You work at that bunters' home? Is that why you've come here – to find out where your girls have got to? You're not that Beatrice that Mr Hazzard was warning me about? Widow Nosey, that's what he called you! Vi – is that who this is? Why did you fetch her here if you knew who she was?'

'I didn't 'ave the faintest bloody clue!' Violet protested. 'She's the same Bea what used to sing with me at the Spread Eagle – 'ow was I to know what she does now? Is this true, Bea? Is that why you wanted to come 'ere? You fuckin' took advantage of me, didn't you? I can't fuckin' believe it!'

Beatrice didn't know what to say. She couldn't deny that she had been working at St Mary Magdalene's, but she didn't know if she ought to protest that Violet had known that she did, and that coming here under the pretence of a social visit had been Violet's idea, and not hers. But Violet gave her a look which she took to mean 'stow it!' and so she said nothing.

'Come on, Bea, let's go,' said Violet, and stepped out onto the porch. But Leda pushed her way in front of Beatrice and said, 'Oh no, you don't, madam! I can't have you going to the traps about this. I've got my clientele to consider. Charlie!'

The flashman came around and gripped Beatrice by the left arm.

'Take your hands off me!' Beatrice demanded. 'I shall have you taken for assault, as well as abduction! Violet, tell this creature to let me go!'

'Oh yes, and why should I?' Violet retorted. 'You've done nothin' but tell me porkies and now even my bestest old friend Coddy 'ere thinks she can't trust me! I'm off!'

With that, she went down the front steps and stalked off along Brydges Street.

Beatrice tried to twist her arm free, but the flashman held even tighter, and pulled her back into the hallway. Leda and the young woman in the pink day gown took hold of Judith and half-pushed her and half-dragged her back to join the rest of the girls.

Once all the girls had shuffled along to the back of the house, and had been herded through a door next to the performance room, Leda Sheridan returned to confront Beatrice.

'If you attempt to harm me, you will face very serious consequences,' Beatrice told her. 'I know a constable at Bow Street who won't rest until you are punished for this.'

'And I know an Old Bailey judge who won't be at all happy that you're trying to spoil his evening's entertainment,' Leda Sheridan replied. 'I shall inform Mr Hazzard that I have you here, and I shall ask him what he wants done with you. I can assure you that you won't enjoy it, no matter what it is. It doesn't pay to interfere in other people's business, madam, especially when it comes to the gentry and to peers of His Majesty's realm.'

'Let me go!' Beatrice repeated, and tried to kick the flashman's shins, but he swung her around and shook her as hard as if she were a dusty carpet.

Leda Sheridan pulled her purse away from her, and then said, 'Take her upstairs, Charlie. The end bedroom. And put the bracelets on her.'

'You can't do this!' Beatrice shouted at her. 'I insist that you let me go!'

'And I insist that you shut your muff,' said Leda Sheridan, between clenched teeth, and returned to her drawing room, dropping Beatrice's purse behind the sofa.

Struggling and kicking, Beatrice was humped up the staircase, and then dragged along the first-floor corridor to the same bedroom where she had discovered Grace. The flashman threw her onto the bed and then fastened a pair of black iron handcuffs onto her wrists.

'You'll be hanged for this, you wretch!' Beatrice spat at him, but all he did was lean over the bed and grin at her, showing her the broken brown stumps of his teeth. Then he left the bedroom, closing the door. She heard him turning the key in the lock and walking away.

She felt both confused and frightened. She could understand why Violet had spoken to her so sharply, but she still felt that she had been badly let down. She didn't know what Leda Sheridan intended to do to her, but she was more worried about Florence now. What would happen to Florence if she could never return to Black Horse Yard to collect her? She would be brought up among prostitutes, and that's if they chose to bring her up at all. They might throw her out onto the streets, and she would have to beg and sleep in doorways like so many other homeless children.

It was growing dark, and the only lights she could see were in the windows of the houses opposite. Even these disappeared one by one as curtains were drawn, or candles extinguished. She tried to tug her hands out of the handcuffs but they were far too tight, and she succeeded only in scraping her wrists.

She closed her eyes and said a prayer. Although she was so frightened, she didn't feel that God had abandoned her, and she also felt that Francis was close. She almost expected to open her eyes and see him standing in the shadows in the corner of the room, smiling at her, and telling her to have courage.

44

She could hear talking, and the sound of a violin being tuned, but she could also faintly hear the chiming of Leda Sheridan's clock, so she knew that two hours had passed. Then she heard girls' voices coming closer, and the bedroom door was unlocked.

Five girls came in, three of them holding candles, and gathered around her bed. She recognized them from the evening when Grace had been murdered – the three holding candles had been naked waitresses, serving drinks and jellies and canapés, while the other two were the lesbian girls who had performed on the stage with the huge ebony phallus.

'What do you want?' Beatrice asked them. 'Please – take these manacles off me and let me go. I promise not to tell the police that you've been keeping me captive.'

Two of the girls tittered and nudged each other, but none of them answered her. After a few moments, Beatrice heard footsteps approaching, and the girls all backed away from the bed so that a newcomer could enter the room.

When she saw who it was, Beatrice was so shocked that she couldn't speak. It was Godfrey Minchin, the young apothecary from the Foundery. He was in his shirtsleeves, with a long-tailed waistcoat the colour of snuff, and his spectacles were perched on top of his balding head.

'Well now, Beatrice!' he said, as if they were already halfway through a conversation. 'This is a *real* pickle you've got yourself into, wouldn't you say?'

He approached the bed and stood beside her. In his left hand he was holding a clear glass bottle with a glass stopper, and in his right he was holding a thick, folded pad of white gauze. He took out the stopper with a squeak, and Beatrice immediately smelled ether.

'Godfrey,' she said, 'I don't know how you're involved with this, but I beg you to reconsider what you're doing.'

'I won't injure you in any way, Beatrice,' Godfrey told her. 'All I'm going to do is put you to sleep, so that you won't have to suffer any indignity.'

'Godfrey – you do understand that what you're doing is a criminal offence, and that you're going to be severely punished for it?'

Godfrey turned the bottle upside-down and shook it until the gauze was soaked with ether.

'Really?' he said. 'I don't believe that it's against the law for an apothecary to anaesthetize a patient who appears to be unwell. In your case, Beatrice, I would say that you have a dangerous case of hysteria, which could well lead to apoplexy and heart failure. I could well plead that it would be criminal of me *not* to put you to sleep.'

'Please, don't. This is insanity.'

'Beatrice, it would be insanity for me to turn down the five pounds that they give me for every patient I treat.'

'But you're not treating patients, Godfrey! You're putting healthy young girls to sleep so that men can have their way with them! And worse! How did those seven girls die – the girls that everybody says were witches? Did you have anything to do with that?'

'I'm not going to argue with you, Beatrice,' said Godfrey. 'I've been sent up here to anaesthetize you and that's what I'm going to do.' With that, he bent over and grasped the hair at the back of Beatrice's head, so that she wouldn't be able to turn her face away when he pressed the gauze pad against her nose and her mouth.

She held her breath for as long as she could, her eyes watering from the fumes, but at last she had to breathe in. The bedroom shrank, and grew dark, and the girls' voices seemed to come from further and further away. At last she blacked out, but she still felt as if she were floating in a starless sky.

I'm dying, she thought. *This is what it's really like to die. No heaven, no angels, no shining lights. Death is nothing but endless darkness.*

When she opened her eyes, she felt cold, and she shivered. Her brain felt as if it had turned into cotton wool, and for a moment she couldn't think where she was or what had happened to her. There was a high plastered ceiling above her, decorated with floral mouldings, and a chandelier with at least a dozen candles in it, so that the room was well-lit. It was draughty, though, which made the candle flames dip, and this had the effect of making the figures on the wallpaper appear to be alive.

The wallpaper was the brightest green, and the figures were men dressed in riding habits, with top hats and crops, and they were sitting astride naked women wearing bridles and bits.

Beatrice could feel something constricting her chest, just under her breasts. She reached down and realized that it was a tan leather strap. She lifted her head and looked down to her feet. No wonder she was feeling so cold – like the women pictured on the wallpaper she too was completely naked. She was lying on a narrow cast-iron bed, on a thin horsehair mattress, pinned down by the strap around her chest, and by two more straps, one across her thighs and another across her ankles.

She looked to her left, and saw that there was another bed, close to hers, and that one of the five girls was lying on it, as naked as she was, but still unconscious. On the far side of that, at right angles, there was yet another bed, and another. By the opposite wall, she could see Judith. All five girls were here, every one of them naked, every one of them motionless. If they hadn't all been breathing, the room could have been mistaken for a mortuary.

Beatrice had no idea how long she had been anaesthetized, but she could see from a triangular gap in the bottle-green curtains that it was still dark outside. From the height of the room she guessed that she was downstairs again now, and she could faintly hear music – the same kind of scraping music that had been playing when Grace had been murdered. The music stopped, and now she thought she could hear people clapping.

She lay back for a while, and then she lifted her head again, to see if it might be possible to loosen the leather straps. But they were at least three inches wide, and far too tight for her to wriggle out of, and their buckles were underneath the bed so that it was impossible for her to reach them.

She looked around. There was a door on the left-hand side of the room, which she guessed must lead out to the hallway, and another door directly in front of her. The music and the applause were coming from behind this door, and she realized that it must be the door beside the stage – the door from which Grace had appeared, followed by the 'nim gimmer' in his pointed white hood.

At least half an hour passed, and then the door from the hallway was abruptly opened. In came Leda Sheridan, wearing an emerald-green gown embroidered with gold stitching, and a green turban with ostrich plumes on top of it. She was followed by a young man wrapped in a grey silk robe and the two girls from the lesbian performance, both in white silk gowns. They had wings made of white goose feathers pinned to their shoulders and gold wire haloes on their heads, so they were clearly intended to look like angels.

Leda Sheridan looked around the room and then came up to Beatrice. She smelled very strongly of some musky perfume.

'Well, well. The Widow Scarlet. It's a pity that your church never taught you to respect the privacy of others,' she said.

'You should release me at once,' Beatrice retorted, although she was finding it hard to catch her breath.

'How can I do that? If I release you, you'll go running off to make a complaint to a magistrate, and don't try to tell me that you won't. Even if you did, it would do you no good, I can promise you. I have too many clients of importance. But it would be certain to cause a most unpleasant scandal, and a great deal of publicity in the papers, and I can't allow that. This house has a reputation to uphold.'

'You, Mrs Sheridan, are a murderess. Nothing more and nothing less. Even if the law doesn't punish you, then the Lord certainly will.'

'I doubt it, Widow Scarlet. The girls who provide our entertainment here are far beyond redemption, and the fate they meet here is all they will ever be fit for. Besides, isn't it a quick and clean demise more desirable than to suffer for years in some wretched rookery, old and half-starved and wracked by the pox?

She turned around and beckoned to the two girls dressed as angels, and then she turned back to Beatrice and said, 'Feel yourself at liberty to report me to the Lord, because you will be meeting him long before I do. Before the next hour is out, if not sooner.'

'I have a small daughter,' said Beatrice. 'Please, you can't leave her motherless.'

'London is full of motherless daughters. All of my girls here are motherless daughters. Yours will no doubt survive, Widow Scarlet, never fear. There are always men with a twitch in their breeches and a shilling in their pocket.'

Beatrice heard the musicians in the next room strike up with 'Lady Lie Near Me'.

'That's our cue,' said Leda Sheridan, and stepped away.

One of the angel girls came up to Beatrice. She might have been beautiful, but her cheeks were pockmarked from smallpox and four of her front teeth were missing and her huge blue eyes were unfocused as if she were half-asleep. She drew a thin, black silk scarf from out of her waistband and pulled it tightly between Beatrice's lips, lifting her head and tying a knot behind the back of her neck to gag her.

Beatrice shook her head violently from side to side and tried to cry out, but all she could manage was muffled, goose-like honks. The scarf tasted of ether and something else musty, like mould or dried semen.

Now the man in the grey silk robe bent down beside her bed and unbuckled her straps. As he unfastened the strap around her chest, she realized who he was – the same man with the rubbery lips who had been raping Grace when she was beheaded. The hair on his head was cropped short, but his dark chest hair curled out of the top of his robe, and the backs of his hands were hairy, too. Close up, she could see that he had a large wart next to his nose, and he had the coldest, deadest eyes that she had ever seen.

She tried to hit him and kick him, but he was far too strong for her. Underneath his slippery silk robe, his muscles felt as hard and curved and sinewy as those of Bramble, the horse that she used to ride in Sutton. He heaved her up off the bed and carried her out through the door, and onto the stage.

The room was crowded. Beatrice turned her face away, because she was too ashamed of her nakedness to see who might be there. But there was loud applause when she was brought in – ribald whoops of encouragement from the men and little shrill screams from the women. The musicians continued to play 'Lady Lie Near Me', faster and faster, and the audience clapped in time to the music. Out of the corner of her eye she could see flushed faces and sparkling jewellery and fans furiously flapping because the room was so airless and hot.

The man laid her down on the oval table in the centre of the stage, and the two angel girls came up and fastened ribbons around her wrists in the same way that Grace had been restrained.

Leda Sheridan came out and held up her green-gloved hands for silence. The musicians stopped playing, although the audience kept on shuffling and laughing and nudging each other.

'My lords, ladies and honourable gentlemen, welcome to yet another spectacular evening of amorous entertainment!' Leda Sheridan sang out. 'Tonight we have a show for you that will exceed in its erotic audacity any performances that you have ever witnessed anywhere, not only in London but in any capital in Europe!'

There was more applause, and cries of 'Brava!' One of the women in the audience swooned, collapsing into her gown like a huge red chrysanthemum, but she was lifted up again by the two men standing either side of her, and they fanned her in the face until she recovered.

'Tonight you will see no fewer than five young virgins – *five!* – deflowered simultaneously on their deathbeds! But to whet your appetites, as a juicy hors d'oeuvre, I give you this delectable female sacrifice – the beautiful Aphrodite!'

The musicians started to play 'The Jovial Broom Man', and as they did so, the two angel girls went up to the hairy man and dragged off his grey silk robe. Men in the audience roared encouragement, while the women screamed.

The hairy man stood at the front of the stage, posing and flexing his muscles in imitation of a Greek wrestler, and then he strutted up and down, waggling his penis.

'What do you think of this truncheon?' he shouted out. 'Any of you ladies like to luncheon on my truncheon?'

Beatrice closed her eyes. *Please, dear God, take away all of my senses. Let me neither see nor hear nor feel anything during this ordeal. Take my mind back to the parsonage in Sutton, on a summer's day, walking hand in hand with Francis down to the stream and smelling the trees and the grass and hearing the vireos whistle.*

But this was a prayer that God didn't answer, or perhaps he didn't hear. Beatrice felt the hairy man grasping her ankles and spreading her legs, and then she heard the table creak as he climbed up onto it. Her throat filled with saliva and behind her gag she had to swallow and swallow which made her feel as if she were drowning.

Edging up the table, the man used his coarse hairy thighs to lever her legs even further apart, and then he opened up her vulva with his thumbs, stretching her labia as wide as he could. She kept on praying inside her head as he prodded at her with the swollen head of his penis, but then he gave a loud grunt and forced himself into her, all the way up to his pubic hair. She was dry, and his penis was enormous, and she couldn't stop herself from letting out a gargle of pain. It was like having a thick wooden pastry pin pushed into her vagina.

The crowd cheered as the hairy man entered her, and then cheered again when he drew himself right out of her again. He brandished his penis in his fist before squashing it back up inside her. Every time he heaved himself forward, her pelvis was knocked against the tabletop, hurting her spine. She felt as helpless as Minnie, Florence's doll, when Florence flung her around the room in a temper.

As his thrusting grew faster and harder, the hairy man started to sweat, and his warm perspiration dropped onto Beatrice's face. He leaned forward and grasped her breasts in both hands, squeezing them hard and pinching her nipples. His thumbnails were coarsely bitten, and she winced every time he dug them in deeper.

Please, dear Lord, let this be over, she prayed, but almost as soon as she thought that, the audience started to chant.

'Nim gimmer! Nim gimmer! Nim gimmer!'

As soon as she heard that, Beatrice was swamped from head to foot with a cold sense of utter dread. She couldn't stop herself from opening her eyes, and there above her, so close that their noses were almost touching, was the sweaty dead-eyed face of the hairy man. When he saw that she was looking up at him, he winked and gave her a rubbery leer.

'Almost there, darling!' he panted. 'Almost there!'

'Nim gimmer!' chanted the audience. 'Nim gimmer!'

From where she was lying on the table, Beatrice couldn't see the door at the side of the stage, but she knew when it had opened because the audience suddenly roared and screamed and stamped on the floor and the musicians began to scrape their instruments even faster, as if they were racing each other.

'Nim gimmer! Nim gimmer! Nim gimmer!'

The hairy man raised his head, and grinned, and nodded, and Beatrice guessed that the tall man in his white robes and pointed hood had appeared.

Pray God it won't hurt too much, having my head cut off. Please let it be quick, and let me feel nothing, and please take care of Florence for me. And Noah, wherever he is. Poor sweet Noah.

The man in the white robes circled around the table until Beatrice could see him, and he stood beside her motionless while the hairy man continued to pant his way closer and closer to a climax. Beatrice could see his eyes blinking behind the holes in his pointed hood like an animal peering out of its lair, and there was a damp patch on the cotton where his mouth was. He must be salivating.

'Nearly, nearly, nearly!' the hairy man gasped, with clear snot swinging from his nose, and the man in the white robes drew out his shiny curved sword.

Beatrice closed her eyes again, expecting to feel the cold blade slicing across her throat. But it was then that she heard a thunderous crash from the hallway, and men shouting.

The musicians abruptly stopped playing, and the audience stopped chanting and clapping. There was more shouting from the hallway, and the loud bang of a pistol shot. The hairy man said, 'God's teeth!' and climbed off her. She opened her eyes in time to see him jumping naked off the stage. The man in the white robes had already vanished.

A surge of panic rippled through the audience. Drunken gentlemen in elegant frock coats and long periwigs were pushing each other to try and reach the door, while women in extravagant gowns were circling around and around hysterically. There was more shouting from the hallway, and the sound of running feet.

Dear God, this was a thousand times more painful and

humiliating than that time when Jonathan Shooks had raped her in her own drawing-room at the parsonage. This hurt so much more, and she was almost deafened by the baying and the screaming of the audience.

'*Stop!*' a man bellowed. '*Everybody remain exactly where you are!*'

Beatrice tugged at the ribbons that were tying her down to the table, but they were knotted too tightly. None of the jostling crowd in the room was taking any notice of her now, and not one of them climbed onto the stage to help her get free.

'I cannot be seen here!' cried a tall man in a pale blue frock coat. 'I can *not* be seen here!' Although he wasn't wearing his long-nosed Venetian mask Beatrice recognized him by his booming voice as the man who had been wearing orange on the night of Grace's murder.

'Get out of my way, damn you!' shouted a fat elderly man with a face spotted with sores, striking at a younger man with his cane. A woman in a high pink wig started screaming, and then fell backwards against the table laden with wine bottles and plates and glasses, and sent them all crashing to the floor. Another woman tripped over her, and then another, until five or six of them were lying in a tangle with their feet kicking and their petticoats showing, all of them shrieking like off-key opera singers.

The chaos was at its height when Jonas Rook strode into the doorway in his swirling cape and his large tricorn hat, accompanied by three Bow Street runners and two watchmen. By the sound of it there were many more officers outside in the hallway.

As soon as he caught sight of Beatrice lying on the table, Jonas Rook sprang up onto the stage, whipped off his dark brown layered cape and draped it over her.

'Widow Scarlet,' he said. 'Here – let me untie you! My dear God, we couldn't have arrived here a second later! What on earth have these devils done to you?'

He took out a clasp knife and deftly cut the ribbons around her wrists, and then he helped her to sit up. She couldn't speak. She was so stunned that she couldn't even burst into tears. She had been so convinced that she was going to have her head cut off that she was shocked to find that she was still alive. She felt as if she had been torn badly between her legs, and the pain was so acute that she kept bending forward to relieve it, but if she could feel pain that meant that she wasn't dead.

'Don't you worry,' said Jonas Rook. 'We'll have to allow some of this carrion to leave, but we'll be taking in all of the principal perpetrators – Mrs Sheridan, for one.'

All Beatrice could do was nod. Nothing mattered to her now, except the gradual realisation that she would be able to go back to Black Horse Yard and take care of Florence.

Jonas Rook sat next to her. He didn't try to put his arm around her but he said, 'You're safe now, Widow Scarlet. You're quite safe. And we'll make sure that none of these vermin ever threaten you again.'

'Thank you,' Beatrice whispered.

There was even more arguing and screaming from the hallway.

'You struck me!' one man shouted out. 'You blackguard! You absolute blackguard! You struck me! Don't you know who I am?'

In spite of this, it sounded to Beatrice as though most of the audience had now been herded out of the house. Some of them were protesting loudly, but she imagined that most of them would want to disperse as quickly and discreetly as possible, before they were recognized by the rabble in the street outside, and their names published in tomorrow's Grub Street newspapers.

'Do you know where your clothes might be?' asked Jonas Rook.

'No, but I suspect upstairs, in the bedroom where they first held me. It's right at the end of the first-floor corridor.'

Just then, though, Violet came into the room. She saw Beatrice and she came hurrying towards her, her arms held out, with a pained expression on her face.

'Oh my stars! Oh, Beatrice! Where's that Coddy? That harridan! That miserable, scraggy, worn-out harlot! I'll scratch 'er fuckin' eyes out!'

She held Beatrice tightly and rocked her from side to side. 'Oh, I'm sorry! I'm so sorry! But I didn't know what else I could do. If I'd told Coddy that I knew 'oo you really was, she'd 'ave done the same to me! I thought the best thing was run over to Bow Street and fetch the traps.'

Jonas Rook said, 'It was just as well you did, madam, or there may well have been lives lost. I'm sorry, too, that it took so long for us to persuade Sir John to issue a general warrant, and to muster our officers, but thank God we arrived here in time.'

He told Violet where Beatrice's clothes might be, and Violet gave Beatrice one more hug and one more 'Sorry, lovey – really, really sorry,' and then she went off to see if she could find them.

One of the constables came out of the door beside the stage looking serious.

'There's five young women in there, sir. All in a state of undress, all spark out, and we can't wake them for love nor money.'

'They're the same five girls that George Hazzard took from St Mary Magdalene's,' Beatrice whispered. 'I believe they've been anaesthetized with ether, which is what they did to me, too, but I think from their condition that they must have been given a much larger dose.'

She paused, and bent forward again to ease her pain. Then she said, 'There's a young apothecary here from the Foundery – Godfrey Minchin. He's bald-headed, with eyeglasses. Ask him what he's given them. If it's ether, they will need mustard flour mixed with warm water, as an emetic, and then cold effusions, and stimulation to wake them up. They need to be taken to hospital urgently, otherwise they could well die.'

'Very well,' said Jonas Rook, and turned back to the constable. 'See if we've picked up this apothecary, and fetch him here. Then tell Frobisher to organize carriages to take these poor girls to Bart's, and send Williams upstairs to fetch down some bedsheets to cover them.'

Violet returned, and she was carrying Beatrice's gown and petticoats and stockings over her arm, and her shoes in her hand. 'There's nobody in the drawing room at present, lovey,' she said. 'You can dress yourself there.'

She took Beatrice's arm and led her to the drawing room. Beatrice had to suck in her breath as she walked, because her stomach hurt so much, but Violet said, 'You'll be all right, Beatrice. You'll get over this. Never let the fuckin' stall-whimpers get the better of you, that's what I always says.'

Beatrice dressed by the fire. She was still bleeding a little, but she used her handkerchief to wipe herself and then threw it onto the coals, where it shrivelled up. She was relieved to find her purse still behind the sofa where Leda Sheridan had dropped it, with her handkerchief and all of her money and even her Toby pistol untouched. When she had fastened the bow in the front of her bodice and patted her hair, she went back out in the hallway. Violet was waiting for her, talking to two of the watchmen. She was about to ask Violet if they should hail a hackney to take them back to Black Horse Yard when she heard shouting from the back of the house, both a man and a woman.

'This is an outrage!' the man kept repeating. 'An absolute bloody outrage! You have no right to detain me – *none*! I shall make a personal complaint to Sir John!'

'And so shall I!' the woman shrilled. 'Breaking into my house like this, into a private function, with no legal cause whatsoever!'

Beatrice saw Leda Sheridan being escorted down the hallway. Two of her ostrich plumes had snapped, and were dangling sideways from the top of her head. She also seemed to have lost one of her shoes, because she was hobbling.

But when the man beside her appeared from behind one of the constables, Beatrice felt as if she were suddenly back in a nightmare. It was the nim gimmer, still wearing his white billowing robe, but without his pointed hood, and it was George Hazzard. He was still shouting, and barging the constables on either side of him with his shoulders, but none of the constables answered him, or even acknowledged that they could hear him, and they continued to march him towards the front door.

Jonas Rook reached Beatrice first. He was breathing hard, but Beatrice could see that he was trying hard not to look triumphant.

'We discovered these two hiding in the larder,' he said. 'There was a third man, who was naked, but he managed to elude us and hop over the garden wall. I presume he was the man who assaulted you.'

'He got away?'

'Yes, but never fear, we'll pick him up, and he'll be riding backwards up Holborn Hill for what he did.'

Beatrice said, 'I need to go back with Violet to see my daughter, and wash, but then I want to go to Bart's to make sure that our girls are all revived.'

'Whatever assistance you require, Widow Scarlet, please let me know instanter. This has been a most rewarding evening, as far as I'm concerned, and I have you to thank more than anybody. I regret only that you had to undergo such an appalling ordeal.'

Beatrice said nothing. She found it hard to take her eyes off George Hazzard. She had been surprised how tall he had appeared, but now she could see that underneath his long white robes he was wearing high-heeled riding boots.

Jonas Rook said, gently, 'You understand that I shall have to question you in due course about the death of Mr Edward Veal, but under the circumstances I very much doubt that you'll be facing any charges. It appears to be a clear case of self-defence against a man who had been assigned to murder you.'

George Hazzard pushed his way forward, glaring at Beatrice with utter hatred.

'Do you know what I wish, widow?' he spat at her. 'I wish these runners hadn't run, but walked, and taken just a minute longer to arrive here. A minute would have been enough! But then I could have had the immense satisfaction of separating your infuriating head from your infernal interfering body, and kicking it across the room!'

'You made one cardinal error, George,' said Beatrice, although her voice was shaking. 'You tried to use superstition to intimidate a woman well versed in science.'

'Science? *Pah!* You're a witch, and that's all there is to it!'

45

It was nearly eight o'clock the following morning when Beatrice arrived at St Bartholomew's Hospital. She hadn't returned with Violet to Black Horse Yard until well after three, and after washing herself and changing into a fresh-laundered petticoat that she had borrowed from Violet, she had sat in a chair in the sitting room beside the still-warm ashes of the fire and fallen asleep for over two hours.

When Florence had woken up, Beatrice had managed to eat a small bowlful of porridge with her, and then sit down and cuddle her and tell her one of her favourite stories, about a duck who could sing opera.

Violet sat on the other side of the sitting room, sewing one of her pincushions and smiling at them both.

'I 'opes you've forgiven me, Beatrice,' she said, after a while.

'Violet, there's nothing to forgive. You saved my life. And I hope you've managed to save those girls' lives, too. I must go to the hospital soon and see if they've recovered.'

'That baldy cully wouldn't say what 'e'd dosed 'em up with, would 'e?'

'No. He didn't want to incriminate himself. But I'm fairly sure it was ether.'

'It can kill you then, ether?'

'It depends how it's administered, and how much. About five or six teaspoons would be enough to kill a young girl.'

'Well, let's 'ope and pray. Don't you worry about little Florrie while you're gone, lovey. I'll take 'er down to Billingsgate Stairs to buy some mackerel. She'll enjoy seein' the fish all flappin' and the crabs all crawlin' around.'

Beatrice entered Bart's Hospital through the main gate, under the supercilious-looking statue of Henry VIII, and walked across the courtyard. It took her almost twenty minutes to find out where the five girls had been taken, but eventually she found them in a small upstairs room overlooking the courtyard, along with three other women who were all suffering from puerperal fever.

They were all still unconscious, although they were breathing, but the wiry-haired Scottish nurse in charge of their room was very pessimistic.

'I'm afraid to say that this is a room which makes many mourners,' she said. She had an alarming cast in her left eye which seemed to make her pessimism even more doom-laden.

'You've bathed them in cold water, and massaged their chests?'

The nurse nodded. 'We shall do so again later. But I don't hold out much hope.'

Beatrice went up to Judith's bed. It seemed to her that Judith was breathing quite normally, and when she felt her pulse, her heart rate was fluttery, but only a little slower than it should have been. She looked across the room at the women with puerperal fever and she could see that their faces were waxy and they were staring at the ceiling as if all they could see was their imminent death.

Dear God, she thought, *why do you make women suffer so much, just for being women? Are you still angry at Eve?*

She sat with Judith and the other girls for a while, but there was nothing else she could do for them except pray. She asked the nurse to send her a message if any of them regained consciousness, and then she walked across to the mortuary. She had been there only once before, when she was a young girl. Her father had been asked to examine a woman who had apparently swallowed poison because the surgeon-apothecaries were unable to agree what poison it was. He had taken Beatrice with him because he had wanted her to see that death was a natural part of life. He always used to tell all of his customers, quite cheerfully, 'The odds on you dying, my friend, are one hundred per cent.'

The mortuary was down at the end of a long, chilly corridor with a marble-mosaic floor. Inside, it was even chillier, and as gloomy as a church, with high leaded windows.

At the far end of the mortuary, the bodies of three of the seven girls were lying on plain wooden tables. A surgeon in a white wig and a black frock coat was standing over one of the bodies, along with his assistant, a young man in shirtsleeves, with hair that was sticking up as if he had just been struck by lightning.

As Beatrice came closer, she could see that the surgeon had cleaved apart the dead girl's chest, exposing her heart and her lungs, and he had opened up her abdomen so that he could take samples of her stomach contents and her bowels. He was spooning faecal matter into a metal dish with all the fastidiousness of a chef serving up pâté de foie gras.

He looked up as Beatrice approached and said, 'May I be of assistance, madam? This mortuary is not open to the public, I'm afraid.'

'Mr Pott,' said Beatrice. 'It's a long time since I was here last, and I was very young, so you doubtless won't remember me. But I'm sure you'll remember my father, who brought me here. Clement Bannister, the apothecary. His shop was on Giltspur Street.'

'But of course!' said Percivall Pott, passing the metal dish to his assistant. 'Clement Bannister was one of the most inventive apothecaries that London has ever known! He came here frequently to assist with post-mortem examinations, especially when we suspected poisons or other noxious substances. He was most inspired, too, when it came to my work on chimney sweeps, and how soot might cause malignancies. Well, well!'

Beatrice stepped forward, right up to the autopsy table, partly to show Percivall Pott that she wasn't squeamish when it came to putrescent, half-disembowelled bodies.

'I'm Beatrice,' she said. 'Beatrice Scarlet now, although I'm sad to say that I'm widowed. The reason I'm here is because of the suspicion that these girls may have been deliberately murdered. I have an interest in finding out if this is true, because I was taking care of them at St Mary Magdalene's Refuge.'

Percivall Pott looked down at the gaping ribcage and shook his head. 'I think the man we need now is your father, so it's very regretful that he's no longer with us. Apart from some superficial bruising, which may have occurred post-mortem, there is no evidence that any of these girls was beaten or stabbed or strangled or drowned or that their death was caused by a physical assault of any kind. There are some superficial blisters around their lips, but nothing more than that. I believe we have to assume that they were poisoned. The question is – what with?'

'Mr Pott, my father taught me everything he knew about poisons. Well – apart from everything he knew about headache pills and cough medicines. Not to mention all of his patented treatments for gout, and consumption, and social infections, and almost every other ailment you can think of.'

'Really? So you're something of a poison expert too?'

'I'm a qualified apothecary, Mr Pott, even though I'm not recognized as such by the Guild.'

Mr Pott nodded across the mortuary to his workbench,

which was cluttered with flasks and retorts and mortars and a flickering oil lamp.

'I've tested for almost all the common poisons so far, but my results have either been negative or inconclusive. First I tested for cyanide, because it degenerates after only a day or two. Even so, cyanide can still leave a lingering smell of bitter almonds in the stomach, and some alkaline burns in the digestive tract, but there was no trace of those. I've also tested for strychnine, belladonna, hemlock and henbane, as well as ether and chloroform and God alone knows what else. Again, no positive results.'

'Arsenic?'

'Arsenic of course, and I found a fairly high level, but not enough I'd say to be fatal. There's arsenic in so many tonics, and women's cosmetics, and in wine, so a measure of arsenic is not at all unusual.'

'What will you be testing for next?'

'To be absolutely honest with you, madam, I have no idea. Some malignant substance killed these unfortunate young women, there's no question of that. They certainly didn't die of any allergy or wasp sting or other natural causes – not all seven of them. But I cannot think what that malignant substance could have been, because I can detect no trace of it.'

Beatrice was silent for a long moment, looking down at the body on the table in front of her, and then across at the other corpse. Its skin was greenish and no longer bloated, but beginning to sag around its sternum. Then she said, 'Do you think I might borrow your equipment, Mr Pott, and try a test for myself?'

'*You*, madam?'

'Please, Mr Pott, call me Beatrice. Or Widow Scarlet, if you still wish to be formal. But, yes, me. I'm not only Clement Bannister's daughter, I'm his heiress. He passed on to me all of his chemical knowledge, all of his inspiration, and all of his enthusiasm to relieve the world's sickness. He was the first person to devise a cure for tenesmus, using frankincense, and I helped him to mix it, when I was only eight years old.'

'Bannister's Bowel Balsam!' said Percivall Pott. 'I do believe my father used to take it. My goodness!'

He smiled, and then he said, 'Why don't you come back this afternoon, Beatrice? I shall be otherwise engaged in the operating theatre, and so you may have this whole mortuary to yourself. David will be here to assist you if you need anything – but please, feel free to use any equipment that you require. It's a pleasure and an honour to have met you.'

Beatrice left, but as she reached the mortuary doors she heard Percivall Pott repeating, 'Bannister's Bowel Balsam. My goodness.'

Before she returned to Bart's that afternoon, Beatrice went to No. 4 Bow Street to see Jonas Rook. The chimpanzee-like doorman knew who she was now, and bowed when she came in.

She could see Jonas Rook through the half-open door of his office, talking to two lawyers. When he looked up and saw her outside, he excused himself immediately and came out to greet her.

'My dear Widow Scarlet. I do hope that you're recovering from that hideous experience.'

Beatrice nodded. She was still very sore, and she had a dull ache in the small of her back, but she didn't yet know herself how she felt about what had happened at Leda Sheridan's. For the time being, all she wanted to do was concentrate on how the seven girls had died, and whether George Hazzard and Leda Sheridan could successfully be prosecuted for killing them.

Jonas Rook said, 'All three will be sent for trial and are held in custody – George Hazzard and Mrs Sheridan and that apothecary, Godfrey Minchin. I'm in the early stages now of preparing the case against them, and if the grand jury approves a true bill I'm hoping we'll be able to bring them up before a judge and jury before the end of the month.'

'That's good news,' said Beatrice. 'Mr Pott has not yet been able to determine the cause of death, so I'm going to the mortuary this afternoon to make some tests myself, and see if we can't prove beyond any doubt that they were responsible. But there is one important thing I have to ask you – can you make sure that Godfrey Michin's apothecary at the Foundery is sealed off as soon as possible, and that nobody is allowed access to it?'

'Of course. I'll make sure that it's done immediately. The general warrant still applies.'

'Thank you,' said Beatrice. 'I strongly suspect he might have been involved in preparing poisons for George Hazzard, and if so his equipment could still bear incriminating traces of it. I don't want anybody to have the opportunity to wash out all of his flasks and destroy any evidence against him.'

'You're a remarkable woman, Widow Scarlet. There's one thing I have to ask you: What is your present address? I will need to contact you from time to time before the trial, and I assume that you will not be returning to Maidenhead Court.'

'For the time being, Florence and I are sharing rooms with Mrs Vickery at Black Horse Yard, by Spittle Market. Where we will go to after that, I haven't yet had time to consider. Perhaps to Birmingham, to stay with my cousin.'

'Black Horse Yard?' said Jonas Rook. 'Forgive me for saying so, but that's a den of iniquity if ever there was one.'

Beatrice couldn't help smiling. 'Perhaps,' she said, 'but there's honour among thieves, and mercy among prostitutes.'

She returned to the mortuary at three o'clock, before it began to grow dark. Percivall Pott's assistant, David, lit the oil lamp for her, and asked her if there was anything she needed.

'Alcohol, please, as well as tartaric acid and lime, and ether. And I will require you to bring out the remains of at least three of the young girls.'

David blinked at her. 'What exactly do you have in mind, Widow Scarlet, if you don't mind my asking?'

'It's a test my father once used, after some parish children were poisoned by eating yew seeds on a walk through Finsbury Fields. I don't know how successful it will be, but Mr Pott seems to have exhausted every other possibility.'

Three dark blue aprons were hanging up by the workbench, and Beatrice took one down and tied it on. Although there was no evidence to support her idea, and no witnesses had yet come forward, she was working on the assumption that George Hazzard had almost immediately taken the seven girls from his factory to Leda Sheridan's brothel. There, they had been poisoned so that they could be seen raped in their death throes in front of an audience. She was sure that the other five girls would have been poisoned in the same way, if Jonas Rook and his officers hadn't intervened.

David wheeled out three bodies, one of which was Jane Webb's. Although they had been kept in a cold store, and preserved with ethanol, they were now in an advanced state of decomposition. Beatrice had prepared for that and brought a handkerchief with her, soaked in Violet's lavender perfume.

She sliced two-inch samples of flesh from the thighs of each of them, laid them on a metal dish and took them over to the workbench. There, while David watched, she dissolved them, in three separate flasks, in alcohol and tartaric acid. Once she had done that, she precipitated the fatty and resinous matter in water and heated it.

She had thought to herself: What poison does George Hazzard have available to him in the greatest quantity, and legitimately, but which no surgeon-apothecary has yet been able to trace? And then she had thought of Katharine, and all the lice in her hair, and how the lice had all been cleared by wrapping her head in tobacco leaves. Head lice were notoriously resistant to all kinds of treatments, such as rosemary and mistletoe and even mercury, but they had been effectively killed by the juices in tobacco.

She knew now that Godfrey Minchin was involved in preparing young girls for Leda Sheridan's necrophiliac performances, and it seemed highly likely that George Hazzard could have employed him to distil liquid from tobacco leaves. Tobacco juice was a very fragile plant alkaloid, but if she could manage to extract it from the seven girls' tissues, and if its residue could also be found in Godfrey's apothecary, Jonas Rook would be well on the way to having all the evidence he needed.

If she could find no traces of tobacco juices, of course, and if the jury were prepared to believe that the seven girls had summoned up Satan, and that Satan had ultimately killed them, then the three accused would go free. Not only that, the Reverend Parsons and Ida Smollett would be able to continue the holy work of St Mary Magdalene's Refuge, rescuing young girls from prostitution and delivering them unto God.

She thought of Jane Webb, delirious on ether fumes, staring at her wide-eyed and saying, '*P'raps I could start all over again, and go back to being a virgin, of sorts.*'

While she was heating the precipitate over the oil lamp's flame, she suddenly found it hard not to cry.

46

Over the next three weeks the weather grew increasingly bitter, and on the day that George Hazzard and Leda Sheridan and Godfrey Minchin were brought up before the Old Bailey, the skies were charcoal-grey and it was sleeting. The courtroom had three tall windows, but it was so dark outside that all of the lamps had to be lit.

The public benches were crowded, and when the defendants were brought out, there was a rustling of paper and a murmuring of voices that sounded like the sea coming in. From where she was sitting in the witness box, Beatrice thought that three of them looked exhausted and ghastly. They had spent three weeks in Newgate Prison, after all, and although they had probably been given preferential treatment, their confinement showed on their faces. They stood together in the dock round-shouldered and sullen, and even when George Hazzard's lawyer John Bellflower came prancing across the courtroom to speak to him, he showed no sign that he had heard what he said, or cared.

Apart from stale sweat and tobacco and wig powder, the Old Bailey smelled strongly of aromatic herbs. Beatrice knew that pot-pourris were arranged around the courtroom to prevent the spread of typhus, or gaol fever, which defendants sometimes brought in with them from Newgate. Some years ago, a prisoner had infected more than sixty people with typhus, including two judges and the Lord Mayor, and they had all died.

After a few minutes, the clerk called out, 'All rise!' and the judge swept in. Beneath his long wig his nose was as sharp as a pickaxe and his eyes were hollow and his lips were tightly pursed. Jonas leaned over to Beatrice and whispered, 'Robert Stokely, High Court judge. Not very happy it's him. He and George Hazzard both belong to White's.'

Beatrice said nothing. Her heart was beating fast. She was the principal witness, and in a few minutes she would have to stand up and give her evidence in front of everybody in this crowded courtroom – not only the hollow-eyed judge but the twelve jurors who were sprawling in their stalls on the right-hand side of the dock chatting to each other, and the public, and all of the clerks and lawyers and shorthand writers who were waiting with their pens poised.

The judge looked across at the dock and said, 'Mr Hazzard, Mr Minchin, Mrs Sheridan. A grand jury has approved a true bill accusing the three of you of manslaughter, in that you deliberately administered a poisonous substance to seven young women from St Mary Magdalene's Refuge for Refractory Females, leading to the deaths of all seven of them. You are further accused of concealing their remains in order to avoid prosecution. How does each of you plead?'

George Hazzard cleared his throat and said, 'I plead *not* guilty, your honour! *Not* guilty! This charge is completely without foundation and has been brought with malicious intent by Mrs Beatrice Scarlet, for reasons that are totally beyond me. She seems to harbour venomous ill-will against me, and has concocted evidence which I am certain this court will dismiss as both ludicrous and far-fetched.'

Leda Sheridan simply sniffed and said, 'Not guilty.'

Godfrey Minchin said, 'Me too. Not guilty, I mean. I had nothing to do with any of this.'

'Widow Scarlet?' said the clerk.

Beatrice stood up. Speaking as clearly as she could, she described how she had visited George Hazzard's tobacco factory looking for Jane Webb and the other girls. She told the jury how she had discovered that the pentagram was drawn in paint, and not in blood, and how she had analyed the goat's hair. She went on to relate how she and James had visited Leda Sheridan's brothel, and how she had witnessed Grace being beheaded.

Inattentive at first, the jury were now sitting up and listening intently. There were gasps and murmurs from the public gallery when she described how Grace had been killed. When she explained how she had returned to Leda Sheridan's with Violet, and how she had been raped, several women in the audience stood up and left.

Beatrice concluded by saying, 'I have no doubt at all that Mr Hazzard and Mrs Sheridan were jointly responsible for abducting those seven girls, and that they were lethally poisoned for the sexual entertainment of a paying audience. I also have no doubt that the Reverend Parsons and Mrs Ida Smollett were both complicit in their abduction and their subsequent murders, and even if they are not standing in front of your honour in this courtroom today, they will surely be judged by God.'

After she had sat down, the courtroom was silent. After a few moments, though, John Bellflower stood up in his wig and his gown, and turned to the jury with a smile on his face as if Beatrice had just told a long and elaborate joke.

'Gentlemen of the jury, I commend you for your patience in listening to the Widow Scarlet's bizarre inventions. However, there is no evidence whatsoever to suggest that my client Mr Hazzard had any hand in the passing of these seven unfortunate young women. He took them from St Mary Magdalene's Refuge in order to give them respectable employment in his tobacco factory. He has financially supported St Mary Magdalene's for many years, and he has rescued countless girls from a life of vice and moral degradation.

'In this particular case, however, the girls performed a ritual which led to them being possessed by the Devil, and becoming a coven of witches. They drew a satanic device on the wall of their dormitory, and they sacrificed a goat. They then demanded that Mr Hazzard take them to Mrs Sheridan's establishment, so that they could pursue their preferred profession of prostitution.'

Jonas Rook stood up and said, 'If that's true, Mr Bellflower, why did Mr Hazzard claim that they had disappeared without trace?'

'Because he was mortally ashamed that he had failed them, sir,' John Bellflower replied. 'He didn't wish to admit that for the first time he had been unable to keep them on the path of moral rectitude.'

'So he took them to Mrs Sheridan's brothel? Is this true, Mrs Sheridan?'

'It is, yes,' said Leda Sheridan. 'But I strongly object to your description of my house as a brothel. I run a highly respectable establishment for the entertainment of highly respectable members of London's society.'

There was laughter and hoots of derision from the public gallery, until Judge Stavely banged his gavel and snapped, 'Silence!'

'Very well, Mr Bellflower,' said Jonas Rook. 'But how did all seven of these girls come to pass away? Can you explain that? And why were they covertly interred in the garden of Mr Hazzard's factory? Why were they given no civil or Christian ceremony, nor public notification?'

'At the time, sir, their passing was a mystery,' said John Bellflower. 'Neither Mr Hazzard nor Mrs Sheridan could explain why they had died. They had been expected one evening to perform in one of Mrs Sheridan's entertainments, but a few minutes before they could appear they were discovered in the ante-room, with all life extinct. Mr Hazzard decided that it would be more discreet if they were taken to Hackney and buried without any ado.'

'You mean that he was concerned that he and Mrs Sheridan might be unjustly accused of having murdered them? And their highly respectable guests might be implicated in a scandal?'

John Bellflower shrugged in his gown like a large crow settling on a fence. 'Exactly. Look at today's proceedings. Utterly without foundation. But – listen! We made a careful study of the post-mortem findings produced by the surgeon at St Bartholomew's, Mr Percivall Pott, and from these I am gratified to say that we have finally discovered the cause of death.'

'Really?' said Jonas Rook. 'Mr Pott concluded that the girls had most likely been poisoned, did he not, but at the same time he admitted that he had been unable to isolate what particular poison it was.'

'Aha! Yes! But he *does* report that he found a substantial level of arsenic in the girls' bodies – perhaps more than could be explained by their use of cosmetic creams or their ingestion of the usual proprietary tonics to prevent venereal diseases or menstrual disorders. I suggest that this arsenic almost certainly killed them, but I agree that we have to ask ourselves where did it come from, this arsenic, and how did it enter their bloodstreams?'

He turned around again, and now he pointed to a red-nosed man sitting at the end of his bench. 'Allow me to introduce my witness, Doctor Josiah Saunders of the Royal College of

Physicians. Doctor Saunders, perhaps you would be good enough to enlighten the court as to your remarkable findings.'

Dr Saunders rose to his feet, and bowed to the judge, and then to the jury. He spoke in a tremulous voice, and Judge Stavely had to ask him twice to speak up, especially as the public gallery was growing restless again.

'When Mr Bellflower showed me the post-mortem findings from Mr Pott, I was reminded of a case late last year, when I was summoned to Limehouse, where a five-year-old boy was gravely ill. I first took his sickness to be croup. He exhibited all the usual symptoms of croup – wracked with pain and unable to swallow, and within a very few hours he was dead. The following evening his two younger siblings also died.'

'Can you get to the point, doctor?' asked Judge Stavely. 'We don't have all day and we have many other cases to consider. And can you speak a little louder?'

'Beg your pardon, your honour. What concerned me about the death of these children was that although the family was living in extremely cramped conditions, cheek-by-jowl with their neighbours, nobody else in that terrace of houses was affected. I examined the water supply and the general sanitation, and there was nothing there to suggest that there was anything injurious to health.

'The only distinctive feature of their house was the wallpaper in the children's bedroom. It was that bright emerald-coloured wallpaper which is known, I believe, as German Green. What gives it such an intense colour is the arsenic used in its printing ink, and it has been suggested for some time now that it can poison those who have decorated their houses with it. Not everybody, necessarily – healthy adults seem to be immune. But children and the elderly, and anybody who is suffering from any kind of debilitation.'

'You are seriously trying to say that these seven girls were killed by *wallpaper*?' asked Jonas Rook.

'I believe it to be irrefutable,' said John Bellflower. 'The ante-room at Mrs Sheridan's in which they were found to be deceased is decorated with an arsenical paper produced by William Windle and Company, and which has been associated with several other sudden deaths since its first production. It seems to me that those girls were difficult and almost impossibly demanding in their behaviour, and that Mr Hazzard and Mrs Sheridan did everything they possibly could to accommodate them. But what they did *not* do was kill them. This was natural death by wallpaper, and I trust the jury will agree with me.'

John Bellflower sat down, and George Hazzard silently clapped his hands together.

Judge Stavely looked up wearily, and said, 'Is that everything? If it is, I will ask the jury to huddle and give me their verdict.'

'By no means everything, your honour!' said Beatrice, standing up again.

'Well?' asked Judge Stavely.

'I spoke to Mr Pott personally and although he *had* found arsenic in the bodies of the seven girls, his opinion was that it was not of sufficient strength to have killed them. As you may have read in his post-mortem report, he was unable to find evidence of *any* poison that could have killed them.'

'*Something* killed them, madam, and if it wasn't arsenic, then what? This is really rather tiresome.'

'With Mr Potts's permission, I examined the girls' bodies myself. I used a test devised by my father to detect the presence of plant alkaloids in human tissue, and I found that the flesh of every one of those girls exuded the oily poisonous juice which can be extracted from tobacco. Without any question at all, that was what killed them.'

'*Tobacco juice?*' frowned Judge Stavely. 'So what inference do you draw from that?'

'No inference, your honour – evidence. There is one defendant in this court who has unlimited access to tobacco leaves – Mr George Hazzard. Mr Hazzard can also draw on the expertise of another defendant in this court who is proficient in chemistry – Mr Godfrey Minchin. Equipment was impounded by law officers from Mr Minchin's apothecary, and that equipment includes numerous jars of tobacco leaves in the process of distillation, and full bottles of tobacco juices.'

Godfrey gripped the railing at the front of the dock and stared at Beatrice in horror. He knew what it would mean if the jury found him guilty of providing George Hazzard with poison – especially since Beatrice had already given evidence that he had anaesthetized her.

'He *made* me!' he screamed, and pointed at George Hazzard. 'He *made* me! He said he would have me beaten if I didn't! He *made* me!'

'*Order!*' shouted Judge Stavely, banging his gavel again. 'This is a court of law, not a bear-pit!'

'He made me! He *made* me! It was him! *And* her! She made me pour it down their throats! It was both of them! They *made* me!'

There was chaos in the courtroom. The jury were all standing up, and now the people in the public gallery were standing up, too, and jabbing their fingers towards the dock, and shouting, 'Guilty! Guilty! Guilty!'

George Hazzard spun around and around, his fists bunched in fury. Beatrice thought that he was going to hit Godfrey, but then he grasped the rail at the front of the dock, and swung himself right over it. He dropped down onto the floor in front of the clerk's table and turned around again, as if he couldn't decide which way to go.

''E's getting away!' somebody shouted. 'Look! 'E's makin' a run for it!'

One of the bailiffs came around the clerk's table – a big man in a tight black uniform. He took hold of George Hazzard's left shoulder and tried to twist him around, but George Hazzard twisted himself back. He drew the sword out of the bailiff's scabbard and without any hesitation he stabbed it into his stomach. The bailiff looked down in surprise, and then tilted forward and pitched face-down onto the clerk's table, scattering blood-spattered documents all over the floor.

Now George Hazzard switched his attention to the witness box, and Beatrice. His face was so scarlet and so contorted with rage with she could hardly recognize him. If the seven girls hadn't really summoned Satan in their dormitory, they had surely done so now.

'*You!*' he roared, walking stiffly towards her, with the bailiff's sword raised. 'You and your evidence! Well, let me tell you this, you scabby jilt! If there's no *you*, there's no evidence! If *you* die, your evidence dies with you!'

Jonas Rook stood up and shouted, 'Drop that! Do you hear me? Drop it!'

He stepped out of the witness box, but George Hazzard lashed the sword from side to side and caught his elbow, ripping right through his sleeve. Jonas Rook said, '*Gah!*' and clenched his teeth in pain and gripped his arm. Blood began dripping quickly through his fingers and onto the floor.

George Hazzard shoved him roughly aside and came up to the steps of the witness box, holding the sword high.

'What about retracting your fanciful evidence, Beatrice? No, I didn't think you would. Not willingly. But this will do, just as well!'

Beatrice felt stone-cold. She had never felt as cold as this in her life, even when she had seen Francis, dead and embalmed. She reached down to her purse and without keeping her eyes off George Hazzard she felt for the butt of her Toby pistol. Before she lifted it out, she pulled back the hammer until she felt it click.

As George Hazzard came up the steps, she took it out and pointed it directly at his face and pulled the trigger. There was a deafening bang and a puff of blue smoke and she felt the pistol jolt in her hand. The ball hit George Hazzard in the right eye, so that it was nothing more than a deep black hole. He stopped, stock-still.

The silence in the courtroom was immense. All that Beatrice could hear was the sleet rattling furiously against the windows. Then the sword fell out of George Hazzard's fingers onto the steps, bouncing on its point and ringing like a bell. He took one unsteady pace back, and then another, and then he fell over backwards with a heavy thump and lay on the floor with his arms spread wide.

Jonas Rook looked down at Beatrice, still clutching his arm. She had never seen such a complicated expression on a man's face before.

'Guilty!' shouted somebody in the public gallery, and at once the cry was taken up all around the courtroom. 'Guilty! Guilty! Guilty!'

47

The next morning, Beatrice was tying up her cape and putting on her bonnet, ready to take Florence out for a walk, when she heard a sharp knocking at the front door downstairs.

Eliza rushed into the sitting room, flung open the window and looked down into the courtyard.

''Oo are you?' she demanded. 'Wodger want?'

Beatrice couldn't hear what the answer was, but when Eliza closed the window she said, 'Two gentlemen for you, Beatrice! Oh yes, *gentlemen* for definite! I'll fetch 'em up, shall I?'

'Please,' said Beatrice, because she was still fastening Florence's cape. 'Did they give you their names?'

'No, but they asked for Widow Scarlet, so they must know you.'

Eliza went down and opened the door, and Beatrice heard voices. Then footsteps came up the stairs, and Jonas Rook came into the sitting room. He looked around as if to say, this isn't quite the kind of place I expected to find you, but he gave her a smile all the same.

'Good morning, Beatrice. And you must be Florence.'

Florence hid herself behind Beatrice's cape, but No-noh trotted up to Jonas Rook and sniffed enthusiastically at his boots.

'I believe I have some news for you, Widow Scarlet,' said

Jonas Rook. 'Two items of news, in fact – some good news and some *very* good news. The good news is that Sir John Fielding is delighted with the outcome of yesterday's court case, regardless of the uproar it has caused. I was not aware of this myself, but apparently Mr Hazzard had exploited his blindness and deceived him into dismissing a serious case of fraud against one of his friends, which would have caused Sir John a great deal of embarrassment, and might even have obliged him to resign as a magistrate.'

'I'm very pleased,' said Beatrice. 'Not pleased that I killed George Hazzard, of course. I can only hope that God forgives me for that.'

'Sir John is certainly pleased, even if God is still making up his mind. He has told me that there are three empty rooms on the fourth floor of No. 4 Bow Street, and he says he would be honoured if you would take up occupancy. He will make sure that they are furnished however you wish, and at his expense. His only request is that you occasionally lend us your talents as an apothecary to solve any mystifying crimes.'

'Really? He's giving us somewhere to live?'

'Completely free of rent, Widow Scarlet. And I am just as pleased as you are, because I will be seeing so much more of you.'

Beatrice turned around to Florence and said, 'Did you hear that, Florrie? We'll be having new rooms of our own! And we can decorate them however we wish!'

'Not with German Green wallpaper, though,' smiled Jonas Rook.

'Please, don't remind me,' said Beatrice. 'But you said you had some *very* good news. What could be better news than that?'

Jonas Rook said, Ah!' and lifted one finger, and then he went back to the sitting-room door. 'You can come in now,' he said, to whoever was waiting outside.

The door opened wider, and Noah came in. His hair was long and braided, and his face was so tanned that he looked like an Indian, and he seemed to have grown three or four inches. He was wearing a brown tweed coat that was at least two sizes too big for him, and almost reached the floor. He stared at Beatrice in silence for five full seconds before he burst into tears, and came stumbling into her arms.

Beatrice sank back into the armchair behind her, sobbing and hugging him close. Florence stood beside them, patting Noah's back and kissing the top of his head.

A voice said, 'Hallo, Cousin Beatrice.'

Beatrice smeared away her tears with her fingertips and saw that it was Jeremy. He too looked suntanned, and his hair was long and tied back with a ribbon.

'You found him!' Beatrice wept. 'Oh, my dear God, Jeremy, you found him!'

Jeremy looked at Jonas Rook and then back at Beatrice. 'I thought it was the least I could do to make amends to you. I found an Ossipee scout in Lower Cohos and I hired him to take me up to New France. It took a while, but Noah wasn't that hard to find when I let the Indians know that I was ready to pay good money for him.'

'Oh Jeremy, I don't know how I can thank you. Noah – look at you! Brown as a berry and all that long hair!'

Florence picked up her puppy and showed him to her brother.

'This is No-noh, too. We called him that because we didn't have you. But now we do. So we'll have to give him a new name, won't we?'

Beatrice stroked the puppy's head and said, 'Yes, you're right, Florrie. Let's call him James.'